Your Inner You

A Novel by

Paul Alexander Fichera

REV 6.1

ALSO BY
PAUL A. FICHERA

www.PaulFichera.com

The Stellar Quest: A Subterranean Adventure

A father and son, in a future where humans no longer inhabit the Earth's surface, visit a once famous, now long abandoned tourist cave in Pennsylvania; it doesn't end well.

Yesterday's Child: An Adventure Through Time

A gifted high school student discovers he can astral travel to the future where he learns humanity's ultimate fate; it falls on him to make it not happen.

Angie's Revenge: A Tale of Many Lifetimes

A newly married thirty-something woman discovers one night she's meant for way more than merely cooking and cleaning … and other wifey things.

Aiden, You've Been Very Bad

"I know what he did, Tracy," Ann Marcella said. "And how many times he's done it. And you're in no condition to go back out there looking like your cat just died."

"How do you know my name?" Tracy Madigan asked, indignantly. "Who are you?"

Ann extended her hand and told her. "Aiden's been cheating on you, hasn't he? And you just found out from your best friend? … I can help." Ann reached into her purse and handed the girl a business card:

GET EVEN, LTD.
"Don't risk Jail, he's not worth it. We'll handle it."

Kayelle's Return: A Sci-Fi at Christmastime

The Nazca Plain in fact stood as a curious strip of land the Inca Indians had used as a painter's canvas upon which they had scribbled twisted patterns and lines into the hard red desert rock. From the ground the lines were meaningless, and as roads went nowhere. Yet from the air they formed patterns and shapes: a condor, a fish, a spider, a monkey. They were believed to have been etched by the Inca themselves, for their gods who they hoped would see them.

Crossing Cassandra: Some Folks Just Shouldn't be Messed With

A playboy is offered the "best sex" of his life by a woman who offers him her daughter's phone number. He's terrible when it comes to his lack of respect for the female gender. And the woman, herself, as gorgeous as she is, has no interest in him. Will he take the bait? We'll see.

AUTHOR'S NOTE

"Do I solemnly swear that the incidents and events you are about to read are what really happened to my protagonist, Keir? Are they the truth, the whole truth, and nothing but the truth, so, help me God?"

"No."

Paul Alexander Fichera
May 1, 2018

Table of Contents

ALSO BY PAUL A. FICHERA 3

AUTHOR'S NOTE.. 6

CHAPTER ONE - The Invitation 9

CHAPTER TWO - Annie's Place.................................. 14

CHAPTER THREE - Autumn...................................... 20

CHAPTER FOUR - A Stroll Through the
Park to Think Things Over 30

CHAPTER FIVE - Prep Work...................................... 40

CHAPTER SIX - There's Always Tomorrow 47

CHAPTER SEVEN - The Calm Before the Storm............. 53

CHAPTER EIGHT - Off to Work 60

CHAPTER NINE - The Future of the Company 76

CHAPTER TEN - Respite 83

CHAPTER ELEVEN - A Tale of Two Thursdays 91

CHAPTER TWELVE - The Holidays
aka There's No Place Like Home 98

CHAPTER THIRTEEN - The Travaglini's...................... 110

CHAPTER FOURTEEN - Christmas Eve, Part One "Sisters." . 120

CHAPTER FIFTEEN - Christmas Eve, Part Two.............. 130

CHAPTER SIXTEEN - Lightening the Mood... Just a Little... 146

CHAPTER SEVENTEEN - A Text from Annie 152

CHAPTER EIGHTEEN - Santa Come and Gone 154

CHAPTER NINETEEN - Christmas Day 166

CHAPTER TWENTY - The Remainder of The Day 182

CHAPTER TWENTY-ONE - A Momentary Return to Sanity .. 188

CHAPTER TWENTY-TWO - A Fond Farewell to
Jim Thorpe, Pa. 196

CHAPTER TWENTY-THREE - Prep for April and
the Excursion 202

CHAPTER TWENTY-FOUR - A Short Hop Across a Very Big
Pond 207

CHAPTER TWENTY-FIVE - The Journey Back 213

CHAPTER TWENTY-SIX - What is real? 224

CHAPTER TWENTY-SEVEN - Cerne Abbas in
Dorset County, England.. 232

CHAPTER TWENTY-EIGHT - The Road Back 238

CHAPTER TWENTY-NINE - Getting Back on Track............. 245

CHAPTER THIRTY - I Am Out of There 252

CHAPTER THIRTY-ONE - Mom and Me One Last Time 256

EPILOGUE - Come What May 260

AFTERWORD 269

CHAPTER ONE -
The Invitation

This doesn't happen very often, I don't suppose. At least as familiar as I would assume it should be it's something I've yet to hear anyone else of my gender complain about it. And maybe it might simply be because they are just too embarrassed to admit it. I'm talking about guys named Eric, Carl or even Robert.

I'm Keir. Keir Adrian Travaglini. And the annoying thing that makes what I'm about to relate today so bothersome is *Adrian*. Not because it's a woman's name for the most part, but because it begins with the letter *"A."* There <u>are</u> guys named *Adrian*. Happily, for me, it's my middle name, rarely spoken aloud and acknowledged by me or known to those I cross paths with. It's when I'm asked to write my name down somewhere that the problem arises. Return mail addressed to *Ms. Keira Travaglini.* I just can't believe this hasn't happened to more guys: First names of a kind like mine that could be effeminized by adding but one extra letter to the end of it.

It reached the point where I would just throw the damn things in the trash in annoyance. I wasn't interested in whatever the senders wanted of me, and the fact that it was addressed to some imaginary woman named *"Keira"* was enough of an incentive for me to just smirk and say, "Straight to the trashcan for you."

In the beginning, it was cute. I would open one and scan the cover letter's opening greeting:

Hi, Keira, how are you today? We at Financial Futures Inc. want to be your go-to location for sound investments and financial security. We just know a woman of your good judgement and common sense knows a thing or two about investing your hard-earned money wisely and I'm sure....

A <u>woman</u> of "my" good judgement and common sense...?

(Assholes.)

I can't be the only male with a name like mine this has ever happened to. And, seriously, among life's many annoyances was this worth getting all bent out of shape over? Just throw it away. What would be the point in writing the company and declaring, *"To whomever screwed up my first name and gender like that: That 'A' at the end of "KEIRA" is my middle initial. There's a gap between that R and that A! I'm male, damnit!"*

(Just throw it away, right?)

It got worse as these sorts of things sometimes tend to do. A new version of this humiliation arrived on my doorstep one day from a company called *Your Inner You.* It was a thick envelope attempting to entice *"Keira"* to consider purchasing product from their fine assortment of women's intimate apparel. And as it happened my girlfriend, *Anita Thrombi* (twenty-something, like me, long brunette hair, to her waist, a great figure, as tall as myself, about five feet eight....) She was visiting on the day it arrived, spotted mail hanging out my apartment's downstairs mailbox and retrieved it. She had to pass the rack of boxes just there to the left of the metal stairway that led up to my place on the second level. She'd gotten my mail for me in the past, so it was no big deal. As she ascended the steps she absently began to sort through the postings and found *Your Inner You's* very large envelope.

"What's this?" I recall her asking, her eyes wide with curiosity as I let her in the door.

I glanced down to what she carried in her hands. "You brought up my mail again," I quipped, innocently. "Thanks." I studied her serious expression, then. "What?"

KEIRA TRAVAGLINI
734 EAST RIVERSIDE DRIVE
APT 34B
PENNS COVE, NJ

"Keira?" she held up for me to read. She started smiling, then, as she regarded my reaction.

I instinctively turned red faced as if I had a secret that had just been revealed.

"Oh crap, Annie, is that another bank trying to get me to open an account with them, and screwing up my first name?" (Her friends, including me, all call Anita, Annie. She prefers *Annie.)*

Annie furrowed her brow at that one and glanced again to the envelope's front. "No..." she answered, confused. *Banks? Banks have been writing you, thinking you're a Keira, for years?"*

"Yeah, for a while now," I nodded, and then realized what she thought was going on. "Annie, no." I made a grab for the envelope; she pulled it away. "It's not what you think. Some idiot company misread my name, and decided my middle initial was the last letter of my first name."

She smirked. "If you say so."

"Come on, Anita. I wouldn't pretend like that. It's another financial company, right? Trying to get me to invest in their company? I thought I was done with all that, once the SOBs got the message that 'Keira' couldn't give a shit about them."

"No," she corrected. "This is a catalog invite to join and order women's undies and bras ... and other good stuff." She glanced to the name again. "I've heard of them." She ripped open the envelope and began inspecting the catalog. "Kind of a *Victoria Secret* knockoff." She nodded. "Some of this stuff looks pretty cute."

"You're kidding?" I furrowed my brow, requesting it. "I thought I was done getting stuff addressed to *Keira.*" I then looked down the correspondence and eventually sighed in despair. "God. I'm receiving catalogue invites like *this* now? *They think I'm a woman?"* I looked up at her then. "You're being mean. I've never even *heard* of this company before."

She smirked again. "I can *see that.*" she giggled. "From the way the cover letter reads, they're trying to entice you to join, to sample some of their fine line of women's ... *unmentionables.* Do you like being mistaken for a '*Keira,*' Keir?"

"*No.* It's embarrassing," I replied. I read the company's name again. "*Your Inner You...*" I huffed in disgust. "It's like with a name like that they're trying to tell me something."

"You want me to throw it away?" she smirked. "Or would you like to look through it first? I know you guys love getting off on the *Victoria Secret* catalog. You want this ... maybe to help you to *amuse yourself* when I'm not around?"

This time I smirked. "No thanks. There's always the internet and porn sites I can assess if I have days like that when I want to ... as you say... *amuse myself* when you're not around."

"Uh huh," she replied. "Then you don't mind if I take it? Some of this stuff I might actually want to order and buy."

"But the invitation is addressed to me— well, *Keira*." I shrugged. "You know what I mean." I nodded.

"Like that would stop them from accepting an order from me? They're looking for customers. Do you really think they care who places an order? But to save all that hassle, I'll just pretend I'm you and send it in with your name on it."

"And girl stuff will come to *my address*, as if I sent for it?"

"No, relax," she replied. "I'll give them mine. They'll just think Keira moved."

She noted, then, the troubled look on my face. "Why not?" she asked.

"Why do I get this feeling, I'm going to get bit in the ass someday over this?"

"I don't know," she replied. "But you know…" she began, pensively. "You *would* make a cute looking girl. I've always thought that."

"What, that I was too pretty to be a boy?"

"Something like that," she replied.

I sighed in exasperation. "Yeah, it's still happening, huh? My mom told me the same thing when I was little. '*You and Kelly look so alike, Keir.*' She'd say that right in front of my sister. My classmates all the time kept telling me I should quit trying so hard to look like a boy, when I wasn't one. I should be wearing tights, knee socks and cute dresses. I was too pretty to be a boy. I wanted to find a hole to crawl into every time I was told that."

"Poor baby," she soothed, approaching me; she began caressing my arms, kneading her fingertips gently up and down my pullover. "I'll bet you were adorable as a kid."

"It was humiliating," I replied. "People constantly kept mistaking me for a girl … a girl who they thought liked dressing in guy clothes."

Anita glanced to the catalog. "I'll bet you'd look pretty good in some of this stuff."

"Does that bother you even a little?" I asked. "I've been told by girls since grade school that I was too girly. Why would they ever want to date me, they'd asked. It would be like hanging out with just another one of their girl buds."

She came forward then and kissed me lightly on the lips. "No, it does not bother me," she replied. "I'm here, and I never said the way you looked turned me off, did I?"

12

"Uh, no," I replied, returning the kiss and kneading my fingers into her waist.

"In fact, if you're willing, when the movie gets out; we can adjourn to my place. I've been meaning to invite you over to test a theory I've been mulling over for quite a while now."

"Why do I not like the sound of that?" I answered, ominously. "You're not just referring to new sex positions, are you?"

"No," she grinned, impishly. "I've got something fun in mind."

"Fun..." I nodded, dreading it. "Just not for me, probably, right?"

She smiled, broadly. "I have a feeling you'll get a real kick out of it. And then after you can fuck the crap out of me in retaliation."

CHAPTER TWO -
Annie's Place

Annie's condo *(Yes, she could afford one)*, resided clear across town in a district reserved for a finer, more affluent class of resident. She and I after the movie ended spent about an hour, soaking in her hot tub. (*Her job at that franchise insurance agency she worked at obviously gave her access to a far more luxurious place to hang her hat than what I could afford with my pathetic job at the local 'The Com-Link' electronics boutique shop.*) I suspect in retrospect she was purposely getting my skin all moist and supple here in the hot tub for whatever she wanted to "try doing" tonight. She cryptically requested we take a shower together after, and we did. Naked and being hit by the warm water of her shower, I was too busy feeling up her body and enjoying every bit of the endeavor, to notice that she had a bottle of Nair hair removal crème on the vanity shelf to my left. When she reached for the Nair and proceeded to open the cap, I got worried.

"What are planning to do with that?" I glanced down at her legs. They obviously didn't need any work done on *them*. (They were gorgeous by the way, long and straight and so smooth and adorable.)

She glanced down at mine, which despite the slight smattering of male hairs up and down them looked quite attractive themselves (though not in good way for a guy.)

I glanced down in the direction she was looking. She was grinning. "Oh, come on, Annie. No."

"It won't hurt," she protested. "And truth tell, it's not like you have a whole lot down there to begin with. It should be child's play to watch it all just rinse off and away."

"Don't I look *girlish* enough?" I protested.

"Yes, but it's not your fault. You told me when we met you were born with an extra X- Chromosome. *Klinefelter's syndrome?"* She attempted to pronounce.

I nodded. "I was born with three x chromosomes and one y, instead of a single 'x' and a 'y'."

"So, you're slowly turning into a woman?"

I grinned and shook my head. "It's more complicated than that and..." I glanced down at my penis, "I don't think so."

"But you are in some ways," she said, touching my nipples. They were surrounded by at this point a growing pair of A-cup breasts. "You really think that ace bandage you wrap around them when you go out in public will fool people forever?"

"Annie," I answered, "I really haven't wanted to think that far ahead."

She nodded. "Please, Keirie?" she asked of the Nair. "Can I do it?"

"I wish you wouldn't call me that," I replied. "My name is *Keir*?"

"Keirie is better. It's fits you better."

"You mean it's more girlish? Use that *Nair* crap on my body and people will think it's the name I prefer."

"Keirie, love, with a body like yours ..." she shook her head ... "whatever those extra X-chromosomes are doing to you, well, let's just say, you don't need any Nair on that cute chest of yours; and those legs of yours look like you're way too old a woman already down there to not be already shaving them. God, you're way too pretty to be a boy." She felt up and down my front, down to my navel and back up again to my chest. "Keirie, if these little boobies of yours get any bigger, you're going to need a bra." She felt down my sides to my middle. "And you're definitely developing some womanly hips and waist action down here." She could feel my torso slanting inward, like a woman's, emphasizing a rounded bottom and butt. "Not much yet," she commented, "but if it gets any worse—"

"I told you, it's a condition I have; my body for some reason didn't get the memo that I was a boy. I know it's doing that down there, and my chest is starting to grow a set of—"

"*We call them 'our girls',*" she said. "You're entering puberty, Keir— *girl puberty.*"

I didn't know what to say to that, didn't want to say anything, so I didn't.

Annie poured some Nair crème into her palm and approached one of my thighs. "This may sting a little, depending on how badly I apply it."

"What else humiliating are you planning on doing to me?"

"I have an outfit in mind I want you to try on. A little work maybe on those eyelashes, mascara, maybe."

"Hey, I have to be at work tomorrow. What are you trying to do to me, get me fired or worse, laughed right out the front door?"

"With your looks, I'll be surprised they weren't half expecting you to experiment like this way before now."

She began to apply it, generously down first my right leg and after, my left, rinsing each off after letting the debilitating cream do its job. The hairs on my right leg melted off my skin and ran down the drain. (Annie's plumbing was in no danger of clogging up from the amount.)

God, that feels weird, I thought as I noted how soft and vulnerable my legs felt with the hair totally expunged. Annie, meanwhile, obviously felt quite pleased by her feminizing work because she began after to knead her fingers lightly up and down my torso, from my developing pair of boobs down to my nether region.

"Oh, look who wants to come out and play," she observed of my … still very young-looking (or not-even-worth-boasting-about) *penis*. She smiled as she took hold of it. "You cute little thing," she told it. "Keirie, are you sure you're even *legal?"*

"I'm *twenty-five,* remember?" I reminded her. "I'm a year older than you."

"You're right, why would you fake stats on your photo ID just to fool your girlfriend?"

"We've been through this before, Annie," I replied. "Will you knock it off?"

"Okay," she smiled.

With the warm water of the shower still cascading down onto us, Annie dropped to her knees and got my *male member* (I'm trying to be delicate here) … to firm up into one of its best *'stances.'* I could see it in Annie's eyes. She wanted the damn thing in her mouth.

I glanced down to what she was doing. She was bringing me to climax in near no time at all. An awful thought suddenly crossed my mind. "Annie, you're not going to make me share after again, are you?"

She glanced up to me, whimsically, and gave me a thumbs-up with her right hand.

Oh, shit.

Damn her.

The worst part of all that was that she knew I kind of not minded.

• • •

"Admit it, you enjoyed that," Annie said to me as we toweled each other off after, atop the mat just outside the shower stall. "I am nuts over you, Keirie."

We were like two females (*and we looked it too),* massaging the moisture from our newly cleansed bodies. "It's time for some real fun now," she said as she kissed me yet again on my lips.

I could still taste the consequence of our prolonged French kiss after her "share" of the blowjob she had just given me. "*Real fun?*" I questioned, dourly. "My mouth feels like I deliberately ejaculated into my own mouth."

"Yeah, well," she began, "if you weren't okay with it, I wouldn't have shared your gift to me with you."

"And now, thanks to you, I'll be tasting that *gift to you* for the next two days."

She grinned. "So, will I."

I wrinkled my nose at her. "That wasn't *all* the humiliating girly type stuff you had in mind for me tonight, was it?"

She shook her head. "You are going to love what I got planned next,*"* she smiled.

Yeah, I kind of doubted that.

• • •

"Ow!" I uttered at one point, as an eyelash hair refused to leave me without putting up some prickly resistance.

"Yeah, yeah," she replied. "Almost done. And stop fidgeting."

She was giving me a complete facial makeover, eyeliner, lashes, mascara, the whole ordeal.

"What am I going to say to the guys and even Sally at the store, tomorrow?" I queried.

"Tell them the truth: your girlfriend, Anita, just wanted to see how pretty you could look."

"Yes," I replied, acidly, "that will satisfy everyone, *absolutely.*"

"There," she said finally. "Now for the clincher." She went over to her bedroom closet and fished out a long brunette wig. "Let's get this on you."

"Oh, fuck, isn't my hair long enough already for whatever way you're planning to strip out any remaining dignity *and maleness* I have left?"

"No. Your mane is long and fluffy enough, I'll give you that, but not for what I have in mind."

Annie set the wig atop my own hair, and worked it into place, and subsequently brushed the long brunette locks to a fine delicate sheen. She then went back to the closet and fished a white top and a burgundy skirt from it and carried them over to me.

"Oh, you're kidding?" I asked. "Why?"

"You gave me the idea when you mentioned earlier how your classmates back in grade school thought you'd make a better-looking little girl than a little boy. I've got the perfect pair of socks and boots to go with it."

She retrieved the ankle boots from the closet floor and fished out a pair of knee socks from one of her bureau drawers. She handed it all to me. "Put these on," she ordered.

"That sounded like a command," I quipped.

"I want to see you in it. Indulge me."

"I suppose you have a bra and a pair of panties to go with it."

"Yes, and I picked up an A-cup, special; just for this day."

I smiled, sarcastically. "Your way of saying you've been planning this for a while."

She smiled in return. "I figure this size 'A' will work fine ... *for now* ... for a girl who's just starting to come into her own."

"I'm going to kill you, you know," I promised her.

She giggled, and then helped me into it, wrapping it around me, front to back, and securing the two cups over my front, imprisoning me in the thing, snapping the fasteners together in the back.

"The panties?" I reminded.

"Oh, who's anxious now?" she asked, giggling.

"We might as well do it right," I said.

"Here you go," she replied, handing me the matching panties *(to the bra)*. "Honestly, though, Keirie, your own briefs would have worked just as well." She retrieved them and held them up before me. "Look at these things."

I glanced first at her and then down at my briefs. I gave her a *Yeah, so?* look.

"They're panties," she stated. "They might as well be. *I* could wear them and be totally convinced they were a pair of mine. Really, Keirie, for someone not happy your body is leaving people thinking you're a girl, *these* aren't helping. They might as well be panties."

"They're not," I defended.

"Actually, I find it kind of cute. No boxers for you. You're giving that body exactly what it wants … *to dress in the same style shit a girl likes against her skin.*"

"Uh huh," I answered. I pulled her panties up to my waist, totally engulfing and concealing any evidence of my masculinity. She was right, the panties neither fit differently or felt any different from the briefs I'd worn prior. The knee socks went on next. They felt weird, soft and wooly, as I pulled them up my newly dehaired lower legs, up to my knees. And the skirt felt equally weird, tickling my upper thighs as it brushed against them so subtly. I finished the outfit, pulling the loose-hanging top over my head and down. Annie tucked part of it under the skirt, and then adjusted my hair (the wig), throwing the bulk of it over my right shoulder.

"Well?" I began, as I stood there in the burgundy socks and matching skirt. "Am I pretty enough for you?" Standing between her bureau and a corner wall, I struck a pose. "I feel like I'm only … *half dressed.*"

She turned very serious. "Oh, my god, Keirie," she said, assessing how I looked.

"What?"

"They were right."

"Who?"

"Your classmates. You were never meant to be born a boy. *What a terrible way to waste a pretty body.*"

CHAPTER THREE - Autumn

It took a while, Annie's using my *Keira* name to order her stuff on-line from *Your Inner You*, but I knew it would one day come back and haunt me. The day began much like any other. I got off early that October day in 2017. The *Com-Link*. There weren't many of them around these days. The company was near bankrupt, close to being sold off, for good maybe this time, not to return. The talk in the store had been ripe with the dismal thought of it all. We might all be looking for other retail work before Christmas. *Best Buy,* maybe. I liked my job. I liked working with electronics, anticipated each year the new Android and Apple smartphones that sent customers scurrying to the be first to trade up. I'd miss all that.

Owing to how "busy" we weren't in the store these days anymore, I had asked permission to head down to the DMV. I needed to update my driver's license, and as in most States here in the U.S., in mine you had to do that in person, with proper ID documents to assure the government you really were you. And of course, there was my mug (my face). It was a photo ID document as well as a permission to drive. It had to be updated every time the thing got renewed. Which meant I had to get my picture taken … again. (*Annie was right about my photo ID*). The last time I had it taken, I'd quipped to the DMV staff that they might just as soon use my class photo from my junior year in high school, taken over ten years earlier. I really had not changed too much in either stature or overall physical maturity. The same dark brown hair; about five feet six inches in height, thereabouts. Kind of a lanky, sinewy build. Honestly, when it comes to physical descriptions of people, I suck at it.

Trust me I hadn't changed much. Twenty-five years old, and I still look like I belong in high school. Unfortunately, thanks to Anita's plucking my eyebrows, they now looked nowhere near as bushy in my new driver's license photo as they had in the prior one. In fact, they made me look downright girly. Where I worked at *Com-link*— they all noticed it as well.

Chuck, the owner, smirked at the news I needed a new photo ID. "With those eyebrows?" he asked. "You want to be reminded of how girly you're capable of looking for the next four years every time a cop asks to see your license? I still can't believe you let Annie do that to you. You must really like her."

"Having her for a girlfriend, has its perks," I only answered.

"Yeah, I bet," he only grinned. "Still, Keirie, you can't afford to look even more girly than you usually do."

"They'll grow back," I protested.

"And then you'll just look like a girl who hasn't plucked her eyebrows in a while. You know it actually works with the rest of you."

And with that quip, I left for the DMV.

• • •

I had contacted Annie while I waited in those god-awful Department of Motor Vehicles metal chairs. Ahead were the nooks where one talked with the DMV agents, had our photos updated, etc. We were assigned a number, told to take a seat, instructed which station to report to when our number was called. It was all so stuffy and serious business-like at the DMV. Everything about the Department of Motor Vehicles sort of came off that way. All business, get in and get out; be thankful you weren't asked to come back tomorrow— this time with the proper documents to complete your application for whatever.

The DMV. Not one of my favorite places to spend a morning … or an afternoon.

And be prepared. You might be there a while.

I heard my name called, eventually. I had done all the preliminary stuff. Got my picture taken, submitted all the proof I was me. I just had to collect my new card, watch the attendant punch a hole in my old one, and inquire how I wished to pay for the renewal.

"Oh my," she remarked as I entered the booth. "I was going to say, *'You can't be a Keira,' but you ARE a boy, right?"*

In truth, what I had heard when my name was called was what sounded like my full name, first and last. I knew it was me who had been called. I simply hadn't heard her add the "a" to the end of *Keir*.

"Yes, I'm a guy." I said in a voice that arguably could go either way. I fingered one of my obviously plucked eyebrows. "My girlfriend did this to me." I took a breath then.

She laughed silently.

"Well, with your voice you could *pass* for a *Keira*," she said, *"but it says here—"*

"No," I answered. I grinned, sheepishly, then glanced down at the documents spread out on the countertop before us. The gap between my first name and my middle initial was clearly present on my new ID card, and there was no question the thing was meant for me: It was my photo on the card *(albeit with moderately plucked eyebrows)*. My stats below the photo identified me as Keir. Apparently, when she'd summoned me, she had only glanced to my name on the folder the thing had been tucked into, not the license itself, and sure enough my name at the top of the folder jammed that "A" too close to the "R" and the poor woman just assumed she was summoning a female to her station.

"That's my middle initial," I corrected her. I nodded then. "This happens a lot."

"Being mistaken for a girl?" she queried.

"Yes, but no," I insisted. "Companies keep mistaking Keir for Keira because they keep forgetting to put a space between the *R* and the *A."*

"I'd call that," she informed me, "the least of your worries. You're not helping your case, going out in public looking...." She waved her hand at me. "Looking too pretty to be a boy. Your girlfriend talked you into letting her pluck your eyebrows? Honestly, you got more going on there than just girly eyebrows." She glanced down then to the license, to my name spaced correctly underneath my photo. "Oh, yeah. 'Keir.' How about that." She studied my face and then glanced again to my ID photo. "Are you sure you're a *boy?"*

I grunted an acknowledgment. "I'm a boy."

"What's the A stand for?" she queried.

I paused with that one. "Adrian." I almost didn't want to tell her.

She snorted. "I was going to suggest you call yourself by your middle name, and sign your documents that way, but *Adrian? Wow.* Was your mother hoping for a daughter?"

I frowned. Sarah Travaglina (my mom) had given birth to three boys prior to finally getting a daughter: Kelly. She was hoping for a second girl to help even the mix.

"Yeah, she kind of was," I lamented.

"You could pass for one." She gathered up my documents and handed them to me. "Here you go now."

"Thanks."

Soon after, I was out the door, back on the road, and headed for town.

• • •

I had promised Annie I'd meet her at the nearby Cracker Barrel around noon. Noon it almost was. Annie as I've mentioned was an insurance agent at one of those independently owned agencies. You've seen them, I'm sure, if you've ever spent some time in the rural districts. They looked from the road like someone's bungalow home. Inside, a few desks replaced conventional furnishings in rooms clearly meant to be rooms in a family dwelling. There was even a kitchen nook somewhere, maybe even complete with a built-in oven. Anyway, as you might guess, it's where I met Annie. We sort of hit it off some time before when I showed up there to make a payment on my auto policy.

As I expected, she was already in the parking lot of Cracker Barrel, waiting for me to arrive. I parked my car beside hers, we greeted one another *(do you really need details?)*, and I felt compelled to tell her about my ordeal at the DMV not a half hour earlier. She was laughing about it all the way across the parking lot and into the building's vestibule.

• • •

"Hello, ladies, can I start you off with some drinks?" the waitress asked as she approached our table. "Oh, sorry," she offered as she realized her error, when she finally *looked* and saw the people she was about to serve. "I guess I wasn't paying attention. I'm sorry, what can I get you two to drink to start you off?"

"Don't apologize," Annie replied to her. "He gets that a lot." She grinned over at me, then. "Severs think we're a couple of girls out for a meal all the time."

The waitress grinned. "Okay."

Annie gave her request then. "Iced tea."

"A root beer," I smiled. It was the first I had spoken. "And yes," I continued, "it happens a lot. I don't know why ... *usually.*" I rubbed one of my eyebrows, and glanced icily at Annie.

As the waitress departed, I heard Annie snicker. I huffed. "Thanks for making this worse by telling her my life story," I said.

Annie shrugged. "You're welcome." And then, "They will grow back, you know," she said of my eyebrows. "And after, people will *still* mistake you for a woman. You must give off a female vibe, on top of everything else."

"I'm getting a little sick of this," I said.

She nodded. "First the woman at the DMV, today, and now our waitress."

24

"She wasn't even looking this way. They never do. They just assume I'm female, even when I'm here with my mom and Kelly. Just one of the girls. It's really starting to feel like it can't just be a coincidence. It keeps happening."

"Are you still getting mail sent to 'Keira'?"

"No, thank God."

"No more financial institutions or insurance companies trying to talk you into being a smart young lady and invest with their company?"

I cocked an eyebrow at her. "No," I simply answered. "Can we change the subject?"

"Well, we could, but I actually got some interesting news. Remember *Your Inner You,* that woman's apparel shop that sent you their catalog?"

"They're still corresponding with you?"

"Well, actually," she answered, "they're still corresponding with *Keira,* but to your question: *yes,* I'm still hearing from them."

"They're still sending 'me' catalogs to *your* place?"

"Yeah, all the time. This bra I'm wearing today.... I ordered it from them. It's nice." She nodded, then. She had no intention of expounding about the bra, and as it lay hidden underneath her wool sweater, I left it at that.

"What's the 'news'?" I asked finally.

"Keira won an all-expenses paid vacation in Europe … for two. Paris, London, Rome."

I smirked. "Really? How did that happen?"

She shrugged. "I guess the last time I ordered I was automatically entered in their contest."

"You mean, *Keira was.*"

"If you insist on splitting hairs."

This time I shrugged. "When for?"

"That's open. We can pick whatever date we want. Within reason, I suppose. I think it has to be within the next twelve months."

"We?"

She shrugged again. "It *is* for two."

"I've never been overseas, and with my salary at The Com-Link I doubt I'll ever make enough money to afford a thing like a trip like that anytime soon. I just hope I still have a job a year from now."

"Your company is doing that badly?"

I nodded, depressingly. "Yeah."

"They'd cover everything. All Keira would have to do is let them do a few promotional shots of her and a friend, if she wants to invite one, at the various locations we'd be booked to visit." She shrugged yet again. "I really wish I'd used my own name when I ordered now. That trip should have been mine."

"Tell them," I suggested. "Are you sure it's not a scam?"

She smiled. "It's a legitimate company. It's no scam."

"So, again, *tell them,* maybe they'll honor it."

"They'll just give the prize to someone else."

"You could explain to them the stupid mistake they made and how much you liked their inventory and … used my bogus name just to keep ordering stuff. Who knows, they might."

"I already contacted them, and said all that. It didn't matter. They said, if there is no Keira, then the prize is invalid and they'll just award it to someone else. *Or back out of awarding it altogether,"* she added, cynically.

"So, I guess as usual it's one of those things like where you think you've hit the jackpot, and then they tell you, *'Oh, no; we're sorry, but this entry is no good. It's invalid.'* Anything to avoid paying out."

Annie hesitated in this next part. "I gave them a *what if…"* she said then.

I did not like the sound of that one at all. "What?" I dreaded.

"I told them, *'I'm not saying this is true, but what if my boyfriend, Keir, wanted to go on that trip as well, and insisted just because you got his name wrong that was no reason to invalidate the award. He is the person you initially contacted thinking he was a woman. He's the one you awarded the prize to.'"* She took a breath. "Again, they reminded me that one of the conditions of the award was that the prizewinner had to agree to be photographed in key locations in Europe wearing some of their … *'intimate apparel."*

"Yeah, that would be amusing, me posing in a bra and panties in *Trafalgar Square* or the *Spanish Steps* in Rome."

"With a little work, I'll bet you could even pose stark naked," she smiled, "and pull it off. Your *girls* are really starting to fill out. It hasn't even been a week since we took that picture of you in my bedroom. You're getting worse even without the supplements. I'll bet even now you would look great in an elegant gown climbing those *Spanish Steps* or being photographed tossing coins in *Trevi Fountain."*

26

"That fountain is famous," I said. "It's been used in a lot of famous movies."

"I know," she said. "And I love that you know that," she replied. "Why?"

"Cause the only straight guys who would bring it up like this are guys on a first date, trying to impress a girl with their sensitivity and elegant sophistication."

"Are you saying being with me is like being out with one of your girlfriends?"

"Yes, you're more girl than you think you are." She reached forward and touched my forehead. *"Up here. You know, if Your Inner You demanded you profile as a female to not embarrass the firm's reputation, you could. We already know you make a convincing young woman.*

"There's a guy in his twenties, I forget his name, Keir; I think he hails from Australia. He's enjoying a hell of a career modeling as both a male AND a female."

"Anita," I emphasized, using her given name. *"No. You're not serious. They'd never go for that, even if I can make a convincing female."*

"I told them you weren't, that I was just giving them a *what if...,"* she replied. "I also told them, *'I'm not saying this is true also, but if Keir made a stink, insisting you awarded him the prize, and he was currently in the process of undergoing a male to female conversion....'* Well, they said, they'd have to see how far along you were. If you were only trying to make a mockery of the whole thing by showing up looking like a laughable substitute for a female, that might make their company look stupid. On the other hand, they considered themselves progressive enough to not only welcome woman customers ordering from them, but ... you know, guys who kind of wished they were also."

"I can't believe we're actually talking about this!" I replied. "Annie, no! It's humiliating enough that I keep being mistaken for a female, when people aren't even looking directly at me."

She nodded. "We *could* pull it off, you know, with minimal prep. I'm thinking of sending them that other shot I took of you a few days ago, you know, in the wig, and on the skateboard?" She retrieved her smartphone and called up the photo.

In it, I was in a local skateboard arena, not so much working the thing *(I was never really all that proficient or enthusiastic about that sort of sport even back when I WAS a kid)*. This was just a shot Annie thought up to show how much like a young post-adolescent girl in her late teens I could pull off resembling in the right outfit, which consisted of a light blue, strapless top that ended just above my ever-developing breasts and extending down to an ultra-short pair of faded denim cut offs that revealed one sexy pair of smooth thighs. *Mine* incredibly. Even I would be convinced as a pair they belonged not on a guy but on an extremely cute young girl. In the photo, I was only using the skateboard as a place to rest my behind, as I stared forward in the reddish-brown wig that draped my breasts. I was gazing absently upon my bare knees and calves, my tiny admittedly girly small feet encased in a pair of black sneaks and white crew socks.

I stared at the photo intently. ***"Don't you dare!"*** I answered of her showing it to anyone.

"Keirie, they might just say yes. That it beats the bad publicity from admitting they made the initial error. Will you at least think about it, Keirie?" she asked me then. "I *really* would love to see Europe at least once before I die."

"With me pretending *that I'm her* the whole time?" I nodded to the "girl" in the photo— *me atop the skateboard* looking like a girl. "I'd have to be pretty desperate."

"They probably wouldn't insist on that, when we were alone, anyway; like after hours in our hotel rooms. It would just be *us*. And seriously, Keir, how pretty do you think they're expecting you to be? *Not that you'd disappoint them."*

"What do you mean?

"You weren't entered in a beauty contest. Just a random drawing of their mostly female customers; they don't expect the winner to be a swimwear model. And I'm sure they have plenty of males buying stuff from their catalogs as well. I guess in that case, they'd either accept that they have to make some kind of exception and honor the win, or get sued for sexual discrimination."

"They why are they being assholes about this win?"

"Because of what happened. They *thought you were a Keira*. If the truth gets out, they'll look stupid. I think if you insist on it, they'd be willing to help in any they can to help you help them protect their image."

"What are they going to do? Foot the bill for a sex change?"

"Keirie, don't be stupid. You just have to look reasonably authentic in probably any touristy shots they take of us walking around. Longshots. It's not like they want you to do formal on-location photo shoots." She nodded. "They take one look at you, the way you look—" She smiled. "You're probably more than they ever would hope for from most guys your age, the way you look."

"I'm not sure I like the sound of that," I confessed.

It was around that time that our drink orders arrived and the waitress asked us what we'd chosen for our lunch order. We told her we would need extra time to choose. She smiled, said *no problem* and said she'd come back.

I had to admit one thing: me pretending to be *Keira* while in Europe caused my heart to pump faster, I could feel it; the tiny hairs of my arms started to tingle. I hated to think what was causing that to happen within my psyche. Where the fuck was all that coming from and why.

Shit.

CHAPTER FOUR –
A Stroll Through the Park to
Think Things Over

I was in my apartment about a week later, off from work for the day, and just moping around. Annie had given me a few days to think about the trip. Why does the universe hate me? If Annie had only just used her own name, maybe the universe—

Maybe the universe what? Awarded <u>her</u> the trip? The universe would have awarded the trip to some other lucky soul.

Right. That was how things usually went. At least, where my luck was concerned; it was as predictable as the sun rising each morning. Yes, an all-expenses paid trip to Europe would go to someone else. It went to me because life really enjoyed fucking with me. I mean, I could say no, easily. But what did I have to look forward to? Yeah, I graduated college, had a degree, a B.A., which wasn't really all that useful. I was working retail, with a firm that could very well go under soon, and if not, would almost certainly initiate another round of store closings and staff firings. I'd been with *The Com-Link* three years since graduating. It had been enough of an income to at least allow me to move out of my parents' place and into an apartment of my own. Of course, it didn't hurt that the old man helped me out a little getting on my feet with the rent for a few months. I truly believed it was because he wanted his youngest kid to get out on his own, and free Dad and Mom up to start enjoying their senior years.

And as for the trip, it wasn't as if anyone was seriously expecting me to do some serious crap to my physique. Stuff like transitional gender hormones and breast implants. I just had to pass for a girl whenever the company photographer showed up to snap off a few promotional shots of Anita and me out on the tourist stops, enjoying ourselves. On the other hand, I'd have to keep a low profile. I wouldn't want someone to take an unusually intense interest in who I was. And then of course there was the plane ride across the Atlantic. Ten hours at least trying to not get unmasked as a fake, a crossdressing male, who liked pretending he was a woman, or worse looking so convincing at it, that guys tried to hit on me during the flight.

Speaking of which—

Passports. Mine would have to read *Keira,* my sex: "Female." My picture on the thing would have to match. And somehow the thing would have to be legal *(or look it).* God, this was not the era to be boarding international flights to port of calls overseas carrying bogus documents. And trying to get back in the U.S. with a passport that claimed I was a *she*? What if they wanted to do a pat down, or wanted me to head to a back room for a more intense strip search? Oh, they would find something on me, all right. A penis where one was not supposed to be. That was the last thing I needed to deal with: Homeland Security wanting to know what I was up to and why. I would need *Your Inner You* to help smooth that one out from the get go. I was intent on hitting them up at the very least for a wig of my own *(not one of Anita's);* a shoulder length woman's wig, and not a cheap ass fake one, something assembled with real human hair. The thing had to look the real thing. I mean, seriously, I could let my own hair grow out even longer than it already was, but to reach any appreciable length would take years.

Yeah, I needed to purchase a wig … *and keep on plucking my eyebrows,* while I was at it; figure out how to apply mascara on my own; eyelashes. Oh, fuck, was I really considering this stuff? I knew the way I was built that mother nature pretty much left me bereft in the masculine physique department. My thin, slender arms. My legs were cute enough to get stares every time I went out in shorts. And now so silky smooth and soft as my legs were, guys would be scratching their heads over me constantly. *"Is that a girl?"*

I needed some air.

A run along the river down in the park might help just fine about now. Yeah….

• • •

Yes sir, the fall colors looked great this time of year, and the way the river was rippling and all one could easily tell just from a photograph that the autumn breeze was up. It was downright bracing and a pleasure on one's bare legs and arms as one jogged the riverfront path. I decided I'd try wearing the same outfit Annie had had me wear for the skateboard photos (minus the wig.) She had let me keep the shorts, top, socks and sneaks. It was all girl stuff, but I asked her if I could have them, just to get used to the idea of what it felt like to be a girl dressed casually for a run in the park and out in public.

I glanced down at myself. Even without the wig, I had long enough hair, that I could easily be mistaken for a girl. A teenage one, actually; one nowhere near a twenty-something young woman, years past her pubescence.

Regarding Anita's request that I *'think about her proposition,'* I wasn't allowing myself to dwell on any of it. At least I kept telling myself that, but in the back of my mind I knew it was just lurking back there, waiting for its chance to rise and demand I do so once more. I stopped to take a breath after a while and sat down upon one of the river-facing benches, those sad things with brushed metal plaques with names on them of people who once lived, whom I never knew, would never know; who had died and at the bequest of their loved ones could have their having lived memorialized here in this riverside park.

"Hey, Keir, how are you?" came a voice suddenly before me, silhouetted by the river's bright glare. I pulled my head forward again and opened my eyes.

"Uh, hey…. Joe, how's it going?"

He was out here, dressed much like myself— in shorts way too short, tracking far up his thighs and near his genitals. Same as me. Only, his body looked typical for a guy, muscled and taunt in a way guys tended to look, especially their legs. Women's legs by contrast, in my opinion anyway, always looked as if they were as child-like as they were when they were all still young girls.

But then so do mine, especially now with not a lick of hair anywhere upon them.

Oh yeah; for the conversation that followed, this should be mentioned as explanation: *Joe Bennington was gay.*

Yeah, we all knew that at the store. He always wanted me to ring his purchases up, or answer questions about whatever he was interested in purchasing. He must have sensed a vibe there as well. You know, the way women regard gay guys as good listeners and conservationists, like their girlfriends, someone you could share intimate knowledge with and know that they'd be supportive. I think the word I'm looking for was: *empathy.* Joe Bennington was an electronics geek. Loved *Star Trek* and *Star Wars.* And all the *X-men* movies.

• • •

"Here comes your admirer," Chuck would always say when Joe came into the store. "I don't know which of you two I worry about more."

"He's not my boyfriend," I would insist. *"I'm not gay."*

• • •

"I haven't seen you in the store in a while," I said to Joe back now in the present and on the park bench. He reminded me a little of Sheldon on the *Big Bang Theory,* tall and wiry, almost gaunt looking with bulging sort of eyes, a lot like the actor, Jim Parsons, who portrayed the character.

"Yeah," Joe Bennington nodded. "I might be in soon. I've been procrastinating all year trading up to the new Samsung S8 phone. Somehow, I can't seem to want to let go of my S7 edge."

"We still have a couple eights left," I answered. "A few plus eights, also."

"Are you guys still in business?"

"For now."

"Want to run with me for a while?"

"Yeah, sure," I replied, as I alighted the bench. We started off down the riverfront.

• • •

"Hey, Keir?" he asked me at some point as we jogged. "You're wearing girl-stuff, you know that, right?"

"It's complicated," I replied. *"Annie gave them to me."*

"To wear?"

"It's complicated," I simply repeated.

"Man, what are you now?" he asked me. "About twenty-two?"

"I'd still be in college if I were that age," I replied. "Twenty-*five*. Why, what are you?"

"Twenty-six. You don't look it."

"Yeah, so everyone keeps telling me. Like those two." I nodded to a couple of older women, senior citizens to be sure, who had parked themselves at a bench further up the other end of the park.

"What did *they* do?" he inquired, focusing on to whom I was referring.

"They asked me how I liked school and if I'd met any cute guys yet."

Joe laughed. "Well, fuck, you *are* dressed like a fifteen-year-old girl."

"It's not funny. A couple weeks ago, my boss, Chuck, at The *Com-Link*...."

"Yeah, I know him," he grunted. "Typical straight guy. Treats me like mother nature really fucked up when she made me."

"You think he's any better with me?" I countered. "With a face and body like mine? Anyway, Chuck took all of us in the store down to that tavern out on Cedar Run road."

He nodded, "I *know* it."

"I think he's prepping us for the day he closes the store for good."

Joe Bennington huffed. "Yeah, that sucks big time. So, what happened at the tavern? Did they card you?"

"The proprietor asked me if I were legal, if I were twenty-one. *'No, I wasn't,'* I told him."

"Why did you tell him *that* for?"

"Just so that could I follow it up with, *'If you'd asked me that four years ago, I could have said yes.'"*

34

Joe had to stop for a second. We'd been jogging at a healthy clip for some time. He snorted a laugh. "How did he take that?"

"He just looked at me, like he didn't believe me, like I was some smart-ass kid still in high school. Then, he looked over at Chuck and asked, '*She's twenty-five?*' Chuck snorted and said, '*No, he's twenty-five.*' The proprietor, I swear, he did a double take. 'And *she's a he?*' The man regarded me again and said, '*Damn, I don't know which lie I believe less, that you're that old or that you're a guy.*' I shrugged my shoulder at him, and answered, '*I was both, last time I checked.*' He had the nerve to glance down at my crotch, and ask, *"Are you sure?"*

"Didn't you tell me you were used to being told that stuff by this point?"

"Do *you* ever get used to the stares you get for being *gay*?"

Joe nodded that he got it. No of course one never did. "Did he serve you whatever you wanted?"

"I don't really drink, you know," I replied. "I ordered a light beer. It still made me dizzy ... a little."

"One *light* beer?"

"What can I say? I'm not a lover of spirits."

"Did you ever think about lifting weights, bulking up?" Joe asked then.

"Why?"

"So, you'd look <u>less</u> like a girl ... you <u>do</u> you know, *a teenage one at that.* You even talk like one."

"Well, I've been practicing," I admitted.

"*Why*?" Joe inquired, puzzled.

"Isn't it obvious?" I asked. "It fits who I am, in my mind, anyway. I like sounding this way."

"So, you wish you'd been born a girl, then?"

"What I *wish* was that mother nature had made up her fricking mind, when she designed me," I said. "Sometimes I do, other times I'm okay being just who I am."

"Are you into guys?"

"I'm straight, okay? No."

"Man, you were meant to be a girl. I mean, come on. Look at you. Most women, the straight ones I've talked, and you know— gay guys like me— women like to confide in, *we're great listeners, interested,* just like their female friends.... Most of them would rather *get it on* with someone who didn't look and feel to them like another one of their girlfriends."

"I thank my good fortune for *Annie; she* thinks I'm fine just as I am."

"You're lucky."

"**You** don't fantasize a roll in the sack with me, do you?" I queried.

"No, you're not my type," he smiled. "Here's some advice though. Don't ever do time. You wouldn't last a day in prison, not with that body. If you weren't into being with guys before, you might not-mind anymore after a stint in the joint."

"So, what are you driving at, Joe?"

"Man, I know a couple of straight guys who probably would fuck you just for how girly you look. And with that face, that body. You ever done that? Stuff like that? Hang out with a guy in that way?"

I came to a dead stop. "No. Why are you asking me a question like that?"

"You don't just look *like a girl,* Keir. You're pretty. I'm surprised guys don't line up asking to get it on with you."

I paused in my reply. "They have; I pointed out to them I had a dick same as them."

"*And?*"

I smirked. "A few answered, '*so what?* '"

He laughed. "Then, what did you do?"

"I got the hell out of there *real fast.* "

"I don't blame you. You're cute enough to fuck, and that's not a put down. So, nothing weird … *ever?*"

"*Uh…* " I hesitated.

"What?"

"Annie insists sometimes, you know, when we do it? That I share the stuff with her after I unload in her … you know, in her mouth? She says, it's only fair."

"Huh."

"Does that mean I'm *gay,* that I don't mind?"

"I don't know. Depends on how you feel about doing it."

"It's semen, it's not like it'll kill me or anything … *and it's mine.*"

"I think you are way more girl than you want to believe you are." He looked me over. "The universe screwed you big time. Couldn't

decide what gender it wanted you to be … and not just physically."
He tapped my forehead. "In there … where you live."

*Christ, now _he_ was imitating Annie, tapping my forehead and
giving me the same FYI spiel.*

"Thanks, Joe, I really needed to hear that, especially today."

"Why, what happened today?"

"Annie wants me to make a decision, if not today, *tomorrow*.
You're going to laugh your ass off over this one."

"No shit, what? *Spill.*"

"You know *Keir* and *Keira* are two names gender-distinguished
by only one extra letter."

"Yeah, so."

"Let's go find a bench. You're going to love this one."

*I told him about **Your Inner You**.*

• • •

"Are you going to do it?" he asked after I'd finished telling him
about the contest I'd unhappily won.

"I haven't decided; I don't know, *maybe*. Why not?" I pulled my
phone from the back pocket of my barely-there denim cutoffs. "I'm
a natural. Look."

Annie had copied onto my smartphone the photo of me sitting
atop the skateboard in the same pair of faded denim cutoffs— barely
covering my upper thighs; a turquoise-blue tight top with a low-cut
neckline and spaghetti straps to keep it from slipping down below
my newly budding cleavage; black sneaks with white outlines atop
a cute pair of white crew socks … and the long reddish-brown wig
that draped my teen-girl cleavage. Those long slender arms of mine
gripping the skateboard, looked so girly; my equally slim smooth
legs dangled to a side off the skateboard as in the photo I
contemplated my clean-shaven thighs. I looked cute, and believable
as all get out. I cued the photo up and showed it to him.

Joe studied the photo, intently, and finally nodded. He glanced
over at me then, in the same outfit, minus the long-haired wig.
"Whose idea was it to add the wig, you or her?"

"*Her,*" I replied. "And then we had sex soon after."

He smirked. "That little penis of yours still *actually works?*"

I blushed. "Fuck off. And *yes*, when it feels like it."

"Your girlfriend likes girls. It sounds to me like she's not yet
willing to admit it to herself. You're the best of both worlds. Good

God, *look at you!"* He continued to study my skateboard photo. *"That's a girl!* Man, if I weren't gay, *I'd* want to fuck you."

I smirked. "I think that IS— like you say— what she likes about me. She kind of acts around me like I'm one of her *girl*friends."

"I like the wig; it suits you." He glanced at my head. "Your real hair is practically as long as that. You might seriously consider getting it styled. It wouldn't take much."

"People mistake me for a girl as it is," I retorted. "Why make things worse?"

"Come on," begged Joe. "That top, those sneaks— that only work on girl's cute little feet— and those girly shorts?" He glanced to me dressed in all of it today. "You're brave coming out here in public in that." He studied the photo more intently. "Are those real?" he asked of my boobs.

"Yeah, they're real."

"Is there a bra under that top?" He glanced to my chest in the same blue top.

"No, that's just me under there."

"I never noticed how developed you were before."

"That's because before now out here in the park or when you saw me at work in the shop I wore an Ace bandage wrapped around my *'girls,'* as Annie calls them, so no one would notice I was slowly developing. They've grown so much in the last few months … and my hips seem to be getting wider as well—"

"Your waistline is getting cuter as well," he remarked. "You're looking pretty good down there."

I simply looked at him. *"Thanks….* Today, I decided *fuck it.* I'm wearing this girly outfit Annie gave me, no bandage, no downplaying what's happening to me. If people notice and mistake me for a girl, *I'm tired of worrying about it."*

"Is all this because of that condition you told me about, the extra female chromosome?"

"It's slowly turning me into a girl."

"Are you taking female hormones to help that out?"

I blushed at the question; so far no one had dared asked me that straight out. "No." I insisted.

"Yeah … okay … if you say so. You're probably lying to me, but to hell with it. I'm not going to push it."

"I'm not lyi—" I started to insist, but he cut me off.

"A trip to Paris, pretending to be *Keira,*" he hypothesized, "it sounds like an adventure."

"But *that* would be '*lying*'," I informed him, finishing my previous declaration. "I'd be pretending to be someone I'm not."

"So? You really think with a body like that, you couldn't pull it off? And besides will anything near as exciting ever come your way again?"

"*It's lying!*" I repeated. "I'm not a *real girl.*"

"Don't be so sure about that."

"What if I *like* the way I am? Annie's great; she's everything I could ever ask for. What more do I need out of life? I'm happy just as I am."

"Keir, I hate to break it to you…" he showed me my skateboard photo again. "*That's* a girl. *You're a girl!*" He nodded. "Embrace it; be one, be what nature intended you to be. Be *your inner you.*"

I could have hit him for that one. "You ought to do standup," I replied. "You're a *fucking comedian.*"

"It's called *irony, Keira….*"

CHAPTER FIVE - Prep Work

"Do we *have* to do this?" I asked Annie about a month later in late November as we entered a local beauty salon. "What will I say to everyone who sees me with my hair done like a woman's? They'll think I'm queer."

Annie grinned as she surveyed my overall *'look,'* head to toe. Under *my* faux leather jacket, I had worn to work that day a deep gray wool pullover, stone-washed charcoal black jeans and tannish-brown boat-dock shoes. My usual *work-at-The Com-Link* attire. But even under the jacket and the pullover, my failing attempts to conceal with an Ace bandage my blossoming set of breasts was hard-put to be concealed. And then there was the matter of my equally blossoming S-shaped figure. My waist had begun by late November to sink inward and my hips were definitely starting to round themselves out.

"Yeah, Keir," Annie answered. "A new hairdo will definitely be the only change you'll have to live down."

"What do you mean?"

"Seriously?" she queried. "Are you that *in denial* or are you *just screwing with me?*"

"Sooner or later," I continued, innocently, "my family will demand I tell them why I'm trying so hard to look like my sister. What will I say to *them*?"

"Okay. *Stay* in denial. Just say, 'Anita wanted to do Europe, and this opportunity was just sitting there for us to take.'"

"Yeah, I don't think that will go down with them all that well."

"Come on," she said, finally, as she walked me over to the coatrack just inside the entrance. She removed her jacket and proceeded to hang it on one of the hooks. It was a faux, spotted white and brown leopard pattern jacket. She reached for the black fake leather jacket I wore over my gray pullover and hung it up for me. She then led me over to the posh benches in the waiting area to sit and wait for the beauticians to acknowledge our arrival.

Annie had worn that day to the agency where she worked a long-sleeved white top with a gold fringe above the nape of her neck, and ringed with horizontal light brown stripes; a matching skirt, burnt orange-brown in hue, which tightly ended mid-thigh around her waist and upper thighs. It was accented with a wide brown belt sporting two ornate ring-shaped clasps. Chocolate brown tights and off-red and tan pumps with a four-inch heel completed the outfit. She struck a pose, purposely I think, to tease me, taking up one whole bench.

(Her legs in the tights and pumps looked great on her by the way.)

"Where am I supposed to sit?" I only asked.

She grinned and then made room.

"Anita…?" a stylist said to Annie as she approached us soon after. "You were a little vague on the telephone yesterday when you called. You said you were bringing in a new client who needed a *full makeover?* For an upcoming occasion?"

Annie nodded. "And today *is* a good day?" she pursued. "You *can* do it all?"

"An ear piercing, nails done, a leg waxing and a better 'do?' *The works?*" The stylist recalled all the requested jobs from memory. "Yeah, today's a slow day. We can do it."

Annie nodded and then glanced over to me. *"It's for him."*

"Oh," the stylist replied as she eyed me. *"Who do we have here?"*

I extended my hand. "Hi, I'm Annie's boyfriend," I said.

She glanced to my "breasts," my face, the rest of me. You'd almost think I was lying about the *boyfriend* part. The stylist glanced to Annie again; Annie grinned and nodded that *the works … for me* was indeed why we were both here today. The stylist ran her fingers through my long hair, to get a feel for what she needed to do. She nodded. "You're very pretty for a boy, aren't you?" she observed of me, then. She turned to Annie again. "You want to make over your boyfriend as a woman— sculptured nails and extensions, pierced ears and style his hair so it looks more feminine?"

Annie simply nodded. "Yeah."

41

"Are you okay with all this, young man?" the stylist asked me.

"Can you chop my manhood off while you're at it?" I asked. "Might as well go all the way."

Annie reached over with her finger and thumb and flicked the side of my face. *"Stop that,"* she ordered. She smiled at the stylist. "He's kidding."

The woman smirked. "We don't do that."

Annie explained to the stylist why we needed it styled. Some firm was doing a pictorial on guys who were unusually female in continence, and her boyfriend here needed to look as female as was feasible.

"If you're trying to look more like a pretty woman, hon," the stylist said to me, directly, *"I don't think you can.* You're already too beautiful to be a boy." She glanced to my breasts, and after— to my budding womanly figure.

"Thanks," I replied, cynically.

"What's your name, sweetie?"

"*Keir*. It's Gaelic. My mom had a thing for *Kyra Sedgwick*, the actress. She was hoping for another girl."

"She came close." She led Annie and me over to her styling chair, and bid me take a seat within it. "My name's Helen by the way."

"Hi," I replied.

"Making you pretty won't be hard at all," she affirmed, starting to go to work. "Was your mom, Keir, disappointed … that you were born a boy?"

"Truthfully?"

"Okay."

"I'm the youngest, three older brothers and an older sister. Mom wanted at least one more, another girl. She kind of encouraged me to go in that direction. Dad hated it, but Mom kind of told him, '*You already have three sons, so shut up!'* I glanced up at her. "She used the F-word, actually, but I was afraid you might get upset if I repeated it."

Helen laughed. "That's okay. She told him to *fuck off,* huh?" She laughed again. "How did your dad take that?"

"He wasn't happy, but Mom pretty much put her foot down. She told him, '*Keir was born with two extra X-chromosomes per pair, you know that. You were there when that specialist told us with Keir's condition he might one day favor my gender over yours, both*

42

physically and mentally. Keir likes it when I dress him like his sister, so let me raise him the way I please."

"I think I've heard of that condition before."

I nodded. "It's very rare, especially my version. Something about two extra X chromosomes per strand, four from Mom, four from Dad. How it will ultimately affect those of us with it is anybody's guess." I angled the fingers of both my hands at my body. "I guess I hit the jackpot."

"Did your mother encourage your exploring your *female* side?"

I turned to Annie, who was hanging on every word. "Yeah, more or less. She would dress me in Kelly's hand-me-downs, Kelly's jeans, tops … her panties, when it was just the three of us alone in the house."

"Dresses, skirts?" she pursued.

I paused on that one, looked at Annie again. "Yeah. We'd all three go shopping, me in one of Kelly's … *outfits*. Sometimes dresses, sometimes shorts and socks. It didn't matter; I looked the real thing, whatever I wore. No one knew I wasn't a real girl."

"Didn't it embarrass you?"

I glanced up at the stylist. "I kind of *liked* being Kelly's little sister…. *I can't believe I'm telling you all this."*

"It's fascinating; I'm glad you are. It's not easy to talk about such things. I'm sorry for you. Sometimes mother nature screws up, does her job wrong. You should have been born straight out a girl."

"Mom more or less raised me as if I were."

"It's wonderful you're so supportive of all this, Anita," the stylist said to Annie. "Most people wouldn't be."

"No. They wouldn't." Annie replied, stiffly. I sensed she was a little miffed by what I had told Helen. "All this time we've been together," she began, "he's never told me any of that. If Keirie is so used to being a girl, and being seen in public as one, don't hold back. Make him so pretty, no one will ever guess he's not the real thing down there."

Helen studied her. "Are you okay, Anita?"

"I didn't know his Mom and sister did all that to him when he was still just a little kid. I'm just having a little difficulty processing it," Annie said. "New information."

"Do you want time to rethink this, try it again another day, after you two have had a chance to talk it over?"

"No, now more than ever, I want it done today. I'm fine with it all."

She glanced to me. "Are you okay with all of this, Keir?"

I shrugged. "I guess."

"How old are you, Keir?"

"I'll be 26 next April," I said.

"You don't look your age," she replied. "You've got great genes."

"It runs in the family," I answered. I was eyeing Annie in concern. My honesty with Helen apparently had taken some of the fun out of this for her.

Helen ran a fingertip down the side of my face. "And you definitely don't profile as a boy. You've got way too pretty features and skin. I'll bet your brothers tortured the hell out of you."

"They called me little Keira, and treated me as if I were their baby sister."

"Yeah, that's what I figured. Brothers. I've got two of them." She snorted, derisively. "They're family, so you got to love them, even if they are brothers. You *got* to love them, I think It says so in the handbook somewhere."

I had to laugh at that and I could see Helen was happy she'd drawn a smile out of me. She turned and called to one of the workers. "Sandra, this young man wants his legs waxed. Can you squeeze him in?"

The other woman glanced to me. I could tell by *her* expression a million thoughts were going through her mind; one, that *he couldn't be a* boy, *he's too pretty.* I'm certain it floated around somewhere as well within that mind of hers. No doubt the request for a leg waxing was not for sports-related applications. This was going to make a guy— who already looked *way* too feminine— look even more so. I could see her thinking it over. She looked— I would say— in her early thirties; blond, with a cut that stopped just shy of her shoulders and hung loosely about her face. "I'll try," she told Helen, ultimately.

Okay," Helen said. "After I'm done with the initial prep, he's all yours." And to me, "And when *she's* finished, we'll see about piercing your ears, and doing up those cute fingers of yours with a nice pattern and extensions. Such slender, tiny hands." She shook her head. "God, you should have been a girl."

Helen got to work straight off. I sighed. I was going to be there a while…

As for doing all this just to take a trip overseas. One might think all this would be a silly exercise. Annie was using the company's products, had done so in a sufficient amount to make her eligible for the contest. Why not just leave it at that? I could tag along as her "companion," and they could just photograph the two of us together among the sites of Europe. Who the fuck would really care?

Your Inner You. They were the ones who would. They'd fucked up, making the error to start with, getting my name all wrong like that. I've come to suspect that since then, they might have used on me one of those popular internet companies that compile information on a person, gleaned from various public-access sources. I suspect that, because I'd been awarded their grand prize; someone at *Your Inner You* might have learned that in addition to my actual name, *Keira* was listed as an *"alias."* Perhaps owing to how many orders Annie had probably made under my name to *Your Inner You*, someone there may have done a check on "Keira" and concluded that I might just be a guy who loved purchasing women's products. YouTube is full of videos of young "guys" who just love revealing to the world just how "female" they can pull off being, with almost minimal work and effort.

Just between you and me, I don't buy at all that the company was worried I might sue them or embarrass them. Annie told me they contacted her and requested images of myself as I look today. I think they probably are amazed by how easily I could pass for a female. Honestly, I think they are secretly planning to make a big deal about it, in their email newsletter, to entice and encourage those customers they know to be … how should I put this: *into playing dress up?* In other words, *guys who secretly wish they'd been born girls.* Hey, it's a source of new revenue, and it's perfect: Order your kinky girl stuff from them, avoid the embarrassment of entering a brick and mortar specialty shop, and being embarrassed within an inch of your life, trying to convince the staff that you're purchasing items of feminine apparel *for yourself.* Go online, order from them, in total privacy.

• • •

Before long my new female "do" was all done. (I'd spent a good while under the hair dryer.) If I didn't feel like a female before, a half hour under that thing pretty much left me little doubt. A beauty saloon's hair dryers were virtually ingrained in human society as intended for women only.

I was then asked to strip to my briefs and prepare for my "leg waxing."

"Okay," Sandra, the *waxing specialist,* quipped as she brushed her fingers over my thighs and calves in prep for stripping.

"What?" I asked.

"You have pretty legs. *Very* pretty. And you shave them too."

"Yeah."

She nodded. "You should let a week, even two, of not-shaving-them pass before trying to wax them. Your leg hairs look about a quarter inch long. I think we'll be all right, but if you really want them gone, you might consider *electrolysis. That* and, you know, investigating what guys who want to transition need to do."

She meant drugs, testosterone blockers and estrogen enhancers.

I glanced to Annie. She only stared at me. "We're not quite there … yet."

The technician nodded. "Okay. Are we stripping your chest as well as your legs?"

I shook my head and glanced down at my now bare chest. "I don't think you need to. There were hairs there just a few weeks ago, but I can't find them anymore. *Only these.*" I cupped my two '*girls,*' and then kneaded them for added effect.

She laughed at that. "Your body has transitioned on its own pretty far." She had heard me tell my story to Helen earlier about the condition I was born with. "Those are a nice set of *breasts* coming in, and the rest of your girlish figure is shaping up nicely. I'd swear I was looking at a girl. You might seriously think about taking estrogen and helping it along. I suspect your body would love it. You are *way* too pretty to be a boy."

I only looked at her and sighed.

CHAPTER SIX –
There's Always Tomorrow

We were in Annie's Subaru BRX, not long after, me in the passenger seat (she was driving). She glanced over at me; I was self-consciously rubbing my thighs under my jeans to alleviate the tingling effects I felt from having them waxed.

"It's your first waxing," she said, observing my discomfort. "That raw feeling will pass."

I nodded over to her. "Where are we going?"

She paused, as if unsure she wanted to answer that question. "To the mall," she finally said.

"Why?"

She faced me. "You need an outfit, Keirie, an outfit from the *women's department*, to wear to work tomorrow!" She glanced to my chest. "You're now showing way too much boob to still wear *that* and get away with it."

I glanced down to my leather jacket, my jeans, the rest of my work outfit. "*Annie*," I began.

"Hasn't Charlie … or at least *Sally*… said *anything*? she asked of my fellow workers at the store. "They haven't said *anything*?"

"Of course, they have," I admitted. "I never looked like a boy. Everyone noticed that the first day I started at the store. I was too pretty, like everyone keeps insisting. I explained about my situation."

"They know?"

I nodded. "They're aware, and they've been commenting for weeks now about how all those extra X's in my genetic makeup seem to be finally *having an effect*."

"It's settled, then," she decided. "You need to start wearing girl stuff."

"Do I have to?" Even to me that sounded like a little kid complaining about hating to get up to go to school.

"We're going to the mall," she declared.

"Are we still watching *Passengers* on Blu-ray tonight at my place? It's in 3D; it's the only way to watch it."

"That's what you're fixating on right now?" she replied. "Boy, you really *are* trying to deny what's happening to you! And *'in 3D?'* No wonder you don't have any money," she said. "You spent it all on that entertainment system of yours. There must be some male left in you … somewhere. I'm surprised your downstairs neighbors don't complain when you crank that thing up." She smiled then. "Yeah. That's still on if you want. It'll be late when it finishes, though." She looked out at the darkening sky. In late November, the day really got late early. "I guess I'm sleeping over; you'll need me to help get dressed in the morning."

"In a full-on *girl outfit*," I stated. I shook my head. "What will Chuck, Sally and the guys think of me coming into work tomorrow looking like that?"

She turned to face me. *"Why hold back at this point? I mean, look at you?"*

"You're angry with me, aren't you?" I abruptly changed the subject with.

She signaled that she was pulling her car off to the breakdown lane, and then once doing so, shut down the engine. "No, Keirie, why would I be?" she said, feigning innocence.

"Look, I'm sorry I never told you about my mom and sister and what they liked doing with and to me," I said. "The truth is, I liked it too. I liked how girl clothes felt on me better than guy stuff. The first time Dad forced me into a suit, I hated it, couldn't wait to get out of the thing. I was so envious of Kelly. Why did she get to wear all those neat clothes, and I had to be stuck in that stuffy old suit; guy shoes, and that tie that felt like someone was trying to hang me with it?"

"Did you tell your dad that?"

I signaled my disgust over that question with a single snort. "Right, like I'd be that stupid. He knew what Mom and Kelly were doing when my brothers and he were away. He wanted to make my life hell for how much I clearly hated being his son. But Mom was always there to give him hell of her own, if he tried."

"And you didn't think I would want to hear about any of this?"

She expected an immediate response, but grew concerned when all she saw on my face was a blank stare. "Keirie?"

"Annie, I can't, not yet," I said. "I'm not ready. This last year with you has been *like heaven*...." I shook my head. "To dredge up again all that from my childhood...." I could feel tears beginning to well up and overflow my eyelids, a single drop tracked down the side of my face. None of that escaped Annie's notice, and I could tell it upset her. "Would you believe me if I said, a part of me was hoping I could just start fresh, no bringing up baggage from my past?"

"I'd be worried for you, for why that was," she replied. She reached over and touched the water rivulet running down my face. "Oh, Keirie, I'm so sorry. I didn't know it was like that."

"Dad hates Kelly because she's a girl. He pretends to like her, kid with her, but he treats her like she hasn't a brain in her head. He's a father who prefers sons. And he sucks at even doing right by the *three* he and Mom gave birth to. And my oldest brother, Craig, always tortured Kelly for being a girl, too. I think Craig so badly wanted Dad's love and validation that he sought to emulate the bastard."

"You said your brothers liked to torture you as a child. Was Craig the worst?"

My facial expression blanked out again. "Annie," I answered after what felt to me like forever, "you're causing something weird to go on in my brain, like it's screaming at me."

She glanced over at me in concern. "What, baby, what's your mind saying?"

"Make her stop," I answered. *"I'm not ready yet."*

For reasons, even I at the time had no explanation for, she nodded, and took a long breath. She reached her hand over to the side of my face and began messaging it. "It's okay. I'll be here for you, when you are," she cryptically replied. "Keirie," she said after several moments of contemplation. "You're at war with yourself, aren't you?"

I only stared at her.

"Your father knows deep down you're female, and you know it also, but like your brother Craig, you feel guilty, don't you, that you're disappointing him? So, you try to compensate, thus the ambivalence, the war going on inside you."

49

"I thought I was the one who majored in Psychology in college?" I grinned.

"You love everything about being a girl, but you're scared to just commit to it."

"I guess that's true," I replied.

"The hell with your father; he sounds like a very sad human being. I feel bad for his soul. He has many lifetimes he must live through before he overcomes this misogyny, this terrible distrust of anyone beyond his sphere of acceptance. And as for the other one, Craig...." She fiddled with the power settings on her dash, and when the interior displays relit, she began to reset her GPS. "Fuck both of them. Let's go buy you a dress."

I grinned, weakly. "That sounds so wrong," I said.

But, I liked the thought, honestly. I could feel the excitement rise all over me the same way it used to when Mom would dress Kelly and me in cute, knee-length dresses, tights and flats, or even in outfits like the one Annie dressed me in for that skateboard photo. I always wished I could own a pair of girl sneaks like those; they just said, "I'm a girl."

Annie looked over at me and grinned. "Wow. Wrong or not, you're getting turned on just by the thought of it, aren't you?"

I nodded. "I really am one of them, aren't I?"

"One of which?" she replied. "One of which them?"

"Those TG freaks my father and Craig keep making fun of. You should have heard the two of them when that sports guy, Bruce-something, changed his name to Caitlyn? And She, they said, had the nerve to list herself as a conservative right-wing Republican? The two of them, hit the channel changer the moment they saw her on the TV for whatever reason. *You damn freak, get off the screen!* they would yell at Caitlyn. They kept wishing bad things would happen to her."

I nodded. "Neither of them, Craig or my father, can stand knowing I was born genetically ... *wrong*. I shook my head. "I'm a fucking she-male. I want to tell them: *get over it, I'm who I am*. But you can see it in their eyes ... in most people's eyes: *You're an abomination. You should never have been allowed to be born.*"

"Then, do it," she replied. "Tell the world you didn't ask to be the person you are, but that it is who you are, and if they can't accept it, that's their problem."

"But, what exactly am I?" I asked. "Am I a woman, because everything I feel and think up here...." I pointed to my scalp, "... tells me I am? Or does that thing between my legs, mean I'm a man?"

"You know what I think?" she smiled. "I think you are even more woman than I am. You have way more X-chromosomes in your cells than I do."

I snorted a tiny laugh. "Stop trying to make me laugh," I begged. "Everything was fine before *'Your Inner You'* made that mistake with my name," I pondered. "In fact, I can barely remember my life before that day you brought that catalogue up to my apartment. Remember?"

She smiled, warmly; and then nodded.

"Do you still want to go with me to Europe?"

"Yes! Keirie, I love you, you've got to know that."

I nodded.

"You're the best of both worlds: a fun-to-be-with boyfriend, *and a girlfriend,* all tied up in one neat bow. And you must know by now: it's that girl part of you that makes me love being with you, not just for the fun sex. I like being with girls."

"So, do I," I said. "Please don't be mad at me for not telling you about my mom before."

"I was miffed, I admit," she revealed. "You trusted confiding to a stranger all that before me."

"I had nothing to lose telling her. You, I wasn't sure you wouldn't leave me."

"Total honesty, now, Keirie," she said, finally. "When did you begin the estrogen regimen? You're on it, I know you are. When did you start transitioning, hon?"

I simply looked at her. "It's that obvious, huh?" I asked.

She nodded.

"In college," I confessed, "seven years ago, when I was eighteen. It was hard at first; I was sharing a dorm room with another student. I had to confide in him my decision to start taking the male blockers and female enhancers. He knew what I was doing; he knew I couldn't resist the urges any longer. I really tried, I did. I explained everything to him, my genetic anomalies. He promised he'd keep my secret, if I kept his."

"He liked guys?" she asked.

51

I nodded. "But he wasn't ready to fully admit it, even to himself. I didn't *out him;* he didn't out me."

"Did you and he ever....?"

I blushed. "Do I have to answer that?"

She smiled. "That's why you like helping me clean up after you climax. He must have *loved you.*"

"He was hoping, because I looked and felt so much like a girl, that maybe he wasn't ... gay."

"And what about you? You didn't suspect about yourself that you might not be—"

"Straight or a guy?" I asked. "I knew. But I wasn't attracted to guys. I kept hoping maybe I might still find a girl who...." I looked intently at her.

"Looks like you found one."

"I was also hoping this *condition* might just *go away.*"

"So, you went online and sent for an estrogen regimen. Great plan there, hon."

"The older I got, the more like a guy I began to feel. I hated it. I needed to stop or slow it down if I could. I just didn't want myself to *man up* any further. I only took a lower dosage at first."

"Mess with shit like estrogen long enough," she nodded, "it's going to have an impact."

"Yeah," I admitted.

"So, you were a freshman in college; that's when you knew what you had to do?"

I nodded. "Hair started appearing on my face and chin. I took one look at it and wanted it gone. Hated everything about it. Everything inside me told me growing hair all over me like a guy was wrong...." I thought about it a second. "No, change that to ... *yucky*...."

"Okay," she decided, pushing the start button on her Subaru. The engine roared back into life. "Let's make your coming out official. Tomorrow's going to be a big day for you. First time dressed full out like a woman since you were little." She twisted the transmission knob, set it in Drive with her foot on the brake pedal, and glanced one last time to me.

"Shall we?"

I nodded.

CHAPTER SEVEN -
The Calm Before the Storm

"I have a pair of *tights* that look just like these," I said to Annie, glancing down at the leggings I now had on upon my legs. Annie had purchased for me— in addition to the outfit I would wear at work tomorrow— a pair of chocolate brown leggings, black, heeled pumps and a sleeveless light brown top.

"Among your secret stash of girl clothes?" she smiled of my reveal about owning my own pair of women's tights.

I nodded sheepishly. "Yeah."

I was sitting cross-legged upon the floor in Annie's bedroom in her condo, as she sorted through her closet for the outfit she'd wear to work the next day. ""Only, they're tights, not leggings," I continued, "they cover my feet like a pair of pantyhose."

"Because they are," Annie said. "Technically, that's what they are: pantyhose."

"Oh," I nodded. "Then I guess I wear pantyhose, like a girl ... *a lot.*" I flexed my left high-heeled ankle slightly and admired the pumps. "These are really cute. I love how nice they look and feel on my feet. Girl's shoes always feel so much lighter, prettier than guys stuff."

"Uh huh," Annie answered, distantly, from inside her closet. "I know," she said.

"You know something else too, don't you?" I said.

Her head momentarily popped out from where it was buried among the hangers and outfits hung up in her closet; she looked at me. "What, Keir?" she asked. "What else do I know?"

"That I have a drawer full of girl's ... *unmentionables* that I wear all the time under my street clothes.*"

"Yes, I know. Do you know *how* I know?" dared Annie.

"You went through my bedroom drawers and found them?" I proposed.

"No," she said. "I once saw your Amazon home page. You forgot to clear it off the screen when you left the room for a second. All those recommendations based on previous purchases and item searches. You scan a lot of stuff meant for women."

"That doesn't mean I buy them," I protested.

She nodded, wisely. "I moved down to your purchase screen." She nodded, again. "You *bought quite a few of them.* And yes ... after that I checked your bedroom drawers. There they all were ... the ones you bought. And all those cute women's shoes in your closet. You love how you look in heels, don't you? *"*

"You knew I was keeping secrets like that from you all these months, didn't you?"

She stopped what she was doing and faced me square on. "Keirie, honey, no guy looks as pretty and feminine as you do unless he likes it. There's no way you weren't encouraging it."

She turned again for her business in the closet; I glanced down again at what I was wearing. "...Annie?"

"What, Keir?"

"I feel like a teeny bopper in this top."

She faced me again. "It works on you. *I* wouldn't want to wear that, not anymore at this age, not *out in public, anyway.*"

"And I CAN? If you can't, I can't;' I'm a year older than you!"

I heard Annie pause to laugh at that as she moved to her bureau and started sorting through her underwear drawer. She stopped and regarded me. "So? Look at you. You're just coming into your own as a woman. You still look like a teenager. Wear it at home, whenever you feel like it. It looks cute on you. Save it for the spring and wear it to work if you dare."

I glanced down at my bare feet in the heels. "*To Work?*" I asked her then. "*Wear this to work* ... and prance around the store *in these heels?* Annie, come on? You're not serious? Wouldn't that be pushing it? My just showing up tomorrow wearing the other outfit is going to go over **wonderfully.**"

"Well, that's the thing, isn't it? You can't wear any of your guy stuff. You'll look stupid. You're a girl, Keirie, own it."

I glanced down at myself in the sleeveless top and leggings, my tiny breasts yet making me look like I belonged in high school. "It'll freak them out," I said of the store's reaction. "And if not my co-workers, what about all the customers when they see me like this?"

"You're not listening," she replied. "It doesn't matter. Keep wearing what you've been wearing, and you'll look like you're in denial. You're a woman, Keira. Keep dressing like *one of the guys*, and *it ain't going to work.*"

"Uh huh," I sighed, ultimately.

"Almost ready to go," she announced. "And then you can wow me with your *Passengers* Blu-ray *in 3D!*"

"Are you mocking my infatuation with 3D movies?"

She laughed.

"Ha ha," I retorted, sticking my tongue at her. "And then after the movie, I suppose we'll make love like a couple of girls?"

"It's only fair," she replied, smiling over at me, and helping me to my feet *(I mean, 'to my high heels').*

"When they see me dressed in *that* tomorrow," I said, grabbing my other "outfit" still in the bags we brought them home in, "I'll never hear the end of it." I extended my sculptured nails in front of me and marveled at how cute my hands looked.

"You'll thank me. Trust me," she only replied. "Now, try that other outfit on. I want to you see in it."

I pondered the thought of me climbing into all that. I was brought back in time in my mind suddenly to all the times Kelly liked to shut me in with her in her bedroom and start dressing me in her clothes. She loved how pretty I looked in them.

· · ·

"God, I wish you were my sister," Kelly used to say almost every time. *"Stay dressed in that and stay my sister, Keira— until night, until Dad and our 'brothers' get home. Tonight, when they all go to sleep, creep into my room; so we can sleep together in matching sleep shirts."* She started stroking my eight-year-old hair. *I'm so glad Mom won't let Dad make you cut that beautiful hair of yours. I love it long. It's almost as long as mine and it's so pretty. Not like guys' hair at all."*

"I'll have to climb down from the top bunk in our bunk beds," I had explained to her about her plans for that night. *"If Craig, Frank or Trevor catch me leaving, they'll tell Dad I've gone to sleep with you again, because I like to pretend we're sisters."*

"You'd rather sleep with me, anyway, wouldn't you?"

55

It embarrassed me to admit it, but I nodded. I smiled. *"Yeah. But if Dad finds out.... You know how he gets."*

"Don't be scared. Pretend you had to get up to use the hallway bathroom, and then couldn't see your way in the dark, couldn't find your way back to your room. I heard you were up, you asked me if I would let you sleep with me again tonight, and I said, 'absolutely Keirie.'"

"You're such an inventive liar, Kelly."

She grinned. *"Okay?"*

"Okay."

"Great. Now, let's go outside to the playhouse and have a tea party. I get to be little Alice from Wonderland, this time. You can be her younger sister."

"Dressed like this," I protested, *"as a girl, outside?"*

On that long-ago day, I recall Kelly had dressed me in her tan jumper, purple tights and blue and white girl's sneaks. I felt like a blueberry tart.

"And then after everyone's gone to bed," she had continued, *"you'll become my sister again and we'll sleep together."*

I recall how much the thought of that made my whole-body quiver.

Kelly had beamed a great smile as she assessed my demeanor. *"You're getting excited just thinking about it, aren't you?*

I blushed. *"Kelly... I'm a boy."*

*"No, you're a girl like me. Your name is Keira. Mom just had to name you Keir so outsiders wouldn't know the truth. You're not my brother. I already **have** three, **and they're jerks.** They're **boys.** You're my baby sister."*

"I am," I recall answering.

"Race you outside," she said, pulling me along with her. *"We're going outside to play in the castle, Mom,"* Kelly hollered to our mother as we reached the front door. She opened it.

Our mother appeared in the foyer to the kitchen, and smiled. *"Another tea party?"*

Kelly nodded, happily.

Mom smiled. "I'll bring you some iced tea and join you maybe in a while, when I'm through in the kitchen."

"Okay," Kelly answered.

"You girls have fun now."

"Kelly?" I paused my sister, at the front door. *"The neighborhood kids will see us,"* I had fretted.

"Keirie, they'll just think you're one of my girlfriends. They won't know. Besides, little sis, the neighborhood kids think you're a girl, already. They're always calling you that."

"And I hate them for it. They <u>know</u> I'm not."

• • •

"Keir?" I heard Annie calling me as if from a long distance away. "Where did you go? It's like I lost you for a moment."

I grinned, removing the gray miniskirt from out of the shopping bag. "I was just remembering something from my past," I said, "with Kelly; when she was ten and I was eight."

"Are you going to keep it a secret?"

"It was just us when we were kids being kids who liked to hang out together."

"I want to hear about it. *But in the car.* On the way to your place."

"It's just a memory; nothing awful happened as a result, not that night, anyway."

"Still…" she decided.

I nodded I would.

"Keir?"

"What?" It was like I was still back there with Kelly in my past.

"The skirt, tights and top? Will you put them on for me?"

I nodded. "Can I have some privacy getting into them?"

"I can't watch you climb into them?"

"Please?"

She smiled. "All right. I'll be in the kitchen.

• • •

The outfit was simple enough in design, quite acceptable for work at an electronics shop, a franchise shop at that. We weren't exactly expected to dress sharply, like it was a Macys or a Gimbels, or a posh place like even Sterns.

Geeks. That's what we were. So, aside from the fact that I was cross-dressing as a woman and showing up for work that way, the outfit was fine.

I slipped off the sleeveless top and then pulled off the leggings. Annie had insisted I wear authentic girl underwear with the outfit, so I didn't need to climb out of them. I put on the white blouse which needed to be buttoned all the way up to my neck, and then pulled over my head the olive, long-sleeve pullover, letting the blouse's cuffs extend beyond it. It fit kind of loose on me; one could barely notice my A-cup *'girls.'* A pair of dark brown opaque nylon tights went on me next, and I slowly bunched up the right *'stocking'* and slowly pulled it up my leg up to my knees and then midway up my thigh. Next the left one, same procedure, finishing by pulling the 'panty' portion of the tights up to just below my navel, snuggling it securely around my waist. I looked down at my nether region entrapped within the nylon tights. My boy junk felt wrong down there, like it had no business even being there. But the way these tights felt against my legs— nylon tights felt even better than wool ones. God, they felt so soft, like I should have been wearing them my whole life and not just starting now.

Finally, I pulled up on to my waist, the mid-thigh length gray skirt; secured it and then stepped into the high heeled tan "high tops," threading the laces all the way to the top and tying them off.

I looked at myself in Annie's full-length mirror. What stared back at me in the reflection was no guy. She was one hell of a pretty girl.

"Oh, they're going to love you at work tomorrow," I told my image in the mirror.

• • •

Annie heard me descend the steps to her condo's first floor, and then gasped as I entered her kitchen. She approached me and hugged me. "Oh, my god, Keira, you're gorgeous. You have no idea how turned on I am right now."

"Oh, that's what I like to hear." I looked down at my genital region. "You know one of these days that thing down there between my legs is going to fade so much, it won't even work anymore. Then, what will we do?"

"What two girls do together when they fall in love with each other."

I giggled, faintly and then whispered. "Why does that always sound so much nicer than the boy version?"

She drew close to my ear as if there were others who might hear. "Less moisture involved," she whispered back.

I laughed, and then glanced around. "I really got to work on my vocal inflections, though."

"Your voice, baby," she returned, caressing the back of my shoulders with her fingers, "hasn't dropped *all that much*. I think you caught it time."

"You mean with *the estrogen regimen?*"

"Back when you were a college freshman. You must have been a late bloomer."

"No, a girl," I offered, "everywhere but down there. You know, the only part of me that *didn't* get the memo?"

"And while it still works, we'll still have fun with it. Wow, you're going to kill tomorrow at the store."

"If they don't just say, '*Out. Freak. You can't come in here dressed like that.*'"

She gave me an encouraging smile. "Let's get going. The day is fading fast."

"Was that from *A Christmas Carol?* I suddenly got an image of George C. Scott as Ebenezer Scrooge going on about time being *precious to him.*"

"Keep being cute, *Keira*. When that movie of yours is over, I'm going to fuck you until we're both hoarse from screaming."

Oh boy.

CHAPTER EIGHT - Off to Work

Annie had lent me one of her coats to wear the next day at work, promising that soon we'd head off to the nearest mall to purchase a whole new wardrobe to replace my old one.

"Do you have any idea how expensive that's going to be?" I asked just before I left in my smart car parked out front the apartment. "Buying all new clothes?"

She was already in her blue Subaru BRX, dressed and ready to head out. "Can't be helped," she had replied. "You've transitioned too far. None of your old stuff fits right on you anymore. It's got to be thrown out. It's time to admit to the world, Keirie, you're *Keira.* Time to *'woman up'.''*

I wrinkled my nose at her. "And if they *won't* accept at work that I'm a 'woman' now?"

"They will," she offered. She looked at me, then. "Last night was fun."

"For me too," I answered.

"*Keir,*" she began then, obviously debating whether she wanted to tell me something. "There's something else, something I kind of did this morning on my phone while I was getting ready."

I didn't like the sound of this. I approached her driver's side window, knelt before and looked at her. "Oh, shit, Annie, what; what did you do?"

"You know that photo I took of you on the skateboard?"

"Yeah…" I began.

"I emailed a copy to '*Your Inner You*'. They requested it. And a second one as well."

"You didn't?" I hoped. I glanced to it.

She did.

Again, on the skateboard, on the same day and location, in this one the camera caught my cute, young girl face, my eyes hidden in this shot by a pair of blue rimmed sunglasses. I looked like a sidewalk skateboard chick ... *in ultra-short denim cutoffs, a turquoise blue tank top, reddish-brown hair (the wig) falling past my shoulders and draping across my cute little A-cup "girls." My cute smooth thighs and knees, tapered to tiny ankles, my feet encased in crew socks and sneaks.*

God, was that really me?

"Humph," I uttered. I wasn't mad; in truth, I was kind of hoping she would. For some reason, dressed as I was today, I felt so great profiling like this in public and finally deciding *fuck it, I don't give a fuck whether people accept me as a female or not,* I wanted the whole world to know that I should have been born one, instead of evolving only so far and no more.

"Are you mad?" she asked, timidly.

I could feel my skirt brushing against the cold metal of the Subaru's door, my nylon tights only mildly shielding my legs against the morning chill. "No," I said, smiling. "It's a great shot."

She brightened. "It *is*, isn't it?"

I studied the image on her smartphone even more intently. "Yeah, it is," I said.

She reached forward to kiss me on the cheek; I leaned toward her to let her. "I was afraid you'd be angry at me."

I shook my head.

"Soon, Keir, you might want to think about applying to the state to change all your documents. You need to make it official. "

"This is all happening so fast," I replied in near a whisper.

She nodded. "It is, but *'Your Inner You'* I think soon will either ask us to forfeit the Europe trip or pick a date. They need to know when to set everything up."

"I wouldn't do it just to please them," I stated. "It's kind of a bold step."

"I know." She kissed me again. "Think about it." She started the car engine, just after. "I got to go, Keir. Don't want to be late."

"Uh huh," I acknowledged.

"I'll call you in about an hour to see how it's going."

I nodded. "I'll probably be in line at the unemployment office by then."

61

Annie laughed at my answer, then backed the BRX out of its parking spot. "Keir? If they *don't accept you as Kiera,*" she said of the staff at *Com-Link,* "fuck 'em. They can't fire you just for dressing like that."

Really? I thought as I watched her car enter the main road, and join the morning traffic.

Really? They can't?

(Want to bet?)

• • •

It had to be the weirdest morning of my life so far. Yes, when I was little with Kelly and my Mom, I would load into the back seat with Kelly, the two of us carrying on like sisters; me eight; Kelly ten; on our way to the movies; to the park; grocery shopping; whatever. People in the neighborhood really believed I was a girl, Kelly's younger sister, Sarah Travaglini's youngest daughter, the baby in the family.

But in those days, I was too young; I was just a passenger in Mom's Nissan Pathfinder. That's right, she drove a minivan, Nissan's noble attempt to make driving one of those ass ugly things cool. I was the youngest of five kids. We needed a fucking bus for Christ's sake, to accommodate all of us, whenever the entire family loaded into one vehicle and headed out somewhere.

But again, I was just a passenger. Today, fully profiling as a woman *(not just hiding a lot of it under my exterior boy clothes),* in a skirt and heels, my hair falling across my face and my chest, my heart racing a mile a minute, I shoehorned my girlish form into the driver's seat of my bite-sized smart car. It was such a fun thing to do, because it *was* bold, daring. *I was really doing this: going out in public dressed as a woman, for all intent and purposes a woman for real.* I looked like one, and in the tights and heels, and that skirt brushing against my upper thighs—like there was never any reason why this should not be a natural thing: I *felt like one.* The only part of me that belied that reality, down there between my legs, wasn't even stirring. As in most of my life, I pretty much had great success living as if it weren't even there, was never there. Hell, the only real pleasure I usually derived from that penis of mine (except for those rare times, like now, that I had a girlfriend) was when I pretended the thing belonged to some other guy who was using it to climax all over me.

Driving in heels. That was new. Had to make sure I didn't misgauge foot pressure on the gas pedal. Not used to being dressed this way. But oh, so electrified by the very thought of being so.

I reached the town center about twenty minutes after leaving the apartment complex, and there it appeared just up the road: *"The Com-Link Electronics Store."*

Slowing the smart car down now to an almost crawl and reminding myself to hit the left turn signal to let others know I was about to turn, I pulled into the shop's small parking lot, out front the building, in search of a parking space. Not at problem doing that at all. The lot was empty; there was no one there yet; save for Sally, who usually got there first in the morning, even before her co-manager, Charles (*Chuck*) Maloney. Not that that meant anything. The *Com-Link* chain of stores was in serious trouble, and had filed twice already for bankruptcy, eventually taken over by other companies who kept the name and inventory. No, if people needed new smartphones from Samsung or Apple, or the latest 4K TV monitor, they usually went across the river to Best Buy, where they'd certainly get way better deals, and save a bundle in the process.

I shut down the engine, took a moment to glance to the store's front entrance, and contemplated just what kind of day awaited me inside.

Now, came the part that made me feel almost light-headed: climbing out of my tiny smart car, in these heels, and walking myself across the asphalt and into the building.

"Here we go," I encouraged myself. "Suicide walk. Entering the building. Into the pits of hell itself. *Why couldn't I delay doing this at least another month?*

It was only November. How I wished I could have put this off until the start of the new year: January 2018. I wish it were 2018, already. A new year, a fresh start and a new phase of my fricking life.

Why did I let Anita talk me into doing this? I must have had a death-wish....

• • •

"Oh, my God!" I heard Sally Kugel exclaim. Even if she did co-manage the place, up until today she had been our only female employee.

63

She was a decent sort of person, I suppose. We got along for the most part. More of a right-wing, conservative, bible-belt sort than I would prefer, but then most of this town, astride the southern New Jersey run of the Delaware River, tended in my opinion to be a tad too *redneck (*for the likes of a sort like me anyway). She was about five-six; a little on the plump side, owing to being now in her mid-forties; short, dirty-blond hair hung off her head and stopped short of her neck. She wore today her usual: a tan knit sweater, blue jeans, comfortable high topped, leather shoes, and very little to no makeup. Still, she was nice enough, most of the time. We got along; I couldn't ask for much more.

She turned from her hunched over inspection of a work order behind the main desk to see me enter the shop's side door. I proceeded then to walk into the shop.

"Hi, Sal," I grinned, weakly. "*It is me.* I had my hair styled, my nails done; and Annie pretty much supervised the rest of my new *'look.'"*

"Oh, my God, Keir, you look…."

She kind of trailed off at that point. She couldn't keep from studying how my chest and torso had developed. "They're real, you know," I said of my boobs. "These aren't falsies or anything else under this bra. They're all mine."

"You're *wearing a **bra?**"*

"Yeeaahh," I replied, drawing the word out slowly. "It's one of the reasons I'm dressed like this today. I reached the point where all my old boy clothes, fit wrong. Remember I told you I'd been taking estrogen for some years now? I guess you could say the girl hormones finally decided to kick in … *big time."*

Her eyes had wandered down to my gray skirt, to where it ended and revealed my cute, smooth thighs under the chocolate brown tights, and my tiny feet and ankles in the leather high tops.

"Keir…" she finally managed to get out. "I don't know what to say. I'm the only one here yet. Chuck hasn't even come in."

I nodded. "Is there anything you want me to do?"

"*Do?* I'm not even sure Chuck will let you continue working here *looking like that!*"

"Well it's also up to you, isn't it? You're co-manager."

"He kind of makes policy you know."

I nodded. "Sal, this is hard enough, as it is," I said of appearing here like this. I approached her, and gestured with my hands down

64

my body's length. "Look at me, Sal? *This is all real.* I cupped my breasts, visible through the material of the olive green top and traced my fingers down my inward slanting waist. "For months now, I've come to work wrapping a cloth *tight* and I mean *really tight* around my upper chest to hide the way my '*girls*' were sprouting." I shook my head. "*It hurt,* and my chest would end up sore and red from doing that. Annie's right. *I'm not doing it anymore.*"

"You said this condition of yours, those extra genes you were born with *might* affect you in later life … *or might not.*"

I nodded. "Uh huh?" I pursued of her.

She shook her head. "Keir, I warned you, taking estrogen to nudge you in this direction might one day push you in the *wrong direction*, turn you into for all appearances a woman."

I grinned weakly. "In the *wrong direction?* I wasn't aiming to transition this far. That wasn't my intent. I just didn't like the thought of becoming more *male* as I got older. And I refused to even consider the medications to help me go that route. My endocrine specialist told me that *was* an option: *testosterone* supplements." I shook my head. "I told him, '*I'd rather be dead. Shoot me now, instead of making me more like the guy that I never wanted to be.* You actually thought there was hope that I'd eventually go that route *or decide to?* Sally, come on; you know how I felt about that. Like I said, I confessed to you years ago my true feelings about which gender I wished I'd been born as.'"

She shook her head and took a deep breath. "God," she mumbled, mostly under her breath.

"What?"

She shook her head again. "I'm not exactly a progressive, you know, when it comes to weird lifestyle choices."

I huffed. "*Lifestyle choices?* Oh fuck, Sal. Don't trot out that ultra-conservative, right-wing *dipshit crap,* please? This is not a *choice!* This is *who I am!* To pretend to be anything *else*, is like trying to see how long you can hold your breath under water." I shook my head. "Sooner or letter you got to quit, you got to *breathe.* The alternative is dying. That's what it's like: asking me to deny my authentic self and watch me slowly die from it.*"

"When Chuck comes in in another hour," she said finally, "I'm not sure I want to be here. He may fire you on the spot. You know how he feels about people who say they're not the gender they were born as. He has a *real* problem with people male or female who don't act *normal*."

"I've been here *three years,*" I said. "Why did he hire me, if he's that much of a *hater*? I've never *looked* all that male since I started. Are you saying, he was trying his best to put up with the way I was?"

"Honestly?" she said.

"Okay."

"He could see you were becoming more and more effeminate in your appearance. He's been saying to me in private, and to Ben and Dave, that he might just get tired of it and ... *let you go.*"

"Really? On what grounds?"

I had my hands on my hips, and the way I was staring at her, the aura I was putting out, *and me in the skirt and tights,* she shook her head. "I can't believe how much you look like a woman," she said. "You even give off that vibe. *And in that skirt* ... I swear if I didn't know better—"

"You *do* know better," I insisted. "That's because *I am a girl.* It's just your personal prejudices stopping you from seeing the me I really am."

"We're an independent shop," she said, back on topic. "Chuck can fire an employee for whatever reason *whenever he chooses.*"

I gave her a cynical smile and said, "He could but he might not appreciate the blowback," I answered. "That would be unfair termination, discrimination. If he *could* do it, why wait until now to do it? *Com-Link Enterprises* might have something to say about it. Sexual discrimination. *Wrongful termination.* Can you imagine the stink I could raise over his firing me *for that—* if he tries?"

"We're a 'franchise' of *Com-Link,*" she reminded. "If they go under, which they might, I'm not sure at this point they would even care. Chuck and I are independents, licensing use of the *Com-Link* name. He'll keep the store open, if he can, for as long as he can, if they go under. He'll find a way to keep the inventory coming in. I don't know, Keir," she shook her head again. "You may be gone before the day is out."

"Sally?"

"What, hon?"

"Look at me? You keep calling me *Keir.* Do I *look* like a *Keir* to you?"

"You really want me to start calling you *Keira?* I thought you said you hated it when junk mail came in addressed to *Keira.*"

"*I did!* Because the reason it kept happening was they got my name wrong. I thought it was cute but at the same time an annoyance."

"Your birth certificate has you down as a male and *Keir.*"

"*Only because Mom had no choice! I was born with a dick. She wanted a girl. Sal, look at me. Do I look like a 'Keir' to you?*"

"Not dressed like that," she huffed.

"There is so much more girl in me than there is guy, you would have to be blind not to see it! *Even up here!*" I touched my forehead.

"I'm not going to say anymore," she finished, going back to her work behind the counter. "You can start with the boxes of new HDMI cables we just got in yesterday. Start putting them on the shelves. Then... I don't know. We'll see what Chuck has to say...."

· · ·

Charles Maloney arrived an hour later. I was on the upstairs floor of the shop, hanging the new Ultra High Definition HDMI cables on the shelves where the old standard HD versions largely accumulated dust; no one was buying them anymore, not from our store, anyway. I heard Chuck open the side door to the store from the parking lot and make his entrance. He took one look at Sally, at the expression on her face, and with not a word exchanged from either of them, a whole conversation, an information exchange seemed to pass between them. I could read it on their faces. She looked up to the second-floor mezzanine, past the wooden set of stairs that led up to where I was, and he turned and looked up. I was along the back wall, where pressed cardboard shelves with *hang 'em up* holes in them supported the various sundry items, cables and connectors, that a customer might occasionally come in for to replace lost or mangled connectors he presently owned.

From where I stood, I could just barely make out Sally's main cashier station, and now Chuck there in front of the four-sided desk that encircled her. If he could see me at all, it wasn't clearly. I decided to approach the waist-high retaining wall, the overlook mezzanine as it were, that opened to a view of the lower floor. I stopped before it, and glanced down at him. All he could see of me because of the retaining wall was my olive-hued top and a part of my gray skirt. I decided I might as well let him see the entire outfit, leave nothing to the imagination; I walked over to the steps and posed just there at the top landing.

My skirt, the whole of it, my tights and high-heeled high tops were now visible for him to review. I could tell he wasn't pleased, but strangely the man behaved as if he half-expected a day like this would arrive eventually. He looked back at Sally and then departed for the stairway, where I was, eying me the whole time as he alighted the steps to the second level. I just remained there at the top of it. I don't know. Either he was going to ream me out and fire my ass straight out, or ... do what he ended up doing. He gave me a vague annoyed glance as he proceeded past me and headed for his office. Recessed among the shelves and *"hang 'em ups"* items showcased along that wall, was a near inconspicuous door with a tiny notice affixed at eye level that read: *"No Admittance: Employees only."* Chuck Maloney quietly opened it, entered, and closed it once more. I remained—*mostly, I supposed, in both relief and shock*— by the stairs, musing over how badly that could have gone between Chuck and me, but thankfully had not.

Sally just looked up at me, silently. I returned her stare, and then went back to my shelf stocking. A little while later Ben and Dave filed in, and they were likewise taken aback by my appearance. I was down in the showroom helping a customer decide which DC car power adapter would work with his old radar detector. I *wanted* to tell him to stop being cheap and just buy a new radar detector. I wanted to walk him over to where they were and try to sell him one. I even went so far as to verbally suggest he do that, but in the end, I showed him what power adaptors we had and he made his purchase. I went to the cashier desk and rang up his purchase.

"Have you worked here long?" he asked, happy he found an adapter that might work with his unit.

I told him, *"I'm new."*

On the back side of the cashier's island, I heard Sally snort in response to my answer. The customer either didn't hear, or not knowing the context of why she had done it, ignored her and it. He was too distracted by the sight of me and that outfit.

The customer nodded then, still apparently wanting to take a final glance at my thighs and knees in the tights behind the counter. "Okay, let's hope this is the right one," he quipped, encouragingly.

"If it doesn't work," I said, in the soft, practiced feminine voice I had labored to master and decided worked convincingly enough some time ago. *(I just never had either the occasion or the courage to use it.)* "...save the receipt. You can always bring it back."

"If it doesn't, I might just buy a new one, like you suggested."

I smiled a cute smile at him, glanced back to Sally, and using my index finger, gestured for him to come closer. I whispered in his ear: "If you do, go to *Best Buy*. Better inventory, and *cheaper*." And then I winked at him.

He laughed, glanced to Sally, who obviously had overheard the exchange, smiled embarrassingly at her, and then told me, "Okay, I'll see you. And thanks."

After he left the store, I glanced back at Sally and stuck my tongue at her. "Hey, we made a sale at least. Honestly, I don't know how we compete at all with the big chains or Amazon."

"If he knew what you were packing between your legs," she retorted, "he might not be so eager to flirt with you."

"At least, dressed like this, guys treat me way better than they ever did when I dressed like a guy. You got to know I sucked at it. It wasn't my fault; physically, I just didn't look convincing dressed as a guy. I looked like a woman, trying to pass herself off as a man." I wrinkled my nose. "In other words, *pathetic.*"

"I never realized how effeminate you could really be," she returned. She took a good look at me. "You really enjoy being in that outfit, don't you?"

I glanced down at myself, made a funny face and nodded. "I have worn a lot of this stuff to work before, you know. You just didn't know it. *Tights, panties, knee socks.* It was nobody's business but mine what I wore under my pants. *"*

"That probably explains it," she quipped.

"What?"

"Why you look so comfortable in those tights."

"Uh huh," I agreed. "I've spent hours in them. It's just a weird feeling going public about it. I mean, I feel so *naked,* so *out there* wearing them ... *in a skirt*. Weird," I shrugged.

"They're pantyhose, you know," she informed me. "You're wearing nylon stockings."

"Opaque *tights*," I clarified. "But you're right, they're just a thicker *denier*. And it's probably the wrong time of year to be in them. My legs feel chilly. I'll wear *sweater tights,* tomorrow. I don't do cold very well. I'm not really a winter person." I laughed, weakly.

She made a spitting sound with her breath.

"What?" I begged of her.

"Denier? Sweater tights? We're just two females chewing the fat, is that what you're aiming for? Two women talking about stuff that only women would know and find relevant."

I only looked at her, wearily. "Not going to do it, huh? I wasn't born down there with the right plumbing. Just going to insist on seeing human beings through one lens and one lens only."

"Guys should be guys, and women the same," she announced.

I sighed. "You're just determined to be *provincial,* aren't you?!" I answered.

"Now, you're just trying to show off you went to college. *Provincial?* You mean old-fashioned in my thinking?"

I took another long breath. "Fine," I decided, "but, did I ever look happy trying to appear normal to you, Sal, with that damn bandage wrapped around my chest? It cut off my breathing, most of the time. I felt like someone was trying to squeeze all the air out of my lungs."

"You should never have begun taking female hormones," she flatly stated. "You wouldn't be having that problem now; you wouldn't be showing like that. You kind of brought that on yourself."

God, what a redneck bitch she could be. You could almost call her a small-town cliché.

"I started taking the hormones *a long time* before coming to work here," I quipped. "If that's advice, Sal, *you're a little late....*"

I glanced behind me to Chuck Maloney's office nook on the second floor. One could look up and see most of his office from the main floor level as its front wall was open. He could easily walk to the edge of it and look down upon the business going on below him. I pondered the thought of him up there and what he was thinking at this point. "If this is my last day," I continued to Sally at length, "if Chuck ever decides to leave his office, make an appearance, and tell me to *leave and never come back, not even as a customer,"* I shrugged, "it would relieve the tension. *On all of us."*

My smartphone rang, all at once, a piece of music from Vivaldi's *Four Seasons Suite* could be heard playing from inside my purse under the cashier's desk. I reached down and retrieved the purse. Annie was calling to see how things were going. I laughed at that and told her what kind of day I had had so far. After our parting, *I love you,* and *I love you back,* we bid our goodbyes and I returned

70

my smartphone to my purse, returning it to where I had stashed it when I first started work.

Afterward, I glanced about the showroom floor and marveled at how many customers presently occupied the store.

Not a fucking one.

"God," I said, "we're really busy."

"It may pick up after noon," Sally Kugel replied. "You never know."

I pondered then the cubbyhole nook also upstairs where Ben and Dave were hiding out.

"If you need me, Sal," I informed her, coldly, "if by some crazy shift in the fabric of reality, a customer comes in, and you need me; can you ring me up?" I pulled my tiny inner shop communicator from the waist of my skirt, where I'd clipped it, under my top. "I want to spend a few minutes talking to the guys. They haven't said a word to me all morning."

"Hoping to get laid?" she snorted.

I just smiled at her. "Did you ever look this cute when you were my age?" I fired back.

• • •

"Hey, guys," I spoke a second after into my little communicator. "Can I come up for a few minutes? Are you busy?"

"Who's this?" Ben answered. "Keir?"

"Fuck off, Ben. You *know* my voice."

"You sound like a chick. Have you been practicing?"

"Yeah, can I come up?" I repeated.

"Sure, why not? Is it busy out there on the floor?"

"Oh, yeah. We may need to hire more sales people we're so busy."

"Well, if your sister, Kelly, ever wanted a job fixing PC's, I'd hire her on the spot, no hesitations."

"Like I'd ever trust you within a million miles of my older sister, you *worm.*"

I was up the steps to the mezzanine soon after. Ben was behind the half door, apparently watching me ascend the steps.

"Hurry up and find a woman," I told him as I reached his cubby. "I don't like the way you're looking at me. Are you sure it's my sister you'd like to do the nasty with?"

71

"You do make a cute girl," he said. "You didn't need to come to work dressed in a skirt to prove that one."

"Thank you, Ben. That's so sweet of you," I replied. I glanced behind me, then, to the floor below. "Sally and Chuck ought to seriously consider putting this pathetic store out of its misery."

"Hell, do that and I might actually need to start working for a living."

Benjamin Linaker, Dave Capuchin's assistant in the computer department, unlatched the half door to their lair and invited me in. It was a cramped little room, filled with half disassembled laptops and PC's, and on the bench on the back wall a very large drive unit to an antique personal computer looked as if it had vomited its guts all over the tabletop before it. I walked over to it, and fingered the thing. "Do they even make this model desktop anymore?"

"What can we do for you, Keir?" asked Dave. "I got to confess, you look *too convincing* dressed like that. It works on you, and you don't know how disturbing that sounds. You do 'girl' well, *too well,* better than most."

"Most of whom?" I answered. I knew what he meant, *guys who wished they were girls,* but I said it anyway. "You didn't mean that as a complement, did you, Dave?" I added before he had a chance to clarify. "Annie and I had a talk about it last night. We came to an agreement that it was time I quit pretending that I … you know."

"Your *girlfriend* put you up to this, you mean," he sought to define.

"It was time; I'd progressed too much! I told you all about that. You've known since I started work here that I had a condition that might just get worse. *It did."*

"And you of course did nothing to *help it out?"*

I looked at Dave. "Look if I want to hear that bullshit I can go back downstairs and get it from Sally. God, what a redneck bitch she can be some days. No, what I've done or not done is *my business.* I'm not discussing it with *either* of you two clowns." I glanced to Ben. *"No offense, Ben."* I said.

He grinned. "Why *are* you up here then, Keir?" he asked.

I shrugged. "You guys at least say hello most days. Why not today? That's very hurtful."

Ben grunted a laugh. "What do you want from us, coming to work in that?"

I frowned. "Well, I didn't wear it, hoping one of you would want to fuck me up my ass because of it, if that's what you're thinking. And I'm dressed like this, because it was time: nothing fits that I used to wear. What did you want me to do, wear Dockers and a pair of loafers? Or a suit, maybe? Have you ever seen me in a suit and tie? I hate it; the way I feel *in it;* like I was never meant to drape shit like that over this body. I hate *men's suits.*"

"Well, now we know why you're up here at least," said Ben of him and Dave.

"You do, why?" I pursued.

"To explain why you're dressed today like a woman. It's your way of telling the world you want to be one."

I smiled. "Have you ever heard me discuss sports with you, Ben?" I asked. "Ever wonder why?"

"We just figured you had no interest in sports," said Dave.

"And you didn't find that a bit unusual, odd?"

"We never thought of you as standard issue," Dave said. "A guy I mean."

I pondered that, puckered my lips and then nodded. "Okay."

"So, are you into guys now?" Dave asked.

I glanced to him. "Well, you're being rude," I told him. "No. I have a girlfriend, remember?" I pretended to smile then and approach him. I touched the collar of his tie-dye T-shirt. "But if you'd like a blowjob, I *could* use the experience learning how."

Dave got a worried look on his face; Ben started laughing his ass off. "She's fucking with you, dude," he told Dave.

I backed away from Dave and laughed. "If I were *really* interested in that, Dave, I'd have touched you somewhere way more *intimate.*" I winked at him. I shook my head. "You guys. *I'm still me.*" I smiled then to Ben. "Oh, and Ben, thanks," I said.

"For what?"

"You called me *She* just now. Thanks. I liked it."

Ben nodded and glanced then to my thighs, at how amazingly *unmanly* they looked for supposedly belonging on a guy. He seemed fascinated by them.

"Cut it out, though, Ben," I warned him then of his antics. "Now, *you're* starting to worry *me.*"

I wasn't looking at your legs," he lied. "I was wondering about your little package you're hiding under that skirt."

73

I glanced down to my nether region, and then up again at him. "Yeah, what about it?"

"Does it still work?" he inquired.

I snorted a laugh. *"So far.* When it wants to."

"Would you prefer we start calling you *'Keira' now?"* asked Dave.

I glanced to him; pondered it. "If you do, I won't hate you for it. Hey, guys, Chuck hasn't spoken to me all morning," I said, finally. "I'm worried when I head out for lunch, like I do regular, he might just tell me not to come back. You guys are typical aging gearheads, but I've always liked shooting the crap with the two of you. It's fun, and you've taught me *way* more about computers than I would have ever learned anywhere else. Chuck, he has issues when it comes to LGBTQ's. He's always making snide remarks, him and Sally both, whenever Joe Bennington comes in."

"He's gay," said Ben.

"So?" I asked.

"He's cool, though. So, nothing."

"But you take my point," I pursued. "Chuck and Sally both … they're not exactly *progressive."*

"You actually made a sale today," said Ben. *"Dressed like that.* That guy … what's his name?"

I shrugged, innocently. "I don't know," I said. "Never saw him before. Probably got off the bridge and just came into town for whatever reason. I never got his name."

"He liked you," Ben said. "He was actually hitting on you."

"All he bought, whoever he was," I said, "was some cheap replacement adapter for his radar detector. If he was really turned on by me, he would have tried asking me out, or acting like he was interested in replacing the unit itself with a new one, just to spend more personal time with me." I faced the two of them. *"And you perverts were watching me on your monitors?* That is how you know I made the sale?"

"Hey," said Ben, "live theater is always preferred over a recording."

I grinned at that. "Yeah, I know he was hitting on me. I kind of liked it, the attention, the validation of my presence in this world. I never really got that before. All I had to do was wear a dress."

"Well for your sake, let's hope he never comes back, thinking you're the real thing down there."

I stared at the two of them, dreamy-eyed, deliberately. "Seriously, do I pass for a female?"

Ben laughed. "Jesus, Keir," he replied. "What do you think? If I didn't know you weren't, looking like that— Don't kid yourself. I used to tell that to Dave all the time. *He's too cute to be a guy. If I ever get drunk enough to not care, I probably might try to do him right out there in the parking lot.*"

I smiled. "Ben, *you are* _really_ starting to worry me. But since you're putting yourself out there like that, I will too. I'm not offended by that, not at all. It's kind of making me goose bump all over." I glanced to my wristwatch and read the time. "Guys, my lunch break is coming up. I'm going to go talk to Chuck. See if I can get him to open up. Tell me one way or another if I still work here."

I glanced back to the two of them, then, as I approached the exit to their cubby hole work area. "If he fires my ass, I just want you both to know that it was fun working with you guys."

CHAPTER NINE –
The Future of the Company

Crossing the mezzanine for Chuck Maloney's office, I glanced to the main floor and to Sally, still idling her time behind the center cash register island. She sensed straight off where I was heading and looked at me, wide-eyed. I smiled down to her and pointed at Chuck's office. She just shook her head and watched me in the skirt, tights and heels, trot my way over to his office.

"You even walk like a girl," she called up to me.

I glanced down at my legs in the tights and heels, as I put one foot in front of the other. I glanced back a her and shrugged.

"You really want to get fired, don't you?" she said.

I gave her a thumbs-up sign and kept going. Glancing, amusingly, upon the *"No Admittance: Employees only,"* notice, I knocked lightly and then opened the recessed door. "Chuck, you got a minute?"

Chuck Maloney was a man of average height, about five-foot eight, a little stout. He had reddish brown hair and geek glasses, black and not that flattering on him. He kind of reminded me a little of Drew Carrey, the former stand-up comedian who these days had hit it big replacing Bob Barker on the daytime American TV game show, *The Price is Right*.

Come to think of it, he also could display Carrey's sense of humor and good nature *(when he wasn't acting like a homophobic jerk or a sexist pig.)* He could be a fun guy to work for most days. Today, wasn't one of those days. And I suppose I had to take the blame for that.

I knocked lightly on the inner edge of the door as I smiled and peeked my head in. "Chuck? Can I come in? It's not like were all that busy out there or anything."

I saw him glance forward over to the half-wall beyond the mezzanine drop and survey the activity in the downstairs showroom. His expression said it all. It looked dead down there, save for Sally, absently perusing the text on an e-reader tablet, on the counter top before her. He swiveled his head back to me.

"Is that what you're planning to wear to the Christmas Party?" Chuck Maloney asked, smiling weakly. He motioned to the folding chair on the other side of his desk. "If not," he continued, "Halloween came and went three weeks ago."

I snorted a laugh. "Oh, good," I answered. "You're amiable."

"You might have given us a heads up," he replied, "before coming in today dressed like that."

I frowned and shrugged. "Look at me, Chuck," I said, briefly standing up and showing off my body. "Would it really matter? Do I really look any worse dressed like this than I looked yesterday?"

I repeated my tale of having to come to work with a tightly wrapped bandage around my boobs for months now to try to conceal their ever-insistent intent to sprout and get bigger.

"What are they up to now a B-cup?"

"Annie and I guess they're still technically 'A'," I replied.

"Hmmm," he replied.

I glanced down at myself and shook my head. "Honestly, Chuck, do I really look all that much like a *guy?*"

He grunted a laugh. "Not in that," he answered. "But there's never been a moment when I believed you ever did."

"So?"

"What do you want, Keir … or do you prefer *Keira,* now?"

"Keir is fine, even Keirie, I don't care. Names are silly. I know who I am. It's still me."

(How many more times today was I going to insist that? I felt like I was Neil Diamond singing one of his old songs, "I am I said, I am I cried, but no one heard me not even the chair.")

"So," he asked, wearily. "You just came in here to bend my ear for a few minutes?"

"Are you really so mad at me for coming to work dressed like this today, that you won't come out and join us out on the floor? It's bleak enough out there as it is."

"Are you really that vain?" he replied.

I frowned at him, wondering what that meant. "What do you mean? Are you going to can me for dressing like this? It's almost time for my lunch break. I just want to know you won't change the locks on the door when it's up and I come back."

He grunted a laugh at that. "You don't know how close to the truth you just were," he said.

"Why?"

"How many sales have we made today?"

I grinned. "I sold a radar power adapter," I said. I shrugged. "It's a slow day."

"Yeah," he said, rising from his chair and urging me to get up and do the same. "So far, it's been

a slow year and if it stays this bad, we're not going to be in business much longer. It doesn't take a genius to see that one coming."

"Oh," I replied.

"You thought my mood was about you?" he asked.

I frowned a yes.

He shook his head. "Man, if I didn't know you weren't, I'd swear I was talking to a woman."

"I think I *kind of am,*" I replied. "My girlfriend sort of made me see that. Not that I haven't always known. My mom wanted *two* daughters. Three boys she said were too many. Four was just God being a bastard."

He laughed. As he was now up from behind the desk and working his way over to the door, he gestured to me to go first. We obviously were headed for the stairs, for the main floor and the cashier island where Sally yet reposed. After we got there, he took a position near Sally, chatted with her a bit and after a while turned to me. "Sally told me this morning when I came in you were dressed like that because according to you none of your old clothes fit anymore."

"Yeah," I admitted. "My jeans and stuff are a little tight around my hips *and up here...*" I pointed to my chest... "for some crazy reason."

Sally snorted at that. "With those hips, that cleavage you're sporting and that tiny waist, I'm surprised you're not hanging out at a street corner in New York, trolling for men."

She was trying to injure me with that, but I simply brightened into a smile. "Is that a complement, Sally?"

Chuck shot her a reproachful look. "Keir," he then said turning to me. "Come to work tomorrow *not in that*. Give it and me a couple weeks to get used to you that way."

"What do I wear?"

"Buy a couple suitable tops, I don't know; and bottoms, slacks, jeans, whatever you want but that will actually fit over that cute butt of yours." He glanced to my shoes. "I suppose the shoes are okay. No one's going to believe you're a guy, anyway; not with that figure." He faced Sally. "Sal, you and Keir take off to the Walmart, don't take all day, but get Keir fixed up. Put it on my account. Just don't go crazy, okay?"

"I really can't wear this anytime soon? It feels really cute on me," I smiled.

Chuck shook his head. "Boy, you better be careful. Some guy sees you walking around looking like that, looking that cute—"

I knew what he meant.

"I think they pretty much know about me here in town," I answered. "But I get where you're going. Even in jeans and top, I don't think I can do all that much to hide this I got going on here," I said of my torso.

"You're going to mind the registers?" asked Sally, "while we're at the *Walmart?*"

Chuck nodded. "It'll take my mind off how badly this ship of ours is going under." He glanced to the second floor and Ben and Dave's cubby. "Might even go up there and shoot the crap with the two nerds. If someone comes in, the door chimer will announce them. You guys have fun."

Sally turned to me. "All right. Let's go. A couple of girls out on a shopping spree. How cliché is that?"

• • •

"Do we take my car or yours?" I asked Sally outside in the lot.

It was December and very brisk out, an oddity so far, this season, as autumn had so far favored warm days over cold this year.

Sally glanced to my smart car, metallic blue; and so tiny and compact it looked as if I had lifted it from one of those kiddy car rides for little kids at amusement parks. "Did you buy that little peanut," she asked, "just to watch people's reaction when you ask that?"

79

"I like it," I replied. "It's a pretty color; good on gas; it even drives great."

"Until a gust of wind gets underneath it," she said. "In which case, I bet it leaves the ground. You're suddenly airborne."

"You're being mean," I said. "So? Your car? We're going in *yours?*"

"You actually think a big girl like me will fit behind the wheel of a midget car like *yours*?"

"I'd be driving," I reminded her.

"It would almost be fun to see how you make out behind the wheel in those heels," she said. She nodded, then. "We're taking *my* car."

Sally's car was a Hyundai Sonata and it was two cars over from mine. She approached the vehicle and it recognized her key fob in her pocket. She never even needed to retrieve the thing. The driver's side door lock mechanism unlocked on its own. She then opened it and pressed the button that opened the passenger side door. "You went all out, didn't you?" I asked, impressed. "The total options package."

"Go on," she said, "get in."

As I settled into the passenger side seat and noted the higher priced leather seats, I couldn't help feeling like *wow, some people are just better off than others.* I glanced down at my tights and ankle boots, picking off a piece of lint I spotted on one of my legs.

"Is this your first time in heels?" Sally asked, glancing down to what I was doing.

I reopened the car door and let go of the piece of lint. I then turned to her and made a face. "No, it isn't," I said. "My mom taught me how to wear them when Kelly and I went out with her places, when we were still kids. Places like the movies and all."

She was about to push the START button, but paused to look at me. *"Your Mom deliberately dressed you as a little girl?"*

I nodded. "I didn't mind. It was fun being out and doing fun stuff with my mom and my sister. We had a ball."

"What did your father have to say about all that?"

I shrugged. "He was never home; he was always away at work."

"What's your father do?"

"Did," I clarified. "He's retired. He owned the *Travaglini Marble and Granite Company;* a quarry initially, before the business expanded worldwide, in Pittsburgh. We hardly ever saw him. He was at the quarry, most of the time, overseeing operations." I shrugged my shoulders. "Mom, Kelly and I saw nowhere near as much of him as my older brothers. When they finished college, all three, he took them into the business. My oldest brother, Craig, runs the business now."

"You guys must be loaded," she mused, shocked.

I grinned. "We are."

"And you drive a thing like that, and work for peanuts ... *here?*"

I nodded. "Yeah."

"Why? You're technically his son, as well. Why aren't you—"

I snorted a laugh. "I was never his son, and he treated me like I was just another useless daughter. He never offered Kelly a position at the company, either. He could give a shit what either of us did with our lives. We're women— Kelly, a real one; me, close enough to count as one as well, as far as he was concerned, anyway."

"You sound like you hate him," she said.

"Oh, God, really? What pray tell gave you that idea?"

"That's the one thing I like about you, Keir," she grinned. "You're sassy. You hate taking shit from anyone."

I laughed. "Thanks?" I looked Sally straight in the eyes then. "Okay? Are we good?"

She pressed the *start* button and the engine kicked over. "Yeah," she answered. "Let's go get you some outfits more designed for a body like yours." She glanced out her window to my tiny smart car. *"But definitely **not in that thing!**"* she laughed as she said it.

"Nobody likes my car," I pouted.

"Well, it's unamerican," she replied, aware of how feminine I had sounded and acted just then. "It's too small. Americans prefer to *go big.*"

"Oh, that's true. *Big.* They're definitely *that*," I said.

A couple of locals were walking the sidewalk immediately ahead of the parking lot and store. Mother and two kids. And not one of them seemed concerned he or she was obese. "I had an uncle," I told Sally, "he's gone now, but before he passed he said of America, *we're getting too thick.* He meant the population, that there were too many of us. But the other way would have applied as well. *We are.* We ought to call it what it is, FAT. Americans are *fat. Big time.*"

Sally snorted, twisting the transmission knob for 'Drive.' "You're a real piece of work, Keir, you know that?"

And with that we left the parking lot. It was near time to close the store by the time we got back, and as it turned out not a single other customer had even bothered to show up.

Yeah, I might not be fired, as I had been sure I would be, but I pretty much knew it wouldn't be long before I'd be back hitting the job listings, looking for work. *Com-Link Enterprises* was hitting the skids big time. Blame online shopping, the ease and appeal of it. Brick and mortar businesses were rapidly becoming a thing of the past.

CHAPTER TEN - Respite

I heard Annie on the metal steps outside my apartment. I heard her insert her spare key into the lock of my front door, twist it until the lock mechanisms disengaged and the door open. She appeared in the hallway soon after, only to see me on my living room couch, a book in my hand.

"Hey," I said, as she approached. "How did it go today?"

She was smiling, amused by the sight of me and the girly-girl outfit I was wearing. It was adorable, one of the cutest crocheted loungewear outfits you might ever want to feel draped against your skin. The white top was a very soft and wooly affair, the matching tights weaved together in a crisscrossed knit pattern, with a pretend leg warmer pattern in light pink on my lower legs. My feet were encased in pinkish, off-white pretend booties, that laced up my feet and ankles in a crisscross pattern that looked positively adorable. One almost had to be female or possessed of soft, feminine skin to truly appreciate the soft cuteness of the entire ensemble.

"Hi?" I posed as a question, as she continued to stare at me.

"What are you reading?" she eventually asked.

"*Peyton Place,* the original novel, by Grace Metalious," I replied. "I thought about downloading it to my *Kindle,* but I remembered I had a book copy in my closet." I inspected the volume's spine. "It's old. I'm not sure if I want to read the whole thing again," I said. I shrugged.

"Uh huh," she acknowledged.

"What?" I asked.

"'*How did it go today?* '" she quoted of me. "You want to know, how it went today *for me?* I was going to ask *how it went for you,* but I'd say, from the way you're dressed and the expression on your face, the day went pretty well."

"Yes," I grinned. "Surprisingly, it went way better than I dared hope.

Annie glided over to the sofa, sat down upon it gingerly and slid over beside me, giving me a full lip on lip kiss. *(You'd swear to look at us we were a pair of authentic girls.)* "So, details, including where that cute outfit you're in came from, and when can I borrow it?"

"Hungh," I uttered, faintly smiling. "After we were done for the day, I went across the river to the mall in Delaware. I've been aware of this outfit for weeks now. I spotted it on Macy's web page."

"And you fell in love with the *look*."

"Well, *look at this thing?*" I asked, rubbing the cashmere fabric of the knit sweater against Annie's face. "It feels as soft as it looks. *I love it.* I took a chance Macy's would stock it in their stores. I had to have it. But until today I wouldn't dare even sort through the sizes, if they did, to find one that would fit. And then I brought it over to the cashier station." I smirked again. "They totally bought me as a female. I knew it would look great on me. So, I bought it. It's lounge wear; I know I won't wear it anywhere but at home and on rainy days when you just want to lay on the couch all day with a good book and laze the hours away."

"Hungh," *she* uttered, mimicking me.

"What?"

She extended her hand to me and started fingering the satiny skin surrounding my lips. "How long have you been taking estrogen now?"

I shrugged. "Seven years…" I frowned. "I think."

She shook her head. "You're a woman, all right. That hormone has gone to your head, affected your brain."

"I like how I feel," I answered.

"Um hmm," she replied. "The only thing wrong with you now is that little boy toy down there. You'll probably want to decide one of these days if you still want it."

"Chuck and Sally didn't fire me," I said.

"They just accepted you as a woman?"

I smirked. "Not all the way. Chuck doesn't want me to wear anything *excessively* girly tomorrow or the day after that, or the day after…." I twirled my hand as if to imply *indefinitely.*

"For how long?"

I frowned. "I don't know. He said a few weeks. To make sure, he sent Sally and me to the Walmart to get a couple less provocative outfits, pants and tops, mostly. Nothing overly girly."

"He wants you to tone it down, not flaunt what's going on with you so hard?"

I nodded. "I don't think he's serious, though. I mean *look at me.* Ben couldn't keep his eyes off my legs in that cute skirt." I laughed. "He said he'd probably even do me if he were drunk and horny enough."

Annie frowned. "You're mine," she reminded me. "I'm not happy to hear a thing like that. In fact, it makes me want to tell him to back off. Go find his own."

"Wow, that almost scares me. I'm just a human being, Annie, just that."

"Not to me."

I frowned and nodded. "Uh, I guess this is where I'm supposed to say *you're more than just that to me as well?*"

"You make it sound like a line of dialog in a play."

"You are," I assured her. I smiled. "You were right about today, though; I killed it from the minute they all saw me. Even with Sally, and she's not one to stray too far into the girly girl nice-y nice category. But it really bothered her how good I looked. I swear, Annie, no one at work ever acted that way toward me before. I wasn't just some pathetic geek employed in a store intended for other geeks. It was as if before I was nothing, no one to make a fuss over. But looking like I did today …" I shook my head. "I mean, damn."

Annie touched the fabric of the wool tights upon my right thigh. "Cute. So, when can I borrow this?" she asked of my get up.

"Well, not today at any rate; I just bought it. Look at me in this? *I'm adorable, and it feels so soft against my body.*" I made a pout then. *"And how fair* is that, anyway? Life gave you everything that went with that beautiful body of yours. It gave me a pretty girly one also, but a little something extra from the other camp. And as a result, up till now, if I tried to wear stuff like this, I'd be stoned as a freak. But no one cares when <u>you</u> go into a store and start sorting through cute lounge wear like this."

"Oh, you poor thing," she coddled, half-heartedly, touching my forehead and running her fingers down my long hair. "So wronged by being born with a little willy."

85

"You want it?" I asked.

"No."

That suddenly reminded me of something. "Oh, hey. I found something in my Blu Ray collection you might get a kick out of. Remember '*For Your Eyes Only?*'"

She frowned. "The Bond movie? Roger Moore? From the seventies?"

I nodded.

"Vaguely. What about it?"

I reached over to the end table to my left and grabbed the remote to my 4K monitor. "I've already got it cued up for you. *Look.*"

The monitor activated to a pool side scene in an opulent villa in Madrid, pretty women in bikinis cavorted about while serving as eye candy for the men also in attendance. On cue, a tall brunette female in a white bikini ascended a ladder, exited the water from screen left and proceeded to skirt the swimming pool's edge as she advanced further into the shot, swishing her hips, smiling and acknowledging another female crossing in the opposite direction.

I hit pause and froze the woman's advance mid-stride.

"Her stage name is Tula," I said. "Carolyn Cossey. There; center screen; walking toward us in the white bikini. That was her first part in a major movie, and she got outed after because she's like me."

"She was born *male?*" queried Annie, amazed.

I nodded. "She was born with *Klinefelter's syndrome,* like me. She had to choose which gender she wanted to be. She chose female. People suddenly knew a Bond girl who really wasn't all girl. It … affected the rest of her movie career."

"Huh. That was what, forty years ago? She must be probably in her sixties by now, I would think."

I agreed. "I would imagine so."

"She's really pretty."

"Mother Nature really knows how to fuck up, doesn't she?"

Annie grabbed my waist and snuggled me up against her. "Yeah, but humanity is improving as the decades' pass, fixing her stupid mistakes. Look at you."

"Yeah," I pondered, somberly. "Look at me."

She sensed something was on my mind. "Have you called your Mom yet?"

"I was going to get around to it," I replied obviously upset over it.

"It's Thanksgiving this Thursday."

"I know." I took hold of her. "We're going to do something special Thursday, right; besides not-watch that stupid Mummers Parade out of Philadelphia?"

"I've got us reservations booked for a nice turkey feast at the little restaurant down by the waterfront in Delaware City."

"Oh, wow. Sounds enchanting. It's sad though, isn't it; neither of us with our families? Isn't that what families are supposed to do on Thanksgiving?"

"Mom and Dad are in Seattle," Annie said of her parents. "I can't get out there just now. They understand."

"It's not me, is it?"

"No. They're okay with our seeing each other. They just want me to be happy. I am. Christmas, maybe. Your Mom and Dad?"

"I'll call Mom Thursday morning, ask her *How's Dad?* And if he's still so: *'fuck that little queer. I don't care if I ever see him.'* Maybe, I'll stop by on Saturday." I concluded.

"And what about your brothers and Kelly?"

"Kelly's in Arizona, I told you that, right?"

Annie nodded. "Two years your senior, still single…"

"…And living," I finished, "in a town called *Jerome*, high up in the mountains above Flagstaff. It used to be a copper mining town once; today it's an artists' community. She works at a little gift shop called *Red Rock Knickknacks* in the center of town. She likes it for the most part; she loves the shop. Amelia, the owner, is a little eccentric, Kelly says; customers are always bitching about her, leaving nasty reviews on Yelp. Not for Kelly, for Amelia. Kelly, they love. Amelia, not so much."

"Boyfriend?"

I shook my head. "Not when I talked to Kelly a month ago. That's when she begged me, *'Come out someday, Keirie, if you can; I miss you.'*

"Will you?"

I shrugged. "With what for money?"

She nodded, pensively.

"Arizona is clear across the country," I said. "A long way to go to escape a life you hate."

"Is that what you think your sister did? She ran?"

I shrugged. "I don't know. Maybe. But I'm not going to lie. I miss her."

"And your brothers?"

"My brothers?" I grimaced. "The older two are married with kids. Trevor's divorced, no kids. Craig and Frank, I think, are spending Thanksgiving at home. Trevor is in Florida; I don't know what he's doing for Thanksgiving. He took the divorce kind of hard, left the family business and opened a pizza shop, somewhere in Tallahassee."

"Pizza?"

I grinned. "Yeah, can you believe that? We *are* Italian, you know, so I guess I can see his reasoning."

"Does he know anything about making pizza?"

"He knows it's one of his favorite meals." I started to snort over that. So, did Annie. "My brothers are all way older than Kelly and me. They were practically adults when Kelly and I were still kids."

"You made a face before," she informed me. "You *grimaced* ... when I mentioned your brothers. *Why?*"

I looked at her, my eyes clearly betraying the sadness behind them. "You caught that, huh? I didn't ask for this condition of mine," I said, "but it kind of upsets my brothers to see me, especially now that the two oldest are raising kids of their own. They prefer their kids didn't spend too much time around me, around their *weird uncle Keir.* '*The little queer,* '" I quoted. "*'Our kids are impressionable at this age. You, looking and acting like that?* '" I shook my head. "One of these days we'll all hook up, even Trevor I suppose; maybe when someone in the family finally passes and we all have to show up for the funeral."

The image of Caroline Cossey on my monitor still hung there frozen. I grabbed my remote again and wiped the image from the screen, which promptly went to black as the unit shut down.

"Dad has a pool," I said, suddenly, reminded of it by the one depicted in the Bond movie. "Maybe *I* should show up at my parent's house in a bikini. Just to piss off my old man."

"Don't say things like that," she asked, touching the strands of hair draping my forehead. "Besides, you'd freeze your little toes off." She reached for one of my feet and began to knead her fingers into the knit crocheting of my embroidered bootie. "Let's go look at some of these *'work' clothes* Sally Kugel picked out for you to wear tomorrow."

I wrinkled my lip. "Why? They're nothing elaborate. Just a few wool sweaters, pullovers and blue jeans."

"They sound perfect," she said, "because I'm sick of being dressed up in tights and a skirt all day." She sighed. "I thought this day would never end."

"Huh," I said. 'How about that?"

"What?" she queried.

"You finally answered my question, remember? '*How was your day?*' It took all this time for you to get around to answering me."

She grabbed me and started tickling and wrestling with me. I fought back and before long the two of us were chittering like a couple of little girls. She left the sofa and grabbed the overnight bag she had left by the door. "I'm going to change. You need to also; you can't go out like that."

"Where're we going?" I asked.

"Just to the diner out on 130. For a decent meal, *for a change.*" I shrugged. "All right."

"Oh, and hey I almost forgot. You're not going to believe this."

"What?" I asked.

"*Your Inner You* emailed me back.*"

I furrowed my brow. "My *skateboard photos?*"

She nodded. "Someone named Evelyn at the company can't believe you're a boy, and already in your mid-twenties at that." Annie hesitated to say the rest of it. "The company wants to do a profile piece, get some professional publicity shots. They're sending a representative down from New York to supervise a shooting session."

"Are you shitting me?" I asked.

Annie smiled. "No. They've got it setup for next week after *Thanksgiving.* Up in *Haddonfield.* Evelyn will be there too, she says. She wants to meet you in person, to see for herself if you're as cute as you look in the photos. I don't think she's convinced they're real." She nodded then soberly. "I think they're planning to milk this one for all it's worth. You and this Carolyn Cossey have something in common. You're both super gorgeous."

"Oh, my God, Annie," I moaned. "They're going to splash my face across the internet."

Annie paused. "I ... don't think *that's* their intention."

"It doesn't matter. They're an online outfit. People see me featured in their newsletter or even their online catalog, with attached commentary, I'm screwed."

Annie shrugged. "We can always say no; turn down the trip; the shoot; all of it; just go about our lives like none of it ever happened."

"No, I don't think at this point, we should *do that* either. I expect to be unemployed by the first of the year. *Com Link*'s going to close. We all know it at work, even Chuck and Sally." I nodded. "This is going to go over huge, I can feel it. '*Keira Travaglini, formerly Keir. She's beautiful. Only one slight problem—she was born a he.*' Okay, do they need me to call and verify? Do I have to do anything?"

"No, just you and I show up in *Haddonfield* next Tuesday, you prepared to be fussed over like a model for Sports Illustrated."

"Oh, my God. I don't fucking believe this," I gasped. I took a long breath and stretched out on the sofa, glancing straight up at the ceiling, my legs propped in the air and against the sofa.

I faced her then. "You're right, let's get out of here for a few hours, enjoy this little fantasy we're living right now of it just being the two of us. For a few hours anyway, until my weird genetics gets splashed all over the internet. Yep, why not?"

We left for the diner soon after.

CHAPTER ELEVEN -
A Tale of Two Thursdays

I suppose I should say something about *Thanksgiving.* It was a nice Thursday, a pleasant one for a change, coming so late in November, and the weather was great as well. And then there was the matter of Annie and me after dinner at the riverside restaurant walking the dock and shorefront just a hundred feet or so from the restaurant and gazing east toward South Jersey across the Delaware Bay.

I could remember in my pre-teen years, *my family,* the seven of us: my three older brothers, Kelly, myself and Mom and Dad; all together at the living room table, Dad at the head of it, presiding over the whole affair, as if he were royalty, leaving Mom of course to tackle the delicate task of eviscerating the cooked turkey in the kitchen, and by that, I mean, he extended to her the honor of carving it, after having spent all morning since sunrise, cooking and preparing the pathetic thing.

God forbid, she would serve it uncarved. My father considered such mundane tasks as food serving and preparation, women's work, even going so far as to tsk tsk talented cooks at the various restaurants he would treat us to on occasion, tsk tsk-ing them for choosing such an unmanly profession as food preparation when they could be out in the work force, getting their hands dirty really putting in a good day's work.

But I digress. I would try my best on those family occasions when I was little to try to dress as a boy for the feast, in pants and a shirt and maybe a sweater if the house was cold. I remember being lambasted for liking when Dad lighted the fireplace, and I could not resist the desire of the added warmth (for he insisted on keeping the heat in the house low to save heating oil) ... the added warmth of crouching so near the fire pit one might suspect I wanted to join the

91

burning logs in the pit itself. I loved being warm. So here again came the taunts: *"You little wimp; can't stand to be cold. You're like a damn housecat, used to being pampered; you're such a girl."*

"Shut up," I would tell my brothers (Craig, usually). But what they didn't know was that while Kelly was dressed in a jumper or a skirt for the occasion (I remember vaguely one being blue) with white tights and maryjanes, she would have me hide under my pants, a pair of her panties and another pair of her white tights to wear under my socks and shoes, so no one would notice I was wearing girls' underthings. That girl loved to dress me as her younger sister, even if she needed to camouflage the activity as surreptitiously as she could. And I of course loved it, the attention from her and all the primping. Of course, wearing the stuff or not, mother nature had done all the real damage. My body profile was way too girly for any guy wardrobe to succeed at defeating Mother Nature's obsession with proving to the world that despite the presence of a male organ between my thighs, this person was in fact one very sweet and cute looking female.

So that was then. Mom and Kelly both made it their mission to not let societal mores, customs and expectations ruin what was obviously a child who by all accounts should have been a member of their own tribe.

• • •

I called Mom this *Thanksgiving* just past, around nine that morning. To wish her a Happy Thanksgiving and to inquire as to how she was doing. Dad of course was retired by this point. He was in his sixties and had done quite well for himself as the owner of his own marble quarry in Pittsburgh, Pennsylvania. It was for a while a family run business with Craig, Frank and Trevor, my three older brothers, executives in the company. But not anymore. Craig, the oldest, now ran the company on his own. That was the primary explanation right there for why Alvin Travaglini, my father, had all those years spent more time away from his family than with it: He was always away, distant cities and towns, managing the business, overseeing the run of the warehouses and the company's general distribution network. The family for all the years that I can recall was always well off as a result. Mom, meanwhile, until she retired a few years back, had worked as a loan officer in the local branch of a major banking institution. Had been with them for near thirty years. The two retired just a few years back, both now in their early sixties. A home situated in the suburbs of *Jim Thorpe* in upstate Pennsylvania, very expensive, a log home in the town's most affluent residential district. Owing to Alvin and Sarah Travaglini's success in their occupations, they could afford it.

What came then of my conversation with my Mom? It was a good one, but not too long of one. Mom knew I had been taking the female sex hormones since I was in college. One couldn't hide the obvious effects it was having on a body that was already skewed toward the female gender anyway by Mother Nature's screwed up genetics. I told her she wouldn't recognize me. She was amazed by my voice, by how high ranged and female timbered it was. I would turn twenty-sixth next April, and still my voice had not descended in timbre appreciatively enough to say that I had yet or probably would ever truly speak with the commanding, mature voice of a strapping young male.

I still sounded like a teenage boy, she meant. One who hadn't yet experienced the aftereffects of male sexual pubescence on one's vocal chords.

"Honey, I'm not sure— with what you've been doing to yourself with those medications— that your voice ever *will* drop. Maybe if you stopped."

"Do you want me to stop, Mom?" I had asked her.

"Keir, honey, if you want to be a female, you know I've always thought it's what you were or should have been since you were born. It's just ... *your father.*"

"Does he know I'm on the line talking with you?"

"He heard the phone ring. He came near when I picked up the land line and read the caller ID profile."

"What did he say when he saw it was me, Mom?" I had asked, a glutton for punishment.

"Oh, Keirie, that's not important."

"It was *that* bad?" I asked.

"*Keir....*"

"Let me guess: *Our little gender confused freak is calling, is he, to wish us a good holiday? And what, is he going to spend the day with that 'girlfriend' of his, doing God knows what together, but nothing that will ever come close to making us grandparents?*"

I had heard a long pause from Mom on the other end.

"Oh my God!" I exclaimed. *"Was I right?"*

"You were close," she answered, sadly. "I answered him: *'You have four grandchildren already between Craig and Frank. You've got plenty, so quit complaining.'*"

"That bastard," I said.

"Keirie don't; not today. It's *Thanksgiving*. Are you and Anita planning a nice time together?"

"Yes, we're going out to a fancy riverfront restaurant later this afternoon."

"Oh, that's nice. She's a nice girl."

"But the fact that she *is a girl* is not enough to satisfy Alvin Travaglini, am I correct?"

"He's disappointed," she replied of my father. "You were born a boy. He's just not able to get passed that you're not exactly on board with being one."

And he can rot in hell for all I care, I had thought to myself.

We pretty much ended the conversation soon after. Mom of course had given me all the latest news there was to be given about my brothers and their families, and of Kelly who had sent her love, Mom said.

And as for my time that day with Annie. It really is not necessary to give a play by play account. We had a nice time, the whole day. Personally, I couldn't have asked for better. Oh, we did of course resemble two females out for a dinner together along the waterfront. That was one of the reasons we chose the locale. It was remote. It was just a shame that the ferry boat shuttle service between New Jersey, Fort Delaware and Delaware City was closed for the fall and winter months, only to open again sometime next spring. We had to take the long way around to get there and back, through Delaware State itself. Fortunately, where we resided, so near the coast, it wasn't that great a burden to just cross the river over the interstate bridge and let Google Maps show us how to weave south for the riverside town.

It was a pleasant dinner. The two of us. Everyone thought we made a pleasant looking couple. *(As two women, of course.)* Neither of us had any intention of dissuading them from that mistake.

• • •

Haddonfield, New Jersey. By all appearances an old-school quaint little villa where specialty shops of all kind abounded. Yeah, it had Yuppie written all over it. Old money. Way too opulent and expensive a neighborhood for most of my or Annie's acquaintances. *Your Inner You* had set us up an appointment with a reputable, local photographer in town center. What they wanted the photos for they hadn't specifically said. Something tells me I was right about them all along. They knew a good opportunity to make money when it dropped into their laps. I suspected they had some interesting plans for the shots they received, if they were as good as they hoped they'd be.

We arrived at the shop around nine on Thursday, to the day a week after Thanksgiving. Parking on the main road through the town's "main drag" was a nightmare. It was the northern extension of the old *Kings Highway,* reputed to be a part of the very route General Mad Anthony Wayne took during the Revolutionary War to drive a herd of cattle up north from where Annie and I hailed in the southern districts. George Washington's troops, starving to death and freezing their buns off in Valley Forge, desperately needed meat to feed the starving troops.

Yes, that was *Kings Highway,* and it ran all the way south to the historic city of Salem.

Jessie Tambour knew his job for certain, and had been briefed on what the mostly woman's apparel magazine wanted from him. It would all be studio work; any exotic backgrounds could always be added later.

Evelyn Tyler, *Your Inner You's* representative from the company, was there to oversee the shoot, to assure the company got the shots it desired. *And meet me.* She knew her job well enough and had sent along with her a makeup woman and various "outfits" for me to wear for the shoot.

When "Evie" took one look at me, I could see it in her eyes. She was astounded and banished from her thoughts any doubts about my authenticity. She knew she'd get some sensational results and that the company would be delighted.

The shoot began quickly enough. I was shown the outfits I was to don, and helped into them. Annie helped as much as they would allow, but I was soon before the makeshift makeup mirror and chair they had brought along and the "work" on my face and body began. Seriously, making me appear convincing as a female, was not that difficult. They merely had to assure that that one inconsistency between my thighs did not dare rise to spoil the illusion. Not that it ever would or could, the poor thing. It really did look as if it were somewhere it didn't belong.

"Hon, your gorgeous," Claudia Delaney, the makeup woman, told me. "This is going to be a breeze."

And it was. We were near done around three. And good thing to. That part of south Jersey gets congested around five o'clock. Haddonfield Road and Kings Highway can be a nightmare to squeeze down with all the cars cramming the somewhat countryfied highways. They weren't exactly wide or a whole lot more than just what you might expect of a big city main street.

Anyway, we got it done.

Not too long after, we got news of when the company had decided we should take our trip, and not to worry about our employments giving us time off. Things had a way of being done when major outfits started throwing their influence around. Chuck, my boss, was given an incentive he couldn't say no to. The same for Annie's boss at the insurance company. She did have leave time coming up soon anyway.

In the meanwhile, we were informed *Your Inner You's* December emailed newsletter over Facebook and YouTube would prominently feature me as the latest contest winner in their European vacation getaway, and most any other internet site you could name that the apparel company had accounts with. I read the advance write up. I swear they were hellbent on making the world know I was a pre-op transitioning male. I never implied anything like that. Seriously.

Here is what they wrote:

She's a beauty, and really a he. You too can look this good as well. There's hope for all. We at Your Inner You are proud to announce this year's winner of our whirlwind tour of Europe. Her name is 'Keira (aka Keir) Adrian Travaglini from Penns Cove, New Jersey. Keira is a pre-op male-to-female, age 25, and currently employed as a sales clerk at The Com-Link. She remains undecided as to her final decisions about transitioning.

The photo that accompanied the writeup showed me standing before a large white boulder (a prop Jessie positioned in front of a green screen set behind me.) He would add later the countryside elements. I was in a simple white tunic top, my brunette wig draping down halfway my front over my right shoulder, a dark gray light jacket, unbuttoned to show off my cleavage and the tunic, a mid-thigh schoolgirl type skirt in a plaid pattern of white and burgundy.

96

And chocolate brown tights. Finishing off the outfit were a pair of dark brown ankle boots.

Fuck it all, I knew they believed they lucked out when they discovered I wasn't really a Keira, but clearly showed I would make a good one. They wanted to make jealous and envious all those wannabe males who liked profiling as females, instill them with the fantasy that buying from *Your Inner You's* catalog may yet bring success to them as well. That's their motto: *"At Your Inner You we strive to help each of you fulfill your quest to attain 'Your Inner You.'"*

"She remains....?" I quoted of their last sentence. *"Undecided ... about her transitioning?"* I ought to sue their asses for putting words in my mouth.

(You're right. There was that waiver, and I was asked to sign it.) Crap.

CHAPTER TWELVE - The Holidays aka There's No Place Like Home

Wouldn't it be fun to believe that? *"There's No Place Like Home?"* Not my home; not these days, not knowing how unwelcome by my old man I would be if I chose to make a return visit which I seldom did these days anymore.

Travaglini Marble and Granite. You should check out our line of marble headstones. *Alvin* and *Sarah Travaglini* were both retired, and seldom home, Mom emailing or texting me from some new location in the States or beyond. They earned it of course, after all the years they put in at their two professions, mostly to see that us kids didn't lose out on any opportunities life might bring our way.

I won't say I was the solitary disappointment of the family, working retail at a failing and obsolete electronics chain. Except for my oldest sibling, Craig, Alvin Travaglini was mostly disappointed in all his offspring, and only two had so far managed to settle down and add to the family with children of their own. Trevor was divorced; my father wasn't so happy with that outcome, not so much; and Kelly and I found marriage a goal neither of us was in any hurry to pursue.

• • •

Annie and I had a sad parting at the airport as her flight was called and I watched her gather up her take on bags and head into the jetway tunnel to her waiting flight out of Philly airport. We hugged one final time, and both of us— fighting not to cry like babies over the parting— hugged that one last time.

"You going to be okay, getting back?" she asked me. I smiled and sniffed, as if I had a cold. So, did she, however.

"I'll be fine," I replied. "And I get to drive that spiffy Subaru of yours back to your condo. That ought to be fun. You even have a garage of your own to park it in."

"Don't be jealous," she chided. "I've asked you to move in with me, dump that place you're staying in all alone."

"You're alone too," I said.

She dropped her carry on's a second to the floor, to take hold of my shoulders. "Yeah, but I worry about you."

I hugged her back. "We'll see," I said. "After the New Year, maybe."

She nodded.

I grinned, then. "I *could* have just driven you in my car, you know."

She tried not to laugh. "Keirie, don't make me cry all over again. I miss you as it is."

"Sorry."

"You and that car. It would barely fit *us*, let alone all my stuff I'm bringing home with me."

"I know," I said.

"God, I wish you were coming with me."

"I wish I was too," I said. "You have no idea how much I'm dreading going home for Christmas, this year for some reason, worse than most years. It's like I already know what's going to happen, and don't want to go through it again. Honestly, Annie..." I shook my head. "I may not even go. I might just stay in my apartment, and watch movies the whole week until New Years'."

"*No!*" she ordered me as she gathered her carry on's again and we both walked over to the line filing into the jetway bridge. "Keirie, they're *your family. Don't do that.*"

"I wish you were there for support. Us two against ... *all of them.*"

"You've come so far this last year," she told me. *"Look at you.* You're beautiful. You know who you are. You're stronger than you think."

"I think meeting you helped a lot," I replied and then smiled, albeit weakly.

So, did she. "Oh, come here," she said, dropping her bags and hugging me yet again. "Kelly's coming in from Arizona, you said," she told me.

I nodded.

"And your Mom's there. And you say, you get along great with your two sisters-in-law."

"Carol and Meg," I sniffed. "I do."

So, did she, sniff, that is. "You'll be fine; you'll see. It'll be great."

I grinned, weakly. "Yeah."

It was her turn next to enter the jetway. She gathered up her bags from the floor yet again. "Well, see you in a week, have a good Christmas."

"I love you, Annie," I thought it important to say. "You've been great."

"Hey, I'm coming back," she assured. "See you in 2018."

Now my eyes were really starting to water up. I smiled and nodded my head. "Bye, Annie. Merry Christmas." I couldn't shake this terrible feeling I had that, whether she did come back or she didn't, things after the new year would never again be the same. Annie continued into the jetway, looking back to me, again and again, as she inched further and further toward the turn that led straight into the jet's interior. She made a final glance back and waved.

And then she was gone, and I remained there near the jetway entrance, feeling as if I'd just bid farewell to an important part of my life. I found my way back to the elevated parking lot, after praying I'd remember where exactly we'd parked the Subaru and on what level of the parking structure. Traffic back to Penns Cove wasn't terrible; I re-entered my apartment when I was finished dropping off Annie's car at her place, and just found myself looking around my living room, feeling like I had no clue what to do next.

Brushing off my family and their wish for a Christmas family reunion would be the height of poor taste; I just couldn't do it. After all, apart from Trevor, who was sort of down in the dumps right now with the end of his marriage, the rest of the family would be there. I was expected to make the trip north to Pennsylvania as well. I was family after all.

But what sort of reception was I headed for looking as female as I did now?

Christmas fell on a Monday this year. Charles Maloney was not about to change his and Sally Kugel's usual ritual of closing early on Saturday, around two in the afternoon. That it was the twenty-third of December and so near the actual holiday, mattered little to him. The volume of traffic into the store, last minute or not, hardly registered as a windfall. Everyone who wanted expensive electronics were across the river in Delaware at the major appliance stores. So, yes, we were getting out at our usual hour. That left me plenty of time to get off work, head home and pack. I had a long drive ahead of me. *Jim Thorpe, Pennsylvania was way up north, a good three hours away.*

Jim Thorpe, Pa.

Jim Thorpe was a cozy little mountain town and the county seat of Carbon County in eastern Pennsylvania, often referred to as *"Switzerland in America"* and *"Gateway to the Poconos,"* and named after the Native American Olympic champion, *Jim Francis Thorpe.* The town fathers named the town in his honor, mostly however to profit from his reputation and the fact that he once lived nearby. An ongoing suit against the town by Jim Thorpe's descendants continued for reclamation rights to his remains. Not yet resolved, Thorpe's descendants insisted his remains be exhumed and relocated to a Native American burial ground.

101

My parents' home resided east of the main town on Germantown Road, in the more sparsely inhabited and expensive part of the residential district. Our family had relocated from Pittsburgh around when my older brothers were old enough to begin pursuing independent lives of their own. The three of them one by one met their future brides, worked for a while in Dad's company and as is wont of most at that age eventually left the proverbial nest. Kelly and I were the only two left to really savor the alpine surroundings, and make no mistake about it, the locale was remote and full of nature. Dad loved being in the Poconos but he couldn't help feeling abandoned by my older brothers' departures. I was no son to him. *And Kelly?* He treated her decently, you could argue; but still in his mind mother nature had cursed her by making her female. The man was a *misogynist,* what else can I say? Fortunately, Kelly and I, by the time of the move to *Jim Thorpe,* were weaving our way through high school. I was already too old to be badgered into becoming a rabid fan of the town's main sport: *White Water Rafting.* As for *Camelback* and *Blue Mountain (those were Ski resorts, just so you know,)* I remained undecided as to whether I was a ski enthusiast *(It's the Poconos. It's what they're famous for)* or just got a rush at the thought of dressing up as a snow bunny.

Craig, Frank and Trevor, my older brothers once dragged me across town to the Jim Thorpe River Adventures, the main resort of the place where enthusiasts could rent rafts and run the rapids. The spring thaw was the best time of year to do that; the waters of the Lehigh River ran swift owing to all the snow melt up in the higher elevations. The Lehigh River Gorge. The four of us went on our way, avoiding for the most part the many boulders and rocks in the river and the occasional rapid, caused mostly *by those very same boulders and rocks.*

(As I said, if you wanted a more thrilling experience, wait for the spring thaw.)

I had fun, but as I kept pointing out to my much older brothers, all in their twenties by that point, I was no sportsman. I just didn't have a thing for paddling a rubber raft down the river.

• • •

My family had not seen me since last Christmas. I called Mom often enough during the preceding year but showing up in person on a regular basis wasn't practical. *Jim Thorpe* was 120 miles north of

102

me; a three-hour drive; longer if traffic conditions sucked. Fortunately, for me, most of the holiday traffic this weekend had already left yesterday. That didn't mean the journey would be a breeze. I was taking the Blue Route, weaving to the north into the hill country of eastern Pennsylvania. It was well known that taking the *Blue Route* meant *you would get where you were going ... eventually.* Luck had a lot to do with when that was.

I left as soon as I could get back to the apartment, get out of the outfit I had worn to work that day, slipped into an outfit a little less 'professional' and was out the front door and on the road. That was around Three in the pm.

Exhausted, tired, pissed *(fucking Blue Route),* and aware of the slow descent of the sun as I threaded into the mountains, I finally reached *Jim Thorpe by six-thirty.* The sun had set an hour and a half before. Two hours my ass, Google Maps. Try it for real, especially two days before Christmas.

• • •

Mom heard me the moment I pulled up. I saw her pull the drape in the living room to a side and peer out, watching me as I pulled my cute, Smart-Car up the drive and parked it out front the car garage.

Home Sweet Home. It should be; I mean, the place was magnificent, all decorated both inside and out for the Christmas Season. The view out the rear window views were especially spectacular, faced the mountains, not Germantown Road nor the remainder of *Jim Thorpe's* residential neighborhood.

But again: *Home Sweet Home?*

Sarah Travaglini appeared in the opening rear door of the house and proceeded to cross the drive for my car. "You made it," she said, as she went in for a hug and a kiss. "It's been so long, Keirie, honey. Merry Christmas." She pulled back to survey what I was wearing, my general appearance. "Oh, my God, honey, look at you! You're *female!* And you're *gorgeous*! Is it *Keira* now?"

I glanced down at myself and then back up at her. I shrugged. "Pretty much, I guess. Merry Christmas to you, Mom. I guess you can say I'm all woman now ... *almost.* I'm cute, aren't I?"

She nodded. "You always were. You were always way too cute to be a boy."

I smiled. "Hi. How have you been?"

She told me. She and Alvin *(daddy, okay?)* had just got back about two weeks earlier tooling around the State of Vermont, drinking in the beauty and splendor of autumn's impact on the countryside. Mom *(Sarah, to anyone else)* was in her early sixties, about five foot eight, a brunette *(okay, basically, a former one; frequent trips to the beauty parlor fixed that problem),* very slim and trim, but then she had time now for her yoga classes and her bike runs with my Dad, to assure she *(and he)* kept death and old age at arm's length as much as could be humanly managed.

"What about you?" she asked me.

"You mean, besides living and dressing full time as a woman now?" I smiled.

Sarah Travaglini grabbed me yet again and hugged me tight. "You always were my youngest daughter, Keirie," she whispered in my ear. "I knew it the whole nine months I was carrying you. I was carrying another girl, I could feel it."

"Great," I answered. "I wish mother nature had got my specs right, and not just settled for this half-assed job result she stuck me with. Mom, Annie and I won a trip to Europe, all expenses paid."

"What?" the news came as a surprise for certain. "How did that happen?"

I told her about *Your Inner You,* how they had screwed up my name, thought me a female and invited me to make purchases from their fine line of inner and outer wear.

"Annie and I figure we'll take it in April, in the Spring, after the weather warms up a little."

"They mistook you for a *Keira?"* she asked.

I laughed. "Yeah. Misread the A in *Adrian* as if they thought it was the last letter in *Keira.* Thanks for *Adrian*, by the way, Mom. Some guys go by their middle name as if it were their first. I couldn't. Thanks a lot, Mom."

She smiled, giggling lightly. "I wanted another daughter."

"Yeah, that's obvious. You came close." I glanced down to my nether region.

Sarah Travaglini snickered, somewhat amused by the whole thing. "I remember you receiving mail like that years ago. And I thought it was just insurance companies that used to do that to you."

"Yeah, well," I began, "I guess receiving junk mail from financial institutions wasn't upsetting enough to me personally. The universe wanted to make sure I got the message: *I should have been a girl.* That prize should have been Annie's alone. She was the one ordering from the catalog, using my ... *alias.*"

"Why didn't she just use her own name?"

I shrugged. "She didn't feel like it. She said it was easier to just order under my name."

"And you just let her *take it,* the invitation to order from their catalog, I mean?"

"What was I going to do with it?" I replied. I thought about that then. "What are you implying, Mom?"

"I think you know," she answered.

"You know, don't you?" I asked, then.

"They already thought you were a girl and both versions of your name are so close, it's really an honest mistake."

"How long have you known, Mom?" I asked, directly.

"That you like ordering women's items over the internet? I've known since your freshman year in college. When you were about eighteen, I'd say."

"And I thought I was being clever, hiding it from everyone."

"Even Kelly knows. We both knew, honey. It's just a female intuition thing, I guess you could say." She smiled.

"Humph," I grunted.

"It's my fault," she suddenly said. "I started you on that craze when you were little. You're used to wearing women's clothes and pretending to be a girl."

"Mom, you know it goes *way* deeper than that."

She nodded again.

"I mean, *look at me!"*

"You're the daughter I always wanted you to be, Keirie. You're actually *too pretty.* Even your voice, you even sound like a daughter. You always did have a pretty voice. *"*

We were inside the house by that point. I found the fireplace lit and roaring away something wonderful. I went over to it, sat delicately upon the raised hearth, and extended my arms to further appreciate its warmth.

"You always did love to be warm, Keirie," she said.

"This was always my favorite thing to do come fall," I agreed, gazing into the fire pit, the flames causing my pupils to shimmer. "Just sit here by the fire and feel it warm me. I loved it." I crooked my head back to where she was standing by the center coffee table.

"The tree looks nice." I glanced to the entire living room. "Dad did a great job. It's so pretty in here, so Christmassy."

"It doesn't take much to pretty up this room," Mom answered. "Look at it. Our living room in our Pittsburgh house never looked even close to like this."

"No, I remember." I mused.

"Aren't you afraid," she asked then, amused, "you'll singe your behind sitting too long on that hearth like that?"

I laughed, silently, rose and walked over to the Christmas tree. "I'm a little wimp, remember?" I replied, lowly, staring at the white tree lights. "No meat on my bones." I faced back to her. "I can't take the cold. Isn't that what Grandpop Gregory used to say?"

"*Gregory Travaglini*," she mused of Dad's father. "He'd been dead now almost twelve years."

I shrugged. "Like father like son," I said of Alvin Travaglini.

(Stop insisting I call him my Dad. I hate him.)

"You and Kelly, Mom," I said to her, then, "you were the only two, who knew I was no guy, *was never meant to be....*" I shook my head. "Dad and Craig, Frank, and Trevor *(My brothers)* .... Is Dad here by any chance?"

"No," she answered. "He went down to Bethlehem to pick up Craig and his family at the airport."

"Wow, Craig took a *commercial flight?*" I said, sitting in one of the two lounge chairs, nearest the fire. Sarah took the other. "Pittsburgh. It's five hours maybe, if you drive. I mean, for God's sake, Mom, it's the same State. Pennsylvania."

"It's a big State, honey," she answered, soberly. "And it's the holiday weekend."

"And his CEO job at Dad's company is so stressful, you mean, that he just wants to kick back and let someone else steer?"

Yes," she replied. "He's under a lot of stress. He complains to Alvin about that all that time."

"My big brother. My Corporate big-wig— who thinks Donald Trump is just what this country needs to make it great again. He's a macho asshole, Mom."

"He's your brother, Keirie," she smiled. "But you're right; he is. But I *can* understand why he'd want to load his family onto a plane. He didn't want to deal with five hours of crossing Pennsylvania *in a car* ... with three young kids in the backseat ... *all boys!*"

I snickered over that. "It'll take Dad about an hour both ways," I said. "Couldn't Craig just rent a car and save Dad the trip?"

Sarah Travaglini grinned, weakly. "Your father wouldn't hear of it."

"No, not for Craig, God forbid. Not Mr. Chairman of the Board. What about Frank and Trevor?"

Sarah Travaglini shrugged. "Frank, Meg and Chloe will show up— they said— Monday, in the morning, for Christmas Mass."

"Are you expecting *all of us* to attend mass?"

"I raised you all Catholic."

"That wasn't my question," I wisecracked, "but— *all of us, correct?*"

She simply looked at me.

"Chloe is twelve, now, right?" I asked of my niece, Frank's daughter.

She nodded. "Almost a teenager."

"Wow," I said. "And what about Trev, Mom?"

She got very sullen at the name. "He's says he's happy. He's going to keep the shop open Thanksgiving."

"Yeah, I can see that," I quipped. "Why roast a turkey for Thanksgiving? Just order a pizza. You think he'd deliver you one, Mom, from Florida, bring it all the way up here?"

She laughed at that, but it was a sad laugh, I could sense it. "No, honey, I don't," she said. "Leaving Rita hit him hard. I just hope he calls. Maybe he will Monday morning."

I glanced out the living room's windows to all the snow on the ground, and then glanced back to the fireplace. "Spending Christmas in Florida; that sucks."

She grinned and nodded. "Trev says it's where he needs to be right now."

"But not Craig," I grinded on *again.* "Not the boss man. Pass up a free meal? Oh, hell no."

Mom shook her head, sadly. "Craig's really made you bitter toward him, hasn't he?"

"He was the worst of the three. They are all three so much older than Kelly and me. You had them almost ten years before conceiving either of the two of us."

"I wanted a daughter," she answered. "One at least. I wasn't going to quit trying till I at least was able to get *one.*"

I nodded. "At least Frank and Trev could look past my girly physique and see me for *who* I was; not just *what, most of the time* ... when Craig wasn't egging them on, calling them girly also if they didn't agree with him and Dad that I was a flat out *little fairy.* And God forbid how mad Craig would get, beat his two younger brothers up, even; if they spent any time around Kelly and me, doing stuff we liked doing just to pass the time."

"Oh, honey, I'm so sorry you had to be put through all that. But your father knows he's as much responsible for your turning out so feminine as am I; it's his DNA in you as well as mine. So, if he wants to hand out blame, he needs to get in line."

I laughed. "He must love that. *Knowing he's part responsible for me being neither all the way female or male.* What if I'd been born with both male and female sex organs down there? What would Dad have done then, *insist you raise me as a boy and ignore all my lady plumbing?*"

"Do we have to do this, honey?" she pleaded, reaching over and placing her hand on my arm on the armrest. "It's Christmas, and I rarely get to see you that much most of the year."

"Salem County, New Jersey is way south of here, Mom. But I might be out of a job soon. That chain is going to throw in the towel any day now. Anita would love nothing more than if I moved in with her."

"She really likes you, doesn't she?"

I nodded. "I'm the best of both worlds, she says."

Mom laughed, weakly. "From what you've told me about her, she sounds nice."

"Yeah, she is. She's really looking forward to taking two weeks off to tour Europe with me."

"April," she repeated.

I nodded. "Even *Your Inner You* agrees we wait for spring. They say it's *way* too cold overseas this time of year."

"Will you be looking for work in the meantime if *Com-link* closes?"

"I doubt it. First off, no one knows when that will happen, if it even does. If it *does*, seriously, who is going to hire me knowing I'm touring Europe for a whole month in just a couple months from now?

She brightened. "Does that mean, you might be moving back in with us?"

"Not if I can help it!" I answered. "No offense to you, Mom. I love you, I love everything about you, you know that. And *Jim Thorpe*. You'd have to be a cold-hearted creep to not appreciate how great it is living way up here in these mountains. And this house, and my old room? Yeah, waking up every morning in this house in this town again would be great. But having to deal with *HIM,* with *Alvin,* and his backward ways? That's kind of a deal breaker."

She snickered. "*Alvin.* You won't even call him *your father?*"

I giggled. "Do I *have to*?"

"*Try* to be nice this weekend," she requested.

I shrugged. "The ball's in his court, Mom. If he's decent to *me ... I will.*"

CHAPTER THIRTEEN -
The Travaglini's

Soon after our talk in the living room, Mom helped me go back out to my car and bring my stuff in. I had a few suitcases; that was another girl-habit I seemed to have been born with and was stuck with: I always overpacked. It had to be a girl thing. I never knew what to leave behind and what to take. I would be there a week; I had managed to finagle that many days out of Chuck Maloney. I would have preferred to have gone back Tuesday, the day after the holiday, but seeing as Kelly would be staying the full week, I loved the thought of spending some time with her. It had been a while. Besides, Craig had to be on-site back at the quarry, Tuesday; he'd be gone. Carolyn and my nephews, though, would stay on to see the New Year come in. Annie would be gone and in Seattle for the whole week, and not return until after the first of the new year.

So, I supposed, welcome again to my old room here in this gorgeous log home amid all the gorgeous scenery that was *Jim Thorpe*.

Carrying the first of my bags up the stairway, I entered my old room and was immediately homesick. The hours I had spent here, and with Kelly. Living here in *Jim Thorpe* in this estate home wasn't like our childhood years and home back in Pittsburgh, me having to share a bunk with three older brothers and hating every moment of it. Imagine just knowing every hour you spent in such a room that it all felt wrong, that if anything a room of my own would be the ideal, but in the meanwhile there was no denying that spending the night talking and enjoying my life and sharing my interests with my sister was way more rewarding than the other.

But anyway, by the time we moved to the mountains of Pennsylvania, Kelly and I were all grown up for the most part, and wanted rooms of our own. This house had rooms to spare, no worry of that.

"What's the matter, Keir?" Mom asked me as I slowly entered my old room.

I simply looked at her. "Annie lives in a condo, and her place isn't half bad. My place…" I shrugged and frowned. "It's all right."

"You miss your old room, don't you?"

"It's like once upon a time you lived in a mansion, which this place for all intent and purposes is, and then you were told you had to move, you were broke. And the only place you could afford to relocate to was a pathetic dump."

"It can't be that bad, honey," she reasoned.

"Your husband's a prick, Mom," I flatly stated.

Sarah Travaglini grinned and shook her head. "Oh, honey, let's get you unpacked."

"Okay," I answered. "It's a shame Dad doesn't realize we have at least one thing in common. *We like log homes.*"

We were putting things away into my old drawers, when Mom noticed the large bit of female items I had packed. When she got to my cache of women's underwear, including bras, she paused to just contemplate them before putting them in an appropriate drawer in my bureau.

"Yeah, I know," I told her. "It isn't like I don't need them. There's no tissue paper stuffed in these things. *They're all me.*" I pointed to my B-cup darlings protruding from my cardigan. "I tried pretending I weren't growing boobs like a girl," I said. "I really did try to pretend it wasn't happening, but … trying to hide the truth just got harder and harder."

"Umm hmmm," she nodded. Studying my very pronounced by this point hips and waist.

I smiled. "No way Dad or Craig or any of them aren't going to be able to tell what effect *Estrogen* over the last almost ten years has had on me."

"You are family, Keirie, don't forget that. They'll get over it."

She reached into the suitcase she was emptying and spotted a pair of women's ankle booties with a low heel and a pretty white dress that went with it. She spread it out in front of her, admiring the wavy, horizontal zig zag lines that tracked around its length. "Oh wow. Were you actually planning to *wear this* this week?"

I nodded. "I was. Like I said, *why not?* This body was built for that dress. When my boss, Chuck, finally accepted how much more I resembled a female than a male, he let me wear it to work. I've actually worn it out in public a few times."

"So, people have *actually* seen you in this? They bought that you belonged in it?"

"I haven't heard any complaints, yet," I coyly answered.

"Can I see you in it?" she asked, then, timidly.

"You want to see me in a dress, Mom?"

She grinned. "Yes, and maybe if there's time we'll take a ride into town, just the two of us, a mother and the daughter she hasn't seen in a while and has missed being with. Just to reintroduce you to the main sights of the town."

"What if Dad and his favorite son get back while we're out?"

She shrugged. "Like you said, Keirie, *dressed in this or anything else, will it really matter?"*

I thought about it. "Okay."

She watched me carefully strip off the leggings, my boots, my cardigan and my top.

"Uh," I paused. I blushed. "I'm in my underwear, Mom, is that okay?" She was just staring at me; I, in a pair of black Jockey brand panties and a matching bra. "Mom?"

"Oh, my God, Keirie," she said, approaching me, and squeezing the crap out of me as she took me, half naked into her arms. "My beautiful little baby girl, all grown up. Look at you."

I smiled down to my bikini briefs. "There is still something down there, Mom, that—"

She squeezed me a second time. "If you want to do something about that, get rid of it, I'll help with whatever financing is needed."

I gaped up at her. "You're serious," I said.

"Never has something as wrong as that belonged somewhere it should never have been."

"Yeah," I slowly agreed. "I wouldn't mind it gone either. I've never really liked having the thing to begin with. Although it does have its fun uses."

"Keirie, honey, aren't you getting a little old to still be doing that?"

''Well, if it's any consolation, Mom, every time I do I was imagining being screwed— I mean, *having sex,* like a girl. It seems to be the only thing that gets it going. I still wouldn't be able to make a baby, make you a grandmother," I said of the surgery.

"I'm already a grandmother," she said. "To a whole tribe of grandchildren, it feels. Does that bother you?"

"That I can never have kids?"

She nodded.

"Honestly, mother, no. The thought of another guy doing that to me, knocking me up like that … I've been a guy, *technically*. I <u>don't really like them.</u>"

"You were robbed of the life you should have had," she said. "They're not all bastards. *Not all.*"

"You'd *really* pay to have me *converted?* " I asked.

"If that's what *you* wanted," she replied.

"God," I replied, "you must have really been depressed when I popped out of you, sporting one of these silly little things between my little legs."

She blushed a little. "I *was* a little disappointed. I got over it."

I huffed, silently, and then peeled myself away from her, and resumed slipping into the outfit, pulled the tights up my legs and over my panties, then wiggled the dress down over my head, past my shoulders. It stopped halfway to my knees. I stepped into the ankle booties last and just struck a pose.

"So, what do you think?" I asked her. I could tell Mom enjoyed the sight of me in the thing.

"*You're wearing that **tonight**,*" she insisted. "We're going out, mother and daughter. Keirie, you were made to wear that dress."

I simply looked at her. "Uh huh."

She took a moment, and then nodded as much to herself as to me. "Give me a minute to put something decent on to replace what I'm wearing," she said of the olive pants and tan pullover she wore with a pair of Mom sneaks and ankle socks. "I'll be downstairs in just a minute, and then we're going out."

"I'll wait for you downstairs," I told her. "I'll be in the living room, my usual place." *By the fire.* "

She kissed me on my forehead. "My beautiful daughter," she replied. "I won't be long." She disappeared then into the hallway and I heard her pad across the hardwood floor for her and Dad's master bedroom.

• • •

I made my way in due course downstairs and over by the fireplace, occasionally glancing to the Christmas tree and out the windows to the snow-laden mountains in the distance. And that was where I was when I got "*outed.*"

I heard the front door open in the front part of the house, some foot stomping to rid accumulated snow from feet—

You will never guess who stepped into the living room not more than a minute after. Dad and Craig took one look at me; they were totally floored. Alvin Travaglini's mouth was open so wide it had to hurt him to abuse his jaw muscles that way.

And from Craig: "*Kelly?*"

I just looked at him. I grinned then. "No. '*Keir*'," I said. "Merry Christmas brother."

"Of, fuck, it *is* you," he said to me. "What the hell have you done to yourself? Are you all the way *fixed . . . even down there?*"

"You mean, is little Keirie still down there? Yeah, he's still in one piece."

"Oh, my God, Keir, why hold back? Jesus, look at you. And I mean, you don't even look wrong, like a queer or a fag in that dress and tights. Holy shit!"

"Don't forget the shoes," I said, pointing to my high-heeled ankle boots. "Aren't they just the cutest things you ever saw?"

"Man, what the fuck's wrong with you?" he asked me.

It was at that point that Carolyn, his wife and their three kids, all boys— the oldest ten— entered the lobby.

"*Craig!*" Carolyn Travaglini cajoled as she approached. "I've asked you not to use those words around the boys; they'll be learning those words themselves soon enough. What are you going on about— *Keir?*" Carolyn asked me then.

"Hi, Carol," I returned.

She was five years Craig's junior, meaning ten years older than myself.

(*Correct. Craig was an old fossil, newly turned forty just two months earlier.*)

"Oh, my God, you're beautiful. I didn't believe you or any guy could get that ... that—"

"*Female?*" I offered my flummoxed sister-in-law. "*Better living through chemistry.* I once heard someone say. You got to love that estrogen.*"

114

"For your sake, I hope there's no downside to taking it," Craig said. "I have read that. It might lead to cancer."

I shook my head. "The docs down in Salem say I'm fine. *I'm good*. Craig, don't. I'm not doing this. You're too old to ack like a jerk, and I'm twenty-five; too old to have to take your nonsense. Okay?"

"Do I have a choice?"

"Call it a request. You're going to be here, I'm told, at least till Tuesday. That's three fucking days—"

"No!" demanded Carolyn, at thirty-five still one hell of a vivacious blond. "No, Keir, not that word, not in front of the children!"

I glanced to my three nephews. I smiled, demurely. "Sorry, guys. Merry Christmas."

They were grinning. The two oldest looked as if they'd heard the 'F' word at least once before and knew exactly to what it referred.

"Sorry, Carol," I replied. "I'll try to watch it. Anyway, I have an idea." Mom had finally finished her business upstairs, and was just now entering the lobby. I called to her. "Mom, are we still heading into town?"

"Well, Keir, honey, maybe…."

"Mom and I were going to celebrate how great I look, especially in this dress and *these shoes*. Like them?" I angled one toward her, like a home shopping network model, demonstrating a line of brownish suede, heeled ankle boots. "Anyone want to see downtown *Jim Thorpe?* It always was a pretty town. Very rustic."

"Keir, brother in law," Carol answered me. She shook her head. "You don't sound like a brother in law, don't even act one."

"You can call me *Keira* or Keirie, if you think Keir feels wrong."

"You always did strike me more as a teenage girl than a boy in his teens when I first met you back all those years ago." Carol glanced around the lobby. "*Here,* in fact, in this house." She faced Craig. "Back first time you brought me home to meet your family. When was that?"

Craig shrugged. "I don't remember," he told her. "It's been a few years."

"You were twenty-five," she informed him. She turned to me. "Keir's age now, am I right?"

I nodded.

"That was, fifteen years ago. God, Craig, you're a typical man, you can't remember anything," Carolyn chided him.

"I remember the important stuff," he curtly replied. "That other stuff is…" *(bullshit. He was going to say it was bullshit. You could see it on his face, but he mentally pulled up short. You could see that too.)*

"Is what … *honey?*" Carolyn replied, feigning innocence.

Nothing. Craig was done, and that also was evident by his expression.

Carolyn faced me again. "You make a cute girl, Keir," she said, amiably.

Again, I nodded. "I get that a lot," I said, "but thanks … *sis.*"

She smiled at me and at my reply. Carolyn then turned once more to address her husband. "This is Stevie's first time here, old enough to walk on his own two legs," she said of their youngest son.

"He's four now, isn't he?" I asked of my nephew.

"Yes," she answered. "You got a better memory than your brother." She glanced to him, annoyingly. "He keeps forgetting."

I grinned over at Craig and shrugged sympathetically. "A lot on your mind, right, big brother?"

"Oh, fuck off you little queer," he spat at me.

"Craig!"

(Time's two.)

Mother and daughter both admonished and then wacked him one on his shoulder.

"*Stop being an ignoramus!*" Carol barked.

"You're in *my* house, Craig," Sarah told him. "You better treat your brother better than that while you're here, or I'll show you the door."

"It's your fault," he chastised his mother. "You *made* him this way."

Carolyn Travaglini whacked him again on his shoulder. "It's Christmas you eff-ing moron; leave that attitude of yours back at the quarry."

"Hey, Carol," he warned her. "Hit me one more time—"

"And what?" *she* warned him. "You want me to tell the world that you're an abusive son of bitch, even to the children? Now, knock it off!"

Sarah turned to her up-till-now-silent husband. "He's *your* son," she told him. "*Talk* to him!"

116

"Craig," Alvin Travaglini called to him, wearily. "Settle down."

Craig nodded. He took a breath.

"We should talk later, brother," I said to him.

He was poised to start up on me all over again, but Carol tapped him once more on his arm as a warning.

I crouched down then to my brother's youngest son. "Hey, Stevie, how are you getting on?" I asked him.

"Are you my aunt now?" he asked, innocently.

I laughed and nodded. "I guess. Pretty much."

"You're pretty," he said.

I turned to Sarah. "So, what do you think, Mom? You, me, Stevie, Doug and Trent? We all take a trip to main street? It's dark as night now— because it *is* night, right? *That* came out stupid. The Christmas decorations along main street ought to be really pretty by this hour."

"You're going to go out in public *dressed like that?*" queried Craig.

I shrugged. "Why not?"

Craig's oldest, Trent, went over to his dad. He was ten and almost as tall as me. But like his dad he was built like a linebacker, someone you just knew would never suffer someone else's bullying. "Uncle Keir even acts like a girl, Dad," he told my brother.

"Does this bother you, Trent?" I called over to him. "Me dressed this way, *and* looking like this?"

"No," he answered. "You're pretty. I've seen guys, Dad has shown them to me, who like to dress up like girls." He shook his head. "They don't look as real as you."

"Thanks," I said to him.

I faced Mom again. "Mom?"

"All right," she said. "As soon as you're settled in, Carol. We can grab a pizza, if you haven't eaten, at *Antonio's* right in town. And Keirie is right; the lights are nice down Broadway this time of year. It's like something out of Dickens." Mom turned to her husband. "Alvy? Do you and your son want to join us as well?"

They both nodded, insisting it was only proper that the entire clan head out.

"Okay, then," Sarah said. "Let's get you guys settled in. The boys can go up in the bed bunk room, top floor. You know the way, you've been there before."

"Yeah," they all answered as one.

"We'll have to figure out how to make more room for when your cousins show up tomorrow, kids," she said to Carol's clan. "So, let's get to it."

Mom started leading Carol back the way they'd entered, for the front of the house, to go retrieve their stuff from Dad's Audi. Craig followed as well, leaving me alone suddenly with *Alvin.*

"Hey, Dad," I said to him. "Craig's a pig, do you agree?" I said of my brother.

Alvin Travaglini didn't answer. Just remained there in the living room, half glancing at me, and the fire pit behind me.

"The room looks nice," I said then. "You did a nice job."

He still said nothing, merely nodded vaguely.

I extended my hand. "You want to shake hands or something?"

"Keir," he absently answered, glancing to my girlish figure. "Nice dress. It works on you. You've filled out *very nicely."* That was not a compliment. If you didn't catch the sarcasm in his voice, my apologies. *"You're even prettier than your sister."* He took my hand then, deliberately applying pressure to let me know how a real man shook hands. "Your hands are soft, like a woman's."

"Always were," I replied.

"You sound like one, too," he continued.

"What would you be like if I had been born all the way like this, and not just *most of the way?"*

"What are you going on about?"

"Look, it's almost Christmas," I told him. "I got to say this. I'm not getting any younger, and neither are you. Are you going to be an asshole toward me for the rest of your life?"

"Just because you're wearing that dress, Keir, and it works on you—" he warned.

"Oh, just save it. You want to be hating on me just because I make a better-looking female than a male, go ahead. It's your loss, not mine."

"Keir," he called suddenly, as I was about to leave him there all alone in the lobby. "Merry Christmas, *son.*"

(Yeah, I caught the emphasis on 'son' as well.)

(Prick.)

"Same to you," I said.

Craig always had an interest in high end entertainment *Man Caves.* You should see how he had his house in Pittsburgh decked out. It made my 4K rig look like something I picked up at a garage sale. Music suddenly flooded the house from Dad's Home Entertainment Center. The house filled with the sounds of the holiday season. Craig had probably keyed in *Pandora* over the internet and one of Dad's Christmas channels.

Sadly, he had activated the system just as once upon a time ten-year-old Gayla Peevey finished insisting she '*wanted a Hippopotamus for Christmas.*' I really liked that song. It was cute and funny. But then another song replaced it. Gayla Peevey I want a hippopotamus for ChristmasGayla Peevey I want a hippopotamus for Christmas

"Oh shit, *that?*" I suddenly said as a very famous, very familiar … *and* _annoying_ _as_ _all_ _hell_ Christmas tune came over the log home's public address.

The Chipmunks Song, featuring Alvin and the Chipmunks.

"Hey, Dad," I said to him, "don't take offense at this. It has nothing to do with you."

"Okay, son, I won't. What's wrong?"

"*I hate that song, always have!* Every time I hear it, I want to kick the guy who wrote it in the balls. Which is probably how he managed to reach all those high notes."

'*I still want a hula hoop,*' Alvin the chipmunk whined.

"Oh, shut the fuck up will you, *Alvin*?" I pleaded. "*Not you, Dad.* **Him**." Alvin the Chipmunk kept insisting he wanted one for Christmas. I looked at my dad then. "What?"

Dad was laughing silently to himself. "I never knew you could be so nasty," he said. "I like that." He heard a few more phrases from the song. "The guy who recorded it— fuck, I don't remember his name after all these years. I was seven, I think, back in the 1950s when that thing was made. He recorded all the vocals himself and then speeded up the tracks to make the voices sound like that, like what people imagine Chipmunks might sound like if they talked.

"You think *you* hate it?" Alvin Travaglini continued. "How would you like hearing ten-year old's when *you* were ten come up to you and shout, '*Alvin? **Alvin?? ALVIN!!!**' And then say, 'come on, man, answer **OKAY!!!** That's your name, right?*' Every time those chipmunk bastards sang that song, I wished they would just *shut the hell up!*"

Wow. Suddenly, we both started laughing over that.

We bonded.

A Christmas Miracle.

CHAPTER FOURTEEN - Christmas Eve, Part One "Sisters."

Jim Thorpe downtown

The trip into town was pleasant enough, but nothing that warranted much in the way of detail. We all, Mom, Dad and I, and Craig's group all descended on *Antonio's* Italian restaurant and treated ourselves to a party pizza, and when we were finished we walked the streets of Broadway, all the way to the courthouse at the end of Broadway where it met Route 209, the dark rise of Flagstaff Mountain hulked its dark presence like a solid wall of rock and forests just there in the near distance beyond the clock tower of the courthouse. I'm not too sure how Craig and my father took the excursion. Mom, Carol and I enjoyed Carol's three young boys; they were still young enough to be awed by the town's alpine ambiance. *Christmas* felt strongly in the air in this town. The Lehigh Scenic Railroad station was right where Broadway met Highway 209 and I couldn't help on this pre-*Christmas Eve night* thinking of Robert Zemeckis's movie, *The Polar Express*. In fact, Saturday, December 23rd, this night, was the final night the *Santa Clause Special* would run. The final *excursion* had rolled out of the station with Santa Clause on board at three that afternoon. It saddened Stevie, Doug and Trent to think they had missed out on riding the train and meeting Santa by so few hours as they had. But they lived so far away in Pittsburgh, it just wasn't practical for their parents to make the trip before tonight.

Not that they would have obtained tickets in time anyway for boarding. Such events usually get booked weeks in advance, as Carol herself knew. A similar Christmas extravaganza could be enjoyed near their hometown in Pittsburgh, *IF* one made reservations early enough, as Carol had. The *Oil Creek and Titusville Railroad* had scheduled two Santa Clause runs, one in late November, the other in early December. Carol had managed *this year* to get advance tickets to the December run. So, her three boys did not lose out.

I hinted earlier that Craig and Dad joined us on this wintry night excursion; they pretty much enjoyed the beers and pepperoni pizza at *Antonio's*, but beyond that, they mostly trailed behind, *(behind us "girls" and my nephews)*. I don't know when I totally began to think of myself as *one of the girls*. It just felt natural, anymore. I must have adopted the new notion of myself when my breasts started coming in and my waist looked like none one would ever find on a guy.

In any case, neither my dad nor my brother spoke to me the whole time we were at *Antonio's* or were downtown in *Jim Thorpe*. They simply couldn't wrap their brains around the notion that I was as much a female as their respective wives.

• • •

Christmas Eve, December 24th. I woke up at dawn the next morning. What a difference it was awakening to a sight out the second-floor terrace of my parent's log home in Jim Thorpe that could only be summarized as nothing less than majestic, the Pocono mountains in the distance, the endless march of forests against their flanks, the dawn-tinted wispy clouds in a clear blue sky. By

121

comparison, back in Penns Cove, out the terrace of my very modest apartment, all that my view looked out upon this time of year were dead reeds with a faint suggestion of the Delaware River off in the distance. And one could smell the river, especially on high humidity days. I would liken the smell to very wet mud.

I took in the fresh mountain air and the sight of the Pocono mountains off in the distance and couldn't help wishing that I too could own a place like this. If only.

I left the terrace eventually *(It was brisk out there)*, slipped off the gray shawl, and remained in my suede LL Bean moccasins, blue sleepshirt (with a large white bunny on the front) and the purple tights I'd slipped on the night before to keep from freezing my toes off. I headed down to the kitchen. I had a good feeling that Mom was already down there, preparing an elaborate breakfast for three growing boys and their dad. And probably for my Dad as well.

(I wasn't wrong.)

• • •

"Hey, Mom, morning," I said, going over to her by the stoves, where she was frying a few eggs. She was in a slightly worn burgundy robe and matching slippers. I gave her a little kiss on the cheek; she made a pretend kiss in the air back, and gave me a *Good morning* back. My hair was all over my face and uncombed, but I still looked cute, like I'd just been through a windstorm.

"You're up early," she said.

I shrugged. "I'm usually the second one to the store back in Penns Cove, so I'm used to being an early bird."

She glanced down to my purple tights. "Someone likes to be warm and look cute when they sleep."

I grinned. "It feels cute wearing these tights to bed, and the house isn't exactly toasty."

"Was your room cold?"

"No. I just like being warm at night, especially in winter, you know that."

"Do you ever wear guy stuff anymore, Keirie?"

'Well, it depends on what you mean by guy stuff, Mom. Underwear? I won't wear boxers at all. Stupid things track so far down a guy's thighs you just know the only reason guys wears such stuff is they don't want anybody to think they like wearing underwear that resembles what women wear. I never threw out my bikini briefs; I didn't have to. I can't feel any difference wearing them and women's panties when I'm in them, anyway. "I shrugged. "The rest? My jeans need to make room for this mid-section of mine. And my tops … well…." I pointed to my boobs. "You're making breakfast … for Dad?" I asked, abruptly changing the subject.

"And the family. Your father and I hit the stores a couple of days ago to stock up for the big event. What can I get you?"

"You know, for me, it's easy. A bowl of cereal and orange juice, and I'm good till noon … at the very least."

"No wonder you can keep that girlish figure of yours."

"Right," I smiled. "You said something last night about me heading down to the airport to collect Kelly."

"Would you?"

"Yeah, I suppose. It might reduce the tension level in this house for a few hours if I make myself scarce. I mean…."

"Oh, come on, brother," said a female voice behind me, suddenly.

Carol, in a white robe over her nightshirt and night booties entered the kitchen and proceeded to greet Mom and me. "Or should I say, *Sis-in law,* from now on?" She surveyed my outfit. "Has anyone else ever seen you dress like that for when you sleep?"

I blushed. "Annie," I answered.

"Your girlfriend," she acknowledged. "That's still on?"

I nodded. "You never met her, right?"

"No, Keirie, you don't come around much, even on holidays."

"Pittsburgh is WAY west of here," I reminded her. "And your husband wouldn't anymore approve of Anita than he would of me. He'd probably call her a stupid name and say she was a waste of a good piece of—"

"Keirie!" said my mom. "Knock that off!"

"Yes, mother." I answered.

"I wasn't just referring to your visiting *us* out west *(in Pittsburgh),"* said my sister-in-law. "Would it kill you to visit your Mom here in Jim Thorpe a little more often than you do? I see her more often than you, and I live clear across the State."

"And I work and live down in South Jersey," I said.

"The kids would like to see more of their—"

"Their *what?"* I interrupted her. "What am I, Carol? Am I a boy or a girl? *In their minds,* in any case. I get it. It's a tense situation. Of course, if a condition like this runs in our *Travaglini* genetics,

123

one of these days the same gene pattern ought to show up again. So, I don't know. Am I possibly confusing the crap out of your boys as to who and what it's okay to be?"

"Kids today," Carol answered, "they'll do fine. Nevermind how backward thinking your brother, my supposed *better half,* can be. Our kids are more evolved than your and my generations, and even Mom's," she said, turning to face Sarah, yet working on the eggs. "Do you need help, Mom?" she asked.

"Could you help me get the waffles out of the fridge and into the toaster?"

Carol indicated that she could.

"And what am I supposed to do," I asked, "sit around and supervise, wait to be served, like a *typical male?*"

"Do you know how to cook?" Carol asked.

I laughed. "Not really. Dad insisted his *sons* not bother with such things— cooking was *women's work.*" I glanced down at myself. "Everything about the way I want to live my life suggests, though, I am not a boy. So, it follows—"

"No, it doesn't!" Carol argued. "Being born female doesn't automatically make you a gourmet in the kitchen," Carol stated. "And God forbid, I like my father-in-law, but that sexist bullshit of his should have gone extinct when the new century came in."

"And then America elected Donald Trump president," I quipped, "and back to the 1950s we've gone."

She smirked. "God, I hope not. And please don't mention that name again today ... *or tomorrow, either.* I hope they impeach that ignorant bastard. Anyway, what I was saying was, I know a lot of girls who couldn't fry an egg right to save their life."

"Keirie, honey," Mom said. "Kelly's flight is getting in around nine. It *is* an hour's drive to Lehigh. Maybe you might hurry and get your breakfast and get ready to head down." She glanced to the clock. "God," she said. "Seven o' clock, already."

"Yeah," I agreed. "I'll scarf down a little juice, some cereal and then get washed up." I glanced out the window to the snow yet covering the countryside and then the clear blue sky. "Not supposed to snow, is it?"

"No," said both women.

"Not according to the report, I heard last night," said Mom.

"Great," I said. "Then I'll have my cereal and git."

"Keir?" asked Mom. "Would *you* like a fried egg? It would only take a minute. Have you had one recently?"

"At the diner."

Carol laughed. "Doesn't *Anita* know how to cook, either?" she asked.

I grinned and shook my head. "Not really. We dine out a lot."

• • •

I arrived at the airport in plenty of time. I finally got my act together, breakfast, a shower and back into the outfit I'd worn when I arrived in *Jim Thorpe*. I was out the door and on my way around eight. It took about an hour. To make sure I didn't get there late, I flipped on my radar detector and hit the gas pedal a little harder than maybe was wise. But I had to book. Naturally, my reward for arriving near nine was that the flight was announced as being a little late. Underneath the dreaded **DELAYED** read the legend: **NEW ARRIVAL TIME: 10:00 AM**. *An hour?* I guess you could call that a *little* late. I found myself walking the concourse. It certainly was a spacious enough facility, but— and this is no complaint— it was no Philly International or John F. Kennedy size operation.

"United Airlines flight 574 out of Philadelphia International now arriving on runway 31," came the announcement near Ten. The short hop from Philly airport was a breeze, compared to the almost five hours one might imagine Kelly had had to travel once departing the airport in Flagstaff, Arizona. But my sister Kelly had arrived, and suddenly there she was:

"Hey, sis," I called to her.

She froze. "*Keir?*"

"Hey, don't say that too loud, okay?" I asked. "For all intent and purposes, it's *Keira,* although *Keirie* sounds neutral enough to work. It's what Mom uses."

She grabbed hold of me and hugged me tightly. "Oh, my God, brother, it's so good to see you! It's been ages. My God, look at you. You're a *girl!*"

"Kelly, will you please quit broadcasting my gender issues all up and down this concourse? I'm self-conscious about being seen in public like this as it is."

"Then, why are you?" she soberly asked.

"Oh, come on, look at me," I begged. "And I'm not even trying hard this morning to come off female."

125

"I always wanted a baby sister," she mused. "God, you're pretty, Keir."

"Uh huh," I deadpanned, "thanks.

"Better living through chemistry, right?" She was referring to the *estrogen* and testosterone inhibiters I'd been taking since college.

"Mother Nature helped," I retorted. "I'd say, she *helped a lot.*"

"I'm not sorry about that," Kelly replied. "I like you this way. I already have *three* brothers."

"How's that persnickety owner of yours at the gift shop treating you?" I asked, changing subjects.

"Amelia and I get along okay," Kelly smiled. "I only wish she'd be a little more civil with the tourists who enter her store. She has a reputation in the town. I'm scared to death to say anything, and she knows it. I don't want to lose the position, telling her to tone it down a little."

"I don't blame you," I replied.

"What about you, Keir? Your last text said you weren't sure you'd still have a job the first of the year."

"It's going to happen, eventually," I answered.

She took a good, long look at me. "My baby *sister,*" she said. She shook her head. "I'll bet you kill in a dress."

"I wasn't sure how far I wanted to take this," I said. "I started on the medications because I could feel masculinity trying to change me. I didn't like it. I only wanted to curtail any real progress in that direction. I got carried away."

"Estrogen supplements will do that to you," she said, "given enough time. And you gave enough." She looked me and up down. "I'll say it again. I bet you kill in a dress."

"Annie pretty much lit a firecracker under my rear. She dragged my ass to the mall and into a boutique store. They never even doubted I was female. Helped me pick out a whole new wardrobe."

"Ooh. Wow," she answered. "That sounds like a *TG reader's* '*wet dream.'* Tell me what else she did to '*do this'.*" She splayed her fingers toward my total package. "But let's collect my bags and find the food court, first; I'm starving. That overpriced crap United serves us on the plane would make a turkey buzzard thumb his beak at it."

I laughed. "All right. Mom's anxious to see you, you know."

"Who's all there so far?"

126

"Just Craig and his family."

"Trevor?" she inquired.

I shook my head. "Mom's a little sad about that."

"Kind of makes me glad I never married any of the losers I thought I might end up with. And Frank?"

"He'll show up with Meg and Chloe Christmas day. Chloe's twelve now, can you believe it?"

Kelly sighed, and glanced down at herself. "Yeah. I can, sadly. We're getting old."

I laughed. "It's good to see you after so long, sis."

"What's Craig been like?" she asked. "Has he been civil at least?"

"To me?" I clarified. "Oh, hell no."

She sighed. "What about Dad? Is he at least decent?"

"I think he was kind of glad Mom asked *me* to collect you."

"Yeah, I'll bet he *loved that*. Get someone else to come get me. How's he been around you?"

"I made him laugh."

"You made a connection? Were you wearing *that* at the time?"

"No. Tights, ankle boots and a dress." I described the outfit to her in detail.

"I'm sorry I missed that," she replied. "I'll bet you rocked in it. You're all girl now, aren't you?

I grinned. "Almost."

She hugged me again. "You brought my coat, I hope, from home, right?" she asked. "Mom remembered to send it with you?" She looked down at the flimsy, very short skirt she wore around her waist, and the knee-high boots that she'd stuffed her bare feet and legs into. She looked great, but way underdressed for the weather here on the east coast.

"That looks great on you," I told her.

"I can't believe how identical we look," she answered. "I bet we could almost pass as twins."

She grabbed her smartphone out of her tiny purse and pulled me up against her, my chin wedged up against hers, for a group selfie.

"Again," I reminded her. "There are significant inconsistencies," I said of my sexuality.

"We used to have fun, as kids," she reminded me, "exploring those *'inconsistencies.'*"

"We had no shame," I suggested. "We were brother and sister for heaven's sake."

"So? And besides, I've *never* thought of you *as* my brother. And my God how great you've filled out."

Just then *my* smartphone sounded. "That's got to be Mom, checking to see if you'd arrived yet." I fished into my handbag and retrieved it. "I called her and said your flight had been delayed. I said I'd keep her updated." I touched the talk icon and spoke into the tiny microphone. "Hi, Mom, yeah, she just came through the gate." I glanced to Kelly. "She wants to say hi."

Kelly smirked, stuffed her phone back in her purse and grabbed mine. "Hey, Mom. Yeah, everything went fine. We left on time out of Flagstaff. It was the Philadelphia terminal. We were late taking off. Yeah...."

We continued down to baggage check, and eventually found the food court. Around noon, we finally went out to the parking lots to find my car.

• • •

Kelly took one look at the vehicle I drove, at how tiny and compact it was, and only stared open-mouthed. "Keirie, *what the hell is that?*"

(Oh, no, not again, I thought.) I grinned. "My car."

"Oh, you got to be kidding!" she replied.

"It's a *smart car.* It gets good mileage," I offered.

"Does it float?"

"Does it *what?* I don't know. Why would it need to do that?"

"Next time you're going over a bridge on a windy day, don't be surprised if you get blown off the deck and into the water."

"Come, on, sis," I implored. "I like it; it suits me. It gets good mileage."

"You said that already," she replied. "Will all my shit fit in that back of that thing?"

I nodded. "I think so."

"Where's the trunk?" she asked.

"It doesn't have one," I deadpanned. "That's where they put the engine. I believe in Europe they say, *the engine's in the boot.*"

Kelly leaned against her passenger side door and started giggling. "Thanks, sis," she said, "I needed a laugh today."

"Why are you making fun of my car?" I pouted. "It gets great mileage."

She started laughing even louder. "It better."

Her stuff, incredibly, did fit in the rear compartment, stacked to the roof. We then loaded

ourselves into it as well.

"Oh, lord," moaned Kelly as she wedged herself into the passenger seat.

"It's a two-seater," I said, conversationally.

She glanced back at all her stuff stacked behind her. She faced me once more and we both started laughing. She grabbed me then, which wasn't easy, in the cramped front of the thing, and gave me a bear hug. "You crack me up, you know that?"

"Yeah," I said. I took hold of the steering wheel, reached down, started the engine, and put the car in gear. "Shall we go?"

"Sure. Don't you need to go in the back, though, and first rewind the rubber band?"

"Kelly?" I asked.

"What, Keir?"

"You're being mean." I broke out into a smile.

Kelly looked about the tiny compartment. "All I can say is, thank God we're both short … *and thin!*"

We pulled out of the parking lot and headed back for home.

CHAPTER FIFTEEN - Christmas Eve, Part Two

Downtown Jim Thorpe

We were back at the Travaglini home by One, and no sooner home Mom and Carol, who had been waiting for us to arrive, requested we save the unpacking of my smart car's back with Kelly's suitcases and last-minute Christmas gifts for after the four of us *girls* got back from a trip to town. *(Kelly had had the bulk of her gifts pre-sent by Federal Express earlier in the month so that they'd be there for Christmas Morning)*. Mom and Carol wished to just walk the streets in the cold, brisk hours before sundown *Christmas Eve* to enjoy the ambiance of a *Jim Thorpe Olde Time Christmas* in the hours leading up to Christmas night. The actual festivals to which the name was associated was yearly held every first and second weekend in

December, so obviously, this was not that, but simply a stroll to view the fruits of that yearly effort and event. It was Sunday; few *(if any at all)* of the small specialty stores up and down the main commerce streets of *Jim Thorpe* would likely be open. It didn't matter, the four of us were mostly interested in enjoying all the fetching Christmas decorations adoring all the exterior facades.

Dad and Craig and the three boys were in Allentown for the day, Alvin treating Craig's three boys to a lunch at a *MacDonald's,* and then a showing of the latest *Star Wars* movie, *"Star Wars: The Last Jedi,"* which had premiered just a few weeks earlier and was still playing in area theaters. Annie and I had caught it two weeks earlier when it first came out. So, preferring to spend the afternoon with my mom, Carol and Kelly, walking the streets of *Jim Thorpe,* didn't leave me feeling like I was missing out on anything memorial. Besides, the movie would probably be out on Blu Ray by spring anyway.

Craig and Alvin considered our plans for the day in their words *'boring as all fuck,'* and as sexist as this all seemed: the *women* staying local and leisurely walking the streets of *Jim Thorpe* while the men headed down to the nearest big city and had what they considered *real fun*— the four of us *"girls"* didn't mind all that much. We chatted on subjects that ranged from the meaning of life, to how long it had been since we'd seen such and such, and who was getting divorced next and who got caught cheating on his wife with the babysitter. That sort of the thing. And truth be told, there was never a time in my lifetime that I could recall where I would have considered a few hours out with the *guys* preferable to the same time spent with the *gals*. It just had always felt way more fun to me.

• • •

Annie called me around midnight from Seattle, which meant it was around nine out there on the west coast. She wished me a merry Christmas, told me how much she missed me already. I pretty much reiterated the same.

Mom, Dad, Craig, Carol and their kids had already gone to bed. Kelly and I were atop her ornate, oak-frame bed, watching *Christmas with the Kranks,* the Tim Allen and Jamie Lee Curtis movie about a husband and wife who decided one Christmas to skip the holiday completely. We were both dressed in sleepshirts and knee socks and LL Bean moccasins, staring up at her thirty-inch

131

LCD monitor, hanging off a support arm bolted to the forward wall. Both of us had chosen to spend the waning hours of Christmas Eve night watching the stupid thing. I liked the film; it was admittedly a fun holiday movie, but I couldn't help finding its nod to social convention and group conformity disturbing. Tim Allen's character wanted to celebrate the holiday that year on a cruise to the Caribbean. To afford the trip, he decided to totally do no decorating or prepare for the upcoming holiday in any way, which infuriated his neighbors. His house stood in stark contrast to their festively trimmed houses, and they did not like his insistence on being different and *skipping Christmas.*

"Actually, this movie sucks," I said, tapping my right foot against Kelly's. "It's all about *conformity.* Yielding to community customs, standards, behavior. Damn one's individuality. It's got *right wing religiosity* written all over it."

"Keir, knock it off," Kelly replied. "It's cute. Stupid, but *cute,*" she insisted. "Quit reading so much into it."

"Yes, big sister," I replied, demurely.

She kicked me back with her left foot against my right one.

"Are you sure you're not tired?" I asked Kelly, then. "You've been up all day, and you must be experiencing some sort of jet lag."

"I am," she said. "But backwards. I'm still on Arizona time. It's nine back there, so I'm quite awake yet. You're okay, aren't you?"

"Yeah," I replied.

That was when my smartphone rang. The fifteen second melody it played was well-known and brought a smile to both of us.

"Peanuts?" mused Kelly. *"Linus and Lucy?"*

"Yeah, so?" I queried. "It's Christmas. I'll change it after New Year's. It's probably Annie."

"You better get it before it sends her to *Voice Mail.*"

I had left the phone on the windowsill to my right. I did my best to reach for it, and almost fell off the bed.

"Are you drunk?" Kelly queried.

"No. Shut up." I needed to physically leave the bed and retrieve it; clicked *talk.* "Hey, Annie, Merry Christmas," I answered in reply to her initial greeting.

"I *miss* you," she whined in a sullen voice.

"I miss you too," I said.

She told me all about her time so far out in Washington State. Her parents were based in Seattle but that was not where the

Thrombi family intended to remain. Annie and her parents *(Annie was an only child)* were spending Christmas with her dad's brother in the old coal mining town of *Roslyn*, a good eighty miles to the east of Seattle. The town was used back in the 1990s for location exteriors on the TV series *Northern Exposure*. Annie went into detail about the weather they were having out there. *(It was snowing right that second out the window of her bedroom in her dad's brother's log home in the outskirts of the town.)*

"It's weird driving through the center of town," she told Keir. "I keep thinking I'm not actually here, but watching a rerun of that old TV series from the nineties."

"I thought that show was set in Alaska," I pondered.

"It *was* set in Alaska," she clarified, "but it was filmed here in Washington State, all the exteriors right here in *Roslyn.*"

"Oh."

"It's midnight there now, isn't it?" Annie asked me.

"Yeah," I acknowledged.

"Good. Remember that present in the pretty red wrapping paper I told you to open at midnight Christmas Eve?"

"Yeah?" I did remember, *just now,* the second she reminded me.

"Where is it? Did you?"

"It's downstairs. No, I haven't opened it. People, Annie, usually wait for morning to open their gifts. You know, to give Santa Claus time to stop by during the night and deliver them? You really want me to go down there and get it? I don't really want to. Can't it wait till morning?"

"No, I need you to try it on now, so that you'll already be wearing it tomorrow morning while you're unwrapping all your Christmas presents, and are thinking of me the whole time you're in it."

"What is it?"

"Open it and find out."

"Annie," I begged.

"Are you in bed?"

"Not my bed," I said. "Kelly's."

"Oh, that's cute," she replied. ***"Hi, Kelly! Merry Christmas,"*** she shouted into her phone. I had to pull my Samsung S8 away from my ear. I glanced over at Kelly. She laughed and in a regular speaking voice, loud enough for my phone's microphone to pick it up, said:

"Hi, Anita. *Merry Christmas!"* Kelly grinned over to me then.

133

"You still there, Keir?" I heard Annie inquire, faintly, from the phone's tiny speaker.

"Yeah," I replied, bringing the phone again up close to my ear. "You almost just blew my eardrum out, Annie. Thanks."

"You're such a wimp," she replied.

"Say hi to Joel when you see him," I told her.

"Joel?" she puzzled.

"Fleischman," I added. "The town's resident physician. He was stuck there for four years, remember … on the show, back in the 1990s?"

"Yeah, you're a riot, love," she told me, "and a nerd. If you're that big a fan, how is it you don't remember the show was filmed right here in Washington State?"

"It's been years since I watched the series on DVD. When it was first made, I was what *one years old?*"

"So, are you and Kel going to spend Christmas night in bed together waiting for Santa Claus to show up?"

"She's blood, Annie, you've got nothing to worry about."

"Did I imply *that?* And that's gross, Keir. You and your sister. But if you two plan on cuddling together like a couple of female siblings, so what? But go get that present! It's after midnight where you are. Put it on! And then email me a picture of it. I want to see you in it."

"It better not be a *teddy,*" I warned her. "Or some frilly negligee thing that's meant to show off my girlie figure. I mean for God's sake, right? You just made me come out with all this to the world two months ago. That's going too far too fast."

"With that body, you'd look gorgeous in either, so what are you so afraid of?"

"You *did* give me a *teddy! For real, right?"*

"No, relax. Just get it, open it, and send me a shot of you in it. You'll love it. Bye."

She hung up the phone abruptly.

"What?" asked Kelly.

"I've got to go downstairs, and hopefully not wake everybody."

"Why?" she pursued.

I told her. And when I reached near the end I added, "She wants you, sis, to take a picture of me in it after and send her a copy."

"Wow, brother," Kelly said to me. "You're her bitch, aren't you?"

"Kelly, shut up," I said.

"Hey, I'm almost jealous. I wish someone loved *me* like that. That girl really likes you. Now go get it. But don't open it until you're back up here. I want to see what it is too, when you open it."

"Yes, big sister, anything you say."

She tapped my leg with her foot. "Go," she said.

I slowly eased myself off her bed and padded out of the room.

. . .

The back stairway down to the first floor deposited me in the common room in the rear side of the house, facing the view of the mountains. Here also, the kitchen and living room also situated this the back side of the house. As I keyed my glance right for the way to the living room and for Annie's gift under the tree, I chanced to glance to my left. My breath froze. I almost wanted to jump out of my skin. A solitary light was on there in the kitchen, a stove overhead work light; very gloomy and sullen was the illumination it cast into that room. Someone was hunched over the kitchen table at the far end of it.

It was my brother. He was naked, save for a pair of boxers. With his toned and muscled arms and hairy chest, he looked like someone a sane person would never want to cross paths with. I tried to be quiet and not draw his attention as I crept rightward for the living room. Curiosity, sad to say, compelled me to take a second glance to the kitchen and to Craig. Our eyes met. He was staring right at me; watched me attend to my business here on the ground floor.

"What are you up for?" he called.

I swear to God, it felt like something straight out of a horror movie. The lighting was just perfect: dark and solemn. All that was missing was a music cue on the soundtrack, heralding the almost certain soon end of my days on Earth. Craig had a bottle in his right hand as he sat slumped forward upon the table, and I was sure in the background someone was sampling Stanley Kubrick's god-awful mood soundtrack from *The Shining*. The air around me suddenly felt so very heavy.

"Craig," I answered lowly.

I wanted out of there; something told me speak nothing more to him; leave. I slowly turned and headed rightward, disappearing from Craig's sight and entered the living room.

It was lit solely by the white lights of the Christmas tree. I went over to it and found Kelly's gift. I really hoped I could just complete my business down here, creep back to the stairs and up again to the second floor and Kelly's bedroom. But a spurious thought in the back of my head told me, no, that's not the way this night would play out. My heart was pounding a mile a minute, as if I had already lived this night once before in some alternate reality, and I wished I could just wish the whole awful memory of it out of my head. But I knew what I would find when I turned and faced back to the living room's entrance. Craig had already crossed the kitchen and was now at the entrance to the living room.

"We don't open gifts until morning," he said. "You're a little early, aren't you?"

I took a breath. "It's from Annie. She wanted me to open it now, midnight."

"Oh," he acknowledged, "your weird girlfriend who can't decide whether she likes fucking guys or other chicks."

"Craig, why are you up?" I asked. "Is everything alright?"

"Why do you care?" he snapped.

I frowned. *This was all so ominously familiar, as if I had lived it all before.* "Honestly?" I said. "I don't. But *you* want to know why I'm down here, and I'm just waiting for you to be done grilling me, so I can go back upstairs and open this thing, like Annie asked me to."

He started coming toward me, intent on taking the gift from my hands. I shielded it behind my back. He saw what I was doing, and like a wild animal, sensed *(or smelled)* trepidation oozing off me *(a polite word for fear, right?)*. He grinned a god-awful grin. He was almost close enough for me to smell our father's best spirits on his breath. Yeah, he was lit alright. "Come on, little brother," he encouraged. "Your girlfriend wants you to open your gift. So, open it. Let's have a look."

The Christmas tree had to be ten feet tall. It lay situated in the extreme left corner wall of the room. Behind it the rear exterior wall was a wall of ornate stained glass panels like something one might find in a church, the top part of it divided by a huge horizontal log that was topped off by an A-frame of glass. Another exterior wall fronted the Christmas tree to my left, and dispersed about the room were various recliners, a sofa, two side by side ottomans, end tables, and a very large coffee table. There was very little wiggle room, space to easily navigate one's way out of it, sort of like a maze. And I was slowly backing myself toward the fireplace.

He kept coming forward. "Come on, bro," he said, smiling. He reached for the gift. "Let's open it."

"You're wasted, aren't you," I told him.

"I'm *drunk?* You think so?"

"Yes," I stated, flatly.

He paused to think about it. "Nah, I feel fine."

"Why?" I asked.

"Why, what?"

"Why are you? It's Christmas night. Why are you down here? Why do you need to get wasted like that of all nights tonight? Is something bothering you?"

"How is it any of your damn business, you little fairy?"

I nodded. "Okay. I'm going back up to bed."

"You mean up with your sleep mate, like old times, huh? Always sneaking out of your bunk and creeping off to Kelly's room, because you'd rather be a girl and sleep with your sister, instead of us guys."

"Yeah, what of it? What do you care?"

"You're a fucking fairy, that's why I care. You're an embarrassment to the family."

"According to you."

"*According to everybody!* I don't give a rat's ass how convincing a girl you make even in that girly getup you're wearing now. You're a freak, a mistake. Nature fucked up when it created you."

"She's done it before," I rebutted. "It's not my fault mother nature gets it wrong as often as she gets it right. Look at you? Are you '*right*'?"

"Damn straight I am!" he insisted.

"Is that why you're here, instead of in bed with Carol? Something not go right between you two? Does she know you're not there? *Does she care?*"

"Why you little son of a bitch!" he flashed. He lunged for me.

I lost Kelly's gift in a heartbeat, tossed it to the coffee table and grabbed the poker from the tool set by the hearth. I whacked him with it.

It didn't stop him. He grabbed me, smacked me hard across the face, and threw me across the two ottomans, lined up one after the other. "*You want to be a girl?*" he yelled. He turned me over onto my stomach, and raked up my sleepshirt, yanking down my underwear. "Let me help you out with that."

"*Get off me, Craig, no!*" I shouted at him. "*What do you think you're doing?*"

"I'm going to fuck you up your ass, or getting ready to," he answered, "that's what I think I'm doing."

I could feel his torso pinning me down under him, and his manhood as yet in his boxers slowly beginning to firm up. There was a dreadful *déjà vu* about this whole situation, as if I were only reliving an event I'd already once before experienced; like in a dream, maybe. But this time, I was not going to let it defeat me … *or him*.

I shut my eyes and steeled myself for the moment he would begin probing my exposed rear and my anus with his penis. I expected to feel him begin to defile me any second then. I blacked out; I must have. At least that is how I remembered it happening. I knew I did not want to accept the indignity of a thing like this. I wanted to just leave this reality, go somewhere else. And I think, *I did do that*…. Black out, I mean. *I think*….

• • •

"*Are you out of your mind, Craig?!! Get off her!*"

But only for an instant, apparently. I snapped back to consciousness once more … in time to hear my father's angry voice fill the room close by. I opened my eyes, creaked my head up and saw my old man raise his right foot and thrust it toward Craig. The anger in my dad's eyes was almost frightening.

Suddenly, Craig wasn't on top of me anymore. I felt his entire form heave sideways toward the sofa. He wound up almost comically finding himself in a reclining position atop it.

"*Jesus Christ, Craig, are you drunk? Have you lost your common sense?*" our dad demanded of Craig.

I gathered myself up, pulled my panties back up and rolled off the ottomans; getting to my feet I retrieved the fireplace poker and lunged for Craig. Someone needed his head cracked open, and I was just mad enough to volunteer.

Dad stopped me. He shook his head no.

"*I did nothing to make him want to do that!*" I yelled. "*He tried to rape me!*"

"But he didn't," Alvin Travaglini answered calmly. "I got here in time."

He did do that, I had to admit. And yet it still felt like I was only dreaming this part, as if my Dad had not got here in time, had in fact not showed up until after Craig had completed his task.

I took a pause to contemplate what almost happened, and then glancing to the poker as yet in my right hand, slowly returned it to the tool stand by the fireplace.

"He's drunk," I informed our father.

Craig was not having any of it; he tried to rise off the sofa and avenge his old man for kicking him like that.

Alvin Travaglini pushed him back with one of his big hands and stood tall before his near naked son. "You move when I tell you to move!" he barked at his son. "You're lucky I showed up when I did. You're the CEO of my company for God's sake, you stupid little shit. You're pathetic. What the hell's the matter with you? She's your sister for fuck's sake."

Wait. Did I get that line, right? Also, Alvin Travaglini had initially ordered my brother to "Get off **her***!" "Her...." Did Dad get my gender wrong? No way had he had an abrupt change of heart about my being part female. I was his son. This made no sense. I swear at this point I could not shake the feeling that this part was all somehow not the way it really went down. Not that I wasn't grateful. If my brother had managed to do what he intended and not be stopped before he could even begin ... I'm not sure I would have survived the trauma of it psychologically. Who in my situation would? But again, Dad referred to me as if I were his daughter. At least that's how I thought he referred to me. Or maybe all these months later, as I write this, I'm just remembering the event wrong.*

As I warned at the beginning of all this, take with a grain of salt anything else I say from here on end.

Craig agreed with his father that remaining on the sofa where he was, was the right thing to do at this juncture and he did so.

"I swear to God, Craig, Christmas Eve of all nights," Alvin Travaglini informed his son.

"Thank you for showing up when you did, Dad," I said to Alvin and meant it. I reached up and kissed him on his forehead. I shook my head in incredulousness, then, and took a deep breath. "I feel like I'm going to pass out."

"Go on up to bed, Keir," he said to me in a low almost kind voice. "You're all right. I'll take care of it from here. And you're welcome. You *are* family, Keir. You don't deserve to be treated this way. A*nd family don't act this way, **right Craig?** Do stuff like this, to family!"*

My Dad shot Craig another sickened look.

I gave my brother a final glance; he wouldn't even look at me. I nodded to my dad and slowly threaded my way out the room for the back stairway and for Kelly's room. Alvin remained hovering over his eldest son like he was warning Craig to attempt no retaliation for getting his butt kicked over to the sofa like that.

"Well?" Alvin said to Craig. "What brought that on?"

"He's a girl," Craig rebutted. "That's what he keeps insisting. I wanted to show him what consequences came with the title."

Alvin grabbed the back of Craig's neck and pulled Craig's head forward toward him. "I don't care how old you are now, you dumb shit. Don't get smart with me! I'll tear you a new asshole any time I choose. Why aren't you in bed with your wife? What's happened, tonight of all nights? Why are you out here? Who said you could raid my wine cellar and drink yourself stupid?"

"Which question would you like me to answer first, Dad?" Craig answered.

"Goddamnit, Craig!" Alvin swore. He grabbed Craig's arm and pulled him off the sofa, catapulting him toward the hallway where I as yet lingered.

"Go on to bed, Keir!" he flashed to me.

"I was hoping you might whoop the shit out of him, like mom said you used to when he was ten and had it coming. I wanted to see that."

"Fuck off, you little queer," Craig said. "You're lucky dad showed up when he did."

I gave Craig a nasty look. "Fuck off yourself, Craig," I returned. "No wonder Carol's thinking about leaving you."

That one cut through Craig like a saber. He lunged for me. Dad held him firm in his grip. *"She told you that?"* Craig said to me. *"You're a liar!"*

I smiled. "Girls share."

"I'm going to kill him, the little fairy," he told our father.

"You're not going to do shit, Craig. Kitchen. *Now!"* Alvin told his son.

140

"Why? *I've already been there.* What are you going to do, Dad, *stick my head under the sink?*"

"Yeah. I just might. Sober you up. First off. Then we need to have a serious talk. You're lucky I don't just take you outside in the freezing cold and beat the fucking shit out of you."

"You could try," he challenged his father.

Craig was quite a hefty soul, but his father, even in his sixties, was no wimp *(not like me)* either. "Don't tempt me," he told his oldest son. Alvin manhandled Craig into the kitchen and forcibly sat him in one of the chairs of the table.

I heard a noise behind me, and from the higher floors I heard Carol, Mom and Kelly slowly descend to the first floor to see what all the commotion had been about; they congregated at the living room entrance where I had remained. They could tell from the condition my sleepshirt and panties were in what Craig had attempted to do to me. Carol flashed an angry gaze at her husband in the kitchen and then joined Mom and Kelly approaching me and taking me into their arms, hoping I might calm down and be all right.

Kelly and I, after, paused halfway up the stairs, curious to see how Dad, Mom and Carol intended to "deal" with Craig's repulsive behavior. Mom left for the cabinet above the side countertop to prepare a pot of coffee to help sober Craig back up.

Carol glared at her father-in-law, like she had some secret history with him that left her bitter. She glanced back to me, me looking so small on the stairs; she gave me the saddest look I have ever seen a person make. "Keir…" she started to say.

I just nodded.

Mom hovered over her oldest son and waited for the coffee in the Keurig to finish brewing. Kelly, beside me, put her hand on my knee and squeezed it. "Are you all right?" she asked me in a near whisper.

"Craig attacked me," I replied, lowly and taking deep breaths. "And I did nothing to provoke it. I was trying to mind my own business. He wanted to fuck me up my ass like I was some damn transgendered street whore trolling for customers."

"Keir?" she said to me, attempting to be very quiet about it.

"What?"

"Don't feel bad. He's done it before."

I studied her. *"You?"*

141

She nodded. "And in my case, he succeeded. No one was around to stop him. Why do you think I like living all the way out west in *Jerome*?"

"When?"

"Back when I was still attending Duquesne."

"He was married by then," I calculated.

She nodded. "I was twenty and babysitting Doug; Trent was three years old. That was in 2010. When Craig and Carol got in after midnight, after their first night out since Doug was born, it was so late I stood the night, and that's when—"

"Shit," I replied. "Oh, God, he didn't? Kel, I'm so sorry."

"And I'm sorry … he almost got you as well," she answered.

"Dad stepped in in time," I said.

She nodded. "Craig's got a problem. Someone should have done something about it back when it happened to me. They didn't."

"Did you tell Carol?"

"No, I never told Carol *or Mom*. But I told *him,"* she said, looking straight at our dad.

Alvin Travaglini sensed he was again being singled out with an angry stare (*this time from Kelly)* from across the way and glanced up at us on the stairs. Kelly just stared him down, coldly.

"What did Dad do about it?" I asked in near a whisper.

"Not a damn thing. Told me to shut up about it. Bought me a *Tesla.* I'm still driving it; I love that car. Its *lithium powered.*" She glanced over at me and smiled morbidly.

"Does that mean I could have hit dad up for one also, had Craig nailed me as well?"

"Is that your heart's desire?"

I snorted a laugh. "No. Was it *yours?*"

She couldn't answer. Tears started forming around the edges of her eyes.

I took Kelly's hand in mind. "Oh, God, Kelly, it must have been horrible."

She nodded. "You're lucky Dad stepped in in time. I hate our brother so much I could go down there right now, grab a steak knife from a drawer and shove it in his goddamn chest."

After that one from her, I felt she needed a hug. I gave her one.

She composed herself after a while, pulled back from me and sniffed. "…What Dad says in this household goes. And if he says, *say nothing ... to anyone ... about this. It's family business. I'll handle it."* She snorted, weakly. "Dad handled it: *His way."*

I stared across the way to my father in the distant kitchen and just shook my head, sadly. "Are you sorry you came home, Kel?" I asked in a near whisper.

"No, I'm not. Apparently, I needed to be here this weekend *for you*. I'm glad I was."

"I'm fine, Kelly. Dad intervened before Craig could get started." I touched her arm then. "But I wasn't there for you when Craig did it to you. I wish I'd known."

"You were away at LaSalle, your freshman year. I was attending Duquesne. I never thought my own brother was capable of a thing like that. Brothers are supposed to protect their sisters from predators like him, not *be one himself."*

"Merry Christmas," I grinned.

She hugged me against her. "I love you, you know that?" she whispered. "We've shared so much over the years. You were my best friend; I could confide *anything* with you. I wasn't forced to grow up all alone in a house full of boys."

"I love you too, Kelly," I said.

We both at that moment looked down and saw our Mom looking straight up at us from the foot of the stairs. We hadn't noticed her before that moment, nor could we say how long she'd been down there listening to us. "Keir, are you all right?"

"I'm fine, Mom," I nodded. I think I just want to go to bed."

"I'm so sorry Craig is like this," Sarah Travaglini said. "I don't know what we should do. I don't know what to say." She looked both at me and Kelly. "I haven't been a very good mother to either of you girls, have I?" she said. "Craig's sick. I should have insisted to your father that we do something about him back when he raped *you*, Kelly."

Kelly flashed over at her. "You *know?"*

She nodded, contritely. "Carol told me," Sarah confessed.

"Carol knew?"

Sarah nodded again. "I was sworn to secrecy. If Craig knew *she knew*, I don't know what he would do to her. Same in my case. Your father with me. Father and Son act decent in public, but they can be mean, your father very guarded and protective, especially when it comes to Craig. This must be eating him up inside. That Craig is like that."

143

Kelly shook her head. "I'll be happy when I fly back out to *Jerome*. I'm half tempted to do it tonight. Fuck this family."

"Keir, what were you doing down here?" Mom asked me.

I explained to her about Kelly's gift. She nodded, withdrew to the living room and retrieved it for me. "Are you two going to be all right?" she asked.

We looked at each other, Kelly and me. I shrugged. "What do you want us to do, Mom? Shall we leave, Kelly and me, try to find a—"

"*No,*" she said. *"At this hour on Christmas Eve? It's even about to snow, from the look of it out there. I don't want either of you to leave."*

"Then what?" Kelly asked.

"You two go to bed," she said to us, handing me the present. "My two girls. *He'll never touch either of you ever again. I promise."*

"What's Dad going to do about this?" I asked Mom, glancing over to Alvin, Craig and Carol in the kitchen. "Craig needs to be locked away somewhere at the very least. Prison for the next thirty years wouldn't upset me."

"Only if *I* had assurances," Kelly interjected, "he'd find out what it was like, himself, to spend all of his sentence as someone's prison bitch, getting anal and oral intercourse regularly."

"Your father could never live with the thought of any of this ever getting out in public. It would ruin him," she mused. "He won't allow that to happen and he's got … *connections*. He knows how to make things go away."

I nodded. "I almost feel sorry for them both," I said. "But that would make me a saint. I'm no saint, Mom."

Sarah Travaglini took a long, deep breath. "Are you really, all right?" she asked.

I smiled, weakly, and then shrugged. "I've been better."

"What about you, Kelly?" Sarah said then. "Something more should have been done about what your brother did to you."

Kelly sighed. "I will never be all right. And I know Dad will never allow me to bring charges against either Craig for what he did to me, or dad for sweeping it under the rug. I just deal with it."

Sarah Travaglini nodded. "What a world we live in anymore," she quipped. "The whole species seems to have lost its mind. I worry most for Stevie, Doug and Trent. And *Chloe*. She's just twelve this year. I stay awake all night some nights just imagining what this world will be like for them by the end of the century." She took us both into her arms and kissed the two of us. "Try to forget this night, kids. Please?"

I grinned, weakly. "No promises, Mom," I replied.

Kelly glanced to me and smiled in agreement; she faced Sarah, then.

Sarah nodded.

Up the stairs we went. And off in the distance, we could hear quiet banter continue back and forth downstairs. Craig was in for a long night. I didn't envy him. I didn't pity him either. If hell really existed, I wouldn't at all be sad to think that one day he'd be down there rotting away for all eternity....

It was only fair.

CHAPTER SIXTEEN - Lightening the Mood... Just a Little

Kelly and I returned to the second floor. "I'll see you in the morning, Kel," I told her, wearily. I turned to continue down the hall to my own bedroom. "I think I need to be alone tonight."

"Keir?" she called, pleadingly. "Don't. *I* don't want to be. Not after what almost happened to you tonight. Sleep with me," she begged. "Please?"

I thought about it. "Annie's probably wondering what's taking me so long to call her back. Do you think I should still bother with this tonight?" I said of Annie's present. "Still text her after?"

"It might help ... to talk to her about what happened when you went down to do what she asked."

"I don't want Annie thinking it all happened because she insisted I go get this thing, whatever it is. And you know, it's weird..." I furrowed my brow, bothered by the next thought. "Somehow, I have this feeling, Craig attacking me tonight was going to happen anyway ... as if it were supposed to happen in one form or another." I faced her head on, then. "How do you live with it, Kel? Craig doing that to you?"

She sighed. "After it happened, I tried to purge myself of it, but It won't wash away, no amount of soup and hot showers can rid you of the memory of it, not up here, not ever." She touched her forehead. "Like I told Mom; it never goes away."

"Does it ever get any better?" I asked.

"You mean *does time heal all wounds?*" she snorted. "Whoever thought that line up ought to be boiled in his own pudding, with a stake of holly through his heart."

146

"Ebenezer Scrooge," I smiled, weakly. *"A Christmas Carol.* We should have watched that tonight instead of Tim Allen in that *Krank* movie…. Craig's always been a pain up my butt all the years I've known him, Kelly. I never dreamed he would one day try to be one for real."

She snorted, weakly. "You always could make me laugh, Keirie," she replied. "You have a weird way of putting things."

I nodded. "I ought to write books," I replied.

• • •

"Oh, wow. Look at that," Kelly said as we entered her room. She approached the eastside window. "It's actually *snowing.* We're having a *white Christmas.* It's so peaceful looking out there."

I nodded. "Annie said it's snowing in *Roslyn* too," I answered.

"Silent Night, Holy Night. All is calm, all is bright," she spoke.

I snorted. "Yeah." I nodded down to Annie's gift as yet in my hand. "Are we really doing this … opening this to see what Annie gave me?" I wrinkled my nose. "Somehow the mood's been ruined."

Kelly shrugged. "Tomorrow morning?"

I frowned. "Annie is expecting a text from me, tonight, though. I suppose if I don't open it tonight, I should at least explain to her why I didn't. Still… I don't know…." I shrugged and felt the weight of the box as I jiggled it in my hand. "It' s got to be clothes."

There was a car door slam outside by the garage. The exterior lighting activated, and still by the window sill, Kelly and I saw Craig (fully dressed now) and Dad enter Dad's Audi to drive Craig to God knows where. "There goes Craig," I said.

We both watched the Audi start, the headlights light, and the car slowly back out of the driveway as swirling snowflakes were caught in the headlights. We glanced to each other as the car left the property.

Mom appeared in the door to Kelly's bedroom. "I thought you two would be in bed by now," she said. Sarah simply gazed upon us in our sleepshirts, moccasins and knee socks. I could almost sense how much we must have resembled a pair of sisters, young ones at that, gaping out the window in search of a man in a red suit, leading a team of reindeer.

"We're still debating whether I should open this tonight or not," I answered of Annie's present.

"Craig and your father just left the house," Sarah replied. "Good riddance to both. It's safe now, Keirie. I wouldn't blame you if you went back downstairs, threw that infernal thing into the fireplace, whatever it is, and burned it."

"It wasn't Annie's fault," I defended of her Christmas present. "It would break Annie's heart if she even suspected we thought she caused what almost happened."

"Well," Sarah only uttered, lowly.

"Hey, Mom," said our sister-in-law, Carol, as she appeared as well in the doorway. "Hey, Keir, Kel. You guys okay?"

We both shrugged, simultaneously.

Carol sighed, heavily. "They left," she said of her husband and father-in-law.

"We saw," I replied.

She shook her head. "I don't know where they went off to. I only know Dad told Craig to get dressed and get going. I feel like making an anonymous call to the police and tell them what happened."

"Better not, though," I cautioned her. "When's the last time you watched *The Godfather* movies?"

"Seriously?" she answered me.

I glanced to my Mom and then back to Carol. "We're Sicilian, remember? Dad didn't just luck into his success. I'm sure he could make your life really a bad one if you went against one of his edicts." I faced Sarah again. "Am I right, Mom?"

Sarah turned to her daughter-in-law. "Carol—"

Caroline nodded. "Don't worry. I won't rat my bastard husband out if you think I'll suffer for it more than Craig ever will."

"Your father-in-law would probably pull some strings and make the whole thing disappear."

"Me as well, probably, right?"

Sarah shrugged.

Carol sighed. "I'm going to try to get some sleep. It's after two in the morning, already."

"Can you sleep?" I asked.

"Can *you,* Keirie, " she asked me.

I shrugged. "I don't know."

"Craig and I had a fight," Carol confessed. "That's what started all this tonight. I guess in a way I'm part to blame for the rest of it going down the way it did. Craig drinks a lot. The stress of being CEO of his Dad's company, I guess." She sighed once more. "Oh, well, I'm going up to check on the boys. Maybe I'll join them. There's an extra bunk. I'm not sure I want to sleep alone tonight."

"Are you and the boys going to leave us in the morning, Carol?" asked Kelly.

"No," she said. "I'm not going to ruin the boys' Christmas just because their Dad is a drunken pervert."

"Merry Christmas to all and to all a goodnight," I quoted.

She snorted, weakly. "I'm seeing a lawyer about divorcing his ass as soon as the new year comes in," she decided. "Fuck Alvin Travaglini, his family pride and his mob connections. I don't care how pissed off it makes him." The exterior lights were still lit outside. She glanced out the window. "Ughh," she said then, observing the snow swirling outside. "A white Christmas. How Currier and Ives."

"How *Thomas* Kinkade*?*" I suggested. "Or even Norman Rockwell."

She approached me in my sleepshirt and socks and cupped my face in her hands. "Goodnight, Keir," she said to me. "You have such a sweet soul for all your rough speak at times. I hope we don't grow distant after I leave that sorry ass excuse of a brother of yours. Merry Christmas. Mom, Kelly. All. I'm going to bed."

We all bid her a goodnight in unison as she left for the third-floor stairwell.

"So," began my Mom after, as she glanced to Annie's present, at the foot of the bed, where I'd left it. "Let's see what your better half gave you that was so special to her she didn't want you to wait till morning to open it."

I nodded, ripped off the bow, and tore the wrapping paper to shreds. It was a simple white cardboard box under the wrapper, with the name *Kohls* atop it. I separated the upper half from the bottom and pulled away the flimsy white tissue paper inside.

It was a red lounge-wear thingy, a jumper, I think. Whatever. Matching knee high booties in a pseudo Scottish pattern completed the ensemble.

"Oh, God, really, Annie?" I asked. I was meant to wear it for leisure around the house, a lot like that white snow bunny outfit I'd bought back in November and loved wearing so much. There was a note in the box. It said, *"That white outfit you love wearing, it's getting old— you always in it, I mean—*

after only two months, hon. You will look adorable in this."

149

I took a breath. "Do you want me to go in the bathroom and put it on?" I asked.

"Stop acting like you're still a boy," my sister told me. "Just take that sleepshirt off and climb into it. Let me take the picture and we can all go to bed. It's not like you have anything under that shirt none of us haven't ever seen, right Mom?"

She smiled, and nodded. "What's the laptop for, honey?" Mom asked me.

I raised the screen part of it up off the keyboard and then the screen lit up, the keyboard's blue keys firing into life. "I'm Skyping Annie." I grabbed my smartphone to text her, give her a heads up to await a Skype call. I turned to Kelly then. "Okay, here," I said, handing her the phone. "Take the picture when I'm done."

I pulled the long-sleeved undergarment up and over me first, and then the red jumper down over my head. It stopped mid-thigh. I pulled off my socks and stepped into the red and brown patterned knee-high booties. Done with all that, I faced my Mom and sister. "Okay?"

There was a beep from my laptop. I had an incoming Skype call. Annie beat me to the punch. I keyed in the command and onto the screen she popped into view. "I got the email, Merry Christmas," she said to me. "It looks *great on you. You are so pretty in that,*" she told me as my laptop's camera caught my image and transmitted it to her. "But I've been waiting for over an hour. I thought maybe you were waiting till Christmas morning to open it. What happened?" She noticed the presence of my Mom and Kelly in the background and the somewhat subdued looks on all three of our faces. "What's wrong?" she asked. "What?"

I set the laptop atop the bureau on the opposite wall to the bed, allowing the unit's camera to include us all in its shot. I then proceeded to tell her what transpired after I went down to retrieve her present. I hated doing so. Not because Annie couldn't handle it. Emotionally, she was way more level-headed than I would ever be. It's just that up to that point the situation had been one I could remain aloof about. Explaining it all to her over Skype, with Mom and Kelly adding additional details, Annie could see in the laptop's high resolution camera pickup that my eyes well welling up and I was beginning to lose my hold on my composure. In other words, the trauma of the whole thing was finally beginning to leak out of the box I'd forced it into. I was starting to cry.

Mom and Kelly, both sat me down on the bed and hovered on either side, attempting to comfort me over the affair.

Sarah Travaglini faced the camera. "We're sorry to dump all this on you, Anita," she said.

"I wish I'd never badgered Keirie into going downstairs. It never would have happened," she said.

"*Don't do that*," begged Sarah. "You couldn't have known. Craig has a problem. I feel like kicking my son a good one in his behind. I'd like to kill him, the way I'm feeling right now."

"Christmas night," Annie mused over Skype. "Of all nights. Oh, Keirie, love," Annie said to me then. "I wish I was there. I feel so useless all the way over here in Washington State."

I tried to clear enough liquid from my eyes and nose to respond. "If you were, he would have attacked you as well, Annie. It bothers him you only date girls."

"Sarah?" Annie called to my Mom.

"What, hon?" she asked.

"Keep that oldest son of yours henceforth as far away from me as humanly possible. If I ever bump into him, when I'm through, he'll be able to insert his man tool in any opening on himself he wishes. It won't be attached anymore. I'll cut it off and personally hand it to him. And he should consider himself getting away easy, losing only that."

"Can you call again in the morning, Anita?" my Mom asked. "I think Keir needs time to come down from all this."

"Yes. Keir, be better," she said. "I love you."

Well that started the tears welling up in my eyes all over again. I tried to smile. "Me too," I croaked out.

Mom rose from beside me on the bed, walked over to the laptop, gave Annie a final goodnight and closed the lid. She glanced back to Kelly and me and just took a long breath. She shook her head and wished us both try to get a good night's sleep.

The snow continued into the night. Craig and Dad, wherever they had gone, would not spend this night at the Travaglini homestead.

CHAPTER SEVENTEEN - A Text from Annie

Annie texted me around seven AM. I groaned as I heard my Samsung S8 beep the familiar notes it did whenever I received a text; I pulled myself halfway off the bed, retrieving my purse from where I'd left it on the floor beside me. Not too far beyond the hour of seven, and time zones being what they are, it was just after four out there in Seattle. Fishing through my purse, managing this time to not fall of the bed, I found my phone and touched the message icon.

Annie's text read as follows:

> ARE YOU OKAY? BEEN THINKING OF YOU ALL NIGHT. I KNOW IT'S EARLY THERE. CAN'T SLEEP.

I texted back.

> ANNIE, I'M FINE. WHAT IS IT, FOUR AM OUT THERE? PLEASE, STOP WORRYING OVER ME. NOTHING HAPPENED. HE ONLY SLAPPED ME AROUND A LITTLE. DAD STOPPED HIM BEFORE ANYTHING EXTREME HAD A CHANCE TO BEGIN. ENJOY YOURSELF IN ROSYLN TODAY.

Her response came right back.

> NOTHING? YOU CALL THAT NOTHING? HE HIT YOU AND TRIED TO RAPE YOU. I WISH I WAS THERE. I WANT TO KILL YOUR BROTHER. HE'S WHY I HATE MEN. THEY SUCK.

And mine:

> WILL YOU PLEASE GO BACK TO SLEEP?

From Annie:
     I LOVE YOU.
Me:
     WHAT YOU SAID. I LUV YOU.
From Annie:
     OKAY. BYE. TALK TO YOU LATER?
     WHEN MY EYES FINALLY OPEN?
Me.
     NOON HERE, NINE THERE. OKAY?
Her:
     OKAY.

I laughed silently to myself and stuffed the phone back in my purse. I then pulled myself back atop the bed and stared straight up at the ceiling.

"She's worried about you, huh?" Kelly spoke from her side of the bed.

"Yeah," I replied. "Did that wake you?"

"I was half awake as it was. No, it's fine. Are you okay?"

I glanced over at her. She had already rolled over and was looking straight at me. "Yes, big sister, I'm fine."

"Okay," she abruptly replied, turning back over to face the other way.

I stared back up at the ceiling and just snorted a laugh.

CHAPTER EIGHTEEN –
Santa Come and Gone

Oh, God, that SUN! ALREADY??? I mused, as its newly risen presence shafted its rays right into the room from the window leftward of me, washing over my face and making it impossible to keep my eyes closed.

Christmas Morning. Kelly and I *had* managed to grab a few hours of sleep, but at sunrise, around seven-fifteen, not fifteen minutes after I received Annie's text, a hurried trio of stomping barefooted youngsters could be heard descending from the third-floor bunk room, down the stairs for the first floor. Craig and Carol's boys were up, and by the sound of them, they were racing each other to be the first into the living room, attack the Christmas tree and relieve it of its treasures encircling its skirt.

As their footfalls faded, I imagined all three were now ganged around the living room Christmas tree, and somewhere in the back of their mind, as they labored to tear into their brightly wrapped gifts, a puzzling thought might just possibly invade the single mindedness of their pursuits. Where's *Dad? Why does it feel as if he's not here?*

I tried to imagine the interior of that living room, the sofas and chairs, ottomans, me lying flat against the two ottomans as Craig forcibly attempted to introduce me to the world of female sexuality, *its kinkier aspects at any rate.* I imagined him successfully entering my only orifice that at present could mimic a woman's vagina, his man tool's gradual thickening and aroused urgency to speed up its thrusts to bring on its eventual release of male reproductive fluid. And then that climatic moment: his semen pumping itself into my very essence as if it were something I should have been allowing to be done to me since I first awakened to what it meant to be an adult human and woman.

And it was at that point that I discovered that imagining all that had given me a rock-hard erection. For God's sake, there was no denying it. *I liked the thought of another male entering me in that way. Not Craig, of course.* I hated my brother. But the sex itself, and me on the receiving end of it? A part of me got a crazy thrill from the very thought of a male of my choice wanting and desiring to do that to me. I had been programmed from infancy to crave a man's tool inside me, to willingly submit to its single-minded intent of leaving with me a sample of its genetic material.

I almost wished this imaginary male somebody would attempt it for real. If he were here now and attempting it, I was certain my own diminutive tool would either beat him to the end game, or follow his own eruption, with a volley of its own. There was only one thing to do: think of other things, inform that penis of mine that now in bed with my sister was neither the time nor the place to be acting this way.

Kelly rolled over, nudging up against me, a position she and I had assumed countless times as pretend "sisters" in the past. In this position, we were practically spooning. Surreptitiously, I inched my hand down to my tiny organ, and pushed it downward, encouraging it to *knock it off.* I rolled over then and faced her. "This would be weird at our age if we were both male," I told her. "Guys *do not do this sort of thing. 'Sleep together in the same bed.'* Some might still say me being half girl, half guy, still makes it weird."

She pulled the covers down to reveal our matching sleepshirts, mine blue, hers pink, our sleek, smooth thighs and knees, and near identical pair of argyle knee socks on our feet to keep us both warm during the long, cold nights. "Keir, we're practically identical," she said. "Yeah, I'm two years older than you, but I swear we could almost pretend to be each other, we look so alike. We're girls, get over it. It's not weird when girls sleep together like this. And besides, we slept together all the time when we were kids," she smiled. "Who cares? I like reminiscing about all those nights when we did this as kids. It was so great to have a bed mate. To not be the only 'girl' in a household full of boys."

Christmas music began playing softly at that point over the log home's public address system. "Mom, maybe?" I asked of the music.

155

"I guess we're up for the day." She made a fake jubilant smile. "It's Christmas. Yay!"

"Yeah, I'm surprised either of us got any sleep at all. Too excited, we were, I guess, to see what Santa Claus left us under the tree."

"When, though, Keirie, was that ever true?" she replied. "We were never excited Christmas morning."

I made a face. "No, but it's fun to imagine that— like most other kids— *we were*," I replied.

She made a face of her own. "By the time you and I were born, dad was about done pretending he cared about kids and their silly beliefs in Santa Claus and the Easter Bunny."

"Yeah," I answered, remembering.

She smirked. "Remember how mad he used to get when Mom bought us matching outfits to wear? We were her two daughters and she intended to rub it in his face. He already had the sons he always wanted."

"But, my God," I said, "he would yell at her for dressing me this way." I grinned. "And she would give it right back. I'm never quite sure why they stayed together all these years. They're so different."

"… I wonder what today will be like," she pondered aloud.

I only nodded, pensively. "Maybe, I should save everybody the tension, all of it, me looking so much now like … like a clone of you, now; and Craig not here, probably wherever he is trying to sober up and decide what happens to his life and his marriage next. And the fact that when Frank and his family get in today, they're going to learn quick enough what Craig did to me and why he's not here. I just know they're all going to blame me."

"Oh, don't say that," she begged.

"They will you know. It's human nature. Craig's not here to suffer any of the icy stares and whispered judgements. *Just me.* "I'm half tempted to just get in my car and head home, *my home.*"

"And leave me here all alone?"

"You're welcome any time, sis. But, you would hate my apartment," I said. I glanced around Kelly's bedroom. "Not one inch of it comes a tenth to looking any near as nice as just this room."

"My place in *Jerome,* Keir, it's probably not much better than yours."

"I'd rather look out a window to mesas and desert rock and smell high desert air," I replied, "any day than swamp grass, reeds and the Delaware River. So, I'd still prefer your place over mine. Maybe," I

156

paused then to contemplate a daring thought, "maybe, instead of your *Tesla* you could have held out maybe for an estate home of your own anywhere you wanted to build it."

"Dear old dad would never have gone for that," Kelly said. "And Craig warned me to shut my trap about what he did to me or he'd see to it I ended up with nothing some day when the estate eventually got divided among all of us kids."

"Sounds like a certain brother of ours is cruising to spend eternity rotting in hell," I quipped.

"I won't shed a single tear for him they day I hear he passes," she replied. "Or any day after it."

"Ouch," I returned.

"I meant what I said last night," she admitted, "*Fuck this family. And fuck that poor excuse for a Dad we were born with. Dad could have at least tried harder to get Trevor to change his mind, spend Christmas up here with his family, not spend it all alone down in Florida.* Trev's got *no one* down there. But no, Dad's pissed at Trevor, for not keeping Rita in line, for not shaming her into staying married to him if anything to avoid embarrassing the family. And then Trev opens *a pizzeria?* Yeah, Trev might just as well have kicked Dad in his Italian pride."

I glanced out the window. The sun had fully cleared the horizon in just the last ten minutes and now gloriously bathed last night's new fallen snow in a brilliant orange-red glow. What a contrast— out there and in here. The world beyond looked so bright and promising, and today being Christmas, so full of the promise of joy and familial reunion. Cold as hell out there, no doubt. But probably way *warmer* in spirit than in this household. A beautiful log home for certain Dad and Mom's home was. But it was only a façade, like a sample home, no genuine purpose for existing, no real use to anyone. Only a pretense.

"I wonder when it stopped snowing," I pondered.

"I think I woke up around four," she said, glancing to the recessed window nook to her right. "The moon was out, and I saw stars mixed in with big fluffy clouds." She shrugged. "Probably around then."

We heard next somewhere down the hall, Mom and Carol talking low and then what must have been at least one of them descending the stairs for the first floor. The second set of footsteps approached our bedroom. We could both tell by the footsteps it had to be Mom.

There came a knock on the door. "Girls?" she called, lowly. "Are you up?"

'Girls.' I wondered if I'd ever be able to accept that that was what I was, a girl. In this century, one that still embraced transphobia and God knows how many other prejudices, insisting I was one seemed like a recipe for disaster.

"Yeah, Mom," said Kelly. "We're awake. Come on in. We're just lying in bed talking about— whatever."

Sarah Travaglini opened the door. "How *are* you two this morning?"

The chocolate brown comforter was still pulled down past our toes, revealing us yet in sleep shirts and knee socks. Mom smiled at the sight of us. "My God, you look like twins." Our hair lengths and styles were near identical, our hair from the night's sleep mostly all in our faces. "My two beautiful daughters," she said then, shaking her head.

"Oh, Mom, *for God's sake,*" I mumbled.

"Keir, stop that," Mom chided. "You *are* my daughter."

Kelly grinned and said, "We're fine, I guess, Mom; all things considering. I mean, considering Craig, *last night.* Is Dad back?"

"No," was her abrupt response. She turned to me. "Kier, are you all right?" she asked me.

I nodded. "Yeah, surprisingly I feel pretty good."

"You two were always meant to grow up together as sisters," she had to comment once more. "I love seeing you both together this way."

"Mom?" began Kelly to Sarah. "Dad?"

She curled her lip. "He called an hour ago to say he took Craig up to the cabin, and he was going to hang around to make sure Craig got settled in okay."

"Well, that tells me everything I need to know," I spat. "He's not coming back today, is he? Why should he? To tell Frank how happy he is Frank left the company to run a kitchen supply store here in Allentown with Meg?"

"Keir," Mom pleaded.

"Are he and Craig going to do some hunting while they're up there? It's why Dad bought that place, wasn't it? To hunt?"

Sarah only gazed at me.

I nodded. "He's not going to lift a finger to stop Craig from possibly abusing anyone else. He's blinded by how important Craig is to him."

"I wish I could say that wasn't true, honey," she said to me, finally, "but I'd be lying if I insisted I didn't think you were right."

"And what about you, Mom?" I asked.

"What do you want me to do, baby?" she asked me. "Leave Alvin?"

"Do you love him?" I asked. "Seriously, you two seem so different. You voted for Hillary. He actually believed Trump's bullshit crap."

Sarah smirked and then lightly laughed. "He's good to me, though; and we have fun. They say, *opposites attract*. 'Occasionally, anyway.' Girls, I've invested too many years in this marriage to dump it now and expect something better is out there just waiting to replace it."

"But he treats Kelly and me like we're useless, like we haven't one useful braincell in our heads."

"I know," she agreed. "He's a *misogynist*. He's old school. But punishing him, by leaving him, would NOT make him change his ways. And if I left him, he'll still be your father. And I seriously believe, he'd blame the two of you for goading me into leaving him. That might only make things worse. Please don't ask me to turn everything on its ear like that. Especially when I think for all involved, it will cause more bad than good." She glanced around herself to the room. "At the very least, I've invested too many years to just throw all this away and *start over."*

"So, is Dad going to be here at all today?" Kelly asked.

She shook her head. "I really don't know, Kelly."

Kelly thought about it and nodded. "Actually, I'm glad," she concluded.

"What are we going to say to Frank when he shows up today," I interjected, "about everything that happened last night?"

"Truthfully, Carol and I are still not sure how to break it to her three boys why their Dad won't be with us today."

"I noticed you didn't say *Merry Christmas* when you first came in, Mom," I observed. "I take it you don't believe it's a merry one, either. Seriously, Mom, will my being here today make things even worse? Should I leave?"

"*No!*" she flashed at me. "Don't you dare blame yourself for what's happened. Craig's got a problem respecting women and women's boundaries."

"But what about me looking like this?" I asked.

"Honey, you're a girl. I should have put my foot down even harder when you were born, back when the specialists explained what was going on with your DNA. I should have raised you as a female full time, not just when we three were all alone in this house."

"*You mean at school?*" I clarified. "Start me off as *Keira* right out of the gate?"

"Yes," she said, affirmatively. "Because *Keira is who you are, and always have been.* Life has been trying to hammer that truth into you for years, baby."

"But what about Frank today, Mom, and his precious Chloe, and me being *as he put it— a confusing distraction to a young girl who's still trying to nail down her identity?*"

"I'll tell him straight to his face, *'you're his sister, accept that or leave',*" she declared. "If Frank's got a problem with you as you are now, I'll tell him he can come back when he's learned to be more *tolerant.*" She glanced then to the tan wicker chair with the burgundy red seat cushions. I had laid Annie's gift to me across it after I undressed to join Kelly in bed.

"Get dressed and join us downstairs, you two; it's Christmas morning. Come see all the nice things I got you, and then whether Alvin shows up or not we've got Catholic Mass at ten."

"Christmas Mass?" I mused. "Must we?" I turned to face Kelly. "I doubt either of us ever even *liked* going to Catholic school, let alone attend Sunday Morning Services, although I always did envy Kelly. She got to wear those cute dresses to Church and those girls' Catholic School uniforms to school every day."

Kelly laughed. "Remember how I used to dress you up in them?" Kelly said of her school uniforms. "You loved climbing into my knee socks and wearing my plaid skirt. You used to cry to me all the time, '*I like what you wear to school better, Kelly.'*" Kelly mimicked my eight-year-old speaking voice from back then. "*'I like the way your skirt tickles my knees when I walk and the feel of your knee socks on my legs. I hate going to school dressed as a boy. I want to go dressed like you.'*"

Mom smiled. "*I remember,*" she uttered, wistfully. "You two looked so cute together in your skirts and knee socks. Alvin took one

160

look at you, Keir, dressed in Kelly's uniform and he hit the roof. *'Get that Goddamn thing off my son!'* he yelled at me. Oh, God, sorry, I shouldn't cuss like that, not on the Lord's birthday, anyway."

"It's all right Mom," I grinned. "That's just how he sounded. You nailed him good. And I think he also said, *'You're encouraging Keir to think it's okay to want to be a girl. No son of mine is going to grow up queer.'* Did I ever tell you, Mom, how much I hate that *son-of-a-bitch* man you married?"

"*Keirie!*" she chided. "He's *your father!* What would the Lord say hearing you say such an awful thing on a day as holy as this one?"

"*To thine on self be true?*" I offered.

Kelly snorted, then busted flat out into laughter. "Good one, Keir," she told me. She faced back to Sarah. "What Keir is implying, Mom," she said. "Your two '*daughters*' are not good Catholics. Catholicism for either of us was never a great fit."

"It's Christmas day, girls," our mother insisted. "Today, you two will *try.*"

"Yes, mother," we both answered, demurely, parodying the way we used to answer her when we were little.

"Very funny," she replied. "Okay, then, you'll be down in a few minutes, right?"

"Yes, mother," we both said again, breaking out into giggles.

Sarah Travaglini shook her and head and huffed.

"Mom?" said Kelly. Sarah paused at the door. "Merry Christmas."

"Ditto, Mom," I added.

Sarah smiled. "Back at you. Merry Christmas to you too. Now get dressed. Frank, Meg and Chloe ought to be getting in sometime this morning. Hopefully, before we leave for Church."

She was gone a second later into the hallway beyond.

Kelly and I turned to each other. We both snorted a laugh and broke out once more with a case of the giggles. "Wow," I said.

"I guess from now on," Kelly replied, "I should quit calling you *Keir.* We're sisters. Any fool can see that."

"Call me whatever you like," I replied. "I don't care."

She reached over and hugged me. "You're my best Christmas present I'm getting this year. A *sister,* for real, like I always wanted. I still wish you'd quit that go-nowhere sales job at *Com-Link* and come live in *Jerome,* with me, work at the store with me. We'd make a great tag team, maybe take Amelia down a little." She shook her head. "Amelia's going to take *Red Rock Knickknacks* right into the cellar if she doesn't stop pissing off the customers with her eccentricities."

"It would break Annie's heart if I just up and left the east coast and her like that."

"Not really," Kelly answered. "I've never met her, except for last night on *Skype* when she called. She genuinely does love you, but she's going to have to accept the fact that you need a life, and the one you have here in the east is coming to an end. If *Com-Link* is soon to be no more as you say it is, she'll have to find a way to make your moving on work if you and she mean that much to her."

"You'd really want you and me to hook up like that; work together at your store *in Arizona?"*

She nodded. *"Yes."*

"You're boss, Kelly, I doubt she'd hire *me,"* I pondered. *"*I'm a freak."

"She knows about you," Kelly said. "I've shown her pictures of you."

"You have? Was I dressed like a little girl in any of them? I know Mom used to get a kick out of snapping photos of us as sisters."

She grinned. "There were a couple like that of you in there as well. I endeavor to be thorough."

"Thanks," I replied, cynically.

"But, mostly, stuff like your high school yearbook picture. You know, when you tried *real hard* to look like a boy, and never really managed to pull it off."

"Are you trying to annoy me on purpose?"

Kelly giggled. "Amelia is just kinky enough to find your predicament interesting. She'd like to hire you, take you on. Especially, *now.*"

I didn't like the sound of that one. "What do you mean, *now?"* I cautiously asked.

Kelly half inched herself off the bed and reached over for the nearest drawer to her in the window stall bureau to her left. The bureau's top shelf also served as a perch to— like a cat— allow one to wistfully repose and stare out the window to the high hills and ridges in the distance. From within the drawer, she pulled out her Android tablet and keyed it on. She touched the screen several times, opening menus until a specific site materialized upon it. I recognized it immediately.

YOUR INNER YOU
Life-styles for Today's Modern Woman

(And below that, headlining a lengthy article detailing the latest winner in their annual European Whirlwind Vacation Getaway Adventure came my photo.

I sighed. *"You saw that?"* I asked her.

"They think you're planning to undergo a complete transformation to female."

I nodded. *"I know,"* I spat. *"I read it!* That company…. I ought to sue them for putting words in my mouth. How did you find that?"

"Amelia found it," Kelly answered. "And showed it to me. She thinks you're beautiful, too beautiful to remain a boy. And from the way *Your Inner You* is trying to exploit your transgender aspect, it's clear they're trying to really attract a new market for their catalog."

"Oh, they made that quite clear, *they are,"* I replied. "They really want to get some mileage out of this trip of Annie's and mine to Europe. It's nuts."

"Well, you're kind of a celebrity in the making, and that intrigues Amelia. As I said, she's just kinky and eccentric enough that she even likes telling customers that I'm your sister."

"That you're my sister?" I gaped.

Kelly smiled. "And that we look so alike."

"Oh, shit," I sighed. "Did you tell *'Amelia'* that we're not true sisters? I still haven't lost that little inconsistency that makes me such an oddity?"

"She doesn't care," Kelly replied. "She's really turned on by the whole prospect. In fact, knowing I have a sister/brother like you that I love so dearly, she would really like to meet you. Oh, and brother? About that little *'inconsistency'* between your legs…." She glanced to it, discretely hidden as it was under both a pair of girl's panties and the sleep shirt.

"What about it?" I got nervous just listening to the way she was putting that.

She started giggling, impishly.

"What?" I asked her, directly.

"Who is Ben?" she asked.

I felt my whole-body flush. "Where did you hear that name?" I asked.

"You talk in your sleep sometimes, like last night."

"What. Did. I. Say?"

"Who is he?"

"We both work at the *Com-link* store in Penns Cove," I answered, finally.

"Does he have a name?"

"Benjamin Linaker," I replied. "He and his co-worker, Dave Capuchin, are our store's laptop and PC experts, translation— our computer *geeks*. I like to shoot the shit, *I mean, talk,* with them when business is slack, which these days is mostly always. Ben's okay."

"Are you attracted to him?"

"What? NO. He's a guy."

"Yeah, so? Does he turn you on? Do you *turn him on?*"

"I ..." I started to answer but got hung up. *"Do I turn him on?* I don't know. Why?"

"Last night," she answered, "you asked him to *finish in your mouth."* She grinned. "You moan like a girl when you're getting it on, you know. You sound just like me. And the way you were puckering your lips in your sleep, you really looked like you were going down on Ben's penis *and liking it."*

I could feel my face flushing. How many different shades of red it took on, I couldn't even begin to imagine."

"So, have you....?" She asked.

"Kelly!" I begged. *"NO.* We work together, just that," I insisted. She smiled a wry smile. "Okay."

"We both have *penises*; it's kind of a deal breaker," I stated.

"But he's interested, am I right?"

I hesitated in my answer. "He said, he'd have to really be wasted, out of his mind; if he were to—"

"Oh," she smiled and then nodded. "He *is* interested; he's thought about you; that's why he said it. A boy likes my baby sister. ...Is he cute?"

I hit her arm. "Kelly, stop it. I never said he liked me, or I *liked him."*

"Craig woke something up inside you, last night, didn't he?" she then confronted me with.

"He tried to rape me," I defended.

164

"But, the thought of a guy doing what he tried? *Ben Linaker maybe?*"

I simply looked at her. I wouldn't give her an answer.

She glanced to my nether region again and noted how my tiny *man-part* nevertheless appeared to be firming up. "Oh, yeah," she nodded. "You liked imagining that. You're getting turned on all over again. I'm calling you *Keira* from now on ... s*is*. You're really my sister. Does Anita know?"

"What?" I asked.

"That the thought of having sex with guys turns you on?"

Again, I hesitated. "I'm not sure."

"Oh boy," she concluded. "Your life just got way more interesting."

CHAPTER NINETEEN –
Christmas Day

Breakfast and after, retire to the living room, where Stevie, Doug and Trent slowly unwound from the euphoria of ripping open all those gifts. The four of us "adults" sought respite in the lounge chairs and sofas, and just watched them in amusement, us in our casual wear outfits. I was in the one Annie meant for me to wear this morning; Kelly, the white one I purchased two months ago in Delaware (she just had to borrow it from me to feel all that soft cashmere and wool against her skin).

There were no adult men in the house *(unless 'I' counted)*. Mom had pulled the wood from the storage nook to the left of the fireplace pit and got it started soon after she rose for the day. It was up and burning brightly by the time Carol's kids descended for their raid of the Christmas Tree's and their presents.

Apparently, my sister-in-law, Carol, told her three kids that her father and grandfather had decided suddenly last night to drive up to Alvin's hunting cabin several miles north of Jim Thorpe and see if they could bag a few deer or whatever struck their fancy.

I'm not sure the three boys bought it, but at least the explanation placated them enough to continue to enjoy the specialness of this dawn after Santa Claus's yearly visit to the world south of the North Pole.

The three of them one by one eventually took the most interesting gifts they had received up to their bunk room upstairs to now enjoy after the enthusiasm of ripping open the boxes the things had come in had waned. The downstairs, in the aftermath of that, besides warming up from the fire, settled back to a peaceful level of comfort and quiet.

"Bye all," Carol said, soon after, as she finished her morning cup of tea and retired for her own guest suite here on the first floor to get washed up for the day.

"Yeah, I guess if we're all heading to Christmas Mass in another hour, I'd better do that too," said Kelly as she also rose from her lounge chair and left for upstairs.

I smiled, weakly, from my own chair and assured everyone when I was ready to, I'd leave to do the same.

I found myself after all alone in the living room, in front of the hearth, my legs crossed in front of me on the floor, just staring to the fire and the way it almost silently fluttered and danced atop the logs in the pit.

I heard Mom enter, after a while, and work her way over to my spot before the hearth. She carried a tray with Christmas cookies laid out upon it and set it down atop the very low and very large, heavy oak coffee table in the room's center.

"Want one?" she asked.

I faced round to her and smiled. "No, I'm fine."

"Are you really, Keir? Fine?"

I shrugged. "I guess."

Sarah joined me on the carpet in front of the fire, the ottomans and chairs having prior been pushed back to make room for the boys as they ransacked the tree.

I glanced to it, the branches and their white bulbs brightly, albeit somberly, illuminating the room in that corner. "My nephews," I mused. "Huh. That was fun to watch ... I guess...." I said of Carol's boys and the way they had attacked the tree and their gifts like a flock of seagulls discovering a bag of French fries carelessly tossed onto the sand at the beach. "Interesting, actually."

I glanced to the presents still unopened: mostly Dad's and Craig's, and several for and from Frank and Meg and the daughter, Chloe, all of which we would all attend to when they finally arrived in a little while hence.

"What, Keir?" asked Mom, caressing the side of my face as she sat on the floor next to me, the tea tray just out of arm's reach. "What was interesting?"

"I don't remember the five of us, Craig, Trevor, Frank, Kelly or me ever being that excited Christmas morning to find what you and Dad left for us under the tree. Maybe because there was nothing to find under there ... or even a tree."

I glanced to the fire in the fire pit then, transfixed by how the flames slowly danced and fluttered in an almost mesmerizing pattern. It helped distract my mind in a subtle almost therapeutic sort of way from the unpleasant things currently holding my life hostage.

"I know, hon," Sarah lamented of our Christmases from our past. "Your brothers were pretty much all grown up, too old to still get excited about opening presents like when they were little by the time you and Kelly were born. And Alvin ... your father...." She frowned, apologetically. "He never really was one for making much of a fuss where Christmas was concerned."

I noted how decked out the living room now looked here in *Jim Thorpe*. It was true. In the days Kelly and I were little in Pittsburg, Dad was virtually never around. Mom did her best, but it just wasn't the same. Not like this.

"This is mostly for show, isn't it?" I observed. "He's a big shot now; he has to act the part. It's mostly to impress his grandkids. Or make it seem to outsiders that that's why he does it now."

"You kids got a bum deal where your childhood was concerned, I'm sorry for that," Sarah said.

"Um," I moaned in acknowledgement. "Thanks for the comforter, Mom. It'll keep me warm this winter, especially when I need to cut back on the heat in the apartment to save money."

Sarah smiled. "You're welcome, honey," she replied. "And if it gets that dire for you in the next couple months, you know where home is. Your old room is just sitting up there."

"Well, let's hope it doesn't. Dad, I don't think, is too pleased I'm here as it is." I changed the subject. "Did the sweater fit all right?"

"Yes, it's just perfect. Thank you, I love it."

"You're welcome," I replied. I couldn't help glance after a while to the two ottomans. "I don't know if I'll ever feel the same about being in this room ever again," I pondered, absently. "It looks so peaceful and rustic. You'd never know Craig tried his best to ruin it all by being a low-life bastard."

"Carol really feels bad for you, Keirie, and angry as hell at Craig."

"For what he did to Kelly as well, right?"

Sarah nodded.

"Is she still planning to leave him?"

"*I don't know if I'm going to leave him, Keira,*" I heard Carol say as she entered the living room, fresh from her shower.

For thirty-five, Carolyn Travaglini looked amazing, and so much more like she was still in her twenties. She used a corner of the very large, square-shaped oak coffee table as a place to sit, then helped herself to a pastry from the tray Sarah had brought in. She was dressed very provocatively in a woolen gray top that hung loosely upon her shoulders and ended just below her mid-section, exposing much of her thighs and white thong, barely covered by the blouse's hem. Strands of her blond hair hung wispy to one side of her youthful face, while most of it lay tied in a bun atop her head. Completing the lounge wear look were a pair of tan, over-the-knee wool socks than accented her youthful legs enticingly.

"It's amazing how sound carries in this house," she informed me.

"Sorry," I said. "It's just—"

She shook her head. "You have no idea how much I'd like to punch that bastard husband of mine right this moment where it will hurt the most."

I grinned. "He might not be able to make any more babies if you do that."

"Fine by me," she replied. "The factory is closed as far as I'm concerned, anyway. If he wants another kid, he's going to find someone else stupid enough to fall for his bullshit." She took a good long look at me, then. "Mom showed me the *Your Inner You* blog," she said to me. "That is some prize they awarded you. When are you planning to go?"

"April."

"I could use a getaway like that, about now," she mused.

I smiled. "I might not have a job by then. So, when I get back, I may have to seriously think about which direction my life should go after that."

"The article said you're considering a sex change."

I chirped a humph and shook my head. "I never said a word about such a thing to them. They put words in my mouth."

"So, you're not?"

I shrugged. "I'll probably do it, eventually. At this point, it's kind of stupid to pretend I wasn't upset being born part male. So, yeah, I can't get too mad at the company for saying a thing like that. It's as if they knew what I would do even before I did."

"I'm happy for you," Carol said. "Put all that *I'm a boy* crap behind you and concentrate on being who you were meant to be and quit suffering people telling you how wrong it is. What do people

169

know, anyway? I'm convinced that if humanity is the most intelligent species on Earth, then this is one dumb planet."

"Oh, Carol," said Sarah. "You're as bad as my daughters."

"I can't help it, Mom," she said. "I married a Lech."

"We've pretty much known that about Craig since we were little," came my sister's voice as she too now entered the living room. She was in a bathrobe, her head and hair wrapped up in a towel. She took a position beside me on the hearth, grabbed a pastry and nibbled at it, half-heartedly. "Do the kids suspect anything?" Kelly asked her.

"The older two do," answered Carol, "Steve, no."

"Has anyone heard of Guy Garcia's book, *The Decline of Men?*" Kelly asked. "I think he's right. Men are in decline and retreat. And they know it. That's why they elected a Neanderthal as our forty-fifth president. It's kind of their last hurrah, like Custer's last stand. They're desperately trying to hold back the winds of change, buck the current, yank us all back upriver from whence we came. And it's only a matter of time. Males like Craig or Dad or that coifed idiot in the White House, they're the last of a dying breed. And as disgusting as they can be, the sooner they go extinct, the better we will all be for it."

"Oh, Kelly," breathed Sarah in exasperation. "This *girl talk* is starting to sound like those women on *The View.*" She glanced around her from her position on the floor beside me and to the room, the tree and the fire. "If only Meg were here … and even Rita. I miss her. I'm so sorry she and Trevor didn't work out. You don't know how much it means to me, how comfortable and great to have most of my girls all here with me in this room like this morning. I hate to see it end."

I issued a subtle laugh. "It's my turn now to go up and get washed," I said. "I suppose we're still on for Church this morning?" I glanced to the mantle clock atop the fireplace. "Ten o'clock, right?"

My mom nodded in the affirmative.

I glanced to it again. "Is there an *Eleven AM Mass* by any chance?" I hoped.

"No, dear. And remember, *we are all going.* I think worse than on most Sundays, *today's* service we really need to attend."

"Today's Monday," I reminded her.

Sarah flashed me an angry glance.

170

I smiled. "I dread heading back to that Church," I added. "I remember from before, when I was still young enough to still be dragged there every Sunday by you Mom. Dad, not so much. We'll probably not witness anything in church today other than zombies reciting the same rote responses they have been taught to recite week after week. I always hated that. It felt so … *phony,* so *contrived.* Like people were just going through the motions. Going to church, not to worship, but because it was … *expected.* Or worse … *required.* You've no idea all those years ago, how much I just wanted to get up and shout to all those parishioners, *do you even know what you're saying, when you recite that stuff? 'The Lord be with you. And with your spirit….'* It wasn't the words, themselves, but the way they *spoke* them, as if they were reading them off a teleprompter. I swear, I thought that they were just phoning it in. I almost wished the priest would say, *'Let's try that response again, but this time make an effort.'* I was so glad when I was finally old enough to say, *I'll skip mass this week if that's okay."*

Sarah seethed as she inhaled a long inward sounding breath.

Kelly almost choked on her pastry, busting into laughter. "Damn, *Keirie!*" she said to me.

"I'm just being honest, mother," I replied.

"A little too honest," Sarah replied. "You agree with your sister, am I right, Kelly?" she asked her.

Kelly shrugged. "Well…" She looked at me. "Kind of … y*eah,"* she nodded.

Sarah took another exasperated breath. "Can you two disbelievers at least *try* to act like you don't hate it there today? St. Joseph's is still a very beautiful old church. I want my family there with me today. As many as *can* attend Mass today, at least. And I want you to *at least* not look like you're not about to make ugly faces because you hate being there so much."

I faced Kelly; she faced me. We shrugged, turned back to Mom and said, "Okay."

Sarah glanced to the mantle and the time. "Oh wow," she exclaimed, "it's nearing nine. We all had better get our behinds in gear, get those kids all washed up, if we're going to make Mass by ten o'clock. And Keirie, you too."

"Me too what, Sarah?" I smiled.

She wasn't amused.

I glanced to Kelly and Carol and got to my feet. "I guess so," I grinned.

• • •

Around the time I popped back downstairs to join Carol's three boys, their mom, my Mom and sister; we had about twenty minutes to spare. The Saint Joseph's Church of *Jim Thorpe* was just across town, not more than ten minutes away, and the town being as small as it was, we hoped the church would not be full. But that was a little naïve, I suppose. The holiday tourists were everywhere, and a lot of them were probably Catholic and what was derisively referred to as holiday service attendees, meaning these people mostly only insisted on attending mass only on special holidays, like Easter and Christmas. So, yeah, Sarah pretty much expected we'd probably have to find room in the back of the church, hopefully a pew, and not have to join the tourist crowd, standing up as they crowded into the walkway behind the last row of pews at the back of the church and the entry vestibule. The one hope we clung to, most of the regulars had already attended the eight and nine AM service.

I made my entrance in gray thigh high cable stitched socks, tan, fur lined ankle boots and a very mini, gray mini-skirt with embroidery stitching that made it somewhat resemble a hand-stitched bedspread wrapped around my upper thighs. Completing the ensemble was a two-sizes too large gray knit sweater.

Carol and the kids only stared as I descended the stairs for the back-door foyer. I glanced down to my gray ensemble. "I'm having a *gray* day," I said of the outfit.

"That's quite a skirt," commented Carol. "You really want people to know you're not a boy."

"She's pretty, mommy," said her youngest, Stevie.

"Yeah," agreed the other two.

"God, I hope the church isn't already brimming over with people. I wonder if we should have tried this a whole hour in advance."

Carol shrugged. "Just as long as Sarah is satisfied, I guess we'll be okay. She just wants us all there."

"Is Dad going to join us at the church, Mom?" asked the middle son, Doug.

"No, I don't think he and your grandpop will make it this year, Dougie."

172

"Why not?"

"Because Mom threw him out, you idiot," said the oldest, Trent. "Last night. They had another fight."

Carol threw her son an angry reproach. He only smiled mischievously.

"Is that true, Mom," Dougie asked. "You and daddy had another fight?"

Carol breathed in exasperation and glanced tiredly at me for emotional support, "Something like that, honey."

"I heard you and Dad arguing, Mom," persisted Trent. "Just before Dad stormed out of your room and went downstairs to do as he usually does— *get drunk.*"

"That's enough, Trent," she spat. "What were you doing, anyway, on the second floor? Your bunk room here in grandpop's house is on the *top* floor."

He blushed and shrugged his shoulders. "I was listening at the stairs to see if there really was a Santa Claus, and if he had visited grand mom's house. Davy at school says there is no such thing as elves and reindeer—"

"That's enough!" she chided him. "If Santa didn't come, which he did, you got everything you asked for, for Christmas, didn't you?

He nodded.

"He waited until he knew you were asleep."

"But Davy said—"

"*Trent,*" she cautioned him, "drop it."

"Yes, Mom," he answered, contritely.

"Mom?" began Dougie, worried. "What's Trent mean? There is a Santa, isn't there?"

Carol Travaglini glanced to her oldest and said. "Happy?" She faced Dougie. "Of course, there is, honey," she told her eight-year-old and second oldest. "Trent is just trying to deflect the issue that he was up when he should have been in bed and asleep. Now, all of you, just stop. Mommy's got a headache, today."

"Yes, Mom," the three replied.

I glanced to Carol and smiled weakly.

She nodded.

"Well, look who looks pretty all dressed up in gray," said Sarah, my Mom, as she descended the stairs.

"I hope I'm not coming off like a hook—" *(Oops, there were young kids present.)* "... like a professional woman. Do I look okay?"

Sarah nodded. "You look wonderful. Don't forget your coat, though, if you're wearing that. It's pretty nippy outside this morning."

"There was snow last night," commented Dougie, interjecting himself into the conversation. "I saw it coming down. I woke up; it was late. Stevie and Trent were already sleeping." He shrugged. "It snowed. I guess, Santa liked that. Made it easier for him to get around. Reindeer like snow."

"Doug, you're a moron," Trent told him.

"Why?" he defended.

"Boys, stop it, now!" insisted Carol.

"Yes, honey," said Sarah to her grandkid, Doug, "It snowed last night for a few hours. It was real pretty, wasn't it? And you went back to sleep again, correct, knowing Santa and his reindeer would appreciate the way the weather was helping Santa finish his deliveries?"

Dougie nodded. "Yes, grand mom," he answered.

"Okay?" she brightened then, glancing to me and Carol. "Are we near ready? We ought to get going. Where's Kelly?"

"Right here, Mom," came Kelly's voice at the top of the stairs as she began her descent. She was dressed in a thick, tan and knit pullover, a very chic brand of slacks, and very expensive looking, and black high heeled pumps with a thick, three-inch heel. She took one look at me. "Show off," she said, as she reached the bottom step.

I nodded to her. "Like it?"

"You're really trying to cheat on Annie, aren't you? The guys at the church today are going there to get some religion, not look at you."

"There's no law that says they're required to. I didn't do it for them; I like how it feels on me."

"Yeah, you're still in that *wearing this girly shit feels great* phase. It'll pass."

"Maybe," I answered.

Shadows suddenly appeared in the glass top of the front door, and the door itself got rapped, gently and delicately, by what sounded like a young, female hand.

"Oh, my, it's got to be your brother, Frank and his family," said Mom. "Wow, that's going to complicate things. We'll have to go in separate cars. It's going to look like an invasion all of us suddenly descending on that tiny church."

"Saint Joseph's?" I inquired.

She nodded.

"Isn't there a bigger one down West Broadway?"

"Yes, Immaculate Conception," Mom said. "It's clear across town, on the other side of the river. St. Joseph's is five minutes away."

I pondered that. "Might be more room, though."

She sighed. "Keirie, open the door."

I did ... and what greeted me was my brother Frank's twelve-year-old daughter, Chloe, and boy had she grown into an attractive young lady. She had an oval, innocent face, a high forehead, and long brunette hair, same as Kelly and myself, dropping down her shoulders and halfway down her arms. A gray and blue striped mini dress ended mid-thigh upon her thin, young legs, a light brownish-tan wide belt divided it around her waist, and down her right shoulder a dark brown handbag hung from a long strap. Competing the outfit were a grayish brown pair of above-the-knee socks and tan ankle boots. She was unquestioningly a very cute young woman, one her parents were quite proud to call their only daughter.

I was afraid to say or do anything; so was Chloe. I wasn't sure if she might scream at the sight of me, dressed like this. We only stared at each other. I hadn't seen my only niece since last Christmas. She'd grown.

Behind her, her mom and dad alighted onto the porch. There were all smiles; they greeted us with much enthusiasm. *"Happy Noel, everybody,"* said an upbeat Frank Travaglini.

(Kisses all around, as one might expect.)

Frank proceeded to kiss his Mom. "You look great," he told her. "Merry Christmas."

(Yeah, that all went back and forth. Everybody knows how that goes. You've all seen it depicted in countless Christmas themed movies and specials. December? By this point, if you were a TV addict you were probably getting sick of all the holiday episodes of your favorite shows. In any case, this sort of thing went on for about another minute, Frank, Meg and Chloe kissing everyone and wishing all a happy Christmas. Not Chloe and Carol's three boys.

175

Chloe was still at that age where she was just getting used to the thought of befriending boys being a good thing. She was a good little Catholic girl, or tried to be, and was a little reserved around boys, especially male cousins, which unfortunately were the only cousins on her father's side she had.)

Chloe purposely said little to Trent, Doug and Stevie; *they were boys after all.* And she had had her fill of boys that age bugging her all through grade school. And even now the ones in middle school were approaching her like she was a trophy they needed to win. Trent was being the most aggressive of this bunch, she saw that right off. At age ten, and yes, she was aware of the ages of her cousins, Trent was already feeling a little like he wanted to let Chloe know she was cute and that as a male he had every right to point that out to her. But her look back at him, said; *you're only ten, back off.* Finished with all the amenities with the other members of my extended family, she turned to me and smiled.

"You're going to be my new aunt Keira soon, aren't you?" she asked, hugging me then. "You are so beautiful."

I hugged her back, totally astounded and confused. I looked at Frank and Meg, fully expected them to be eyeing me with abject rejection, but there was no such air about either of them. My brother Frank smiled over at me. "Yeah, Keir," he said. "I always thought you were way too pretty and nice, like Kelly, to be another one of my brothers. You've really filled out, haven't you?"

"Uh, yeah," I answered. "Hey, Frank? Merry Christmas."

"Same to you." He approached me and kissed me. "Chloe has been eager to see you."

"You explained what was going on with me, genetically?"

He nodded. "I didn't have a choice, after she found that blog from that apparel company, copied over and over on Twitter, Facebook and everywhere else stuff turns up these days on the internet. You're an online celebrity. You've no idea how many hits that photo of you on their blog has accumulated."

I explained yet again the company took liberties with my future intentions where my future plans were concerned.

"When are you going to change all the way, Aunt Keirie?" Chloe asked.

I just stood there stunned. "Uh," I attempted to begin.

Trent suddenly groaned out an *"Oh, shit. Girls are so stupid."*

176

Chloe flashed over at him and let him have it. "*Shut up, you little twerp,*" she chided him. "*Go play with yourself.* Oh, that's right, you can't yet, can you? You're only ten. *You're still a little boy.* What do you know about life? You still believe there's a Santa Claus!"

"*No, I don't—*" he checked himself, worried he might anger his Mom again with his newfound understanding of such things and the impact of it all on his younger brothers and *their beliefs.* "Shut up, yourself, '*Chloe,*' he told her, emphasizing her *female* name. 'You're just a useless girl. You're not my equal."

Right, I thought. *Your father is teaching you well, Trent. You're well on your way to growing up a misogynist pig, just like him.*

"I'm taller than you ... *and older!*" Chloe rebutted. "I can knock you across this room without even straining myself to do it, you smart-ass little snot-nosed—"

"*Try it,*" he dared her.

"*Hey,* you two *knock it off!*" said Frank. "It's Christmas."

"Honey, we got to go," said Sarah to her son. "We don't want to get there after Mass already starts."

"Okay, Mom. Honestly, we got here as soon as we could." He shook his head. "It's a long way up from Allentown into these mountains."

"Yeah," she said. "We all won't fit in one car, Frank."

He smiled. "A shame you sold the van," he said.

Sarah laughed. "That thing went to the wreckers' *years ago.*"

"Yeah, but I remember that mangy old thing," he replied, wistfully. "That was a hell of a vehicle, a lot of fun. Right, Kelly, Keir?"

Kelly smiled fondly. Before I had a chance to respond, Chloe chimed in. "*Keira,*" she corrected her father. "She's a *girl,* Daddy. Call her *Keira.*"

"Yes, honey," Frank smiled to his daughter. "I won't forget again."

I just shook my head. *I felt like a circus freak show attraction.*

And my twelve-year-old niece, now apparently enlightened to my situation, was no doubt intrigued by me; I was a refreshing change from the blasé predictability of everyone else she knew. This new young generation did not as a collective whole hold with the old beliefs that this LGBT stuff was somehow an abomination against God himself. It some ways it was like the new fad; the new thing. In others, it heralded the beginning of a new outlook on humanity. And that was a good thing. If so, I was happy to do my part.

We were out the door soon after, Mom locking it behind us.

"Can I sit beside you and aunt Kelly?" Chloe asked me as she took my and my sister's hands and held onto them as we headed out the door.

"Well," said Kelly. "I don't think there's room for us all like that in the same car. Your grand mom wants to take her Mercedes and it can only fit so many. You may have to ride over with your Mom and Dad."

She glanced over at me. "There's room for you, Keira, in the back … with me."

I got a fun thought. "I tell you what," I replied. I fished into my handbag for my smart car's keys. "Chloe?"

"Yes, aunt Keira?"

"How would you like to ride with me in *that?*"

Chloe froze a second, studying the tiny vehicle in the driveway I called my car.

"It's only a two-seater," I said. "Kelly can't come with us. It can only hold two."

Her face abruptly brightened. "Oh, that is so cute," my niece replied. "Can we?"

"If your dad and mom say it's okay," I replied.

Frank was listening and turned his gaze to my vehicle. He couldn't help laughing. "Keirie," he said, "what the heck did you buy *that* for?"

"I think it's cute," I replied. "It's fun to drive."

"Yeah, until a strong gust of wind blows *you* and *it* off the road."

"It's not that bad, and you're only the umpteenth person to say that. You remind me of *Ralphie's* parents and all the adults around him in that dumb movie."

"What are you talking about?"

"Today's Christmas. All day long that annoying *A Christmas Story* movie is going to run on cable and DirecTV, and the tag line to that movie is—"

"*You can't have a BB gun for Christmas, Ralphie,*" said Chloe. "*You'll shoot an eye out.*"

"Yes, sweetie, that's right. Very good. Same thing, Frank. People always say it: '*Don't buy that car; it ain't safe. The first slick road you meet, first strong wind, and you'll wind up upside down in a ditch somewhere.'* That really gets old. My little car is safe enough. I got all the way up here to *Jim Thorpe* from *Penns Cove.*" I nodded. "It's safe enough."

"Can I, dad?" asked Chloe. "I want to ride with Keira."

"Okay, honey, yes you can ride with your Aunt Keira."

I hit the key fob to open the door locks. Chloe ran to the passenger side door and proceeded to climb in. I playfully punched Frank in the side. "She's got you wrapped around her little finger, hasn't she?"

"Yes, she does," abruptly interjected my sister-in-law, Meg, as she approached. Meg Travaglini, formerly Megan Lewinsky, was as tall as myself, about five feet seven, reddish-brown hair, down to her waist and in her early thirties. A good figure, which she kept very trim and tight, she sported classy jewelry upon her wrists and neck. Under her faux gray fur-lined coat, she wore smoky-gray slacks, red, high-heeled pumps, and I couldn't tell you what top she wore with it. It was below freezing, and she looked very snug in her winter coat. I would have to at the very least wait until after we were inside the church to describe for you the remainder of her outfit, and only *if* that near century old church building now had adequate heating. The Roman Catholic Church, *Immaculate Conception,* down Broadway, across town, was probably more modern and more accommodating, but … *Mom preferred Saint Joseph's.* I remember always freezing my behind off in that drafty old building back in my mid-teens, those days before I up and quit attending mass. It's kind of small and it's been around a lot longer than Immaculate Conception, I believe.

Meg watched her only child settle into the cramped interior of my car. Chloe was enjoying checking out all the little dashboard doohickeys that came included with the standard accessory package.

"She's my little angel," Frank replied, placing his arm around Meg and snugging her tight against him. "We love her to death."

"She's great," said Meg, "and smart too. I wish I could say the same for Craig's oldest. He's as dumb and mean-spirited as his dad. Like father, like son, I suppose."

"Like father, like son and *Alvin,*" offered Frank, referring to his father. Meg chuckled, gave her husband a little squeeze with her own arm around him, and then detached from him. "I'll go start the car."

"Okay, hon," he said, as she then left for their BMW. Frank then turned toward me and in confidence, said, "Take care of my little girl in that bite-sized golf cart of yours you call a car."

"I will," I promised.

"Can I say something, Keir?" he abruptly added, as I started off. I shrugged and faced back. "What?"

"I'm sorry for the way my brothers and I tortured you when we were kids. I didn't want to, you know that, don't you?"

I nodded. "I knew; you tried to make it up to me, whenever Craig wasn't around to bully you."

Frank nodded. "I was afraid of Craig."

I nodded. "Yeah, I know that. He's a bastard, we both know it."

"You were always as pretty as your sister, maybe even prettier."

"That's not fair. I don't want to make it a competition between Kelly and me. We get along so well. She accepts me as her sister without reservation. She always has."

"Like Mom," he said.

"Yeah," I answered. "Frank?"

"Yeah?"

I nodded. "We got to go."

"You're right. Keirie, where *is* Dad and Craig?"

I sighed. "They aren't here," I informed him.

"Where are they?"

"The hunting cabin, you know, up in the—"

"*I know* where it is. *The hunting cabin? Why today?* Why go up there? What's going on?"

"We don't have time to get into it, brother. We're going to be late. Don't ask Carol. That would be …" I grimaced, "*not good.* Just don't."

"*Why?*" he fretted. "*What happened?*"

I nodded. "Ask Kelly to ride with you and Meg. She might tell you, explain why our father and brother aren't here. Craig for all I care *can rot in hell.*"

I saw him walk over to Mom's Mercedes, open the front passenger side door and speak with Kelly. I can guess what he said to her, for soon after she turned to Sarah, I saw Kelly's lips mouth some words that I imagined was an explanation of why she was riding to church with Frank and Meg, and then subsequently leave Mom's Mercedes to climb into the back seat of Frank's BMW.

180

Frank spoke a few words more to the two women in the car with him, and thereafter took his place in the front passenger side seat as Meg behind the wheel revved the BMW's engine and put the transmission in gear.

I buckled myself into my own vehicle, looked over to Chloe to make sure she was buckled in as well, and smiled to her. "Okay?"

"Um hmmm," she chirped, enthusiastically. "This is going to be fun."

CHAPTER TWENTY -
The Remainder of The Day

The trip down Germantown Road and toward the suburban housing district on this the east side of the two concrete highway bridges spanning the Lehigh River was not a long one, and the worst part about that was that the heater in my smart car barely had time to warm up the interior. So, Chloe and I kind of shivered the whole trip to the church. We were glad when we turned off Fifth Street onto North Street and in the view ahead appeared St. Joseph's just down the way from the Lutheran Church and nestled among modest two story houses. It seemed a very tightly compacted neighborhood with the mountains prominent far off in the distance.

The church was a gray stone affair, with the familiar steeple and bell tower. Parking on North Street looked rather limited. The church from all appearances had no real parking lot. One seemed to need to parallel park on the side of the road where one could find an empty spot.

Chloe and I joined Kelly and her parents as they found a place down the way a bit and walked back up to the church entrance. Chloe wanted all three of us *"girls"* to hold hands. We did.

"Sis?" I said to Kelly, across from Chloe as we all met up with Mom and her group and trudged up the stairs to the vestibule of the Church.

She only glanced to me. She nodded, severely.

"That bad, huh?" I mouthed silently.

She nodded.

Chloe looked at the two of us, and our silent attempts at concealed conversing. "Is everything okay?" she asked us.

"It's nothing bad, Chloe," said Kelly.

"You know how you hate your cousin, Trent?" I asked my niece in a hushed voice.

"He's an asshole," she whispered back.

"His dad is our older brother," I said.

She nodded. "I know."

"Your Uncle Craig is an even bigger asshole," I told her.

Chloe giggled. "You're funny, Aunt Keira," she said.

"Do you like him?" I asked. "Does he treat you okay?"

"He's not my favorite uncle, if that's what you mean. I don't care about him one way or the other. He lives way out in Pittsburgh, so does Trent, so it doesn't really bother me. I don't have to suffer Trent's company except on the occasional holiday."

"Yep, that's about right."

"Okay, that's enough, you two," said Meg, as we entered the church proper. "Save it for later." We all searched for an available pew.

She seemed, Meg did, kind of in a more subdued mood now, not so lively and festive. Kelly just nodded, and then shook her head, as if to say, '*Yeah, I just delivered some heavy shit on both of them.*'

We found an empty pew. It wasn't that hard to find a place to sit. I had a feeling most of the Catholics currently residing or visiting the *Jim Thorpe* area had chosen instead to visit the other *Catholic* church across town.

The services began not too long after.

• • •

The Mass lasted near an hour, and I probably exaggerated before. It wasn't *that* cold inside the church. But I was feeling cold, none-the-less. My brother Frank would not look at me. He couldn't have been angry with me, or anything of that sort. I mean, *what had I done?* I certainly hadn't encouraged Craig to molest me like he tried. I was sure, it wasn't that. My brother Frank really was nothing like his older brother. He was sensitive, empathic, a good man to father a daughter and be sympathetic to her plight in life. No, Frank Travaglini did not look angry; he looked upset, to the point where he might even want to leave the church and get emotional, silently, over the whole ordeal involving his mean-ass older brother.

We all filed out of the building and back into the cold air of that late December morning. It was near eleven by now, and almost time for the next service to begin. Which meant out of courtesy to the next group who wished to attend Christmas Mass, we should all hop in our cars and leave to make room on the side streets for them.

"Well," said my Mom after the service. "That went well, didn't it? It was a lovely sermon."

"Yes," said Carolyn. "It was lovely. That's a lovely old church." She looked out at the mountains in the distance, and the houses lining both sides of North Street. "This is a pretty neighborhood."

"Shall we go? Get started on the meal?"

"Yeah," she replied. "Trent, Doug, Steve, you boys were pretty quiet and decent inside for a change, thank you."

They mostly nodded and grasped their arms. They were shivering.

"So, who's all riding with whom?" asked Mom. "The same group going back?"

"Chloe," interjected Frank, speaking up, finally. "You ride with Mom this time and whoever wants to crowd into our car. I'm heading back with Keirie."

"Oh," I processed. "Okay. You might feel a little constricted."

"I'm driving, if you don't mind."

Frank was almost six feet tall. I grinned. "You in my tiny car, ought to be interesting."

We all loaded into our respective cars and subsequently pulled away from the curbs. There was a very large open space up the way just next door from the Lutheran Church. A large rectangular shaped building, which seemed nevertheless way too small for the lot surrounding it, inhabited the lot's middle. There were spaces meant for parking marked out only on the extreme edges. A stone wall with a white fence made of PVC plastic runner boards and posts sat atop it. I mention all this because no sooner did Frank approach it that he pulled over into the large empty space and parked my car along the stone wall. He shut off the engine.

"I wish you hadn't done that," I said of shutting off my car. "It's going to take this car the whole trip just to start to get warm as it is. It's freezing in here."

"Fine," he said. He started the engine up once more.

"Are you mad at me?" I asked. "Kelly told you what happened, I gather."

My brother was seriously trying to keep from losing his hold on his emotions. I could see his eyes were watery. He reached over and gave me a hug. "I'm going to kill that son-of-a-bitch brother of ours, next time I see him."

I hugged my brother back. We both were having trouble seeing clearly. My eyes as well were starting to well up. "I wasn't sure how you'd take it," I told him.

"Does Mom know?" he asked.

I nodded. "Yeah. Carol too. She practically told him to pack his shit and get out."

"And that's when our father decided he needed to treat his *golden child* to a visit to the hunting cabin, Christmas Night?"

"Yes. You don't think he's going to reprimand Craig either, do you? Our dad, I mean?"

"Hell, no," answered Frank. "He lets that dumb shit brother of ours get away with most anything. The old man has paid off more law enforcement officers and judges than a few to keep that kid from being locked up. He's had more DUI's pending against him than anyone would ever want. Why he still owns a license to get around, there's only one explanation."

"Dad," I said.

He nodded. "Greasing the wheels, making the charges just go away. That's the advantage, I suppose, of being a successful businessman and entrepreneur ... *with connections*." He glanced at me.

I nodded. "*Those kind*," I affirmed. "The *Godfather* theme is going to be stuck in my head all day now," I added, sadly. "Thanks, Frank."

"Huh," he snorted, smiling. "When Alvin Travaglini speaks, people listen, give him whatever he asks, and if it's to bail your shit-ass drunk ass son out of jail, then that too."

"I don't know what's going to happen this week," I told Frank then. "I'm scared to death that if Dad returns home the first thing he'll demand is that I get the "F" out of his home. It's all my fault Craig lost his self-control over his libido. I should never have accepted Mom's invitation, especially when I was planning a pseudo sort of *'coming out'* event to the family."

"You have nothing to be guilty about," Frank said. "Don't forget. I'm raising a daughter. I know when I'm in the company these days of a female human being." He nodded. "You fill that criteria very well. Even my daughter sees it; even Meg. If they accept you, that's all the endorsement I need."

"Thank you, Frank. I wish Trevor had come up from Florida. It doesn't seem right, somehow, his staying down there. Like he should be ashamed, just because his marriage to Rita collapsed."

"You staying away as well, wouldn't have been right, either. Whatever our mob connected old man thinks, you are family, and if he can't accept you for the person you are, male or female, then that's on him."

"He's in good company, thinking the way he does. Especially now in this country, after the last major election."

"Yeah, I'm still trying to get over that one," he said of our country's newly elected leader. He looked at me. "Kelly said Dad showed up just in time. But are you okay?"

I shrugged. "I got to give that one to the old man," I said. "He came through for me." I nodded. "I'll live."

"Are you planning to undergo, you know, the what do you call it?"

"Sexual reassignment surgery?" I shrugged. "I don't know. It's an extreme step."

"No going back, after," Frank said, nodding.

"Yes. It is. Did you know, Frank, about Kelly? What Craig succeeded in doing to her?"

He faced me. "*Kelly?*"

I shuddered. "Oh, God. *She didn't tell you that part?*"

"When?"

"Back when she was still a student at Duquesne."

"And I'm just hearing about it now?"

"I just found out yesterday. Oh, Frank, I didn't know. I shouldn't have told you."

"You're right, you shouldn't have, cause now I'm going to have to kill my brother. Jesus, fucking Craig, son of a bitch. Who else knows?"

"Mom, Dad and Carolyn."

Frank shook his head, dismally. "I could see why Kelly didn't want to mention that in front of Meg and myself."

"Are you going to be okay?" I asked him.

"I'm fine," he nodded. "Craig might not be the next time I see him."

"He's built like a Mack truck, Frank. And then there's his defender, his bodyguard."

He nodded, *"Dear old Dad."* He put the car in gear and pulled back onto the road once more.

It wasn't long until the Travaglini home loomed on the horizon. However, there *was one* additional vehicle not there earlier that now was parked in the driveway.

Not good.

CHAPTER TWENTY-ONE - A Momentary Return to Sanity

I contemplated the house before me. Craig and Dad were back. Why would they come back? It was not a complication I wanted to confront.

"Oh, God, *why* are they here?" I asked my brother.

"If I know our father," Frank answered, "he's decided to deal with everything *his way.*"

"He had five kids," I replied. "Do the rest of us *even matter?* Or was he— as far as he was concerned— done after he got his first *'male'* heir?"

"I've been thinking that since I was five," admitted Frank.

"Frank, I can't explain this, but I don't want to go back in there."

"No one's going to hurt you, Keira, don't be scared."

"But I am scared," I admitted. "I'm suddenly shaking all over, as if— if I go back in there *now*— I'll need to *deal with things* I'm not ready to. Why can't we just start the car, and drive around all this beautiful countryside for a while? Let the situation settle down a little *in there?*"

Frank smiled, strangely, almost as if it suddenly weren't even really him in the car with me. "It doesn't work that way. You're scared, Keira, because you're getting close now."

"Close?" I furrowed my brow. *"To what?"*

"To coming back to us … from your long sleep."

"Frank…" I replied and had to stop. I simply looked at him. *"What are you talking about?"*

He took my hand and patted it. "No one is putting a gun to your head, Keira," he said. "Come in when you're ready. We'll all be inside waiting for you...."

Waiting for **me**?

He opened my smart car's driver side door, and stepped part way out. He had the strangest look on his face, almost as if he were not quite real. "It's been months, now, baby sister, and we want you to come back to us." He nodded then. "We all know you will. Like I said, when you're ready."

"Frank," I cautioned him, touching his arm. "Don't go in that house. Be careful against those two. Craig and Dad. They were never nice to any of us."

"You don't have to tell *me*." He smiled. "I'll be fine."

He extricated himself from my sardine can of a car and approached the front door. I found myself only reluctantly removing myself as well out from the passenger side seat. Frank seemed not to concern himself with me and my hesitation at that point. He was entering the house, as I was still just crossing the yard from the garage and all the cars parked in front of it and the back door.

Even before reaching that door, I could hear the shouting. It was my father's voice, mainly.

"This is my house," he declared, **"and MY family. We take care of our own in this family. We don't call the authorities, we don't coddle misfits and do nothing members. And we don't toss off our wedding vows just because we think we've made an error. You hear me, Carol? You married my son, till death do you part. You're not going anywhere!"**

• • •

Without knowing how I had managed it, or when I made the decision to do so, I found that I had walked to the right side of the back of the house. There was a patio entrance to a guest bedroom on the first floor. I had this desire to go upstairs, hastily toss all my clothes back into my suitcase, and leave, go back to New Jersey. Wait for Annie to return from Seattle, return to where I still possessed a sane existence; I might soon be out of work and penniless, but I least back there, I had Annie and I was content.

I glanced up to the second floor, the bedroom patio balcony where I needed to be and I swear I saw an image of *myself* up there out on the deck just beyond my old bedroom.

189

I just had to look a second time.

• • •

I guess not.

I must be going crazy, hallucinating now, seeing things. There was no one there, certainly not a double of myself. That might be, were it Kelly up there outside my bedroom, but we weren't *that* much alike. I'd know if it were her. And besides, Kelly was not here. She was nowhere on the property. I don't know how I knew that, but I did. All that was out there on the first of the two wooden patio decks was snow, lightly lining the wooden log railings, and the deck itself. All that beautiful wood and long logs, and gray stone running up the right side of the house, featured predominantly on the lowest floor and its own stone patio. God, my father may have been a terrible human being, but he had built my Mom one beautiful home up here in *Jim Thorpe*. It almost made me want to cry to just up and leave it yet again. Run away, that was. I really thought I could do it this time.

As I said, there were patio doors out a downstairs guest bedroom there on the left, in front of that wooden hot tub. I headed over for it. I only hoped the doors weren't locked.

They weren't.

• • •

"Fuck you, you mean old son of a bitch. You're lucky I haven't killed him yet; you're lucky he hasn't killed *me*, yet," I heard my sister-in-law, Carolyn, reply as I entered from the guest bedroom patio. All the adults, apparently, were gathered together in the kitchen. **"...You're not forcing me to stay with that philandering dick of a son of yours...."**

Alvin, aka Dear Old Dad. Carolyn was laying into my dad. Good, the bastard needed it; he had it coming.

"... just because you see it as a slap in the face to your family honor. He's a terrible father to his kids, and a thousand times worse with me than you are with Sarah."

Wow, why did that sound familiar? I thought, as I opened the doors and crept in. I searched the front side of the house quickly, finding no one, not even the kids, here on the first floor. The elders

190

must have sent them all upstairs to their rooms, to let the adults have one of their *discussions*.

"Carol," Craig's voice filtered back to me; it was eerily calm.

"No," Carolyn replied. "You don't get a voice in this discussion. You raped *both of your sisters*. **Both**! Stone drunk both times; the kids and I were home both times when you did it. And you expect me to just be a dutiful wife and say nothing, just *yes dear* you and continue to open my legs for whenever you get horny and want me to let you fuck me as well. I am sick and tired of the sight of you."

Both of us? "Carolyn no, you got that wrong," I whispered to myself. "Only Kelly. Dad got there in time, stopped Craig from nailing me as well. *But you **know that!**"*

I was suddenly feeling very agitated, as if my whole body were alive with a thousand needles or fire ants crawling all up and down it.

Nope, not yet, I thought, *I'm not going near that kitchen. I'm not ready; I'm not ready for whatever I'll learn there.* I reached a back stairway up to the second floor and crept up it for my old bedroom. I didn't figure on finding who I did waiting for me up there: *Chloe.*

She had been waiting for me, as if she knew here I would end up. This was a complication I was not anticipating. "Chloe?" I asked. "Why are you in here for?"

"I don't know," she shrugged. "I am. Our parents are arguing."

"Yeah," I said. "Even mine. Suddenly, that makes me feel like a kid as well. And I'm supposed to be an adult."

"Mom and Aunt Kelly told me what Uncle Craig did to you." She ran up to me. "I'm so sorry," she said, starting to cry. "That must have been so horrible."

"He *almost* done to me," I sought to clarify. "He didn't succeed, Chloe. Do you know about such things?"

She pulled back and looked at me. "Why? Why didn't you press charges? Why didn't you go to the hospital, to check to make sure you were fine? Why didn't the authorities arrest Uncle Craig for doing that to you? Why is everybody so blasé about it all? I don't understand."

I shrugged. "Tell you a secret," I whispered to her. "I don't know why, either, why everyone is so blasé, as you said; but I'm glad they are. I'm glad I am. I'd go insane, otherwise. I just want everything to be fine like it was before with my friend, Annie, back in Jersey."

"But Uncle Craig raped you," she countered, sniffing back a tear.

191

"No, he didn't. Your Grandad stopped him."

She sniffed. *"He did?"*

"Yes!" I insisted. "Chloe, do you know about those sorts of things? What your uncle Craig was trying to do to me?"

"Yes. I'm twelve, Aunt Keira. I have to watch out for that sort of thing among the boys in my school."

I shook my head. "Kids develop way sooner than they ever did even in my generation. I feel bad for your generation."

"Why, Aunt Keira?"

"Oh, Chloe, honey, call me Keirie. It's easier. Aunt, Uncle. Oral and anal sex." I shook my head. "At your age, you should still be just coming off believing in kid's stuff, like thinking all those characters walking around in Disneyworld are real cartoon characters."

"Keirie?" she timidly called me.

I smiled. I nodded then.

"That's baby stuff at my age. I mean, kids my age still like Disneyworld, but we know those figures walking around are just actors, actresses in costumes."

"Again," I sighed, "your generation grows up too fast. You've even got your period already, haven't you?"

I could tell that by how developed at age twelve she already was.

"A year ago," she said. "It was yucky, but at least I knew it was coming."

"Your Mom?" I smiled.

She shook her head. "Cindy, my best friend told me it would happen."

I sighed again. "God, you make me feel old," I told her.

"Aunt Keirie," she began, "are you up here because you're still not ready to *deal with the truth?* Are you going to pack and go back to New Jersey?"

"How do you know I'm up here for that?" I asked her.

She didn't respond. "Grandpop Alvin," she answered instead. "He's been screaming. Doug and Steven are still young. They're upstairs and yet they can hear good. They're crying; they know Aunt Carol and Uncle Craig are going to separate, get divorced. They're upset."

"And Trent?"

She huffed. "He says he hopes Dad gets custody of all three of them. Who wants to be raised, he said, by only a mommy. He'd rather grow up with his Dad."

"So, the fact that his parents might be breaking up, itself, doesn't bother him?"

"No. But as I was saying. Grandpop Alvin. He was screaming that he wants you out of here. He wants Uncle Frank to leave too. He hates Uncle Trevor, just because he went to live in Florida."

"And open a pizza shop," I added.

"Was that so bad?"

"To a man like my Dad? It's the behavior of a person who gives up."

"Aunt Keira, why are men such jerks?"

"Hon, I don't know the answer to that; I'm as clueless as you."

"That's because you're no more a boy than I am. Aunt Keira, can I help you pack?"

I thought about that. "Okay, if you want. But I don't want the family to know I'm leaving."

"Why?"

I breathed heavily. "That's a hard one to answer. I'm worried that if I stay, everything will change. And *listen to them down there*." I requested of her; I shook my head. "It doesn't feel like this change will be a good thing."

"Can I come with you?"

"Oh, Chloe," I said, shocked. "If your father knew I said yes, he'd never trust me again. I'm being irresponsible leaving without telling anybody as it is."

"You're running away?"

"Yes, like a child. It's totally an irresponsible and an anti-grownup thing to do."

"I want to see south Jersey."

"Why?" I asked her. "There's nothing worth seeing down there, where I live anyway. It's mostly marshland. And everything is closed today. You'll be bored."

"Do you have a PlayStation?"

"Yeah. It's practically required to be a member of my generation."

"A 4K TV?"

I sensed where she was going with all this. "Okay, help me pack, and we'll sneak back out the way I came in."

She smiled. "Okay."

• • •

As we were leaving through the same downstairs guest bedroom doors I had entered the house through, off in the distance, Chloe and I heard her father's voice, loud and very angry;

"I came here this holiday for Mom's sake, because she begged me to," we both heard Chloe's dad, my brother, Frank, declare.

"My Dad is yelling at your Dad," Chloe said.

I nodded.

"Meg wasn't up for it!" Frank continued, *"but she couldn't stand Mom's disappointment year after year when we turned Mom down. But why she stays with you is a mystery. You **deserve to rot in hell.**"*

I just looked at Chloe.

"Wow," said Chloe.

"He stole that line from me," I informed my niece. "That's what I said to him about your grandpop just a few minutes ago." I cupped my hand around my mouth like a megaphone and shouted, *"You're stealing my line, Frank!"*

Chloe cupped her hand as she snorted a laugh. "You're fun, Aunt Keira," she said. "God, I've always thought you were a fun aunt."

Not long after that we loaded *(or should I say stuffed?)* our four suitcases into the back of my Smart Car, got in and started the engine. It was a very quiet engine for not being an electric, still I couldn't help wondering if anyone in the kitchen noted when my vehicle started moving out of the driveway and down the road. The parked cars were easily viewed out by the garage from the kitchen. I'm sure they saw us.

• • •

Once hitting highway 209, I touched the phone icon of my car's touchscreen, which through its USB port was connected to my Samsung S8. I paged through the listings *(I was offered by the system only a limited number of calls to page through while the car was in motion)*. Still, I found Frank's cell phone number and touched the screen.

"Hey, Frank, hi, it's Keira," I said. "Chloe was bored, wanting to go somewhere. Everything is closed, and I was sure I had overstayed my welcome anyway. I'm taking her to my place in New

194

Jersey. I hope it's all right. She really is not taking well the way all you guys are fighting. Do you think you'll put an end to it soon? Oh, and tell Dad, *Keira* told him, for the way he treated all of us kids growing up, tell him, *he can go fuck himself.* Okay, bye."

Chloe giggled her ass off over that little message I left on Frank's phone.

"Okay," I said to my niece. "If we can get home in time, we might still be able to catch one of the airings of *A Christmas Story.*"

"Oh, God, please let's not," Chloe begged. "I'm so sick and tired of that movie. All they do is run it over and over all Christmas Day.

"You got it," I replied. "No Ralphie and his stupid BB gun."

We reached Penns Cove by three in the afternoon. Meg and Frank showed up three hours later.

CHAPTER TWENTY-TWO – A Fond Farewell to Jim Thorpe, Pa.

Just to state it for the record: My pleasant little time with my niece in South Jersey wasn't bad. I took her to see the same Star Wars movie at the closest nearby theater to Penns Cove that my dad and brother had taken Craig's three kids to go see in Allentown, Pa. Chloe hadn't seen it yet, and this was my way of telling my dad and brother that one didn't need to be male and a geek to like a movie like that one. Meg and Frank showed up at my apartment near seven to collect her. Chloe and I had been back long before then. Her parents weren't even pissed that I had absconded with their daughter and forced them to drive two hours out of the way to get her back. We all went out to dinner at a restaurant nearby that had the decency to remain open on Christmas Day.

I had hoped to spend the next four days all alone in my apartment, until Annie returned after Christmas. But Frank would hear nothing of that. He had called ahead, he said, and managed to book a room at the nearby Holiday Inn down the road. They had a few rooms vacant. Frank said he trusted me to be on my best behavior, and that if Chloe wanted to stay with me in the apartment that night that would be fine. He trusted me. The next morning, he said, both of us be ready, though, he and Meg would show up early to collect us, go out have a nice breakfast, Tuesday, the day after Christmas, and then begin the long drive back to their home in Allentown.

"You don't have to put yourself out like that," I said of taking me in for a week. "Annie will be back next Tuesday." I shrugged and glanced around the apartment. "I'll find something to do this week."

"What about the store?" Frank asked.

"It'll open tomorrow," I replied. "But I took the week off. I know," I nodded. "I hadn't figured I'd be back here so soon."

"Well, then it's settled," said my brother. "You're coming with us."

"Frank," I replied, "I'm a big girl. I don't need to be looked after."

(I didn't even process at that time, that I had referred to myself as a female without taking even a second to pause over the declaration. Thinking back on it now, it creeps me out why I did not.)

"Do it for Chloe," he replied. "She wants you there, right, honey?"

Chloe didn't hesitate to say, "Absolutely. Can she?"

"Meg and I are trusting you with our little girl tonight, *Aunt Keira,* " he said. "We'll be here around eight. Be ready to go. You'll behave, right babe?" he said to his daughter.

She nodded.

"Okay, see you guys. Have fun."

He and Meg left soon after.

"Oh shit," I suddenly exclaimed after they left.

"What?" Chloe asked.

"Annie."

"Your girlfriend?"

I nodded. "I promised to call her at noon. I totally forgot."

"I'm sure she'll forgive you. You've been through a lot the last two days."

"Can you give me a few minutes? My God, what time is it already?"

"Almost ten," Chloe answered.

I shook my head. "I'll bet we'll all remember this Christmas for years."

"Has she sent you any texts?"

"I don't know. I never even checked. Probably," I answered. "Let me call her. She's probably frantic."

No, Annie understood; she just assumed that I was having a somewhat passable good time with my family. I hated to inform her different. I explained how the day had in fact started out well, until we returned from church and found my father and decrepit brother back. I told her how I had crept out of the house, unnoticed, except for my niece, Chloe, who insisted I take her as well out of that hell hole.

"Good for you," Annie replied. "That took guts to do that. I'm proud of you. So, Allentown, huh? It's nice up there, so I've heard."

"It's not *Jim Thorpe*," I replied. "But it's not so much *where you go*, it's the people you know there."

"Why isn't that creep brother of yours in jail?" she asked.

"Dad has a lot of influence. He knows what strings to pull."

"I hope they both get what they deserve in the end," Annie said.

"*Karmas a bitch,* so I've always been told."

"Yes, it is," she replied. "God, I wish I were leaving today and not a week from now. It's killing me."

"Annie, I'll be fine. Frank won't let Dad or Craig anywhere near me."

We ended the call soon after that, and as it was getting very late, Chloe and I found we still were not sleepy, but instead grabbed my copy of Robert Zemeckis's "*A Christmas Carol*" in 3D on Blu Ray. It was half cartoon, but it was fun watching the thing. Went it was done, we both retired to my bedroom and spent the night together in my bed.

Next morning, of course, right on time at eight, Frank and Meg returned. We left shortly after for a breakfast at the nearest diner, and then took off in Frank's car for Allentown.

It was a pleasant week with the three of them. So, I suppose it wasn't a total wreck of a holiday week after all.

And now to catch us up: whatever pleasant holiday getaway my mom and dad had hoped for at the Travaglini homestead in *Jim Thorpe* never happened. Everyone went home. The attending parties were in no mood to pretend a family like theirs would stand for such a farce.

Frank and Meg had used my running away with their daughter as an excuse to leave as well before things got so ugly at Mom and Dad's place, the authorities might have had to be called. Meg and Frank had told Alvin at one point to shove it, invited Mom to leave our dad, come stay with them and Chloe. Mom thank them, but declined. Carolyn, I learned from Frank and Meg, slapped Craig a hard one across his face and announced she was divorcing him as soon as she could get the papers written up. She was leaving him. "Don't come back to the house. I'll have signed a restraining order against you by then. I don't care where you go, just don't come back to the house. I don't want you anywhere near our three kids. No judge in the world would grant you even visitation rights, not with your past."

She then went upstairs to order her kids to pack. The younger two, Doug and Stevie, gave no protest at all; in truth, their father frightened the crap out of them. They were almost glad to not be further subjected to a man who was as mean as he was. It was Trent who tried to resist his mother's decision to separate the family.

"Look, Trent," she told him, *"you're coming with me, even if I have to grab you by the scruff of your neck and haul your ass out of this house. PACK. NOW."*

Carolyn was about to call for an Uber to drive her and the kids to the airport, when she broached to Sarah the possibility of Mom leaving with her and the kids as well. She asked Sarah to join her and the kids back at the house in Pittsburgh and try to salvage what one might of the remaining holiday week. Or at the very least, she said, please give her and the kids a lift back to the airport?

"Forget the airport," Sarah told her daughter-in-law. "I could use the drive time to clear my head. We'll take my Mercedes."

"All the way to *Pittsburgh?"* clarified Alvin Travaglini, who would not let his wife out of his sight, following her from room to room.

"It's my car, isn't it?" she barked at him.

"What of it?" he replied.

"Fuck off, that's what of it."

"Why are you talking to me like that?" he shot back.

"It's this way, Alvin. You don't love your kids; you treat them like property, like tools, *your tools!* If you were a decent man, you'd do whatever you needed to protect them from predators. I've always been leery of Craig, he was so like you, but now he belongs in rehab or in jail. Alvin, who's next? Chloe? Is he going to fuck her next when she gets old enough?"

"I can handle Craig."

"Oh, you've done a wonderful job so far. I'm driving Carolyn and the kids to Pittsburgh, and then whatever happens with you and me, we'll see."

"I don't like this," he said.

She snorted. "Yeah, well, you should have thought through your decisions better, stopped to consider the consequences. I actually feel sorry for you, for what might be coming."

Sarah bid Alvin all the luck the coming week, she had a feeling he'd need it, and went upstairs to pack a suitcase. Carol went up to help her, while the women ordered the three boys to wait up in their room. When all was ready, Sarah and the four loaded into her Mercedes and it being around One PM by then, the four of them left for the long drive back to Pittsburgh. That left only Alvin and his favorite offspring to make do on their own in the now abandoned *Travaglini* home.

As it might be expected *(or hoped)*, bad things eventually do happen to terrible people, and Craig's troubles were only beginning. The charges against him for rape against a member of his own family were only the first of it. Investigations into the working conditions at the quarries owned by *Travaglini Marble and Granite* by OSHA arose. Then, the Federal Trade Commission became interested in the company's financial dealings. With a signed subpoena by a federal judge, officers of the court showed up at Craig and Alvin's main offices and took whatever possibly incriminating relevant documents they could get their hands on. In the process, all business operations at Dad's company was shut down, pending the outcome of the investigation. Craig and his financial officers at the company weren't exactly working only one set of books. It took some months but eventually, both father and son found themselves standing before review boards and were facing possible jail time.

And Mom? She loved that log home in *Jim Thorpe. (Who wouldn't? It was the one really nice thing Alvin had ever found the time in his pre-retirement years to give her.)* She had the house all to herself. I visited to be sure during the next few months before Annie and I left for our whirlwind tour of Europe. I needed not worry about my dad showing up to want me gone again from his premises; he had more important things to worry about by then and was seldom home.

And that pray tell finally takes us into the new year, 2018. What happened with *Com-link,* the company my franchise store was affiliated with? Seriously, a company as in trouble as that electronics firm was, could only remain above water for only so long. By the end of January, there was a **Closed** sign on the side entrance door to the store and the place looked very much like several main drive business establishments in Penns Cove looked these days: *emptied, gutted, totally devoid of all life and activity,* like their best days were now behind them, and only the universe knew what future if any lay before them.

CHAPTER TWENTY-THREE - Prep for April and the Excursion

It is said, as one aged, time seemed to just speed up. The days of the week flew by with unbridled urgency; by the time one could afford to look up from one's busy life, the realization was not an easy one that an entire week (*or month for that matter*) had come and gone. The days themselves were recalled as only momentary fragments of select hours, minutes, even seconds. It was possible to seriously wonder if one were even "present" in those days now forever gone, for the memories of what one did was clouded by the even sadder realization that as one aged, his or her ability to remember became less and less trustworthy.

But I was twenty-six, and such things had no business being matters I need be mindful of, and yet I would like to say, *I was.* But I can't even do that. January slid into February, into March, and April was suddenly just there, announcing itself on the calendar as if all the prior months' pages had somehow slipped off the calendar and scurried away, intent on never returning or explain where or even why they had gone, and in so much of a hurry.

I was passing through the first months of the new year as I believed an older person might, seeing the days fly by as if they were only telephone poles moving past one's passenger car train window as the train itself moved down the track to its inevitable destination.

My week spent with Chloe and her parents had been a good one, and I even conversed with Mom during the whole of it to find how she was managing away from Alvin in the days following her trial separation from him. I was back in Penns Cove before I even knew it.

Work resumed at *Com-Link*, the routine of each day, checking inventory and making the occasional sale, just seemed to fall into its slot in my life, as if the brief respite from it for the Christmas break had never even occurred. I was back in my regular life in the armpit of south Jersey, so near the run of the Delaware River and its oftentimes muddy presence reminding me that as a State, the river pretty much cut New Jersey off from the remainder of the country. And maybe one day in the future, the rising seas of the Atlantic would swell the Delaware River's girth and pretty much swallow up Penns Cove in total under its rising tides, while to the East perhaps the Atlantic Ocean itself little by little whittled away at the coastline and cut further and further into the fifty-mile length of solid ground that separated the ocean from the waters of the Delaware to the south and west.

My time with Annie was back as well to its regular rhythm, with *one* defining difference. My sexual antics with her just were not as satisfying as they once had been. I liked being with her, but I did not like the presence of my male tool between my legs, and her desire to continue to make use of it became an increasing irritant for me. I couldn't leave from my brain the memory of what my brother, Craig, almost did to me in *Jim Thorpe,* and the thought that there had always been something kind of thrilling or fun about the thought of being on the receiving end of such a sex act rather than the other way around.

It was during these weeks of January of 2018, that the news of *Com-Links* demise finally hit our store. Prep began very soon after to stage a mostly what I would call a pathetic *going out of business* sale. *"Everything Must Go!"*

As if....

As if anyone at that point really gave two shits about what we were trying to unload on the public as we cleaned out our inventory. And it was during this time, one morning in one of those five weeks of January 2018 that I was back alone with Ben in his and Dave's computer nook in the mezzanine area upstairs that I couldn't help mentioning my difficulties with being entirely satisfied with my *female-on-female* antics with my girlfriend.

"Really?" Ben had commented. "You're curious," he pursued, "about all you've missed being born with that little boy toy between your legs?"

I wanted to say something nasty in return to him for the way he was making light of my unhappy plight. Instead, I simply said, "Yes."

"But I'm not drunk," he said.

"And I'm no guy," I retorted, "and we both know it. So, fuck me and quit making excuses."

Let's just say— *(because I don't want to go too much into detail at this juncture)*— that old Ben pretty much knew what I was implying, and we were all alone in the nook upstairs. Dave, his co-operator of the computer nook up here, would be out for the morning, leaving Ben in charge of the computer station during his brief absence, and of course by this point virtually no one even bothered to enter our store these days anymore as it turned out. The public could clearly see the *Going out of business* signs emblazoned out front the building, and I suppose people considered it only a matter of time until we were gone anyway, so hardly anyone even bothered to come in in those last days.

As you can imagine, Ben was up for it as well. No way did he doubt that he was in the presence of a female, as opposed to a female *wannabe,* a fetching one at that, and there I was dressed in a pretty powder blue cashmere pullover, and black slacks and matching high heeled pumps. I seemed sexy enough, and he was more than willing. I dropped down onto my knees and reached up for the zipper to his tan khakis slacks and delicately removed his tool from its restraint behind his tight mid-thigh reaching spandex trunks.

My own tool between my own legs reacted as I imagined the neural receptors in some true female genitalia would respond, and I could feel it telling me that this was a very welcome situation that was the very sort of thing all previous fantasies of such an act would pale against by comparison. I found myself savoring the feel of every inch of his six-inch manhood. *(By what law would it say he would need to have anything other than an average male length down there? He was adequate; it was a penis. Was I disappointed? Not in the least bit. I knew the thing would rise to the occasion and complete the task I sought.)*

I worked on him swiftly, aware that Chuck Maloney or Sally Kugel might knock on the closed door to the cramped space at any time, wondering why both the upper and lower door halves were closed. It was a blow job, and it had been a while since I'd found myself curious in this way as I had back in college with my then roommate, Doug Decanter. I suppose it was like they say about riding a bicycle, once done you always know how. Ben apparently had no complaints. It wasn't long before he was cupping the top of my head in his hands and pumping me with his tool on his own, leaving me to just cup my lips and feel the shaft of his organ plow into my mouth as if it were a genuine vagina the thing was servicing.

He tensed up finally, and I could feel his penis begin to spasm as his load poured into my mouth, spurt after spurt. I liked it. I swallowed most of it, some back flushed out onto my chin and dripped onto the solid wood floor.

I wiped the residual off my chin and lips and smiled up to him. "Thanks," I said.

"Anytime," he smiled back. "So, do you think your Annie would be up for a threesome sometime?"

"Yeah, no," I replied, cynically, "maybe we better just keep what we just did— for now anyway— our little secret."

He shrugged. "Okay. Will you be back?"

As it turned out, no. We didn't do it again; the business of shutting down the store just took up too much of our attention. The subsequent goodbyes, good luck wishes given out to all gathered on the final day was probably the most sad and tearful. It was over, my last day. I spent it returning to the municipal park, the one in warmer days I would visit to work out the kinks in my joints, take a run around the park, get thoroughly worked up before heading back to the store. That day, I simply sat at a park bench by the sea wall and watched cars in the distance on the Memorial bridge. I watched them slowly traverse the long decking of the two spans over the river.

I almost wished Joe Bennington, my gay friend, was still in the neighborhood, but as I later learned, he had moved away shortly after the first of the year. To where, no one seemed to recall ever asking.

No, I never told Annie about my little *"thing"* with Ben Linaker. I didn't have to. She pretty much knew I was becoming bored with just female on female sex, but we were both preoccupied with our jobs and the planning of the trip to Europe.

And this finally is what I meant at the start of this section or *chapter of my story. Time.* It went quickly. Before I knew what had happened, it was April already, and the departure date was rapidly approaching. I can't even recall exactly how and when I managed to have my name and official stats, birth certificate and my driver's license ID all altered to reflect my change from *Keir* to *Keira.*

The trip to the DMV was the cute affair; returning there with all my new stats to have all my driving documents changed to reflect the new me, a new photo ID needed to be made to be able to eventually board the plane to our first stop in Rome.

The same woman— who months earlier had questioned my being the Keira she mistakenly mistook me for, all because it was so easy to misread the space between *Keir* and the first letter of *Adrian,* my middle name— remembered the earlier incident.

"I remember you," she said to me. "Oh, my God, wow." She glanced to the image on my old photo ID and compared it to how I looked now. This day I wore a red turtleneck sweater and a pair of blue denim jeans with a pair of running shoes. "So, it's *Keira* for real, this time?"

"All legal and everything."

"Are you all the way with this new look?"

(She meant fixed.)

I frowned up at her. "No, maybe someday."

"I never did believe you were a *Keir.*"

"Me neither," I replied, as I gathered up all my new ID documents.

"Good luck," she told me as I left her tiny compartment.

CHAPTER TWENTY-FOUR - A Short Hop Across a Very Big Pond

Whatever mileage '*Your Inner You*' had hoped to get out of my looking the way I did, didn't in the end really amount to much, not with the public. I was no celebrity; I never believed I would be. Had I been a model or a media celebrity already and my true *situation* down there between my legs had been outed in a scandal sheet somewhere, *maybe* some real traction might have arisen by how naturally female I looked and for the most part always had looked. But this was a very depressing spate of years stealing its way through American society. LGBT rights and privileges. I wouldn't say in the year 2018, the United States was a proudly progressive place. And with the current administration in Washington lording over all three branches of the government for the most part, I sincerely doubted I would ever be considered a champion for an individual's right to live his or her life as he/she desired.

Annie and I hired an airport Uber to take us to Philly International and from there we would board a connecting flight at JFK for Rome, our first stop on our whirlwind trip. With all my documents properly declaring me to be the person I seemed to be *(from a visual inspection at least)* everything seemed to go down very fine at the various security checkpoints. I almost thought it would be a real hoot if an agent had insisted on a pat down or a full body X-ray scan to check to see if I were carrying on my person any illegal substances. It would almost be fun to explain that my little inconsistency between my legs was nobody's business but mine. For all intents and purposes, I was now legally *Keira Adrian Travaglini*, whether my old man wanted to accept that fact or not.

. . .

'Your Inner You' really wanted this trip to be a big deal for Annie and myself, as we were informed both a local photographer attached to their Italian division in Rome and a translator/guide would meet us upon arrival and escort us to our first-class accommodation at the hotel del Rome just up the way from the Colosseum. The on-line apparel outfit was really hoping my success at transitioning from male to female would inspire many other wannabe-types out there into finding *Your Inner You's* site and avail themselves of *Your Inner You's* on-line catalogue. The days of such individuals risking shame and embarrassment— or worse, incarceration— purchasing items legally or flat-out shoplifting them and either way facing society's disgust over you and its disapproval was pretty much no longer necessary thanks to sites like *Your Inner You.*

As for me, successfully boarding the United Airlines New York to Rome Direct Flight, out of JFK, brought me great personal relief, especially when the flight left the tarmac and was airborne. I was home free. No more worries that this was all going to blow up in my face.

. . .

"You've been awfully quiet most of the trip," said Annie to me halfway across the Atlantic. "You've said little to nothing since we left New York."

This was one of things I hated about air travel: if I weren't personally steering the airplane, there was nothing to do but try to sit still in one's seat and just *wait ... wait* for when the aircraft deposited you where you wished to be and allowed you to get on with your life.

I yawned as I pulled my glance away from the tiny window port to my right and faced her. I shrugged. "I'm sorry," I answered. "A lot on my mind, I suppose. Just lost in my thoughts, I suppose."

"Is it me?"

"You? Annie, you've been there for me through all of it, all the hard decisions, some you even made for me when I wasn't ready to make them on my own. No, you've been great. No one could ask for a better person to exist in her life."

I placed my hand over top of hers on the armrest between us. The man, I believe he said his name was Bob-something, across the

208

aisle to our left, glanced over to Annie and me as I did so. I had tried to keep my voice low, but that would only work so well and little more, in such a confined space as the interior of this United Airlines Boeing 787. I wondered if he suspected the two of us were lovers or something. If he did, he had the decency to keep it to himself.

"Then, why are you so subdued?" she asked. "Seriously, baby," she said.

(Mister pretending-to-not-be-listening glanced at us again at that one from Annie.)

"Do you want the window seat?" I asked, as I glanced again to the slight sprinkling of billowy clouds wafting along far below us and casting shadows on the waters of the Atlantic.

"Not yet," she replied. "You can enjoy it."

I laughed. "Are you just saying that because there's nothing down there right now worth even looking at?" I asked. "Look at it down there. It's been just like that for hours, just an endless s expanse of water, no end in sight, not a trace of land."

"Do you want to change seats?"

I shook my head. "We're fine for now."

"So, what are you thinking?"

"Our lives are back east, back in that direction," I pointed, indicating the rear of the plane. "It's like I'm not just physically abandoning my life back there but saying farewell to that whole reality I lived back there as me. Like I'm never going to see it again; this reality I've known … *with you*…. It feels as if someone stamped an expiration date on it."

"Well, that's depressing," she replied. "Are you tired of your life with me?"

"No, Annie," I insisted. "You're everything to me. This last year since we met … *in fact about a year ago now, last April* … I've never been happier, and that despite having a man for a father I detest like you wouldn't believe, a brother who deserves to be in jail, and *is heading there* I'm happy to say, just not for what he did to me, and a personal career path I took that ran itself right into the ground when *Com-Link* folded."

"Well, you knew that was going to happen, eventually."

"Kelly still wants me to work with her in *Jerome* for *Red Rock Knickknacks*."

Annie nodded. *"Arizona.* Well, if that's where your life is meant to go next then I guess it is. You have to do what's best for you."

209

"But what about us?"

"I don't know," Annie returned. "I can't just up and leave my position at the insurance agency. You could always move in with me, I've suggested that before."

I shook my head. "Mom has been helping me out with the rent on my apartment, since the store closed, but she makes it quite clear she'd like me to move back home, at least for the time being. And I *have* spent a lot of my days of late in *Jim Thorpe,* keeping her company. She's lonely, now that she kicked my old man out. Moving in with you and unemployed…." I shrugged. "Is that what you really want, I mean, *really,* at this point in your life?"

"You'll find another job eventually."

I shook my head. "No offense, but Penns Cove is dying; it's been doing it for more than fifty years, ever since the bridge span to Delaware replaced the ferry boat service back in the 1950s. The best move for me at this point feels like it's *Red Rock Knickknacks,* working alongside Kelly."

"Our time is coming to an end?" she feared to suggest.

I nodded, heavily. "Don't you think?"

"I don't want it to end," she said.

"What are we going to do, get married? There are still only a few States in this country that even allow that sort of thing." I shook my head. "I would say yes to that, if it felt like it was in my future. But to be honest, I can't see my future. It's just black, like what happens to the screen after the final credits roll at the end of a movie."

"God, Keirie. This is supposed to be an exciting adventure—*for both of us.* Two weeks in Europe, visiting some of the most romantic and picturesque places on Earth. Neither of us have ever really been able to afford a trip like this. You should be excited. Think of all the new things we're going to see, new people we'll meet."

"That's the other thing," I answered. *"This trip.* It doesn't feel *real.* It feels more like a dream. A dream that will end soon somewhere on the horizon ahead of us."

"You're worrying me, love, you know that?" she replied. "I've never heard you talk this way before. You were all excited about this trip, even last night. Couldn't wait for it begin."

"And then there's that," I nodded, sadly.

"What?" she feared to ask.

"Did last night really happen?"

"You mean, what we did?"

210

"The day itself, or any of the days, since…."

"Since, when?"

"Last Christmas? Nothing has felt real since last Christmas."

"Keirie, in all seriousness, you haven't really been you *since* last Christmas."

"Ever since Craig assaulted me, though outwards and even perhaps consciously I've been putting up a *good face,* shrugging what he did to me off as basically *no big deal.* But it is a big deal; he's done it before. He deserves to rot in prison for the rest of his sorry life for it all. And ever since that night, Christmas eve, it's as if I've only been '*observing*' my life ever since, like it's only been passing in front of me, and I've not really been living it."

She nodded, encouragingly. "It's a phase you're in. It'll pass."

I sighed. "I hope so."

"Do you think maybe after that *thing* with your brother, maybe you should have, I don't know, seen somebody?"

"Maybe, I should have; but I didn't, did I?"

"You still could."

I took a breath. "Somehow doing even *that* doesn't feel in my future either. I have to ask you a question, Annie, and I *really* need you to answer."

"What? What's the question?"

"*Are you real? Is any of this? Me, you, this plane, our life this last year together? Is this nothing more than just a dream I've been having?*"

A terrible paleness seemed to cross her complexion, not because it might be true, but because the seriousness with which I had posed the question, suggested things with me were not quite right with me.

"I feel like I'm in an episode of *The Twilight Zone,*" I said then.

She touched my arm. "I'm here. I'm real," she said. She looked up to the 787's interior. "This is as real as anything could be. You're really here, Keirie." She glanced to the tiny window port beside me. "That's real water, ocean below us. We over it and en route for Rome."

I nodded. "I wish this feeling that none of it was really real would just stop hovering somewhere in the air all around me." I smiled, then. "You know what?"

"What Keirie?

"I'm fine. Forget I said anything."

She smiled. "Okay."

211

I kissed her. I'm going to close my eyes for a while. Do you want to switch seats?"

"No, that's all right," she replied. "I'm fine here for now, very comfortable. I'll tell you when I want to switch."

"Okay," I replied in near a whisper, and kissed her again. "I love you, Annie, I really do. I've enjoyed my year with you. It's been great."

"It's been great for me too," she whispered back.

I settled my head against the window, my face pressed against the glass and for a second or two watched the clouds just hang there above the ocean, seemingly mere inches above the blue water. Almost imperceptibly I saw them work their way rearward and eastward, back for the United States.

I heard a creak to my left; imagined the slightly balding fellow in the brown turtleneck and gray slacks across from us lean over into the aisle to speak quietly to Annie. I heard him say to her: "*Your friend sounds like she's not all there.*"

"*She's had a rough last few months.*" I heard Annie say. "*She'll be okay once we land; this trip is a dream come true for both of us. Her mood will change after we touch down in Rome.*"

"Hey, Annie?" I whispered over to her, my eyes as yet closed. She leaned back over, her head very near against my own. I opened my eyes briefly and smiled at her. "Tell that guy to mind his own fucking business."

Our flight continued on for the straits of Gibraltar and our first port of call in Rome, Italy. Our whirlwind European getaway was just beginning.

But still that feeling of finality never left me. It just kept haunting me.

CHAPTER TWENTY-FIVE - The Journey Back

"Keirie? Keirie, hon, please wake up, you've been asleep way too long," I heard Annie's voice call to me sometime later. It seemed very much later in fact. *And it was very odd.* I no longer felt the motion of the plane souring over a mile above the Atlantic. In fact, I felt no motion at all, just the succulent seat cushions of this incredible, beautifully appointed aircraft *787 Dreamliner.* But even that felt wrong, like I was no longer in an aircraft souring high amid the clouds over a mile above the ocean.

I felt Annie touch my arm, not to stir me awake, but more to just make physical contact as if to let me know she was there and concerned.

But concerned about what?

"Are we in Rome, yet?" I asked Annie.

"Baby sister will you please come back to us now?" I heard Annie ask.

I puzzled over that. "Annie, I never noticed that before," I commented. "You sound so much like Kelly. That's so weird."

Nothing felt right, suddenly. The plane was no longer airborne. I opened my eyes to glance over at Annie and saw—

An empty plane. An empty seat where Annie should have been sitting.

And then I looked down at myself. I was no longer dressed in slacks and a comfortable dark brown pullover sweater, but instead the lounge wear outfit Annie had bought me for Christmas. And after that reveal, *"Annie?" I called. "Annie???"* I pulled myself up out of my seat to glance around the remainder of the aircraft.

Nothing. No one. It was totally empty, and the plane was no longer in flight. I looked out my tiny window port once more, and saw yet another impossible thing:

The Travaglini homestead. My parent's house and beyond it: *Jim Thorpe.*

The rightward face of the Travaglini homestead was what presented itself in the window port; patio doors led into a first-floor guest bedroom, a hot tub, round and encased in a circular wooden frame fronted a stone porch just before it. I got a profound sense of Déjà vu, as if I were not really watching the scene out a window of an aircraft, but instead were only recalling an earlier moment when I dreamt the same scene of me approaching the house, surreptitiously, seeking a side entrance to avoid the heated exchanges of words I knew were being tossed in the Travaglini kitchen by other members of my family. The image was repeating itself all over again. I looked up to the second-floor balcony railing. There again, was an apparition of *me*, my arms draped over the balcony railing, as I wistfully pondered the peace and quiet of this secluded mountain resort town. I saw it was me for sure this time, and it quaked my very being.

The Me on the balcony looked at me; she looked right at me, as if she knew I was spying on her from inside the aircraft. I was gazing upon a doubleganger of my own self, and she gazed back.

I had mentioned to Annie that my life since last Christmas Day had felt like an episode of *The Twilight Zone* and now apparently, it was coming true. Why was there a version of myself up there on the balcony of my parent's home? Why was I even back here in *Jim Thorpe*? And it was winter again, not early spring as it should be.

Winter ended a month ago. We were in April now. But even worse than that, was the remembering. I had seen this image of my parents' house, that fateful Christmas morning, when I left *Jim Thorpe* for my apartment in *Penns Cove*. Just as now, a vision of myself standing in that exact same spot on the second-floor balcony, gazed off into the new morning's rise. And quite frankly from that moment on I never really believed again that what I experienced, what I thought was real, really was.

I looked back to the interior of the empty aircraft all around me, then out again to *Jim* Thorpe and my parents' home— *to assure I wasn't imagining things.* But I had to be *imagining things,* because when I looked again out to the balcony railing, this time *"the other*

214

me" WAS ME.... I was no longer inside the *787 Dreamliner*. My hands draped the balcony railing; I was *her*, the *me* upon the second-floor balcony of my parents' log home in *Jim Thorpe*, gazing absently upon the wilderness countryside beyond the town's outermost suburban limits. There was no sign of the *787 Dreamliner*, no indication that an apparition such as it could or would ever manage to find itself reposing within so unlikely a location.

None of this made any sense; I knew I must be dreaming or hallucinating this whole thing. But damn it all, it felt so *real*, like I was present *for real* on the terrace balcony outside my old *Jim Thorpe* bedroom.

It was Christmas of 2017 all over again. I recalled my prior decision that day when Frank and I had returned from Christmas Day Mass, my decision to run away, not deal with the heated exchanges proceeding a floor below me in my parents' kitchen—*pack my bags and flee back to the safety of my apartment in Penns Cove, New Jersey and the dream that by doing so all would be fine, that my life might resume as it had for months now.* Perhaps, I had even conjured up the fantasy that my niece, Chloe, had been waiting for me right here in this very bedroom, and then joined me as I left for *Penns Cove*. There was no sign of her this time; if she remained yet within this house, it was probably in some other part of it.

Perhaps none of this was real. Then or even now. Perhaps … *everything I had experienced since Greg's attack Christmas Eve, had been nothing more than a dream,* all of it. In truth, none of it ever felt real to me, as if it had all been a delusion, one I had created to mask whatever it was I was attempting to forget. Somehow, despite all that, the heated exchanges going on downstairs in the kitchen felt like maybe **they were real**. I hadn't wanted to confront what I might learn if I went down there. I still didn't wish to. *It wouldn't be pretty.* But perhaps I would just keep circling back to this moment in time if I continued to resist confronting it.

What truly sucks is the realization that some things you just have to do, pleasant or otherwise.

• • •

"This is my house," declared my father, **"*and MY family*. We take care of our own in this family. We don't call the authorities, we don't coddle misfits and do-nothing members. And we *don't* toss**

off our wedding vows just because we think we've made an error. You hear me, Carol? You married my son, till death do you part. You're not going anywhere!"

"Fuck you, you son of a bitch," My sister-in-law replied. "You're lucky I haven't killed him yet; you're lucky he hasn't killed *me*, yet. You're not forcing me to stay with that philandering dick of a son of yours, just because you see it as a slap in the face to your family honor. He's a terrible father to his kids, and a thousand times worse with me than you with Sarah."

"Carol," came a calmer voice. Craig.

"No," she replied. "*You* don't get a voice in this discussion. You raped *both* of your sisters. **Both of them.** Stone drunk both times; the kids and I were home both times when you did it. And you expect me to just be a dutiful wife and say nothing, just *yes dear* you and continue to open my legs for whenever you get horny and want me to let you fuck me as well. I am sick and tired of the sight of you." She faced Alvin Travaglini again. "And as for you! *You* made it quite clear it was in my best interest seven years ago to remain married to that son of yours when he raped **his own sister!** First Kelly, now Keira, and you're still insisting *you'll handle it.* And according to you, I'm supposed to *just stay in line?"*

"I will not put up with any more talk like that from *you*," said my father, "I don't care if my grandkids are upstairs and listening to every word. What I say in this family goes, you got that?"

"No," calmly exclaimed my brother, Frank, as he entered the kitchen. *"No, she doesn't 'got that,' Dad. And neither do I."*

"Stay out of this Frank," said Alvin Travaglini to his second oldest son. "Why are you even still in town? Why aren't you back in Allentown, running that *'store'* of yours?"

"Oh, that's just so *you*, isn't it? You sad excuse for a human being," spit Frank. "Your youngest is in the hospital, she won't wake up, she's been molested by a member of her own family, and you're here, instead of there by her side, insisting *you've got it all covered.* Well, not this time, Dad, *not this time."*

Something was different. Frank was *not* dressed for Christmas Mass. Nothing he said or did suggested that he and I had just returned from St. Joseph's Church down the way. And apparently, he was talking about me, *in a hospital of all things,* as if Christmas Morning had gone down way different than how I recalled it. I didn't understand. I looked out the window to the cars parked out back. My smart car was not there among them. And as I surveyed the members of my family here in the Travaglini kitchen, I also noted that my sister, *Kelly,* was not in attendance. None of this made any sense. What day was this and where were *Kelly and me*? I crept further toward the kitchen and glanced to a knickknack calendar Sarah had placed as an ornament on a countertop.

The day after *Christmas,* I noted. I glanced to myself, in the lounge wear jumper with the mitten pockets. *Oh, Jesus Christ,* I thought to myself. *What am I, dead? Did I die that night Craig raped me?*

But he didn't rape me. Dad stopped him; he got there in time. Right?

"What's going on?" I shouted to everyone in the room. But not a one of them looked up. Not a one of them heard me. As far as any them were concerned, I wasn't even there.

"How is Keira this morning?" Sarah asked Frank, a worried expression on her face.

"No change," he answered. "Kelly's with her. Refuses to leave her side." Frank faced our father once again. *"Why aren't you there? Are you even planning to at least pretend to care?"* He faced Craig, then, leaning as yet against the kitchen's twin stoves. "And why is *he* still free to come and go? Why isn't his sorry ass behind bars?"

"Dad bailed him out," Carol informed her brother-in-law.

217

Frank grinned and nodded cynically to his father. "Still covering for him, huh?"

"Is Keira going to be okay?" Craig inquired.

"You don't get to ask that question," Frank informed him. "You are one lousy piece of garbage, you know that?"

"Watch it, Frank," Craig warned him. "I'm pretty broken up about all this myself."

"You are? You mean, two days later, you're finally sober?"

Craig made a move for him.

"Yeah, come on, you lousy prick. Just try it."

*"**Knock it off, both of you!**"* ordered our dad, getting between my brothers.

"If Keira doesn't wake up soon, I'm coming for you," Frank promised Craig. He turned to our dad, then. "You bailed him out of jail. That's what you care more about? Keeping a lid on it all?"

"**I have to,**" Alvin Travaglini replied. "I'm the only one who gets it: *we're a family. Family sticks together.*"

"Frank, honey, maybe we should go," said Meg Travaglini, newly entering the room, after descending from the second floor. "The kids can hear you all, you know? Even Chloe, she's upstairs, crying her eyes out for Keira. Frank, we don't need this, let's just go."

"First, tell Dad, Meg," Frank said to his wife, "what you told me about Craig."

"Frank, no, aren't things in this family bad enough already?"

"Tell me what?" barked Alvin.

Meg was standing right beside her husband, near the entrance, and unbeknown to her, right near where I apparently invisibly reposed. She steeled herself to answer her husband's request. "Dad," she said, meekly, "Rita left Trevor because Craig tried to attack her too."

Alvin turned to his oldest.

"And he came on to me about a year after Frank and I married, that fourth of July picnic back in 2006. Right out there by the pool. I slapped him in the face."

"Oh, Meg, I'm so sorry," said Carol. She glared at her husband, then. She slapped him hard. "You really disgust me, you piece of shit."

"It's okay, Carol," said Frank. "Just be smart from here on and put as much distance between yourself and that disgusting brother of mine." He faced Megan, then. "Go call Chloe. Tell her we're leaving." He faced Mom, then. "I'm sorry, Mom, but we're out of here."

Sarah Travaglini blinked her eyes once and only nodded, forlornly.

"I talked to Keira's doctor," he said to her. "'Physically,' he said, 'she's fine.' At least, getting pregnant is something Keira won't have to fret over, if she ever awakens." He turned to his brother again. "What is it with you and rear end sex? I remember one night, when we were still kids, you climbed into my bunk and thought you were being a smart ass. That's when the old man came in and wanted to know what all the shouting was about. What was I supposed to say to him, *Craig tried to fuck me up my ass, the queer?* God, brother, you're one sick character."

"Shut up you little prick," Craig told his brother. "And that didn't happen. You must have dreamt it."

"*It happened!*" Frank told him. "You really think I would make a thing like that up? Keira couldn't fight you off, like I could. Kelly neither.*" Frank took a deep breath. "The doctor thinks our Keira has suffered a possible complete mental break with reality. He thinks when she is eventually ready to wake up, she'll probably need therapy, maybe months of it, to come to terms with what's happened to her."

Sarah faced her husband. "And all you care about is sweeping Craig's messes under the rug," she told him. "Alvin, I was wrong about you. This attitude of yours, I just can't forgive."

"Is, that, right?" he flashed back at her. "You mean, I have to deal with *you* as well? Keira's going to be fine. She'll get over it. Just like her sister. I'll give Keira whatever she wants to placate her."

Sarah walked over to her husband and smacked him. "Get out of my house, you son of a bitch," she ordered him.

"It's my house, too," he replied. "And this is how this is going down. Craig is not going to jail for this. Do you realize how much I had to put out to bail 'our' son out of jail when the cops showed up and hauled Craig away like a common criminal? He's the CEO of my company. He's the only one of my goddamn sons who has what it takes to run my company. I've now got to grease some serious palms to make all this go away. Craig is *not* going to trial for this. It will ruin the family name, and all that goes with it."

Sarah Travaglini approached her son, shaking her head, and getting right in his face, she slapped him. "I forgave you for what you did to Kelly." She shook her head again. "Keira can't press charges against you, right now; *but I will.*"

Megan returned from upstairs and informed her husband that their daughter would be down in a second. Frank nodded and turned to leave. He paused to reflect and faced his father one last time. "Old man, I never told you why I left your precious company." He nodded. "Now, would be a good time."

"I already know why," Alvin Travaglini replied. "You couldn't cut it managing a big corporation. *You* or Trevor."

"I won't speak for Trevor," Frank calmly replied. "But hear this, you'll get a kick of out of it. You want to know why I up and moved Meg and Chloe to Allentown and opened my own business with Meg? Do you remember that convention I attended five years ago in Cleveland, promoting our company's latest line of granite tops? I bumped into an acquaintance of yours, mister king of the marble and granite business himself, *Marble Man John.* Largest distributor on the east coast."

Alvin nodded. "John DeSimone, a good businessman, a model for all of us, what about him?"

"He said you insulted his family *and your own* at the same time."

"How?" Alvin Travaglini queried of his son.

"You were going on about Jerry and Henry DeSimone, his two boys, recall it yet?"

"I told him I admired their abilities, they made excellent executive officers in his company, they were smart, shrewd, had good heads on their shoulders. How was that an insult?"

"You told him, 'I'D GIVE ALL FIVE OF MY KIDS FOR JUST ONE OF YOUR BOYS.' Yeah? Is it ... coming back to you, yet, old man, what you said?"

Alvin Travaglini found himself shuffling as he placed his hands down on the kitchen table. "So, he took that wrong," he defended of his words. "I didn't mean it as an insult."

"You implied that not one of us kids, *your offspring, your family,* meant shit. And as for all *his kids*, all you saw in them was how good as workers they were. *Not their value as human beings.* What are any of us to you, you miserable bastard, just pieces of equipment? Do we only exist just to make your life better? Do you even give a shit about any of us?"

Craig Travaglini pulled himself up all the way up from his slouching position by the sinks. "You really said a thing like that, Dad? None of us? You'd trade all of us, just to have offspring who could make you the envy of your peers, like John DeSimone, *Mister Marble and Granite?"*

"Craig," he replied, lowly. "Not now."

"Screw you," he told his father. "I bust my ass for that company of yours, and I don't really give two shits about quarry pits."

"You're not smart enough to do much else," Alvin informed him. "I started that business. All you had to do was be capable, not screw things up."

"But you'd still trade me in for a better model, if you could, right?"

"Why are you two," he said of his two sons, "making that dumb comment of mine such a big deal?"

"It's why I left with my family, you damn jerk!" said Frank. "And what about Trev? You think he's down there in Florida, just to enjoy the climate? He wanted to put as much distance between you and him as was possible. And Kelly? She moved to Arizona. I'm in Allentown. Yeah, kids move away. *But not your kids!* They needed to get as far away from you as possible. Who can blame them? As a Dad, you *suck!* And Keira, she was just another daughter, like her sister. Of no real use. She follows a boy down to South Jersey, it doesn't pan out, gets a job down there and you could give a royal shit about what happens to her. Hey, Craig, remember Dad's favorite line he used to use on us all the time, you, me and Trevor? *Make yourself useful?*

"A Christmas reunion?" Frank concluded then. *"This family?* I came here this holiday for Mom's sake, because she begged me to. Meg wasn't up for it, but she couldn't stand Mom's disappointment year after year when we turned her down. But why she stays with you is a mystery. *You deserve to rot in hell."*

"I said that," I said, aloud, knowing full well no one would hear me. **"You stole my line again, Frank. And what's all this talk of me being *a real girl, raped for real,* or unconscious and in the hospital? I'm fine. *What are you all talking about?* Craig was arrested? Dad bailed him out? *In what universe did all that happen?"*** I finished with.

221

There was a scream just then out in the common room just off the kitchen. We all turned, including me. It was Chloe at the foot of the stairs. She was staring right at me.

"Chloe, what in the hell?" Meg asked, leaving again for her. Chloe had descended with her bags and was preparing to head out to the car.

"Aunt Keira?" my niece called to me. *"Mom, can't you see her?"*

"Who?"

"Aunt Keira! She's right there!" She frowned then, observing the red jumper and knee-high booties I was wearing. "But why are you dressed like that, Aunt Keira?" she asked me, directly. "That's what you were wearing when I visited you in the hospital yesterday."

Instinctively, Meg Travaglini turned to where her daughter was pointing. She saw nothing. I meanwhile left the kitchen and slowly approached my niece. "Chloe," I said to her. "You can *see me?"*

"Yes," she replied. "Why? Can't anyone else?"

I glanced to all the other adults back in the kitchen. Chloe followed my glance and realized everyone in attendance thought she was nuts, hallucinating.

Chloe faced back to me. "You're my favorite aunt in all the world. You know that. I love being around you almost as much as Mom."

"I'm your *almost* Aunt Keira, you mean," I smiled.

She frowned at that one. *"Almost?* What does that mean?"

"Chloe?" called her grandmother, Sarah, frowning, approaching her, putting her hand on her shoulder, and staring— unbeknown to her— right at me. *"Who* are you talking to? There's no one there."

Chloe tried to touch me, and saw her fingers go right through my lounge jumper outfit.

I saw the very frightened look on her face immediately. And now for real I was sure of one thing. My body was not here, and *It was time for me to make myself scarce.*

"Oh, my God, she just vanished," exclaimed Chloe. *"She's dead; she died, didn't she?"*

How I managed to make myself suddenly invisible was unknown to me, but, apparently, I did. I was still there, observing it all as if it were in a dream I was having. Meg tried to console her daughter, envelope her in her arms and press Chloe's head against her bosom. "Honey, shush now. Aunt Kelly is in the hospital with

Aunt Keira. She's not dead. If there were word, Aunt Kelly would call. I'm sure your Aunt Keira is still with us."

"I've seen enough true-life ghost stories on TV, mom," Chloe rebutted. "I know how it works. I saw her, right here, right in this room. She was with us. But we frightened her away. That means, she died; her soul left her body."

Meg hugged her daughter even tighter. "Honey, you don't know that. You're just upset. We all are."

Chloe ripped herself away from her mother's comforting grasp and flashed an angry gaze upon everyone else in the kitchen. I could read the rage on Chloe's face as she faced her elders. "**I hate all of you,** *especially you, uncle Craig! You're a monster."*

She grabbed her bags, and ran for the back door, out for her parent's car.

"A monster." Frank grinned to his older brother and shook his head. "She got that one right," he told Craig.

And me? All my being told me I wasn't dead; I couldn't be. But a real girl? Really, I was? And in a coma? God, I hoped I hadn't died. What I needed to do was go find my body and see about knitting me and it back together again.

If that was still even possible.

CHAPTER TWENTY-SIX -
What is real?

It was back: the low drone of an aircraft in flight, the slight sway of the floor beneath me, suggesting a plane aloft in the air, the ambiance of being surrounded by a pressurized cabin full of other souls, sitting or milling about, their lives in suspension until some point in the future when they could disembark and continue with their humdrum lives.

I opened my eyes and looked around me. *"Oh, shit,"* I thought. *"Not this **again**?*

As if awakening from a dream, around me was the Boeing 787 *Dreamliner* jet outbound for Europe, first stop allegedly Rome. I didn't buy it for a second.

Had what I'd just witnessed back last Christmas in my parents' house only been a dream?

*Bullshit. That was real; **this** wasn't. Why was I back here? I should be scouring Carbon County, Pennsylvania, in search of my unconscious body, what hospital or by this time what mental facility it was wasting away within.*

I must be dead, I thought, I can't tell what's real, what's now, when's now, and what's only a figment of my imagination.

This was one hell of a gorgeous plane. Boeing should be proud. I glanced around the interior and to all the people *allegedly* sharing this flight with Anita Thrombi and me. I had seen photos of this plane's interior on Bing and Google. Even what little I could see from where I sat told me these were high-tech, no-expense-spared accommodations.

Your Inner You was a real, online women's apparel company, that much I knew to be true. But this contest, that I had never heard of before, I seriously doubted it ever existed, or that I had ever won any such thing. I couldn't believe that a company like *Your Inner You* would allow Annie and me to fly in such a ritzy plane. It had to be super expensive. Surely, there were cheaper airlines and flights to Europe.

But here again I was, supposedly on my way to Rome, Italy, a contest winner, and right beside me in the aisle seat to my right was Annie Thrombi, her eyes closed as she leaned back in her seat. She suddenly sensed I was up; opened her eyes, glanced over at me and smiled affectionately.

"Well, I see you're awake," she observed of me. "You've been asleep for quite a while."

"A very long while I suspect," I answered, icily. "And I really wish I'd wake up now. I suspect it's been months."

"What are you talking about?" she frowned.

"*Am I*, Annie?" I coldly replied. "*Awake*, I mean? Why am I back here?"

"Why are you back…." Her words just sort of trailed off as confusion passed across her face."How did we meet, Annie?"

She creased her brow. "How… *You know*, at the agency. You were there to renew your policy, make a payment, and we just…"

"What?"

"I don't know," she repeated. "We clicked."

"Was I a boy or a girl?"

That same nosy rosy across the aisle from us looked over again. I exhaled in annoyance and leaned forward to confront him. "Look, *Bob*, is that your name?"

He nodded and then smiled.

"At this point, I don't even care about you, because frankly, I don't believe you're real. *Or any of this.* So, do me a favor, put on a pair of headphones, listen to a symphony, Bob Seeger, put on a movie, do something but stop listening, will you? It's rude."

"Keirie, what's the matter with you?" Annie asked me.

"I'm going to the restroom to check myself out."

She nodded, amiably. "All right."

I shook my head. "I'm not going there because I have to pee," I informed her. "But if I did, I'd need at this point to check what equipment I have on me. Do I do it standing up or sitting down?" I forcibly slipped around her into the aisle and sought out the nearest bathroom down the way. I glanced casually to all the passengers who were engrossed in their little worlds, glancing out the window ports to the ocean below, or watching the tiny monitors in the seat backs in front of them, or scanning their tablets and laptops. In other words, they were attending to their own affairs. It must have been the determined, somewhat miffed look on my face that led a few of them to glance at me as I passed on my way to the massive compartment's rear and the nearest bathroom.

"Hey, doll," I heard one teen kid say, looking up from his video game antics on his laptop, "Hi, what's your name?"

"Hi, yourself," I replied, "and never mind."

The bathrooms were occupied, naturally. It was a long flight across the Atlantic. *Oh, I'm good,* I thought. *Details, even the people look like real human beings, with real lives that are sending them across the Atlantic to the European continent.*

"Why am I doing this to myself?" I asked, lowly. "Why don't I just wake up now? I'm sick of pretending." I glanced to Annie far up the compartment. She was smiling back at me, as I leaned in my jeans and brown top and sneaks against the opposing wall to the bathroom stall I wished to enter, impatiently wishing whoever would finish his or her business in the stall and leave it so I could enter it.

"Excuse me, miss, are you okay?" a passing female flight attendant asked me as she read the perturbed look on my face.

I forced a smile onto my face. "Yeah," I said, amiably. And then in a near whisper. "I just *have to go.*"

The pretty blond flight attendant smiled back. "Well, I'm sure it won't be too much longer."

"Hope so," I grinned.

If I am having an 'out of body' experience, or if I'm already dead, and this is me between where I was and where I'm meant to be heading next, I got to admit this is a lot more exciting than working at Com-Link ever was.

I frowned to myself. *I did work there, didn't I? What did Mom say? I had a thing some guy and followed him to Penns Cove— got a job there while he and I.... Oh, fuck, I don't know. What is the real event, and what is just me compensating with this whole fantasy of being half guy with a dick and all just to not 'deal' with what Craig did to me? Am I a real girl or an almost one? And Oh my God.... Did Craig really do it? Did Dad not get there in time?*

I glanced down at myself.

*If none of this is real than **I'm** not actually here, either. So, pulling my pants down to have a look, might not prove anything at all.*

The *"occupied"* designation on the LED readout across from me on the john, changed to *"open."* A slightly paunchy man who looked in his early fifties and was dressed in a pair of Bermuda shorts and a vertically green striped white shirt and god-help him, sandals with black socks emerged from the tiny compartment and smiled at me. "Hi. You're a cute one, aren't you? Sorry, I took so long." He glanced behind him. "It's all yours." He slipped past me and returned to his seat up the way.

"He was flirting with you," said another young woman, about my age, who approached and looked as if she too needed to use one of the handful of restroom facilities in the plane.

I cringed. "He's a little too older, right?"

Guys always stare like that," she said. "It's the price we thin girls pay for being thin and cute, like you and me."

I grinned. "I'll just be a sec," I told her.

"It's okay. I can wait. I'm sure the person in the other one ought to be exiting soon as well, in case."

"Um hmmm," I nodded, as I entered the stall.

I shut and secured the door behind me, and immediately faced the cramped interior. If I was still male down there and had to pee, it would be an interesting affair to try to do so and get my aim at the little receptacle for that properly. "How in God's name," I asked myself aloud, "do *mile high members* pull off sex in here, two at a time? There's barely room for one."

I unfastened the belt buckle to my jeans, pulled down the zipper, and slowly eased the pants down off my lushly rounded feminine hips. That just left my navy-blue Jockey brand panties, and already even before pulling them down my porcelain smooth and white thighs, I knew the answer: *There was no bulge.* I looked like a female in a pair of panties, *not a pre-op transgendered male trying his best to pull off the same look.* But just to verify it, I grabbed the top elastic rim of the panties and delicately slid them down off my hips.

"Yep," I said, lowly, to myself. *"I'm a girl. It's gone."* I kneaded my finger around the edges of my slit and had no doubt that it was an authentic vagina.

"So, what does that prove?" I asked my reflection in the mirror. "Even if this flight across the Atlantic is only a delusion, this at least proves *that. None of this is real.* I'm not some wannabe girl a real woman named Anita Thrombi fell in love with because she liked boys who looked like girls. If this were a real flight across the Atlantic, then I'd still be sporting the same equipment down there I had when I got up this morning. And when was that? Is this April of 2018 or December 2017?" I shook my head, though.

Either way, I told myself, none of this is real."

I left the john and smiled to the young woman who was still waiting outside. "Okay," I said.

"That was quick," she said.

"It was, wasn't it?" I returned. "I'm Keira by the way."

"That's a pretty name," she said.

"Thanks."

"I'm Madelynn."

"Maddy?"

"To my friends," she nodded.

"Enjoying the plane ride?" I asked.

"Yeah," she answered, slipping hurriedly past me. "Sorry, but now I really got to get in there."

Before I even had a chance to wish her good luck, she shut the door behind her. I headed back for my seat beside Annie.

• • •

Annie was just looking at me, eyes wide, and so full of affection toward me. "Is everything all right?" she asked.

I smiled. "Yeah, it's great."

"Okay," she replied, leaning back in her seat. "These seats are really nice, aren't they?"

"I would hope they would be," I answered. "Ten hours in the air across the Atlantic to Rome, that could do a real job on one's behind after the first couple."

"Yeah," she agreed.

"Did I ask you this question already?"

"What, Keirie?"

"Are you really here? Are any of us?"

"Why are you back on that?"

"So, I *did* ask you that?"

228

"Hours ago, right before you said you needed a nap. Keirie, what's happening with you? Why are you acting like this, suddenly?"

"I'm a real girl, did you know that?" I cryptically answered.

"As I've always said since the beginning, a year ago, when we met—"

"At your *agency?*" I reiterated.

She nodded. "A year ago, this month.

"So, it is April."

"Keira, what is going on?"

"In the bathroom, just now. I'm real. You know?"

It was as if she were a character in a video game who had no answer to a question not in her programming. "What?"

I nodded. "Yeah. Real. A real vagina down there. And my memories of being a real woman had better return to me soon, because eventually I'll need them to help me know what to do when my next period arrives."

Her lips were slightly parted, as if she had no idea how to respond to a statement like that.

"I need my memories back," I said to her. "I suspect months have passed by now, and based on what I heard my family saying, or what they said, four months ago the day after Christmas, I never got over Craig fucking me in my rear end. And I think I know why he went in the back door like that." I nodded. "He left his condoms in the guest bedroom downstairs he and Carol were in Christmas Eve." I nodded even more assuredly. "His three boys were asleep in their bunk beds two floors up, awaiting Santa Claus's arrival, and as much of Dad's good stuff as that brother of mine was downing, I'd say he and Carol on Christmas Eve had one doozy of a fight. He stormed out of the bedroom, raided our dad's wine cellar and just nursed a bottle of Jack Daniels or whatever the hell it was while slowly getting soused in one of Mom's kitchen table chairs. Until I showed up the living room, in my cute little ..." I thought about it. I nodded. "I was already wearing that gift of yours, the one with the mitten pockets and cute knee-high booties. He just lost it, Craig. He didn't care if I was his sister, that didn't stop him seven years ago when he attacked Kelly." I shook my head again. "He did." I looked down at myself toward my female genitalia. "He started down there. I started to scream, and he ... turned me on my back, and said something like, *'Can't risk you getting pregnant on me, went through that headache with your sister. I better use the rear entrance."* I shook my head one last time.

"Annie, none of my ever being born a guy was ever *real*. None of *this* is real. How do I know that? Because if it was, I'd still have a little willy down there between my legs."

I glanced to all the other passengers aboard the plane. "Are they even real people? Let's see."

"What are you going to do?" fretted Annie.

"I'm going to ask them to get up and leave the plane."

"Are you nuts?" she queried. "You can't blurt out a thing like that. Security will tackle you so fast, you won't know what hit you."

"Not if this all is just a coma-induced hallucination."

I took a breath and opened my mouth to speak.

"Keira don't!" she pleaded. "Don't do that. You've come so far, don't involve them."

"But they're not real."

She wrinkled her lip. "Maybe there are, maybe they aren't."

"Okay," I considered. "Something else, then." I glanced to the endless expanse of the Atlantic Ocean far below our flight. "I'm sick of this endless water scene. Can I change it?"

"You?" she replied. "No."

"Can you?"

"To what?" she asked.

"You can, can you?" I smiled. "Change the scene below us to one I read about once that I thought was a real hoot."

I leaned over to her and whispered it in her ear. She laughed, silently. I turned then to glance once again out the window port.

Suddenly the scene below me changed to one of green land, a quiet English village and rolling hills. I smiled. "Holy shit," I whispered. "Un-fucking- believable. Annie, *look."* I invited her to look past me to the scene now passing us by far below.

She did and immediately began to laugh. "Yeah, that's *it* all right," she replied.

We were passing over a hillside, upon which in white chalk outlines a relief of a male warrior, or what was called a *geoglyph,* was etched in large strokes, intended to be seen from the air or from great distances away. He wielded a wooden club in his right hand, drawn for combat, and except for a few strap-like outlines upon his chest and torso the man was totally nude. He was known as the

Cerne Abbas Giant, aka the Rude Man of Cerne Abbas in Dorset, England, a very famous local tourist attraction.

Famous, for one very good reason: At some point, after its initial etching, according to historical sources I had read, someone altered the torso region and added a very large and erect male organ pointing upward, his testicles proudly displayed and everything.

Adults and children alike, visited the geoglyph just to stand atop the foreskin head of the warrior's very long penis. Local women in the area believed that standing upon the warrior's proudly erect sex organ enhanced their potency and ensured that the next time they and their men mated children might be successfully conceived.

I could feel Annie's breasts and shoulder pressing against my left arm and shoulder as she peered down at the image. *"You're a naughty little girl, aren't you?"* she pursued, humorously. "Of all the gorgeous sights in Europe you could request, you chose *this*?"

I turned my head to face her. She was smiling at me.

"You're not Anita Thrombi, are you?"

"No, I am not." She shook her head. "Congratulations, Keira Travaglini. You're finally getting over the trauma of what your brother did to you all those months ago. And yes, he really did it. Your father never reached you in time."

The tender empathic smile she gave me seemed almost ethereal. I just knew she was way more than the human being she pretended to be.

"I— I mean, *we*— are not really here, are we?" I faced back to the passengers sharing this flight with us. "Can you make them *all* disappear?"

"I can do better. This is *their* flight, Keira. We're just along for the ride. Most of them will never even remember us, that we were ever here."

"Even *him?*" I said of Bob across the aisle from us.

He glanced over and smiled at us. We were— after all— two-gorgeous, twenty-something, American females.

"Even him," she assured me. "I'll see to that."

"Who are you? Are you an *angel?*"

"Helping spirit," she answered

She glanced down at the Dorset countryside below us, and suddenly she and I were no longer aboard a plane bound for Italy. We were instead standing upon a hill overlooking the *Cerne Abbas Giant* geoglyph just up the way upon the next hillside.

CHAPTER TWENTY-SEVEN - Cerne Abbas in Dorset County, England

"My name is *Ariana,*" the woman pretending to be Annie Thrombi proclaimed as the two of us landed upon a valley overlooking the hillside of *The Rude Man of Cerne Abbas.*

There was a flash of light, and suddenly the female I once thought was Anita (Annie) Thrombi dissolved in a cloud of incandescent white. An energy mass hovered briefly in the air just off the ground, it billowed and sparkled as if charged with multi kilowatts of energy. It then gathered itself inward, imploding one might say, until it was no larger than a psychic's crystal ball. It slowly approached me.

My instinctive impulse was to recoil from it; I tried not to.

"Do not be frightened of me in this form," the orb then asked, not in words but as thoughts in my head. *"I am an immortal, a being of pure sentient energy. I am ageless; I travel through time as easily as you pass from one room in your home to another."*

The orb then expanded once again and proceeded to re-coalesce into the form of yet another Earth female, one presenting in a flowing and white evening gown, with a long train that billowed like a sail in the wind. I was speechless in the presence of such ethereal beauty. Ariana was truly heavenly, and it radiated off her like eternity itself.

"Does this form please you?"

"Yes," I replied, in near a whisper. "Very much. You're beautiful. I have only one question."

"What is it?"

"Can others see us?"

"At present only you."

"But how can I be here?" I queried. "My body is somewhere back in the States, unconscious, I would imagine."

"They perceive your presence even though it is not genuine. You seem to be here. For them that is all they require. Let us go," she said as she smiled.

"Where?"

"She faced round to the glyph on the distant hillside. "There," she said. "you wish, if only for the whimsy of it, to do as others and stand upon his enormous male appendage."

"Is doing that silly, Ariana?" I queried of standing upon the stretch of ground the glyph figure's groin encompassed.

"No sillier than other such silly things," she cryptically answered. "There *is helpful* energy emanating from this site. That is why this site was chosen. Its creators thought only to cast their whimsy upon this hill. They did not realize the gift they were bestowing upon others. Here, was where it needed to be drawn to draw others. Any positive energy added to what you possess on your own should be welcomed for the gift that it is."

She extended her ethereal hand for me to take, and there was no sense of her only being a manifestation only; she seemed as real as me.

"Come," Ariana requested of me, "let us advance forward. I so rarely get to do this."

"You've spent a year in my company, have you not?" I inquired. "Pretending to be *Annie?*" I creased my brow. "Why Anita Thrombi, by the way. *Why her?* I've only seen her maybe once or twice each year to renew my insurance, when I'm too lazy to mail the payment to the parent company. *Why her?*"

"Why not her? Assuming an earthly guise— as this Anita— worked well into the cure scenario I wove around your unconscious mind to help rid you of any remaining trauma left behind by your brother's uninvited advances.... And no, Keira, it did not take a year," she told me, then. "It only seemed a year to your mind. It has only been a few months, since that awful Christmas Eve." She shook her head. "With all the good cheer and positive emotion that arises that one day each year, leave it to a troubled soul like your sibling brother to mar it in such a way. But, you'll see, bad deeds have a way of coming back around, eventually, and nipping the offender in his own behind. He will suffer consequences."

I crinkled my nose. "Was I really such a baby about getting plowed up my rear end, like that? It wasn't the first time, you know? I smiled. "I have been around … *a little.*"

She laughed, amiably, and nodded. "It was your brother, Craig, and you were rightfully outraged. That was not a gratuitous exchange, Keira. *He attacked you.*" She smiled then, wistfully. "Your memory of yourself as Keira is returning."

I nodded. "I can feel it doing so," I replied. "Ariana, did I ever press charges against Craig?" She indicated no. "You've not regained consciousness since that night."

I sighed, forlornly. "I thought so, I knew it," I replied. "I'm locked away somewhere in a mental institution. I can almost sense it, my body there," I said. "Just lying there, and me, the essence of my very identity, gone from it, as if my body were only an empty vessel." I glanced up to this lovely apparition of a human form. "Because you were there to weave a different reality for me, one that allowed me to relive that night Craig did that to me, and this time, alter what happened just enough that I wouldn't get so upset over it. And all my family were gathered around me, and gave me support, were there to help me just get over it. But it wasn't real, was it? Any of it? All those months?"

"It was as real for you as it needed to be. What is real, when you really stop to think about it?"

I grinned over that one. A person could go crazy just pondering that even a little, such an innocent question.

"You will soon awaken from your state of spiritual retreat," she then informed me, and all will be fine. If I may so in advance, Keira Travaglini, you are very welcome."

"I owe you more than you could ever know," I replied.

She mimicked a human shrug. "It's what I do."

· · ·

On the dirt trail, up to the hill where the Cerne Abbas Giant reposed, and surrounded by lush wild-growing vegetation, a sign and wire fence suddenly attempted to prevent our further advance:

Due to Severe Erosion
of the hillside, visitors are
asked to not advance beyond this fence.
The best view of the Giant is from

The LAY-BY on the northern
End of the village.

"According to that," I told Ariana, "this is as far as we can go."

She laughed. "We're not really here, not like everyone else."

"But they'll see me," I replied.

She touched the middle of my turtleneck. "Now they won't," she said.

At the top, finally, and not even a little winded, I paused to take in the village that was Cerne Abbas and the green and rolling fields that surrounded it. At my feet, just down the way from where I stood, was the massive phallic image of the warrior glyph. I contemplated the thought of how this thing looked from overhead, and here at the hill's top only meters from the relief of the warrior's massive penis. I had only to walk just a few steps more down the hill to reach his foreskin tip.

"Have at it," smiled Ariana.

"This feels so stupid," I said. "Nothing will actually happen."

"You'll feel different about yourself, if only because you will *desire* it to be true of yourself from this day on."

I went the last few steps and stood upon the very tip of this monstrous penis. I stood tall and straight upon it, imagining I could feel positive chakra energy welling up from the ground and recharging my soul. I closed my eyes and felt the wondrous blue sky and gorgeous sunlight upon my face, and heard the new season of spring filling the air all around me. I raised a single eyelid only slightly to catch Ariana watching and waiting, and I grinned over at her. "I am really accomplishing *anything*?"

"Absolutely," she replied. "Your chakra points along your astral body are drinking in the energy. You won't believe how much more alive you look as a result."

"Am I done?"

"You'll know when you are."

I glanced to the hill's bottom, and to the sight of several tourists, slowly ascending the hill to do what Ariana and I were up here doing, and I thought, *I guess they missed the warnings to stay off the hill. Or ignored them. Which was probably more likely.*

I did not want their intrusion at this point, even if they had no knowledge of my presence up here. I stepped off the grassy mound embossed by the rounded chalk outlines, and joined Ariana at the base of the phallic glyph. This glyph warrior had two very rounded and healthy-looking testicles flaking either side of the rising shaft.

"We're done," I declared, smiling to Ariana.

"Then, we shall go now."

"Back to where my body lies unconscious somewhere in Pennsylvania?"

"Yes. You do not wish it to remain in that state, indefinitely, do you?"

"No, but I know that when I awaken you will leave me after, won't you?" I replied. "Ariana, I have no idea if the real Annie Thrombi is as nice and as fun to be around as you, but I'll miss you in my life."

"And I'll miss you, but you no longer have need of me, and I have others who also require my assistance."

"Can't we spend a little while longer out here in *Dorset?*" I asked. "I mean, you were prepared to spend two more weeks with me touring Europe. I've read and seen pictures of Dorset, England on the internet. The coastline is especially pretty. *Can we?* I mean, have a little fun sightseeing? You're entitled to time off occasionally, aren't you?"

She smiled very broadly. "But after, we must see to knitting your spirit back together with that earthly vessel you get around with in this universe."

I agreed to that.

The other hill climbers below us were by this point almost upon us. They never saw us, and never even knew when we left.

• • •

Surrounding by an endless blue sea, an orange-brown protrusion of land crept away from the long shoreline below us, jutted out a hundred feet or so into the English Channel and ended in an arch, like an upside-down horseshoe.

"Oh, my God, that's awesome," I exclaimed.

"It is called *Durdle Door,*" Ariana said. *"I thought you might enjoy it."*

I envy you, I told her in my mind. *You can go anyplace at will, and anywhere in TIME; physical impediments mean nothing to you.*

She smiled and faced me. *"I was as you, once, as I have already said,"* she spoke to me aloud. "I went by many names: *Angelica,*

Lori, Danielle … even *Daniel*." She grinned at that last one. "Don't despair, little one; your time will come."

CHAPTER TWENTY-EIGHT - The Road Back

In the dead of night, in the cover of darkness, from high overhead Ariana and I approached a hospital only partially known to me to reside in nearby Lehighton, Pa. just south of *Jim Thorpe* about five miles. We were drifting among the clouds like two *lost boys* in the Peter Pan story, Ariana's flowing white gown fluttering and billowing behind her like a super hero's cape, me apparently once more in the lounge wear outfit with the cute red and brown jumper and matching knee-high booties whose pockets were in the shape of mittens.

Ariana smiled over at me, our extended left and right hands, knitted in each other's. "Do you like the outfit I gave you for Christmas? It looks cute on you," she said of the wine-colored garment with brown accents. She looked so very much like a spectral manifestation, adrift among the clouds, one adrift in the night, I could almost imagine her out here, seeking new souls to haunt and terrify.

"This wasn't a gift from you, was it?" I replied, not in words but with my thoughts. "Not in the conscious world where I've been a girl all my life." I added.

"True, but I still think it looks good on you."

Though neither of us spoke a word out loud, I could hear Ariana's side of the conversation in my mind, and she by her replies suggested she received mine as well. I clearly heard her now tell me that my body resided there below us in that Lehighton district hospital. We descended, skirting the largely by this hour deserted parking lots, and finding entry through a side door that looked as if it were only a metal outline painted gray, with no door knob or any other exterior apparent means to open it. We didn't need to open it;

238

we simply slipped through it and were at once inside, in a narrow and dully lit corridor that tracked backward a way until angling off to the left and into the bowels of this very large and multi-leveled facility

Wards and departments, nursing stations and wings, up one floor and to the next, we passed through floors and ceilings as if they were only images of floors and ceilings, were not real at all; we slipped through them with no hint of hindrance or effort. And in a wing clearly advertised as existing for the care and treatment of the mentally disabled, we turned for it and threaded down the corridor of this special wing until passing a klatch of females pausing in their continuous rounds to chat quietly among themselves. They were doing so in tones so low and hushed one might imagine that this was not a place filled with living humans at all, but of those who had recently passed on: a *morgue*. The lighting was dark, the air filled with the solemnity one might imagine it possessing at hours far past midnight. And moving now as *(unseen by them)* apparitions that floated mere inches off the ground, as opposed to merely walking, we moved down past their station as one might expect lost, newly deceased souls might aimlessly do as they haunted the facility where they had met their end. We went unseen, although I suspect at one point an attending nurse looked up as we passed and frowned as she mentally sniffed the air around her, as if something about it was not right. Even a chill, seemed to come to her person, as she grabbed her arms and shivered, frowning as she did as if to question why.

"Helen, what's wrong?" came a co-worker in attendance.

She shook her arms, almost imperceptibly, and then followed that with a shake of her head. "Weird," she said. "I suddenly felt a chill, like something just walked past us."

"Maybe it did," came another. "This wouldn't be the first haunted hospital. Psychics, I've read, hate visiting hospitals for all the deceased spirts still roaming the corridors."

"Oh, good, that's what I need to be thinking now at this dead hour of the night," said the one called Hellen, as the others smiled and chuckled. To my mind their banter was the proverbial hospital equivalent of *whistling past the graveyard.*

I glanced casually at Ariana and she just nodded, equally amused by the women's conversations.

We proceeded on into the wing where even I at this point sensed my physical body reposed somewhere up ahead. We came to it, at last, and then slipped through the door, again as if it were only an imagined barrier and not one to be reckoned with.

It was a mostly spartan appointed room, no frills, I mean. A low hospital bed, a few cards and a flower or two adorned the window ledge just atop the room's heating, cooling unit; a solitary adjustable height serving table, seen in a thousand rooms in as many hospitals, lay sideways against the bed, pushed out of the way for now.

There I was, beneath a single white blanket. Apparently, I was being kept nourished and hydrated, but not at present, for there were no signs of any intravenous tubes running into my arm; nor were there heart monitors attached to a readout monitor, checking my body functions from electrodes attached to my physical body.

I faced Ariana. "Are they doing *nothing* for me?" I asked.

"Your body is being kept alive, that is all they can do."

"I hate IV's," I said. And glancing to two containers currently sitting together atop a metal nightstand behind the bed, a pee pot and bed pan, I wrinkled my nose and announced, "And I absolutely detest those things."

"Are you ready?" Ariana only answered.

"Do I just step into the thing?"

She smiled and nodded. "It couldn't be easier."

I glanced once at my lifeless form on the bed and then at Ariana. "This is goodbye, isn't it?"

She nodded. "It is time. I have finished what I came to do in your behalf. I should tell you, however, there is one change you will henceforth notice about your life within that vessel."

"What?"

"You have not been imprisoned within it, as are most alive on this world. You have roamed free for what has seemed an endless time."

"A year," I nodded. "To me it was last April. That's when Annie and I... *I mean, you and I...* first met."

"Those I have visited as I have you, never feel wholly stuck ever again in their bodies."

"You mean, I can leave whenever I want, go wherever I want?"

"As your skill in doing so improves, the further from your body can you travel."

"Well, that's something, isn't it?"

She smiled, sadly. "Take care, Keira."

"Wait," I begged. "Will I ever see you out there? Will you promise me I might meet up with you again?"

"I won't rule out that possibility," she answered. "But concentrate for now in getting your earthly lifetime back on track. Oh, and I have a message for your sister, Kelly."

I frowned, "Kelly?"

She nodded. "Tell her to tell Amelia, Angelica Matchelli says hello."

"Angelica?" I asked.

Ariana smiled, weakly. "Amelia will know the name."

I nodded, and slowly climbed onto the bed; I settled back onto my body. I let the knitting of my astral and corporeal body take hold. I can't rightly say when and how the transition occurred, how much time elapsed, but when I opened my eyes, it was in fact my physical body's eyes; I tried very awkwardly to acclimate myself once more to the limitations of mobility that came with being an organic living being. I slowly rose to a sitting position, glancing around the room in the dreadful darkness, a darkness soothed only by the distant streetlights out beyond the hospital grounds in Lehighton, Pennsylvania. Slowly, I adjusted to my human eyes and their night vision capacities. The room was empty, save for me.

Ariana was gone.

Still getting used to the muscles and ligaments of my legs and arms, I searched the room for a way to turn on the lights. Behind the bed was a long horizontal light fixture with a long florescent tube and a long white cord that just hung off its right side. I reached back for and pulled on the cord. The light unit flickered on, and that dreadful florescent white color, inherently lacking in wavelengths of red light, filled the room, casting the room's scant furnishings in drab red drained colors. Speaking of drab, I caught the sight of me in a drab blue hospital gown peppered with gray rectangles here and there, tied in the back of course, hanging so loosely upon my body I always wondered why these things were supposed to be considered normal hospital bed wear. But it permitted me to easily pull the hem of it up to reveal—

"*Yuck,*" I spoke aloud, aware of how scratchy and course my voice sounded. I probably hadn't spoken aloud to anyone in months. A capped off tube led into my stomach, protruding from just above my belly button; it likened itself to me to an outdoor water faucet attached to the side of a house. *My feeding tube,* I realized. "What

241

did you expect, Keira?" I whispered to myself. "That better not leave a scar when they take it out."

Beneath it, a pair of *Depends* possessed my middle like I was a damn infant or something. It obviously was a fresh one, not yet soiled in any way. Apparently, it had been changed and me cleaned up like a newborn, one not yet potty trained, not too long before.

"How many months have they had to do this for me?" I wondered aloud. "*Ick.*"

I slipped the Depends down and off me, tossing them out into the room. With them gone, and me totally naked down there, I could now easily ascertain that I was in fact a girl. There were no undesired protrusions *(meaning: male genitalia)* creating a nauseating nuisance to my person present between my legs. I scanned the room for signs of a closet, and saw it way by the door. I grabbed my legs and helped them slide off the bed and onto the floor, steadying myself upon the floor after so long not using the muscles and ligaments within them to walk on my own. I noticed at that moment on my left wrist a capped off IV needle stuck in my skin, probably for the next time I needed to be re-nourished and rehydrated. I wished I could just pull the damn thing out, but I had no doubt very soon that would be accomplished by a qualified member of this staff.

I needed to pee, and this tiny room did in fact have a small bathroom just off to the right. I went for the closet first and opened it, revealing the red and brown jumper with the pair of mitten styled pockets on a hanger, the matching booties were on the floor of the thing, and on the shelf above it, underwear, a single purple pair of panties and a matching bra. I grabbed the two of them and headed for the restroom, did my business, for the first time in months obviously like an adult female, and aware as I did so that I could never remember a time when I would ever have conceived peeing standing up like a guy.

Finishing off with those earthly ablutions, I rinsed off my hands in the sink and glanced to my hair, which looked as if I seriously needed to attend to it, big time. It was all over the place, suggesting for time unknown I could not care a lick about it. Everything about me said *female,* even the cute, narrow contour of my feet and toes. Not that in that pretend world of Ariana's, as Keir, I ever had to suffer the look of a male with oversized feet. I must have spent a good ten minutes just reacquainting myself with the silky smoothness of my skin everywhere upon my person, and the pretty and slim shape of my arms and forearms. I almost felt like I had never been human before, and was still struck by the incredible wonder and novelty of being thus.

Eventually, I returned to the room, and looked about the place. I said it was spartan. Aside from the red and brown jumper outfit with the mitten pockets and knee-high booties I now insisted on wearing in the stead of that stupid hospital "gown," the room was not meant to be inhabited by someone either in their right mind or even conscious.

I found no way to call out, no phone; my purse and smartphone were nowhere, and as I expected, this being the mental patient wing, the exit door was locked from the other side, trapping me inside. And I desperately wanted to let someone know that I was back now among the living, and in the real world. But how was I to do that?

I *could* wait till morning and make a case for my being well enough to kiss off this prison of a place. My Mom had probably been the one who had signed me in as a resident, I imagined. I needed to get a message to her that I was fine, wanted out, the sooner the better. I did not want the shrinks in this establishment insisting I tell them of my hallucinations about being Keir and living with and in love with a perfect stranger, named Anita Thrombi. They would say I manufactured that entire scenario to replace the true events of my life which I did not want to accept happened: *what Craig did to me,* and that maybe I should remain here or another such competent facility that could help me work through my having needed to invent such a tragic substitute lifetime as that of *Keir Travaglini,* a transgendered person, and his love affair with a totally imagined version of a woman he barely even knew. If I could prove to them that I no longer believed, seriously, that any of it had happened, maybe then they *might* contact my mother, and suggest that then and only then might I be able to function once more in the real world.

Fuck all that, I thought. *Think, Keira, think.*

I could try banging on the door to summon a nurse, but that might only result in my being given a sedative to calm me down and whatever other drugs this establishment might be using on me to try and get me back to the world of the living.

And then I wondered....

I faced the bed again, approached it and laid back down, face up upon it. I closed my eyes and imagined I could leave this body, just as Ariana had said, as easily as removing a wet suit or a spacesuit. I

243

concentrated and thought I could feel myself slip right up and out. When I told myself to look where I might be, I saw only the ceiling tiles. They were only inches from my eyes. I was hovering up near the ceiling. I flipped myself around and had to laugh. No sooner had I reunited with that pretty human body of mine that I had once again departed it. My body looked as vacated as before. I floated myself down to it and landed on the side of the bed beside it, contemplating it, awed by the fact that that was me in this lifetime.

Okay, I thought. *Now to leave this room.* And the quickest way to do that was to go straight out that window. *What floor was this?*

I peered forward past the HVAC unit and determined, based on how far down the parking lot pavement appeared to be, that I must be at least on the fifth floor, if this place even had as many floors as that. I was really that high up off the ground level. I felt a thought come to me. *Oh, you got to kidding? That's a long way down.*

But I glanced again to my vacated body on the bed, and for a second felt bad. It was cruel to leave it behind, stuck here in this locked room. But I needed to contact the outside world, and I wasn't about to trust this staff to make a timely call to my loved ones that I had awakened and wanted out. No, I needed to contact someone, someone who could see me and know that I was really present in their midst, not a dream figure he or she was having.

I smiled. I knew who that would be. Allentown, Pa. was a good thirty miles south of here, I was sure. My first astral projection solo. *Oh, boy.* I faced back to my body on the bed, and said to it, *"I'll be back."* I then steeled my courage to suspend myself so many feet above the ground beyond the hospital building and shoved myself right out the window, into the starry night.

Chloe, I thought. *You saw me once before. Only you, when no one else could. Let's hope that wasn't just a fluke.*

Allentown, Pa. and the residence of Frank and Megan Travaglini. I knew the way.

CHAPTER TWENTY-NINE - Getting Back on Track

Traveling by air when you were your own aircraft, and the countryside below looking like so much great open land, it was like sailing over the landscape in a hand glider and wondering where in fact you were just in case a downdraft took you out of the sky abruptly. There were a few reliable constants such as familiar highways and interstates and the Lehigh River snaking down through Lehighton and through Allentown. Where I needed to go was a residential area called Westwood Heights in East Allentown. And aside from following a natural landmark like the Lehigh River all the way from Lehighton to Allentown, I might find it far more beneficial to track onto the Pennsylvania Turnpike, Route 476, hug the roadway from an appreciable height and keep coming down to street level to occasionally read the road signs to help me navigate, until I reached where I wanted to be.

The residence of
Frank and Sarah Travaglini.

The dawn was not too far away when I finally ended my flight. I just went through the front door, in search of Chloe's bedroom. I knew at this hour she would not be up and preparing for yet another boring day at the nearby Catholic middle school. I spotted a calendar in Frank's study. It was not yet April at all in this the real world, but as yet only March of 2018, and just after six in the AM. Chloe would soon be up to prepare for school, and her parents would be leaving as well to start the day at their shop in town.

Chloe lay soundly asleep in her bedroom. It was a pretty powder blue room, with a Queen size bed, very roomy for such a young girl, an ornate headboard and footboard of oak with large rounded newel posts at all four corners and a chocolate brown bedspread. There was a stuffed animal toy giraffe sitting proudly atop her high chest of drawers and several varieties of toy cats on the floor. And Teiger, the Blue Persian male kitty her father and Mom had bought for her two years before, curled up in a furry ball right near her chest and face, her long hair draping the kitty very delicately.

I approached the two of them. Teiger recognized me; cats know when they are in the presence of cat lovers, and even in this state, he was not averse to my presence. I suspect that as a cat he was used to otherworldly manifestations from time to time invading the peace of his homestead. As with any feline, suddenly staring intently off to a corner of the room as they were often wont to do— where to the naked eye there appeared to be nothing— an intuitive person was left to sense that maybe her kitty cat had zeroed in on something not seeable by humans, but clearly there and alarming one's kitty.

"Hey, Teiger," I called to him.

He started to purr. Chloe, near awake by this hour, smiled at the sound of his purring and ran her hand against his blue fur. "Hi, hon," she said to him. "Is it morning yet?"

"Chloe," I called lowly. "Chloe? You saw and heard me once, last Christmas, please hear and see me now? I need to tell you— and through you everyone else— that I'm fine, okay. Chloe?"

"Aunt Keira?" Chloe queried. "You're here? You're still in the hospital, aren't you?"

She opened her eyes, and almost jumped out of her skin.

"Oh, dear God!" she wailed. *"Aunt Keira?"*

Glancing down at myself, I saw that like ghostly female spirits depicted in your typical ghost movie, I profiled as draped in a flowing white gown, like something I might wear one day were I to ever get married. Why would I manifest myself in this gown? It was so cliché. I suppose because it felt appropriate.

You must admit though: this astral out of body stuff was fun, right?

"It's me, Chloe. I'm here; *don't cry out!* You'll alarm your parents."

"I insisted I saw you Christmas day to Mom, Dad, Grandma Sarah. They didn't believe me."

"What about your Uncle Craig or your grand pop, Alvin?"

"They both thought I was nuts," she replied. "Am I really seeing you? Are you dead?"

I giggled. "No. Chloe, I'm back from my long sleep. A beautiful helping spirit helped me recover from what Uncle Craig did to me. I'm okay now. She made me all better. Chloe, I'm ready to leave that hospital. I could go back right now and re-enter my human body, but it's trapped inside that locked room, and even though I'm only now aware that I've been there for …" *(I took a mental note of Frank's office calendar)* "...three months!* I hate that place. Chloe, I need you to tell your Mom to call my Mom and beg her to sign me out of there. She has the authority, I believe. Can you help me?"

Chloe, in her tan pajama top and bottoms, gave her cat a pet and worked her way around his refusal to move out of the way, eventually sliding off the bed mattress and onto the floor to approach me. She reached out her hand to touch my ethereal presence.

"You're like a ghost," she observed. ""You look like *Josette du Pres* when she appeared to *Victoria Winters* in that *Dark Shadows* movie I saw a few years ago."

I smiled. "But I'm not dead. I'm just *out of my body.*"

"Can you teach *me* how to do that?" she asked.

I shrugged. "I'm not even sure I know how I *know how* I know how to do it. But, yeah, I'll give it a shot. I assume Mom had me committed to the psych ward at Lehighton General, when it became obvious, I supposed, that I had slipped into some sort of coma or fugue state. Chloe, until I spoke with you Christmas morning, I didn't know I was born a real girl."

"Aunt Keira," she began, hesitantly, "I told my mom what you said, that you said you were only an *almost girl.* What did that mean?"

I explained to Chloe how *Ariana* had weaved around me an entire fantasy reality in my mind, or maybe it might even have been an alternate reality timeline.

"Like in that Star Trek movie, when Mr. Spock changed everything by going back in time?"

I smiled again. "Could be like that, I don't know. It felt real to me. To help me heal, Chloe; Ariana created around me a fantasy that I was born not quite all the way female, but only mostly."

She furrowed her brow. "You mean you were half boy?"

I shook my head. "In that false scenario I was stuck in, I was born with a man's biological…"

"Oh, dear God," she stopped me short. "I would hate that if I were born with one of those. You're so beautiful, Aunt Keira. Were you as pretty— as a ..."

"As a boy?" I finished. "You would never believe I had been born with a male part, a guy's—"

"Please don't say it," she begged. "I hate those things."

I started to laugh. "You're still not quite a woman," I said. "You might feel differently about *those things* in another year or two."

She cringed. "They scare me. They're so ... *rude*. Why do guys like to do that with us girls? Get their fluid all over our faces and down there, so that we could make a baby, even if we aren't ready?"

"So, you know all about that?"

"Of course, I do. I'm almost thirteen. My friends and I like exploring the internet. The sites say only come here if you're older than eighteen, but all you have to do is say *yes, you are,* and—"

I drew my hand up to stop her. "I get it," I said. "Do your parents know you visit those ... they're porn sites, mostly, Chloe."

"I know," she answered. "But it's both fascinating and *gross* what grownups like doing."

I laughed even more. "I wish I was here in the flesh; I'd love to hug you right now."

"You're my favorite aunt, Aunt Keira."

"I'm also your baptism *godmother."*

"Oh, yeah," she thought, beaming. *"I have a fairy godmother."*

I glanced down at my ethereal presence. "I'm *not* a fairy, Chloe. And I'm not a ghost, either."

"But I doubt even one of *my* friends," Chloe replied, "have an aunt who can appear to her like you can."

I grunted a humph. "Fat good it does me. I can't even extricate myself from a locked door."

"Aunt Keira, are you all better now?"

"Yes," I said. "I'm ready to blow that mother fuc— that place."

"It's not so bad there. It's actually a pretty nice place," Chloe said.

"It probably is," I agreed. "I wouldn't know. I haven't actually been there in spirit."

"You mean, you've been like now, out of your body?"

I shrugged. "Or something for all intent and purposes like that."

"Chloe!" came a voice suddenly, and the sound of footsteps coming up the hall. "Honey, who are you talking to?"

(Chloe's Mom, Megan.)

"I better go," I said.

"No, not yet. Wait."

"Chloe?" came the sound again of Megan, as she opened the door. "Chlo…"

My sister in law stared directly at me. *"Holy mother of God!"* she spoke, making a quick sign of the cross against her chest.

"You can see me too now?" I asked my sister in law.

"Keira?"

"I'm not dead, but I'm back, in my right mind, I mean. I'm over what Craig did to me. I'm fine. And this is something I'm just now able to do, because of it all. Will you tell Mom to get me the—"

I grinned, sheepishly. "I was going to use the F-word. Sorry. Tell Sarah to sign me out of that place, like *today,* if she can?"

"Are you even alive?" she returned.

"Yes, *now,* please, Meg? *Tell Sarah?* Tell her, *I'm fine, and I'm ready to come home."* I paused. "I have to leave now, I think. This is my first time traveling out of my body like this on my own, and I think I'm getting tired without Ariana's energy assists to help me stay out here. I've got to go. Please, sis, get me out of that place. *Today, if possible!"*

Megan Travaglini, like her daughter had, approached me, and waved her hand through my ethereal presence. "I'm not sure I'm really awake and seeing this. This can't be real."

"It **is,** Mom," said Chloe. "I told you I saw her last Christmas."

"Yes, you did do that, baby," Meg told her daughter.

"To you two," I informed them, "that happened months ago. To me, it only happened yesterday. Time is relative and even meaningless in this state, if you stay out here long enough. I'm going to re-enter my body, but I don't want those people giving me stuff to make me stupid or unresponsive, or whatever. I just want out of there. Okay?"

"She's really here," nodded Meg to Chloe, disbelieving the words even as she spoke them. "My sister in law. And I can actually *see her."*

"Mom?" Chloe begged with her cute wide brown eyes.

"I'll call Sarah this morning." Meg shook her head. "She'll never believe this."

"You both see me," I answered. "Do you honestly believe you *both* are simply dreaming this?"

"No, we both can't be, can we?"

"Today?" I asked again for the— I lost count how many times.

"Your Mom and I will be there this morning to see you in the flesh for ourselves."

"I'm coming too!" insisted Chloe.

"You have school."

"I'll miss a day," insisted my niece. "My aunt needs me. *She chose me.* I'm coming too."

"Okay," I replied. "I'll be expecting you all, then."

And I promptly vanished from amid them.

· · ·

Not too long after that, one of the nurses was doing her rounds, and looking through the small window in my room's exit door. She couldn't believe the sight of me, not only up but over by the window and gazing out at the dawn. She opened the door and came in.

I faced back at her. "Hi," I said, "good morning. I'm Keira."

"Oh, my God, *you're up*," she said. "And *talking*."

I laughed. I held up my wrist with the IV needle still stuck in it. "Can you get this damn annoying thing off me? I don't need it. I'm fine."

"Do you know my name?" she asked.

I shook my head. "No, I can't lie about that. I'm still trying to process being stuck in this place behind a locked door for the last three months."

"You're aware of the passage of time?"

"I know it's March now."

"My name is Sandra," the nurse told me. "And in those times when I spoke with you, when it looked like you might be coming back to us, you kept insisting you were a male named Keir."

"What do you want me to say about that?" I replied. "So, I wasn't completely catatonic all the time?"

"Most of the time," she answered. "You mean, you just decided to come back to us, to wake up?"

I nodded. "Yes. And I could use a decent meal, if you would be so kind." I glanced down at my stomach. *"Could you also get this sickening thing out of me?"*

"That's your feeding tube."

I nodded. "I know."

"It's been keeping you alive for the last three months."

"Well, I'm awake now. I'd like it gone, please. *And this with it.*" I pointed again to the IV in my wrist.

"I'll need your doctor's authorization to remove them," she answered.

Of course, you do, I thought. "I don't need them anymore," I informed her. "I'm back."

She nodded her head in agreement, and left a few minutes later, promising to get the current physician on my team, presently on staff, to come visit me asap. The entire staff, she predicted, would be shocked beyond belief to hear the news of my sudden awaking.

CHAPTER THIRTY - I Am Out of There

The current physician on staff showed up during the day, showing up more out of curiosity than anything else. He had been told I was alert and in full possession of my faculties; he came because he wanted to make an on-sight verification for himself. There were people peering into my locked door for the next several hours, awed over how animated and alert I now was as I sat atop the bed, my mind seemingly lost in thought.

I was promised the feeding tube would be removed promptly and I could go back on solid food this very night; it would be my first taste of solid food in three months. My doctor, a Kevin Lavender, MD, doctor of Psychiatry, promised he would get right on it. With his approval, a nurse entered and removed both the IV from my wrist and the feeding tube. I was happy to say goodbye to both. When I asked why I couldn't perhaps be allowed to leave the room and dine with the other troubled souls who were just sane enough to not need to be confined to a bedroom, Kevin Lavender said he would see to that being ordered done as well.

When I inquired why he was being so cooperative with all my requests he told me about the other shocking thing that had occurred during the day and morning. My Mom, seemingly out of the blue, had called to check on my condition and to inform the staff that she and two guests were coming to the hospital to see me.

• • •

"It's peculiar that you should call on today of all days," Keven Lavender had said to my mom, she told me later.

"Why is that, Dr. Keven?" she had asked him.

252

"Ordinarily, I'd tell you there was no change, that your daughter remained in what appeared to be a semi-comatose state, and that all you might do is just sit beside her, keep up the hand holding and stimulation efforts, talking to her, singing the songs you know she'd recognize, mention the news you would discuss with her, anything to try to bring her back to the waking world.

"Mrs. Travaglini, your daughter has made a miraculous recovery. She's suddenly alert and talking, demanding solid food, I'm told, and to be let out of that room."

"That's wonderful," my Mom said she told the man. "How soon can she come home?"

"Well, I want to examine her first, to see for myself just how really well she suddenly is now. And then I think the next thing would be to make sure she hasn't suffered any motor control loss from the weeks she's been unconscious. Therapy to get her limbs limbered up again, improve her agility at walking and getting around. That sort of thing."

"Dr. Kevin, if my baby has finally awakened, that means she's gotten over what my rotten son did to her. I'd like her home with me, she can recover just fine under my care."

"And that may very well be just the thing for her, but let's give it a day at least to see how she's coming along. I should have a talk with her to see what her general disposition is."

"Will you at least release her from confinement in that room? She's not a criminal in solitary, I mean."

"Well, that was never really the case," he defended. "Every day, though she remained in a catatonic trance, for whatever reason, a staff member got her out of her bed, dressed in the lounge wear you got for her, and wheeled her out to the common room, to hear the sounds of hospital staff and other patients milling about all around her, external stimuli it was hoped might encourage her to *wake up.*"

"I *know* all this," Sarah claimed she had insisted to Lavender with impatience. *"And now?"*

"The initial reports I've been given suggest she's doing pretty well. If true, I see no reason *not* to rescind the confinement protocols."

"So, it will be taken care of before we come round?"

"Of course. When do you think that will be?"

"You're right down the road from *Jim Thorpe,"* Sarah said. "I can be there in the next half hour, myself, if I need be. My daughter

253

in law and my grandchild want to meet up with me. They're coming up from Allentown. That will take them at least an hour. We' should be there within the next two hours. Figure on three of us."

"Are you sure that many isn't a bit much so soon?" he asked.

"I'm sure. My niece wants to see her aunt Keira. She's been upset about her situation ever since last Christmas."

"And what's the status of your son and your husband, if I may ask?" he inquired.

"Neither are any longer in the picture," Sarah Travaglini coldly informed Kevin Lavender. "In fact, my son is in jail. And his father is facing possible jail time soon as well. Meanwhile, he's found himself a small condo a couple towns away. I threw him out."

"That's bad for them," said Lavender, "but probably good for your daughter's recovery, neither being around to remind her of the incident last Christmas."

"Yes, and good riddance to both," Sarah spat.

"Okay, I'll release her from confinement status. The exercise just moving about the halls and terraces of the facility might actually do her muscles good."

"Work on the release papers as well," my Mom told him. "I want my daughter out of there, if she's doing that well, by week's end at the latest."

"If all goes as it seems to, I think that will be entirely possible and likely."

"Goodbye," my Mom had said to him and hung up.

• • •

Kevin Lavender smiled as he finished relating to me his version of his conversation with my Mom. "So," he concluded. "Let's get you out of here and ready to meet your family."

"Let's," I replied.

"Are you still troubled by what happened last Christmas? Do you want to talk about it?"

I shrugged. "No. I'm pretty much over it. I hope though for Craig's sake, I never meet that brother of mine ever again. I'm tempted to go online, purchase a dildo, and see how he likes it."

Lavender laughed. "Okay, then," he said. He patted my hand. "Good to see you back among the living."

I couldn't have been more pleased with the way it had all gone down.

• • •

By the end of the week I was out of there and home again. But not for long was I back in Jim Thorpe. I had no intention of remaining on the east coast, indefinitely. In the meantime, I had a lot of catching up to do.

CHAPTER THIRTY-ONE - Mom and Me One Last Time

My old life as Keira Adrian Travaglini pretty much settled back to what it had been before that awful Christmas Day of 2017.

One of the first things I did after my release from hospital was to return to Penns Cove and look around. I just had to see what had become of my old place of employment. It seemed so sad, the building, just sitting there, shuttered, and abandoned. Only a *for rent or lease* sign now adorned the building's front where *The Com-Link logo* once reposed. Chuck and Sally had indeed been forced to close the failing electronics boutique just after the first of the year. My apartment on the other side of town still had most of my stuff inside. Mom had been keeping up the rent for me during my time away. Stepping through the entry foyer to the living room hit me immediately with a flood of memories: two conflicting ones at that. The memory of my time here as Keira, working at the *Com-Link* before the stuff with Craig in *Jim Thorpe* last Christmas went down. The times in the supposed alternate timeline spent here with *Annie*— here and at her apartment across town. All that other reality— it felt almost as if only a dream now. Still, me all those months living here as myself and wondering through all my Keira time here if this was all my life was ever going to be, that felt only a dream now as well. It was the past, only memories of a life lived and behind me. I couldn't help smiling forlornly at the thought of that as I slowly moved into the room and headed for the remainder of the apartment. I needed to inform the manager that I was leaving, and over the next few weeks I moved the items that represented my physical life out one at a time.

Initially, as I recovered and began writing about my experiences while in a coma, I accepted Sarah's invitation to move back into my old room at the log home in *Jim Thorpe*. At least for a little while. She was all alone now after having given my dad the boot. I made it clear to her however that the move back home was only temporary. I planned to relocate and join Kelly in *Jerome,* Arizona, work with Kelly at Amelia Slattery's *Red Rock Knickknacks* store as Kelly even in this reality/timeline had requested of me.

"I'm getting the two realities all mixed up in my head," I said. "But Kelly wants me to join her out there. She asked me if I would again when I spoke to her a few days ago. She was with me the whole time in the hospital those first couple of days."

"I know," Mom acknowledged. "And she was upset that she had to leave after the first of the new year, to head back to Arizona." Sarah shrugged. "But what could she do? Who knew when you'd finally wake up?"

I nodded, somberly. "I felt her there, you know. Somehow, I'm aware of her being there." I frowned. "God, I wish I could have awakened sooner than three months later."

Sarah nodded, wistfully.

"We look so much alike, she and I," I said. "Kelly said Amelia, the shop owner, is just loopy enough in her new age thinking to find hiring me an okay thing. Especially after Kelly told Amelia what *Ariana* said to tell her—"

"About this *Angelica Matchelli* woman who lived so long ago in *Jerome?"*

Mom had read my journal. I smiled. "Yeah, she really lived, Mom," I said. "And *Ariana* implied Angelica was one of her many past Earthplane incarnations."

Sarah Travaglini huffed. "That doesn't put your *Ariana* in the best light in that case," she mused. "A prostitute in an old-west brothel."

I smirked. "And what were you, maybe, in a past life that might shock you to find out you were," I queried.

My Mom only regarded me, and a paleness seemed to drift over her complexion. I suspected the thought of it rattled her a little. "All my kids want to leave me, leave the East coast," she said then, shifting the conversation to a less angst-provoking topic.

"Frank and Meg, Mom, are just thirty minutes away … in Allentown. We're not *all* trying to put an entire country between us, you and this town."

"Keirie, honey," she insisted, then. "I'm okay with you leaving to join your sister out there, if that's what you believe is what's right for you now, but … you'll need better transportation."

I wrinkled my brow at her.

"You're not driving that glorified golf cart you drive all the way to Arizona. And not if you're seriously planning to take my granddaughter along for the ride with you. I won't allow it. And if Meg has any sense, she'll forbid her daughter accompanying you as well."

When Chloe learned of my plans to leave for Arizona, she was heartbroken. She had become so attached to me in the last few months, that the thought of my moving permanently away devasted her. Until … one day about a week ago, she descended from her bedroom during one of my visits, still upset, but bravely queried if maybe she could join me on my trip out west, at least for the summer.

"Can I, mom?" She had implored of Meg. *"Keirie?"* Chloe had smiled over at me.

I smirked at my mother. "What do you propose then?" I answered. "You want to buy me a new automobile … with Dad's money?"

She grinned back. "Yes. With Alvin's money. It's the least that son of a bitch can do for his youngest daughter after all you've been through."

"What model would you approve of, Mom?"

"I trust your judgement," she replied. "Whatever you like… I still can't believe you were right about Alvin," she told me then. "How you could possibly know he'd get into this much trouble? It's as if…."

"… as if I'd seen an advance script of what the next few months would be like?" I finished for her.

"Keira, that is so upsetting," she uttered in a troubled tone.

"You're beginning to seriously think," I proposed, "that maybe there really are supernatural entities out there in the universe, who have God-like abilities, and who may in fact be the real inspiration for all of humanity's religious beliefs."

She just looked at me. "If I told Father Bessley what you claim happened to you, and what this *Ariana* claims she was before she evolved into an omniscient being, he'd almost want to ban you

258

forever from ever again stepping into his or any other Catholic Church. He'd call that blasphemy."

"And now?" I pursued of her.

"I'm just not sure what I think now. Thanks, Keirie. You've threatened everything I ever took for granted about the nature of the universe."

"It wasn't like I was trying, Mom," I said.

EPILOGUE -
Come What May

"This car is so neat," said Chloe as we tooled down the rustic highways and backroads of South Jersey at the start of our journey west. "Grammy Sarah actually let you buy a car as neat as this?"

I grinned and nodded. "She said I could trade the smart car in for whatever I liked. It's a Tesla model 3," I informed her. "Actually, it's an early production model. Elon Musk is still trying to get his new *'hey look what I just made'* off the ground. Mom used your grandpop's old connections to put me up near the top of the list. This thing is fresh off the assembly line."

"And all electric," Chloe replied. "No engine, no smelly gas to pour into it. Just rechargeable batteries and motors to drive the wheels. This is really super. I'm glad mom's letting me do this, go with you out west to visit Aunt Kelly, at least till school starts again next fall." She glanced to the huge LCD readout screen in the center of the Tesla's forward dash. "Wow. This is going to be fun, Aunt Keira. It's like being in a spaceship. And you can't even tell it's on. It's so quiet."

"I know," I smiled. "I love it."

"It's weird driving a car so quiet. Driving this all the way to your Aunt Kelly's, is going to be interesting. I can't wait for the first time this thing tells me to pull over and directs me to the nearest recharge station." I laughed at that, and then glanced to the sunroof above me and the extended forward window view. This car with its abundance of overhead glass really gave one an amble view of the world around one.

"I miss your old car, though," Chloe confessed. "It was cute."

"Yeah, it was," I replied. "Driving it was fun. The other you from the other realm got a real kick out of it also."

Chloe frowned. *"Was she real?* Seriously, Aunt Keira, the thought of another me out there somewhere in an alternate universe … it really creeps me out."

I shrugged my shoulder. "I don't know if she was real, Chloe. I may never know."

• • •

The sign out front of the tiny house just up the road from us read:

STATE FARM
INSURANCE
Katherine B. McGarry
A licensed independent Agent.

"Oh, wow," Chloe exclaimed then as I let off the accelerator and prepared to pull in. "Is that…?"

"Yes," I responded. "I just have to stop in and fix a small insurance problem."

"Aunt Keira," Chloe suddenly said then. "This is where the real Anita Thrombi works, doesn't she? This is where you know her from."

I glanced to my niece and nodded. "I know. I'm a little nervous about maybe running into her again ... *the real her.* But ... I need to take care of this, before we get started." I glanced ahead for a parking space, spotting Anita's Subaru BMX just to the right of the entrance door. "Oh, God," I moaned. *"She's here! That's her car!* I'd know it anywhere. *I've even driven the damn thing! Damn it to hell."*

"You mean one like it…" Chloe answered soberly. "In that—"

"Other realm," I nodded. I faced Chloe again. "I'm not sure now I really want to do this."

Chloe faced me. "I want to meet her," she replied.

I glared at her. "And say *what* to her?"

Chloe shrugged, grinning sheepishly. *"Hi, Annie?"*

Chloe grinned over at me; I couldn't help laughing. "You're so much like Kelly and me, it scares me," I replied.

261

Chloe nodded and reached for the door release; she opened her passenger side door. It was summer. Chloe and I both were in very short shorts and sandals, me in a tank top, and she in a spandex top that ended just above her belly button.

I watched her head up the tiny concrete steps to the door, turn and face back to me, still in the car. I sighed, and clicked myself out of my seat belt, tossed it aside, and opened my driver side door. I opened the house's front door, and entered first. In front of us were makeshift dividers, designed to simulate a pretend vestibule into an interior that reminded me more of the interior of a mobile home. To our left was a work station, more of a record keeping center with a desk and computer atop it. Two work stations manned by agents went off in the other direction. This forward section of the small house looked as if in the original design plans this would have been partitioned out for dining and living areas. Of the two desks meant to be occupied by an agent, one was; the other currently was not. The occupied one, as luck would have it, was manned by Anita Thrombi. I always thought she was an adorable looking young woman.

• • •

"Hi," greeted Anita as Chloe and I approached. "How can we be of help today? It's *Keira*, isn't it?" she asked.

"Yes," I answered, chilled to hear her now very familiar and friendly voice in my ears once more.

"You used to drive a little mini car, didn't you? I remember that about you."

"A smart car, yes," I nodded.

"Yeah. I remember the first time you pulled in with it," Anita said. "I thought wow that's tiny. And you looked so cute behind the wheel of it."

"It was a fun car," I agreed, smiling.

Anita glanced to her left and out the window to my Tesla. "Wow, that looks sporty."

"It's a Tesla Model 3. Electric. They're only a few yet available."

"Expensive?" she queried.

"… Yeah," I said. "It's not the base model. I kind of got carried away with the options package." I shrugged.

She nodded. "Nice."

"Thanks," I replied.

"Hi, there," Anita Thrombi said to Chloe. "And how old are you, young lady?"

"Thirteen," she answered, timidly.

"Just this month," I added.

"Oh? Well, happy birthday!" Anita told her.

"Thanks," Chloe only answered.

"This is Chloe, my niece," I told Anita.

Anita nodded and smiled over to her.

Wow, she's cute, I heard Chloe say. She hadn't spoken it. I heard it as clearly in my mind as if she had said it aloud. Chloe knew I had gotten it; she smiled, knowing we both had a new way of talking among ourselves. My mouth flew open in amazement.

Anita regarded the two of us, suspiciously, as if something weird was transgressing between us two females. "Is there something I can help you with today, Keira?" she asked me. "Everything go okay with the insurance transfer? Registration? Plates? Title?"

I shrugged my shoulder. "That all went fine," I said. "*This is the problem....*" I handed her my insurance card. Anita glanced to it. It looked fine to her at first, but then she read it again.

Keir A. Travaglini

"Oh, my," she said. "How did they make a mistake like that?" She glanced at me again. "You don't look like a *Keir*."

"What?" said Chloe. "Can I see that?" Anita handed it to her and Chloe snorted a laugh as she looked at me. "You mean, *it happened for real ... here ... in our universe?*"

Anita Thrombi regarded her, a weird expression passing across her face at Chloe's strange comment.

I just laughed and shook my head. I took hold of it from Chloe and handed it back to Ms. Thrombi. "Chloe and I are starting out today on a weeklong drive to Arizona. We'll be there most of the summer. I'm probably moving out there permanent. If for any reason, I'm stopped by a policeman and he sees my name like that he might think it's not mine."

"We wouldn't want that. He'll ask for your driver's license. It's written correct on there, isn't it?"

I nodded.

"So, at least he won't accuse you of using a bogus insurance card, but he'll probably insist you get it fixed right off."

"Probably," I agreed.

"I can make you a temporary card with it right," she said, as she pulled up my insurance stats and found my file. "This will just take a second, and then you guys can be on your way."

"Okay," I replied, unable to take my eyes off her. She was so much physically exactly like I remembered her from my *'experience.'* "Forgive me for staring," I said. "It's just that you look so familiar."

Chloe glanced to me, fighting the urge to smile.

"Do you know me from somewhere else?" Anita inquired.

"Just from here," I replied. "Just here."

There was a noise from the printer behind her; Anita reached back and pulled out the new insurance card documents. "That should do it. I'll notify the parent company, tell them to fix it in their records, and you should be mailed a replacement card in about a week or two."

"Uh," I began. "That address is no longer valid. I don't live there anymore."

She nodded. "Do you know where in Arizona you might be staying, or if you give me your email address we can probably send you a digital version for you to print out. And once you're settled out there, you might think about letting us know your new address."

"I will, thanks Annie," I said.

Chloe shot me another glance; *her* mouth this time agape.

"Excuse me?" Anita Thrombi said, glancing at her name on the little name plaque on her desk. "Did you just call me *Annie?* People I know, know I like to be called by that name, but *how did you know that?"*

I froze.

"She guessed," spoke up Chloe, quickly, before I had a chance to think up a lie. "My aunt Keira and I are kind of psychic; we're good guessers... For instance, let me prove it to you."

"All right," Anita answered, curious.

"You don't come from here, originally. Your family lives in Seattle; you have relatives in a little town called *Roslyn,* the town used in that old TV series from before I was born."

All her good humor all at once died from Annie's face. "Okay, that's too weird," she replied, coldly. "How could you possibly guess that? Unless you two have been digging into my personal life on one of those *Your Private Info* sites on the internet."

I faced my niece. "Chloe, why did you do that?"

Chloe faced Anita. "You need Keira's email," she said. "This will all make sense to you, pretty soon; you'll see."

I knew immediately what Chloe meant by that. I faced back to Anita. "I went through a thing a few months ago," I told her. "My oldest brother forced himself on me. It was in the news; you may have heard about it. He's in jail now; he even forced himself on my sister, almost eight years ago now. I was unconscious for more than three months."

"Oh, God," Anita replied, her demeanor suddenly softening. "I'm so sorry to hear that, Keira. That's so awful, a thing like that. To have family behave like that."

"Yes. I wrote a book about what I hallucinated during the three months that I was unresponsive. I uploaded it to Amazon. If you give me your email address, I'll send you a free copy to read. It will explain everything. Let's just say for reasons I can't explain I cast you as an important character in my delusions."

"Why?" she asked. "I wouldn't know you from Eve, and I imagine you wouldn't either."

"Well, I did. It's all explained in the *memoir*. Can I send you a copy?"

"All right, if you want. This is really creeping me out, I should tell you both. But I promise I'll give it a quick read."

"Oh, you'll read it a lot slower than that," guaranteed Chloe. "You will." Chloe requested my smartphone. "You older generation types," she said. "You don't know half of what my generation does about texting and emails and stuff and how to do it." She knew where a copy of my memoir was accessible via The Cloud, called it up and asked Anita if she could lend Chloe her smartphone for a second.

By this point, Anita Thrombi was so numbed by this whole encounter with the two of us, she just dumbly handed it to my niece. Chloe expertly opened the phone's menus up, asked Anita to— without showing Chloe or me— enter her private Microsoft password, and once Chloe knew she was in, she again took Anita's phone and tapped it against my own. My memoir file transferred a copy of itself to Anita's phone in an instant.

"There," Chloe said. "All done. Enjoy. It was good to see you, Annie. I'm glad I got to meet the real you." She faced me, then. "Aunt Keira?"

I nodded, vaguely. "Uh, yeah. Sorry about all this, Anita," I said. "We're weird but not dangerous. That memoir will probably make your hair stand on end, but it will explain everything. Okay, Chloe. We have a long drive ahead of us if we want to make Virginia and I-40 sometime before nightfall. We better get going. Thank you, Anita. For all your help."

"My pleasure."

"Bye," I told her.

"Bye," Anita Thrombi replied, making a quick glance at the old insurance card she chose to keep." Bye, Keira."

• • •

We were on the road soon after, and heading for the interstate bridge between New Jersey and Delaware to begin the long journey down south to eventually reach the beginning of the cross-country thruway christened Interstate 40.

"Keira," said Chloe. "Aunt Keira, are you okay? You look like you're crying."

"Chloe, please," I begged. "Don't talk; I'm trying to see the road and my eyes… I mean, that was Ariana, not Annie all those months I thought I was Keir/Keira in that other reality, but the real Annie just now… Ariana copied her perfectly. It was like it *was her*. I almost wanted to just hug her and thank her for being there when I needed her all that time. And Chloe… I'm not gay. I like guys. And yet."

"She's a human being, Aunt Keira," said Chloe. "What difference does that make? You like her, don't you?"

"Yeah," I admitted. "I do. We'd probably in that alternate universe would have been besties, best friends."

"You'll probably see her again," Chloe replied. "In fact, I wouldn't doubt before the summer's over, she'll figure out where in Arizona you're staying with Aunt Kelly and come see you."

I sniffed and glanced over at her, the beginnings of droplets of water starting to run down the sides of my nose. "How do you know that?" I asked her, attempting to smile.

"Because I'm talking to you right now, Aunt Keira, but I'm still seeing Annie back in her office. She's already starting to flip through the file."

"You're kidding me," I replied. "You can *see her?* You can do that?"

"I'm surprised you haven't tried it. You taught me."

"Chloe, I haven't taught you much of anything. Like I told you before, I don't even know how I do what I can do now, thanks to Ariana."

"Well, I caught it whatever you can do now, because so can I; and like I said, this Annie, this one, is back there in her office right this minute, reading your file. I can even tell where she is in the file:

Oh Good, Sanity.
My Journey Back to the Hell
We call Normal.

A Memoir by
Keira Adrian Travaglini,

...Chloe recited to me.

To Annie and Ariana
Thank you for being there when I needed you both.

• • •

How I managed to get us all the way over to the other side of the bridge span without driving straight off and into the Delaware River, I'll never know. Just the thought that Annie Thrombi was reading the memoir's dedication was getting me right where I lived. But let's just say, it got better after a while. Chloe and I continued southward, for now; and eventually when we hit I-40, we veered off and headed due west.

We were on our way....

AFTERWORD

The backstory alluded to in *Your Inner You* about Danielle and Roger Tigerson, Angelica Matchelli and the higher realm spiritual being, *Ariana,* is detailed in my prior novel, *Angie's Revenge: A Tale of Many Lifetimes.* If you want to learn more about them, the novel is available on *Kindle* for downloading and can be purchased for $2.99 directly from my site **www.PaulFichera.com**.

The Author in a 1986 photo (when he was 35)

And on a weekend getaway
With friends to go
Whitewater rafting in
Jim Thorpe

www.ingramcontent.com/pod-product-compliance
Lightning Source LLC
Chambersburg PA
CBHW022032240626